Linda Grant was born in Liverpool and now lives in London. Her first novel, *The Cast Iron Shore*, won the David Higham First Novel Prize and was shortlisted for the Guardian Fiction Prize. Her second novel, *When I Lived in Modern Times*, won the Orange Prize for Fiction. She is also the author of *Sexing the Millennium: A Political History of the Sexual Revolution* and *Remind Me Who I Am, Again*, a family memoir.

LINDA GRANT

Still Here

LITTLE, BROWN

A *Little, Brown* Book

First published in Great Britain in 2002
by Little, Brown

Copyright © Linda Grant 2002

Photograph of Albert Docks, Liverpool © Chistian Smith

The moral right of the author has been asserted.

A CIP catalogue record for this book
is available from the British Library.

ISBN 0 316 86995 8 (hbk)
ISBN 0 316 85993 1 (pbk)

Typeset in Goudy by M Rules
Printed and bound in Great Britain by
Clays Ltd, St Ives plc

Little, Brown
An imprint of
Time Warner Books UK
Brettenham House
Lancaster Place
London WC2E 7EN

www.TimeWarnerBooks.co.uk

To Natasha, Mark and Clara

Alix

From the river the city seemed like a colossus. The sky was heavy with rain and the wind was sharp. Salt and tar were in our throats, our eyes were stinging. Seabirds were screaming in the sky and the ships' horns boomed along the estuary; behind us was the emptiness of the sea. The pilot boat went out and came back in, guiding the ships through the invisible channels in the sand and silt. Lashed to them by metal cables, the tugs hauled the leviathans into port. The city bore down on the shore, the dock brought the water into land and closed in on it four-square. Everything was immense: the warehouses, the harbour board, the shipping lines, the insurance firms, our two cathedrals, all made the skyline and beyond them our magnificent temple of Zion. The city spoke in tongues and when it didn't speak it shouted.

Yet for all we had here, some of us felt a wrench when we looked westwards out to sea towards the Atlantic. We were yearning for something even bigger still. We had inconsolable longings in us for the city across the ocean. We were its blueprint. It was our completion. Some of us went, some of us stayed, but even separated, we were part of the same need to turn away from England. For a hundred years my family has been trying to get to America. In each generation someone tries and fails, or makes it, and, for one reason or another, comes back again. We cannot get over the feeling that England is an interim stage. America! We still have inside us the immigrant, greenhorn fever of our grandparents for the country where the personality expands to fill the emptiness of the continent instead of shrinking into itself, shrivelling for want of air and light. We have an itch. We want to talk big, think big, make it big, be big people without jostling every day for elbow room.

One day, my brother Sam rang me to say that our mother was going to die, perhaps that night. I know of people who hear from a telephone call months later that a parent is dead, and they shrug and say, 'I really hadn't seen him for years.' Apparently it is possible to pull free of the ropes that tether you to your family; but not for my brother and me. We had a history. My second home, the former agricultural labourer's cottage in the Périgord with its garden of lilac and lavender, sunflowers and geraniums – where Sam stood with his hands in his jeans' pockets, flinching as a neighbour's cat came and rubbed up against his leg and said, 'From *shtetl* to *shtetl* in two generations, Alix' – was off the Rebick map. It was insignificant. What *could* it mean? It had no meaning. It was all make-believe, like the articles knocked out to sell to French housewives in a shop we walked past in Bordeaux called the Romantic Englishwoman. 'I don't suppose they named that after *you*.'

I drove to the airport at Bergerac and flew to Paris. It was March, a windy spring day. A certain numbness overtakes you when you hear bad news that you can do nothing about, and you settle into a sequence of routine actions, without pausing to think of their moral appropriateness. At Orly I bought a Cartier watch for myself in the departure lounge while I waited for my connection to Manchester. I looked at all the other things I could buy there, Gucci handbags, Bally shoes, Godiva chocolates, and I badly wanted these things as I had once *had to have* a boy doll dressed in the kilt of a Highlander, seen behind the glass of a kiosk in a London hotel when I was a child, and my father had said, 'What's the matter with you? What are you going to do with that rubbish when you get home? Give me an explanation for why you want it and I'll buy it for you.' But I had no explanation. My eyes were bigger than my head. 'Be serious, Alix,' my father warned me. He meant that we should have reasons for what we did and what we desired. 'Make your case.' I know exactly what he would have thought of the Cartier watch, the Gucci handbags, the Bally shoes: 'Good-quality products, I'll give them that, but you only want to buy them because they've got you, you're bored. You're climbing on to a death machine and you're certainly not going to think about what you're doing, so you empty your mind. And when you empty your mind in a place like this, what comes along to fill it? Shoes and handbags and chocolates.'

Across the Channel England was green below and grey above, and I was reminded of those months of low cloud, brown light, light in its old age, pressing down on my head like a roof. This was one of the reasons why I had left and bought the cottage in France. It was the dimness of the light that made me turn against the land of my birth. In my seat I ate a second in-flight snack, though I wasn't hungry, and drank a second glass of free champagne, though my head hurt slightly from the first, but I was travelling business class and it was there, to be taken, and being rich is still a novelty to me since the company my grandfather founded and my mother continued – the manufacture of a renowned and expensive face cream, a 'best-kept-secret' among those who each month studied with diligence the pages of *Vogue* and *Harper's and Queen* – had been bought out for six million dollars four years ago by the American cosmetics conglomerate, Rose Rosen, and my brother and I each took a fifty-fifty share. I tried to read the papers, absorb myself in peace talks and hostage-takings, events to which I had come in the middle, having rarely seen a newspaper or listened to the radio in France (part of my programme of immersion in the Greek classics) but my mother's face was in my mind, as I had last seen her, eight months before, entirely indifferent to my presence, calm and void. Everything, the clothes she wore, the wedding ring slack on her finger, the bones of those hands, the oval nails, the threepenny-bit scar above her thumb knuckle, entirely familiar, all known, yet the substance that animated them was opaque.

'Where is she?' Sam wanted to know. 'Where is she all day? Is she back in Dresden, Alix, what do you think?' But I didn't know and neither did the doctors.

At the barrier, dressed as always in jeans, white shirt, white leather Nikes, he was waiting, pulled me to him with a strong arm, held me, me stooping a little for his embrace. I smelt his skin, the musky male odour of Pears soap, Chanel aftershave and whatever the male hormones were that had been fizzing through the body of my brother since his teens. 'Hi, kiddo,' he said to me.

'Hi.'

He did not age. *I* aged, not him. He had the same build at fifty-two as he had had when he was ten years old, never a geeky kid, not at all, not even at thirteen and fourteen when boys and girls begin to sprout like wet spring lawns. There was meat on his bones, his uncles would tell him, packed in a small, punchy, heavy-shouldered frame. He smiled at me, that Rebick smile revealing the wolfish yellow teeth, the humour, the tenderness of all the Rebick men who cried in movies, let their tears dry on their faces, unashamed.

Anyone but us would have driven from Manchester to Liverpool in silence, each alone with the thoughts we had of our mother and the impending death and of our loss and what it would mean to us, but all we know how to *do* is talk. Our mother had been very silent for a long time. A psychologist might want to make something of this, that she had finally retreated from the barrage of noise that the Rebicks made, the cacophony of words, the pointlessness of it all. But we were realists, we knew the loss of speech was part of her condition.

'How is she?'

They had come to her room that morning. She was lying with her eyes open. Her breathing was hoarse. Nurse O'Dwyer lifted her up against the pillows. The smell of hot urine rose from the sheets.

'Alix, it's pitiful, just awful. She's sitting in her chair. I come in and she's fiddling around with her crotch. I can't believe it, I thought . . . I really believed for a minute she's playing with herself. My own mother sitting there in full view doing . . . and I say to the nurse, "Hey, what's this?" And she says, "Oh, no, Mr Rebick, it's the incontinence pad, she's not used to it and—"'

'Stop!' I cried, my foot jammed against the car's floor. 'I don't want to hear any more. This indignity, this—'

'You *have* to hear. Then O'Dwyer starts holding my hand, squeezing it and says, "Mr Rebick, don't question God's mercy," and I turn round and say, "Why? What's that shyster doing to her now?" And old man Levy comes past and hears and do you know what he says to me? He says, "That's no way to talk about the

God of your forefathers who brought us out of the land of Egypt and delivered us from slavery.'"

I could not smile because I saw my mother as she was once, the young woman of my childhood precise in all her movements, with lustrous copper hair, whose waves coiled around the brush, elegant in Susan Small or Jaeger, who looked with shining eyes at her handsome husband, the doctor, who walked like a god through the city, St Saul, the saviour of sick children, who promised her every day of his life that one day, sooner or later, he would take her away from the dark continent to America, where happiness was written into the Constitution and there was a limited supply of history.

I know it's true, she was a difficult woman, Lotte Rebick, my Mamma. She was undoubtedly damaged by her wartime experience, by being thrust on to a train at Dresden station at the age of fourteen, never to have a proper home again with her parents. She was angry and sad. She was sometimes demented by sorrow and regret, but let me tell you, *I was born into love.* Held in my mother's arms wrapped in a bathtime towel, the lilac scent of talcum powder rising warm from my skin, the pages of a picture book open before her on the table: from this tight swaddling grew the story of Jack, of the cow and the beans and the plant that rose up from it with green and curling leaves and the giant who lived in the clouds with his wife. Words. New or familiar. What is bean? Like in soup. Where is the cow? Here. Bad giant. Yes. Smack him. Yes, he has a broken head. Kiss it better? No, we don't kiss bad giants better. The walnut radiogram played waltzes and polkas and Mamma hummed and sang. In my barred cot my rabbit guarded me. No giants came near. The nightlight hummed. Mamma told me a little lullaby and my eyes closed. She walked to the door but it did not shut. My eyes opened. Mamma standing darkened, back-lit by the hall light, a velvet shape with her hands clasped together. 'Nothing terrible will ever happen to you, baby. Your daddy will see to that. All safe. All safe now. Sssh. *Einschlafen, mein Liebling.*'

South past the cast-iron shore, inland a mile or two, my mother was in the old people's home, a red sandstone monstrosity knocked up with fake turrets and crenellations, built, according to a plaque in the entrance hall, by a cotton merchant around the time that the city was engorged with wealth, when the river was full of masted schooners and the first steam liners, the raw cotton stowed in ships sailing up the Manchester Ship Canal to where the Lancashire mills were going at full production, and little mill girls in clogs spun and spun until their fingers bled.

A picture of the house in its heyday shows the entire cast of characters assembled on the lawn for the photographer: pater-familias, face buried in his beard, unreadable; washed-out mother, half dead from child-bearing; doe-eyed daughters in pinafores and hair reaching their shoulders like Alice in my childhood story book; jaunty young sons, dipping a hand into the pocket of a Norfolk jacket, unaware of what life had in store for boys born in the 1890s – dead at the Somme or Passchendaele; and 'tween-maids and parlour-maids and butlers and all sorts. It was the self-confidence of them that struck you: they knew who they were and by what God-given right they were there, on the shores of the river Mersey. They knew their place, members of the rapidly rising bourgeoisie propelled upwards on a blast of boiling white steam from the chimneys of the industrial revolu-tion. They were powering their way into the future, into the twentieth century, rolling in on a tide of sugar and cotton and (until recently) slaves. In their stiff suits and impossible dresses, hardly able to believe their grandparents once tilled the Lancashire earth, these grandchildren of an almost forgotten rural English ancestry were thrusting modernists, playing with their new toys: steam engines, horseless carriages, flying machines. They were the forerunners of an American state of mind.

All gone, totally swept away, and in their place, the house was full of old Jews.

Little girls who had skipped rope on the cobblestones of Brownlow Hill; their older sisters, the first Jewish flappers, who went to the pictures to see Mary Pickford and Clara Bow and defied their parents with lipstick and rouge, 'my own daughter leaving the house like a prostitute'; the barefoot kids whose parents sat at home mumbling into a prayerbook or pushed handcarts up and down the hill and spoke only as much English as they needed to know to tell the authorities what they wanted to hear – they were old, old people now, the same age as the grandparents of those young pogrom immigrants who left Russia and Poland and the Ukraine at the turn of the century in the years after the Kishniev massacre.

When I first walked into the home four years ago I was impressed by the scale of its public rooms and I didn't immediately make the connection with a hotel that puts its best furniture in the lobby: only when you have signed the visitors' book and taken your key do they show you the meaner cubicles, the stained bedspreads, the chipped Formica headboard, the desolate view from the window where you will lie awake at night, sleepless, listening to the knocking pipes, the timbers shifting. A grandfather clock with spidery hands and a walnut case ticks abruptly in the entrance hall. Gold-framed mirrors adorn the walls, as well as tame, inoffensive pictures of blameless, soothing water-lilies. Various plaques announce donations and endowments, and a whole breeze-block extension (built by eight years of fund-raising banquets, tombolas, raffles, charity golf tournaments and jumble sales) leads off to the right where up-to-the-minute *en suite* rooms offer the ultimate in luxury for these old people, who are hoisted into bed at night by thin Irish girls, scaly feet eased out of slippers, nightgowns slipped on over their bent heads. In the upper atmosphere competing brands of air-freshener wage war with their different chemical odours. Beyond the entrance hall, another grand, high-ceilinged room. A mahogany sideboard holds numerous silver menorahs and Friday-night candlesticks, some brought over on the boat from the Old Country by the mothers of the inmates, wrapped in a linen tablecloth, rolled up in the bottom of a cardboard suitcase and preserved right through to the far end of the century when the silver has been polished down to the brass.

But now, in March, freezing winds blow across the estuary. Afternoon has drawn in. The long day ends, the lamps are lit, the TV turned on, the visitors depart and a new life takes over, the private night world of the home. Tonight someone may die, because on any night death is always possible. The company is not static, it changes all the time. It is an illusion that these are the same old people sitting in the same chairs with the same chapped legs and swollen feet. I see them in motion: a line are waiting to depart and another line are waiting to enter, and the line stretches back well beyond the doors and I see myself there, and see you there. The home is not asleep, it is not motionless at all, it is a place where dramatic events happen . . . the most violent thing of all happens here: death comes by, once or twice a week, and wrenches someone from their chair.

If I could, I would reverse time. I would poke the old people on the shoulder and make them stand up, throw down their sticks, push away their zimmer frames, tear off their old-people's clothes, see the colour return to them, give them rosy cheeks and brown hair, the bosoms and chests rise up, the spines elongate – watch them grow again, inch by inch, until they regain their full height as the vigorous adults they once were in the fifties and sixties, the prime of their lives, and watch them leave, just walk out the door and get on a bus home. I'd crank the clock back, turning the hands with all my force so they would become young wives, their hands clotted with dough, sweat shining on their faces as they kneaded and sifted and baked biscuits and cakes for their children. They fatten those pink cheeks so that they never resemble the starved, rickety street kids, whose mothers don't know how to feed a growing child and give them 'tea' of bread and dripping instead of a meal with soup and chicken and potatoes and vegetables and strudel, which all day throughout the rest of their lives will form fatty plaques around their hearts, until death calls out, '*Next.*' We are obliterated now, their children, we are not born, but are eggs clutched in adolescent ovaries like tiny pearls, unspent sperm in boyish testicles, just dropped, and they are almost children themselves, thirties kids trying to make a living in the Great Depression and making one, because they stuck together, were hard workers, gave each other a hand. Wherever they colonised a new neighbourhood, moving outwards from Brownlow Hill, inching into the suburbs, they built themselves a synagogue with money they raised from whatever was spare in their wages. Everything was organisation, committees, plans, *surging* into the future. Not bound by any class system, for when the workers told them that they knew their place, they thought, But I have no place. They were immigrants. Things could go either way. But always they were propelled forward by the sheer energy of the immigrant, for whom there is no safety net to catch them when they fall.

Further back, further back I would go, the hand turns in only one direction and I make them vomit over the side of the boat, the first time any of them has ever set foot on the uncertain, unstable, treacherous sea. And then the curtain comes down, darkness falls because before Liverpool, before the century that has just ended, there's nothing. Only the tiniest scrap of memory handed on and torn, so that the ink of the writing fades and the creases in the paper wipe out whatever was once there and we must fill in the blanks with our own imaginations and what we know from the historians who went to eastern Europe after the collapse of Communism and resurrected towns and villages from the ashes of history.

Before the Jews came, before even that bearded patriarch, the Liverpool ship-owner or insurance merchant or sugar magnate who built this absurd, overweening house, even before the Irish came, Liverpool was a few streets and a semi-derelict castle put up in the time of King John. Where my father would one day grow up, on Brownlow Hill, there is a hill but no Brownlow for it to be named after. Windmills stand, their vanes turning, their stones grinding; corn grows on the farmlands, which will one day house the teeming tens of thousands living in the worst squalor in Europe, and the corn makes flour and the flour makes the daily bread of the people of the emerging port. To the north, where the first wet docks are beginning to reclaim the sand-dunes, horses race on Whitsunday, their manes tearing the sea wind. Salt is in your mouth and your hair and you can taste it on the back of your hand with the tip of your tongue. Behind you is the village of Everton, whose beacon looks out over the Mersey on which the wooden ships will sail to America with cargoes of slaves and back again with cargoes of raw sugar. And before that? A fishing village on a tidal inlet of the river, which flows quite fast through shining silver beaches, and beyond them, a wooded ridge of red sandstone, because in Liverpool even the rock comes from the sea.

Within my mother's body, the doctor observed, time was also being reversed. Unable to walk or speak or control her bladder or bowels, she cried when she was in pain and slept when she was not. God walked about her, turning off the lights. Around lunchtime, while I had shopped for Cartier watches at Orly, my mother, Lotte Rebick, had had a strange period of animation.

She lay in her chair and her hands made fluttering gestures as if she was beckoning or addressing invisible friends. Her mouth moved without sound in a continuous monologue. She was taking up again her end of a conversation that had fallen silent three years ago when she put an end to speech. Every morning in the home she spent a long time dressing, a long time creaming her face and applying her lipstick, straightening the seams of stockings that were visible to her alone, in her mind's eye. She wore a little chiffon scarf around her neck to conceal the ruins of a throat my father had wanted to kiss and kiss when they were first courting, just after the war when he was a young ex-serviceman smashing Mosley's fascists with his bare hands. For four years my mother had descended like a queen to the first meal of the day, would eat sparingly, still following the regime she had begun as a young bride. Then, resisting every attempt at conversation or therapeutic interaction by the staff ('How are *you* today?'), she would sit bolt upright in her chair staring into the middle distance. Nothing moved her, not the reminiscence work, not the singalongs.

> *Sally, Sally, pride of our alley,*
> *You mean the whole world to me.*
> *Sally, Sally, don't ever wander*
> *Away from the alley and me.*

There were many wanderers in the home. They wandered up and down the corridors, but not our mother. Her brain is very, very damaged, the doctor said to us. It was hard to know what remained. Mary O'Dwyer injected her with antibiotics and the bacteria died for a few hours or went to set up house somewhere else. But then it came back, always it came back, and the urine that seeped from her body stank and with each breath her lungs banged against her ribs like iron hammers. Mamma was dying in full view of the others and of their relatives, their sons and daughters and noisy grandchildren. Care assistants walked past with sponges and cups of tea and boxes of tissues. Her nose stood out like a sharpened beak in her sunken face and her eyes were grey and filmed. Her lips were slack and askew. A smell came off her, an odour of disinfectant masking waste materials. She was half-way through the door into the other world. The biochemical processes that would render her body back to the earth were already beginning. Horror. Disgust. My mother rotting before my eyes, her hand rotting in mine.

'Sam, my God, what . . .'

She was hot, she was burning up with feverish infections.

'It's terrible, just awful.' We cannot bear too much reality, not even Sam who deals with nothing else.

'When did you see her last?'

'Sunday. She was nothing like this, nothing. She was just like when you last saw her. Exactly the same for three years, identical, the same every day, now this.'

'What's happened?'

'I don't know. I'm fucked if I know.'

'What did the doctor say?'

'A stroke, he thinks, strokes happening every half-hour. *Felling* her.'

'How long?'

'He can't say. Could be any minute, could be weeks.'

Levy came over. He squinted at me, his eyes red and watering. 'Is it Alix Rebick?'

'Yes.'

'You come home to see your mother?'

'Yes.'

'I remember when your father first brought her back to Liverpool after the war,' he said, feeling in his pocket for the cigarettes that weren't there because the doctor had made him stop smoking after last year's coronary. Still his fingers twitched in the lining, closing on emptiness. 'She was a picture, a doll. A little girl, I can see her now.'

'She was twenty-three,' I said. To hell with these second-hand memories of my mother, I wanted to be alone with my own, of watching her sit in front of her dressing-table mirror on the satin stool, massaging her face with the special cleansing cream that had come with her from Dresden, and me saying, 'Mamma, am I old enough yet to use the special cream?' Because I knew she had something to teach me, that there was a lesson I was waiting to learn, eager for it, rushing ahead precociously towards woman-hood. And always the answer, 'On your sixteenth birthday. Not a day before, not a day later.'

'All the boys were in love with her but she was a married woman, already. A shame. Anyone would have had her.'

And walked off, shaking his head, his newspaper clamped under a stiff arm, an eighty-five-year-old man with a dowager's hump and tartan carpet slippers who used to sell ladies' dresses in three shops in Walton, West Derby and Fazackerley. *Schmatte* shops, outfits that came apart at the seams after one wearing, 'Because there's no quality, no workmanship, you only pay for what you get, Alix, but I'm not selling them a garment like your mother would wear because for that they would have no appreciation.'

Sam turned to me, the face of sorrow, and said, 'Shall we sing to her?' For she always sang to us: we were a family who sang. We gathered round the gramophone, a hefty, leather-covered box, and listened to our parents' records, show tunes, from Judy Garland all the way to Barbra Streisand, American, of course, because it was America, my father said, who had given the world the popular song. We sang 'Somewhere Over The Rainbow' and 'Some Enchanted Evening' and 'I've Grown Accustomed To Her Face' and 'Surrey With The Fringe On Top'. My father's baritone, my mother's wavering soprano, my own firmer, louder contralto and Sam, who said he was tone deaf but only because he loved to hear *us* sing, a chorus of voices filling the house, attempting rudimentary harmonies, the Rebick choir of loud-mouths sweetly singing together.

Mamma is weary, weary of this hard life in which so much has been lost. Sam and I sit, each holding a hand in one of hers, and I am crying until I think my heart will break at this *thing* that lies in its chair, this scabby rag that is supposed to be my mother.

We sit until close to midnight. The nurse comes over and tells us to go home, get some rest, and this is the end of my first day back in the city. We drive downtown to my brother's flat in the Albert Dock, I get undressed, in the bathroom cleanse my face with the special cream, holding the flannel against my skin just as Mamma taught me on my sixteenth birthday so long ago, climb between the white sheets in the spare room, while outside the Mersey flows past me from the granite hills of the Pennines down to the turbid sea.

When I was a child I heard the loud, echoing horns of the ocean-going liners pulling out on a midnight tide and their lights turned the river gold and the funnels sang the song of our city. For the Mersey ran out to Liverpool Bay, and our bay led to the Irish Sea, and our sea opened up to the Atlantic Ocean and our ocean touched the shores of Mexico and all the way down to the bottom of the world. All the old Jews, every one, like their nurses and helpers ('Angels! Florence Nightingale's bog-Irish bitches, more like') had come from over the water. In our city everything comes from the sea. The Irish girls wheel the old Jews out along the promenade at Otterspool, and the old Jews look at the river and hear the ships' sirens and the foghorns and the motors of the tugs and the pilot boats. 'In your dreams,' the care assistants say, for there are no more ships on the Mersey, or at least not very many and they only go as far as the container port at Seaforth.

The old Jews knew they wouldn't be there much longer, watching the river. They were bound for the other side, the unknown peninsula. That they were still there at all was a miracle. It was the same with the city: it was hanging around long after anyone had any further use for it. My mother was dying on the banks of the Mersey, in a derelict town, the worst place in the country, the very worst. Yes, it's depressing. But it's not the story, only the beginning of the story. When I came back to see my mother I fell in love. Me – the arrogant, angry, wilful, sarcastic daughter of Liverpool and of Saul and Lotte Rebick.

At the time of these events, this explosive thing that happened to me, I had just returned, the previous month, from India. I had not gone there to seek spiritual enlightenment, far from it: I had no plans to sit at the feet of a guru or reach a more evolved mode of consciousness. The last thing I was looking for was transcendence; I had enough of that at home in France. I went out as part of the administrative team that was doing the documentation research for the restoration and preservation of a synagogue in Cochin. There are Jews in India, a few still remain. They say they are the descendants of King Solomon's sailors, shipwrecked in Biblical days, though perhaps the truth is they arrived from Spain or Portugal around the time of the great expulsion, the same year Columbus discovered America, as it happens. I have no opinion either way about where they came from or how they got there; the only thing that interests me is that in the sixteenth century they built their synagogue where women in saris still come to sing the old songs of my race, mumble the same prayers as my mother and father said.

It is a *mitzvah*, what I do, a good deed. I travel the world and visit old buildings, in Fez, in Hungary, in Poland, in France, in Montenegro. I see synagogues that are warehouses, storerooms, cinemas, department stores, cattle sheds. I am in a team with architects and engineers who give me their opinion about whether such a structure could be restored, and I write a report that is circulated to rich Jews around the world telling them of the community that once was and is now, if any of it remains, and what has been lost and what might be regained. I tell them, *We can resurrect something from the ashes of history, we can make it live again.* Look. Here is its current state, here's an artist's impression of what could be once more. You want to see this come to life? Give me your money. I write reports that are very, very persuasive. I say, There are a million evils in the world, believe me, I know. Cancer, Aids, malnutrition, war, the illegal occupation of territories, refugees rotting in camps, discrimination, torture, crimes against women and children – rape, incest, paedophilia, infibulation – and against animals, whole species about to vanish from the earth. It's terrible what goes on, and in my time I have studied cruelty and sadism, have looked at photographs few other people have seen, which are kept locked in police files, have lain awake at night and, like Jacob wrestling with the angel, have been overcome by thoughts about our nature, that evil perhaps exists independently of the human mind, bound into the atomic structure of matter. But this little project, this harmless pinprick of good, I believe in with all my heart.

I stood in the street in Cochin, in that ferocious sunlight, overwhelmed by the scent of pepper, tamarind, cinnamon, cloves, nutmeg, cardamom, ginger, turmeric, entered the synagogue, the warm tiles beneath my feet, gazed up at the branched brass lamps, felt the tremor of shuffling feet behind me, some kind of bells clanging outside, heard the old words unscroll in my mind, *Shema Yisrael, adonai elohaynu, adonai echad.* Hear, O Israel, the Lord our God, the Lord is One. A pitifully small handful of men and women saying that every day, when they rise in the morning, a speck of dust in India. Hear, O Israel . . . and God answers back, What the hell are you doing there? I grew up on the most westerly margins of the continent of Europe, so nearly there, nearly in America. I am still here, as my city is, and as those few surviving synagogues, by some miracle, are still there too, and the Jews of Cochin.

The day Sam rang to tell me to come home because Mamma was dying, I was doing the preparatory work for the next project.

A synagogue with frescoes had been discovered in a remote village in Romania, where it had been used since the end of the war as a warehouse for storing plums, which they make into a famous local jam. There is, I know, only a finite number of restorable synagogues in Europe, yet every time a new one is documented I feel the same deep astonishment at what manages to survive and in what form it does so. The little *shul*, when I looked it up on the map, was only a few miles on the other side of the former Soviet border, east of the Carpathian mountains and within half a day's drive from a town. It gave my heart a sudden shock to see it written there, fixed, identifiable, capable of cartography. Kishniev! Where it all started, the landslide of Jews leaving the east after the two pogroms – terrible atrocities, mass murder, rape – my father's parents among that flight, and even here there is still, I had found out, a Jewish community. Who decides to stay, who decides to leave? Who thinks they made the right choice and at what stage do they realise they did not? What makes a person still a Jew after seventy years of Communist government where their very selves are officially denied? 'There were Jews here once,' a man said to me, in a village in Slovakia. 'Where did they go?' I asked him. 'They evaporated, like the dew on the fields and on the backs of my sheep,' he replied. 'Dew returns every morning,' I told him angrily (through our interpreter, a girl we brought with us from Prague who wore frosted-pink lipstick and weighed down her neck with a heavy gold cross). 'Yes,' he said, 'but my fields and my sheep are here all the time, we never come and go. It doesn't matter who is the government, or if you build roads, me and my family don't budge.'

Waiting for Mamma to die, I needed to be back in Romania once again where it was clear to me who I was and what I was for. Immersed in my work it is easier to bear the absence of attachments. To be a single woman at the age of forty-nine is no laughing matter, to fear that love and erotic desire will now and in the future always be a thing of the past. It is bearable, but only with a great deal of mental ingenuity.

I had a lust problem. With no boyfriend, no lover, no marriage, no relationship, I was raging inside. Then I fell temporarily into the grip of a conviction, that I could transcend desire by attaining peace of mind – liberation from sexual urges – through sheer willpower. I bought a house outside a village near Bergerac in southern France. Alone there I had forcibly made myself practise silence, which turned out to be an almighty struggle against fidgeting and jumping up to run to the window if a car came down the lane. I would lie on my couch and listen to the clock tick in that absolute stillness, my breath toiling in my chest; even the padding of a cat's feet on the concrete path behind the house became audible to me. It was an exercise, a force of will, not to fall asleep with the sheer boredom of it, this Zen, trance-like state I was trying to induce, a suspension of self by brute force. Meditation lasted only minutes, sometimes seconds, and gave way to easy slumber, to dreams of cities shimmering in a heatwave, frantic streets, tall buildings with glass lifts shooting up and down. When I went outside, the sky was high and white and silent. The grass made little noise. The dry earth kept its thoughts to itself.

The first summer I lay in a hammock absorbed in the heady, nerveless scent of lilac and lavender, geraniums and sunflowers, alluring on a hot summer afternoon at the aperitif hour. But the next year I was losing interest in my house with its whitewashed walls, the weathered green paint on its buckling front door, the gravel path, the swimming-pool already lightly misted with a green scum of algae, the mosquitoes swarming above the surface. In the third, I didn't go out into the garden at all and, watching from the window, saw things die or choke other things, lead energetic rampant lives; the hammock rotted in the winter rain and the mist of algae turned into a thick emerald carpet. The elemental struggle for survival took over my garden, green-blooded battles raged. I noted that stubborn, simple, single-minded plants like moss prevailed.

When I moved to France I thought the countryside would teach me to be alone and to be alone with myself. I was looking at a life that was bound to be spent alone, without intimate companionship, and I had been convinced that I should master the art of solitude. But it's a lie to pretend that you don't need love when you do, a heinous crime. *I grew up loved.* Everywhere I turn I hear people telling me, 'I was an abused child.' Books on the subject sell like crazy: everyone imagines that the worst happened to them. Not me. Not Sam. Our parents adored us. Everything under the sun was striving and seeking and toiling and succeeding or going under, and I had three million dollars in the bank and was to attain a state of grace by sitting in my garden shelling peas. At this still point I was supposed to be seeing into the heart of mystery, to find that God loves small and humble things and actions, and inside I was screaming, *I want, I want, I want.* Nirvana you could keep, the whole of eastern philosophy that transcended *I want* you could keep.

What do I want? *Rapture.* When do I want it? *Now.*

Mamma lay first in her chair, then in bed breathing, hoarse echoing sounds that reverberated round her chest. Every day we sat together, Sam and me, in her breeze-block room, our young selves looking down at us from the walls, in the days when we thought it *obvious* that we should have a mother, and that she should be cajoled, ignored, defied, laughed at for her antiquated habits. Her arms raised behind her head pinning her heavy dark hair into a French pleat, wearing a rubber girdle to hold in her already slim figure, her modest A-line skirts never above the knee, collecting string and paper long after nothing was on the ration and everything was plentiful, taking to the floor with my father at weddings and dinner dances, slowly circling the room in a stately waltz. And respected her when certain things were mentioned on the radio or television and she would say, 'Please, I do not wish to hear.'

We sat beside her, turning the pages of books, newspapers, drank coffee, waited.

'Look, was that a movement?'

'I didn't see. What happened?'

'I thought . . . No. It was nothing.'

'Her breathing is worse.'

'Yes. She's really hammering.'

The sheets and blankets were neatly folded over her, the window closed tight against the wind, the floor spotless, by her bed a photograph of the four of us on the beach in the South of France, in the fifties, my brother's arm round me, in imitation of our father whose own hands clutched our mother's shoulders as she sat in her swimsuit, crisp dark hair, moving in the sea breeze, leaning forward applying oil to her legs, laughing. And only in her eyes the sorrow that bore down on her every day and made itself known to my brother and me in those moments when her hand fell out of ours and she stopped what she was doing and began to cry. '*Mutter, Vater, wo bist du?*' 'Daddy, is there something wrong with Mummy?' 'Why?' 'She let go of my hand when we were crossing the road and she told me *always* to keep tight hold of her.' 'And then what happened, darling? Come here, sit on my knee.' 'She was walking along but she was crying, not like I cried when I fell over the lawnmower and cut my leg, but just tears on her face, why?' 'Because your mother has lost *her* mother and father and she misses them, and her brother too.' 'Where did she lose them?' 'A place where a lot of people got lost.'

Sometimes we would hear slow feet shuffle through the hall and a heavy figure would knock and say, 'Sam, Alix? Can I come in?'

Sam would jump up. 'Mrs Gelfer, take my chair.'

'Only a minute. I can't stay. I have the musical memories class before lunch. Ah, look at her, she's skin and bone, God help me.'

'Don't cry.'

'How can I help it? I remember them. Who could forget? Your father so handsome, you should have seen. And a doctor . . . How hard he worked at school, always his head over his books and never came out to play. The brothers saw to that because he was going to America, your father. After poor Ike got knocked back because of his TB, it had to be Saul, we were so sure he'd go to America, and then look what happens. Two years after the war ends he brings the most gorgeous girl home to meet his mother. Everyone could see at once she was a lady, that she'd been brought up with servants, like a princess, and one thing led to another. You were born, Sam, then you, Alix, and still they didn't leave Liverpool and here she is, that doll, like this. Oh, look at her . . . it breaks my heart. But she has two good children, you've been a wonderful son, Sam, a wonderful son with your own three *kinder*, wonderful too, and you, Alix, well, you know what they say, none to make you laugh, none to make you cry. Not married yet?'

'No.'

'You seeing someone?'

'No.'

'Well, darling, don't leave it too late, you're no spring chicken.'

I flinched. Sam saw my face. 'Forgive her,' he mouthed. I nodded. She gripped the arms of the chair and stood; I ran and lifted her zimmer frame towards her. She made a massive turn, in her flowered dress, knitted slippers on her feet, Ida Gelfer, who was eighty-three and whose son, Simon, had died at the age of twenty-two in 1969 in a motorbike accident while tripping on LSD on his way back from the Isle of Wight rock festival, something that Ida would never understand if she lived to two hundred. And all in the name of what? Of some kind of youth rebellion that she had read about in the papers, a rebellion of kids who had everything against parents who had once had nothing and were *happy*. That was the killer. For we were so happy when we were children, she told me, happy to be alive, happy not to be in Poland like our cousins who stayed behind, happy even to have a chance to join the army and go and fight the Germans, instead of being lined up and taken away by them.

'Sam,' she said, holding on to the door-frame, 'you know I don't bear a grudge.'

'I know you don't.'

'It was my fault, I should never have let my Harry go out that night, I should have insisted, put my foot down. It wasn't safe. The *schvartzes* were still going crazy, stealing everything they could lay their hands on, the fires everywhere, my God, it was like the blitz, and the police didn't know how to handle it at all. He said to me, "Listen, Ida, they had their fun last night, now they're sitting at home watching the TVs they nicked *last night*," and I said, "Okay, Harry, whatever you say," because *Coronation Street* was just starting and I didn't want to have a row with him. And then the next thing I know the phone rings from the hospital. But when they came up in court, and you said what you said to me, "Everyone has to have a defence, that's the law," I knew you were right. But still I say they should have known, an old man, what his heart would be like.' She turned at the door. 'Will you come and see me one day, after you've been with your mother?'

'Of course,' we cried. But we never did, we were so glad to escape from the home after our two hours was up, when Sam drove back to town and walked into his office, that raised-heel walk of his, head first, not feet first into any room, still in his jeans and Nikes with a suit hung up behind the door, which he changed into when he went to court or visited a client in the police cells or prison, and said what he said every day to the usual collection of druggies, prozzies, dealers, burglars, muggers, joyriders, ram-raiders, insurance scammers and wrongful arrests. 'Hey, what's happening?' He always had music playing in his waiting room whether his clients liked it or not. He was on a campaign of re-education, trying to eliminate rap and hip-hop with a counter-programme of soul and Motown and blues: James Brown, Marvin Gaye, Sam Cooke. 'Brother, brother, brother, there's too many of you dying,' he would sing, as he drove his Saab (then two years ago, the Merc) through the wide streets of our city, seeing it as Detroit without the summer heat, the gagging humidity.

Each day Sam and I watched by the bed and each evening Mary O'Dwyer said, 'I don't think your mother will be with us tomorrow, my dears.' And yet she was, she always was. We would sit in the office with her and Dr Mooney, a Belfast man, in Pringle sweater and corduroys, whose square red hands were laid on my mother's body, pressing her abdomen, feeling her internal organs through sour, milky skin. Outside in the hall, a girl was singing this song:

> *If you ever go across the sea to Ireland*
> *Be it at the closing of the day*
> *Just to see once more the moonlight over Claddagh*
> *And watch the sun go down on Galway Bay.*
>
> *Now the strangers came and tried to teach us their way*
> *And blamed us too for being what we are,*
> *Sure, they might as well go chasing after moonbeams,*
> *Or light a penny candle from a star!*
>
> *And if there's going to be a life hereafter,*
> *And somehow sure I know there's bound to be;*
> *I will ask of God to let me make my Heaven*
> *In that dear land across the Irish Sea.*

'The true song of sentimental exiled Irishmen everywhere,' said Dr Mooney. 'Now, in the version I remember, from when I was a medical student, it was "... and watch the *suds* go down on Galway Bay".'

'That's Mrs Friedman she's singing to,' said Mary O'Dwyer. 'A terrible case, Doctor. She was a girl in Auschwitz, and when the care workers here took her to the showers she thought she was being brought to the gas chamber and screamed and pleaded and begged the girls to spare her life. We have to give her a sponge bath once a week, in her bed, so she smells, of course, but I believe she is happy. I have got Agnes to sit all day and sing Irish lullabies to her to calm her down.'

'I got on the boat for Holyhead in 1973, and I've never once set foot on Irish soil ever since,' Mooney said, drinking his coffee from a rose-petalled china cup. 'I'm fond of the Jewish people for there's not a drop of Celtic blood in them. You're a very pragmatic race, I like that. There's little romance in you, a good thing, I believe. You know what Shaw said about us? The Irish drink too much and think too little, and the Jews drink too little and think too much.'

Pans clanged in the kitchen, the heavy rubber wheels of a trolley echoed in the halls. Someone was crying as an infant cries – mewling, it's called – and a voice said, 'Now then, Leah, your daughter-in-law will be in to see you today, won't that be nice?'

'And is your wife Irish, too?'

'She is, but she's trying to squeeze the romance out of herself. She works in pathology, she sees inside the human heart, but not the way the poets intended it.'

'You'll retire back to Ireland, Dr Mooney, just see if you don't,' Mary O'Dwyer said to him, laying a hand on his arm.

'Never. My wife has a fancy for Florida. She likes the heat, you see. She loves the look of a palm tree.'

'My!' said Mary O'Dwyer, opening her eyes wide. 'I went to Disneyworld once, but I never thought of settling there. Though I have some cousins in New Jersey, I believe, and my husband's brother lives in Boston. Have you been to America, Mr Rebick?'

'Yeah. My wife and I lived there for a few months, back in the seventies.'

'What made you want to come back?'

'Couldn't get work permits.'

'Do you visit often now?'

'Nah. Haven't set foot in the place for years. We'd got married young, had kids young, couldn't afford it, then never got round to it, and now the three of them have left home we could go but my wife isn't interested any more. She likes to ski and I like to keep her happy.'

'And you, Miss Rebick, have you been to America?' Mary O'Dwyer asked me.

'Yes, many times. It's not what it's cracked up to be.'

'You should tell that to the illegal immigrants that come in. We saw them in Miami, the Cuban people, all speaking Spanish, that was a surprise to us. Not a word of English some of them, though they'd been there twenty years or more. And their own clubs and restaurants and films . . .'

'Like us,' said Dr Mooney. 'I mean the Irish here in England.'

'And us,' said Sam.

'I nearly married an American once,' I said. 'I won't say he was the love of my life because he wasn't. I can't even remember why I wanted to marry him except it was that time when it seems the obvious thing because all of your friends are doing it. I met him at an academic conference, he was a lawyer who specialised in cases to do with native Americans, very passionate and committed to his work . . .'

'You mean he was a Red Indian himself?'

'No, no, not at all. Potato-famine Irish was his ancestry, same as you, I suppose. Anyway, he'd moved from New Jersey to live in Seattle but this was long before Microsoft and Bill Gates, when Washington State was the most godforsaken hole, absolutely the back of beyond, logging country. I went out to see if I would like it there, he had an amazing house on Puget Sound, right on the edge of the water and I was wowed, I really was. We'd sit out in the evening on the porch with our drinks looking at the lights on the boats in the harbour and I thought, Okay, he may not be Mr Right but we get along fine and between us we will have some very interesting-looking children, without a doubt. But on the very first weekend he took me wilderness camping. Now, you have no idea how much it rains in the Pacific North West. In half an hour we were sodden, the tent was dripping, the sleeping-bags damp. We hit some place and he says, "Look!" And I said, "At what?" I *am* looking but all there is are pine trees, nothing else, just these spruces, as far as the eye can see. The visual monotony! I told him I would marry him if we could live somewhere civilised like San Francisco or preferably New York but he wouldn't hear of it. He said those places weren't the true America, the America of the pioneer. So that was that.'

'You must have had many proposals in your time,' said Mary O'Dwyer, pouring me another cup of coffee from the electric machine.

'No. Just that one, as it happens.'

'She's had her share of boyfriends, though,' Sam interrupted. 'She was never short.'

'I nearly got married and I nearly became an American. I could still become an American, Rose Rosen offered me a job, but I doubt if I'll marry.'

'That's right. A woman doesn't need a man. She can stand on her own two feet.'

'Yes,' said Dr Mooney. 'It's a very different situation for women these days. Even in Ireland things are improving no end.'

'All my sisters in Limerick are on the Pill,' Mary O'Dwyer added. 'Of course, they dare not tell our mother, for she's still old-fashioned in that respect, but the priest must guess and he says nothing.'

'My wife works in a women's centre in Bootle,' Sam said. 'She does a family-planning clinic. She thinks nothing has changed at all.'

'It's marvellous what your family has done for the Liverpool people,' Mary O'Dwyer told us.

My mother did not die that night, or the next, not the one after that, either. She stayed with us many days longer until we began to expect that death would not come at all.

One day Sam said, at breakfast, 'I want to invite someone to dinner.'

'Who's that?' my sister-in-law Melanie said.

'An American. I met him at the gym, a real treadmill schlepper.'

'Is he married?'

'I don't know, I didn't ask.'

'Did he wear a wedding ring?'

'I didn't look.'

'What's he doing here?'

'He's building a hotel.'

'What kind of hotel?'

'I don't know.'

'So what did you talk about?'

'Our running speeds. The weights we could pull. How we'd spent years walking round thinking we still looked like we looked at twenty-two and the shock you get when this thing appears where your stomach used to be. One of the twenty-year-old instructors comes up to him and asks if he'd like to join a class called Awesome Abs and the guy looks at him and says, "Listen,

I'm never going to be awesome anything, physically." And the instructor is baffled and I'm killing myself with laughter.'

'Why not?' Melanie said. 'What shall I make?'

Sam looked at me. 'Alix?'

She was a terrible cook, just awful. She regarded the kitchen as a place of unending toil, a factory in which she was the sole worker, day in, day out. Meals had to be produced on time and to fit in with the requirements of a grown man who didn't care what he ate as long as it was ready when he got home from court, a son who would eat nothing but pizza if they let him and two teenage girls each with her own faddy diet. Melanie faced ovens and grills and hotplates, ingredients that went off if not prepared at once, recipes she couldn't follow written for people with three hands. For a year after they were married she cried every time she went into the kitchen, until Sam came home one day and found her standing sobbing, frozen peas bouncing across the floor, the torn bag in her hand. She had an iron will, could make herself eat next to nothing or not eat at all one day and the next drink only vegetable juice, 'to detox'. Food was fuel; what she ate was the minimum number of calories she needed to keep her going. Sweet things didn't interest her. And Sam took her in his arms and told her that she need never go into the kitchen again, they would live off raw steaks and raw eggs and glasses of milk and bread and fruit, nothing that needed any preparation, if that was what it took to make her happy. But she struggled on, mastering simple recipes like Bolognese sauce and chilli and just once assembled eggs, anchovies, lemon and oil and in front of our eyes made, from scratch, a Caesar salad.

'I'll tell you what,' I said, 'why don't I cook?'

What else was there to do in France? To drive, every morning, to the nearest small town, which is Lalinde, and go from shop to shop, buy bread and brioche, lamb, poussins, *moules*, St Jacques, tomatoes, chicory, Roquefort, raspberries, chocolate, Merlot – at first I had been enchanted with the prosaic task of shopping made poetic. Everything in France that was for sale was presented as if it were a work of art, and living in France itself was, I believed at first, its own kind of art form. The asparagus held in bunches, the silver gleam of mackerel, the wild strawberries red as babies' mouths, the knobbly lemons still tinged with green; the smell of herbs, lavender and rosemary and chervil, heightened the sensation of being alive on one of our hot blue June days before the tourists arrived from Paris and England, and I would meet my new friends for coffee and we would exchange recipes. 'Delia Smith, not serious about food, but Elizabeth David, of course . . . knew the woman she bought . . . and Claudia Roden, whose classic dish . . . and going back to Brillat-Savarin . . .' I did learn to cook. I was invited to dinner parties and gave them in return, and recipes were asked for so I can only assume the compliments were sincere, but food overwhelmed me. The pointlessness of cooking overwhelmed me: you sweated, you struggled, you created, and then someone, perhaps yourself, came along and ate what you had made and what was left? Washing-up.

None the less, it was something to do while we waited for Mamma to die, so in my brother's flat, I said I would make dinner for this unknown American, whose name was Joseph Shields.

But in the afternoon, when I had bought chickens and lemons and chocolate and Sam was holding in his hands a bottle of Médoc I'd brought back from France, Mooney rang and picking up the phone Sam heard him say, 'Shall we end it?'

'You mean,' Sam replied, 'do we want you to kill our mother for us?'

'It's like there's a rusted gate in my mind,' he told me, when he'd ended the call with 'You've got to be joking, haven't you? Now fuck off.'

'Have you tried to open it?'

'Yes. I've pushed, but it won't budge.'

We went straight to the home, sat by Mamma's bed and looked at her. 'He's right in one way,' Sam said, pointing at our mother's panting form making a little ripple in the bed-covers. 'This isn't life.'

'So what is it, Sam?' I asked, turning on him.

But my big brother – the lawyer who knows everything – didn't know what state of heaven or hell our mother was in, and neither did I.

'Do you want her to linger like this?' Mooney begged us that evening, called out by Mary O'Dwyer. He was wiping away a morsel of his supper from his mouth with a royal blue handkerchief.

'Why?' Sam asked him, his temper rising in his throat. 'Are they short of a bed? Is some other old biddy needing it? There's no difference in the money, you know. We'll go on paying even if she's not doing your reminiscence classes and your raffia weaving and your old-time singalongs. Our cash is still good.'

'Or can't you stand looking at her face a second longer?' I chipped in. 'Because *we* can. If you think I've nothing better to do than sit with my dying mother, you're right. I haven't. I'll sit there until hell freezes over.'

'Miss Rebick, please, think of *her* for a minute. There may be some pain, some discomfort, there's no way in the world of telling. She's had no solid food for weeks, she can't swallow any more, she's starving to death. The best we can do is get a little water down her. She'll fade away eventually but the truth is she should have been long dead. It's our modern antibiotics that are keeping her alive. The flu is on her chest, that's why she's hammering, the pneumonia will come next. Will you put her through more? If we give her an injection of morphine now, it will ease her suffering, but she's so weak, she won't last the night. Believe me, I've seen murder, my little brother went to the Provos. I've a reverence for life, and I won't refer a woman for an abortion, I'll give her the name of someone who will, but I will not put my own name on the form – excuse me, I didn't mean any disrespect to your late father, a wonderful doctor by all accounts though I only really knew of him after he retired. Now with your mother, there's no future, no one's going to come running through the door waving a serum in a glass bottle, like you see in the old films, shouting that he's found a cure. She's on her deathbed. Let her go over to the other side now, for pity's sake.'

'Why?' I cried scornfully. 'Do you think anything's waiting for her there?'

'Personally, yes, though I don't know what your mother believed. But life here must end, it *must* end. That is the law of the universe. There is no immortality for any of us on this earth.'

'Don't talk to me about the law,' said Sam, but it was only because he felt himself up against an almighty adversary and it was unbearable not to have the last word.

'Go home and sleep on it,' said Mary O'Dwyer. We stood up and shook the doctor's hand and Sam apologised for both of us, for our anger and our sarcasm, and Mooney clasped my shoulder. Warmth spread through me. Then he turned and went home to his wife.

In Sam's new flat, in the dockside development, we came up in the lift and walked along the echoing corridors. Sam turned his key in the lock. If I was back living in the *shtetl*, he had moved straight into the sweatshop. They hadn't even painted the brick walls. Iron columns held the place up. The furniture was the kind you looked at rather than sat in. The dining-table chairs alone were excruciating.

'Sam,' I had said, when I first saw it, 'it's stunning. I can't imagine how much you would have to spend to achieve this simplicity.'

'A fortune.'

The windows ran from floor to ceiling and wherever you looked the river was in front of you. Rainclouds hung over the Wirral. Shafts of weak sunlight illuminated the water. The seagulls made the old familiar sound, the shrieks and stutters that rent the lower throb of the traffic along the dock road.

'You know my problem, don't you?' he said.

'What?'

'What is going on here is that I'm being required not to offer a defence but to make a judgement, to switch sides, and it goes against the grain with me after all these years, Alix. What do *you* think? You're the expert in murder.'

It's true, there are certain things I know about death that years of study have taught me. We sat down at the kitchen table. I looked at my hands, saw the blood-red polish on my nails, saw Sam's bitten ones, these small dead lucent shells on our living skin. Our bodies thrummed with life like power cables. 'Well, we need to ask ourselves what Dad would have done in the same circumstances. I suppose he would have mentioned *tzadakah*, which conceptually contains the ideas of both justice and charity. He would have wanted to know, is this a just act? Is it a compassionate one?'

'To the second, I don't know. As for justice, we have to speak about what's lawful. I suppose Mooney wouldn't have suggested it if it wasn't legal. They must do this kind of thing all the time.'

'Is it euthanasia?'

'I don't know that either, all I know is that it's a death sentence. It's not so much that he's asking us to kill her as telling us, "You have the power to say when she'll die, to name the day."'

'Oh for God's sake, put the poor woman out of her misery, will you?' Melanie shouted. I'd barely seen her in the room. She was standing stock still at the door, her small body rigid with anger, her hair electrified about her face. 'Stop talking, will you, for once in your lives? There's nothing *to* talk about, it's not a talk-ing business. Don't make an intellectual argument out of it. I cannot stand to see Lotte like that. I know six women in Bootle alone who have said to me, "Mrs Rebick, your father-in-law helped my mother or my father or whoever it was to pass on." And if that's what *he* would have done, then it's good enough for me.'

Darkness was on the river. The uncurtained windows showed the lights of Birkenhead and the shadows of the shipyards deep-ening on the water. Everything I saw was dying, the city's population thickly flowing south. The Docks and Harbours Board and the docks themselves, the insurance buildings, the blackened, blasted warehouses along the waterfront, the cranes and piers, and a mile or so inland, those hulking brutes, the two cathedrals, all dead entities.

In my story there is no magic realism, no flights of butterflies above a grave, no unicorns, no mermaids, no ghosts, no demons, no fairies, no wizards, no sorcerers, no spirit world at all. Here in the port and on the river there is only the iron law of the tides and the weather.

We sat up all night talking – about the world and its wrongs, about the scams and the skives, about our memories of a past when we were kids and had two parents who loved us, each in his or her own very different fashion.

'Do you remember the time Mamma came to the school par-ents' day in a *cartwheel hat*?'

'It was black and white straw.'

'And her black and white pearls.'

'Have you ever forgiven her for making such a show of you in front of your friends?'

'Never in a million years.'

'You pushed me off the top of the sand-dunes at Ainsdale once.'

'You were trying to bury me on the beach.'

'And I was rolling over and over, curled up, my mouth full of grit and Mamma was standing at the bottom with her sunglasses on and she was shrieking and Daddy was laughing and saying that no harm had come to me, but she picked me up and wouldn't let go of me for the whole of the day.'

'Oh, you baby, Mamma's baby.'

Mamma among us, always there, always *soignée*, prettier than anyone else's mother. Mamma asleep in the afternoons with the curtains drawn, the streets quiet, woken by a ship's horn on the river or a train coming down the track to Grassendale. Mamma bending over Robert Carrier's cookbook, announcing, 'I think tonight I will make an onion tart from Alsace. Look, Alix, at the picture of it here.' Mamma standing by a zebra's cage at the zoo: 'Sam, the striped horse is eating his lunch, come and see.' Mamma doing the books, totalling the figures. 'Saul, we have sold fourteen per cent more jars this month than in April. And not only that. I have an order from a lady in Paris! She writes that her sister-in-law in Hampshire gave her a jar and she has used it up, she must have another. We are international!' Mamma with her reparations papers, the ash from her cigarette falling on the pages. Mamma bending down and leaving a scarlet mouth on my cheek, the scent of Blue Grass perfume on her wrists and neck and violet lozenges on her breath. Mamma crying, '*Naughty* child, I will smack you – no, I will *thrash* you – if you . . .' and Daddy standing in the doorway, blocking the light, saying, 'Lotte, a word.' And Mamma and Daddy behind locked doors, Mamma groaning and crying, and Sam hammering on the door with six-year-old fists, 'Daddy, why are you hurting Mamma?' And my mother flushed and dishevelled in her nightdress with Swiss embroidery at the yoke, opening the door and saying, 'Sam, go back to bed this very minute. I am very angry with you. Of course Daddy is not hurting me, do not ever think such a thing.'

At dawn, Sam said, 'Let's go for a drive.'

We drove away from the waterfront round the one-way system, across the overpass that lets you down on to Lime Street; past the concrete funnel of the Catholic cathedral, crowned in thorns of iron; through Toxteth, where roadworks were causing a diversion around Falkner Square, whose Georgian mansions form a white fortress against the chaos; circled Sefton Park where I once kissed boys in the fretted shadow of the palm house; hurried along Smithdown Road, past the hospitals and their consequence, the boneyard. Past Penny Lane we entered wide, empty boulevards lined with early-flowering cherry trees, bands of bronze around their trunks. Through Speke, past the car factories at Halewood, until we reached the place where the Runcorn bridge crossed the Mersey mudflats at low tide. And everything I saw came towards me with its hands held out, saying, 'Do you remember, don't you remember?' . . . *Of course* I remembered, I remembered everything. I saw myself at fifteen walking these streets, not afraid of anything, because no one had ever taught me to *be* afraid, Alix on the verge. Running with her tennis racquet to the bus, hair flying about her face, breasts already heavy on her chest, so impatient, so cross, so easy to laughter, so little need to cry – and the girl I was then turned sharply to look at me, that kid in her denim mini-skirt, the round-toed patent shoes, the brown polo-necked jumper. She was still here, still in Liverpool! I hadn't known, I thought she'd died long ago, and been replaced by the successive stages of a self that even then was itching to move on, move away, because it was in the nature of this place on the edge of the Atlantic to promise that if you were a restless girl not a tree – had legs instead of roots – somewhere else was waiting for you.

And all the time Sam kept up the Rebick riff.

'Still smoking?'

'Yeah.'

'Gimme one.'

'You too?'

'Why not?'

'It's a con, you know. The government put cancer in the cig-arettes for a few years but then they stopped. It was the Tories who first did it under Heath but Labour reversed the policy. I'm telling you, it's the God's honest truth.'

'Now why, Sam, would the Conservatives put cancer in the cigarettes?'

'Too many workers. The country didn't need all that many any more. Of course, it killed off some of their own voters but it was a small price to pay in the long term. You remember how the unemployment rate kept going down? That was because the workers were dying off from lung cancer. But cigarettes are safe as houses now. '

'Well, that's a relief.'

We got out of the car and breathed the fumes of fifty years of industry, of car manufacture, potato-crisp production, the pro-cessing of chemicals at Rio Tinto Zinc. The wind was biting, blowing up the estuary from the sea. 'It's so cold,' I said.

'You've gone soft. It's just fresh.'

Down on the banks of the river, there was a smell of mud and the bridge above us shuddered. Across the other side lay Cheshire, and that was something else entirely.

'"If you ever go across the sea to Ireland,"' my brother sang.

I said, 'Have you ever been to Ireland?'

'No.'

'Me neither. What do you think it's like?'

'No idea. I never thought about it. Alix, what are we going to do?'

'We've got to let him.'

'Yeah, I know, you're right.'

'*Melanie* is right.'

'She always is.'

'You got a good one, there.'

'So everyone tells me.'

'How do you make it work?'

'What?'

'Your marriage.'

'Sheer bloody-mindedness, I suppose.'

'On whose part?'

But Sam just said, 'Your shoes are covered in mud. They look expensive, you'll ruin them. Come on, let's get out of here.'

In the morning we rang Mooney.

'You can go ahead,' Sam told him.

'And is your sister in agreement?'

'Yes, and my wife. We've discussed it thoroughly.'

'Then I would advise you to ring your synagogue – it won't take long at all and I understand you'll need to have the funeral within the day.'

Mary O'Dwyer injected our mother with morphine while we sat and watched. The needle went into her left thigh. Then . . . the roses on her curtains blanched! The water in the glass by her bed where her teeth had been for five weeks dried up in an instant! No, they didn't, none of these fanciful events occurred because this is Liverpool, where there is no room for fairy stories and if a miracle occurs it's not a babyish one. And yet still things happen that I cannot explain.

The needle went in, there was a little sigh. Six or seven minutes later, when the opium was entering her brain, my mother opened her mouth and spoke. She said four words in a clear voice, the voice I hadn't heard for three and a half years. 'Hol' die Fabrik zurück.' Birds sang in the garden, bees buzzed. An old man screamed in the corridor as the nurse hoisted him into a contraption that would wheel him to the bathroom.

'What did she say?' cried Mary O'Dwyer.

'Get the factory back.'

'A factory?'

I looked up from my mother's dying face. 'There used to be a factory, in Dresden, a long time ago.'

'And what became of it?'

'It was appropriated. We don't know.'

'Perhaps she'll speak again. I told you, Mr Rebick, about God's miracles and his mercy. Has she another message for you?'

'No, no.' The past revolves around us like the planets.

She died in the early hours, exactly as Mooney told us she would. There's a big difference between being alive and being dead, though I can't say what it is. When the nurse pulled away the sheet the next morning and I saw her, without breath, there was no doubt that she was no longer living. One minute your heart is beating, however feebly. Your chest rises and falls, the blood circulates through your arteries and veins and the flower-like networks of tiny branches invisible beneath the skin. Then all this activity just stops and who are you left with then?

'Where did she *go*, Alix?'

Sam, the women from the Chevra Kaddisha came and, with the utmost tenderness, they raised her limbs and gently washed her shattered body and they wrapped her in linen and they bound each wrist seven times with linen strips and they placed a mask of gauze over her face and a handful of earth from the land of Israel beside her, and she went into a hole in the ground in a pine box with rope handles, not ten hours after she was dead. And you saw it yourself and you heard what the rabbi told us, that she's in heaven now, with her mother and her father and her brother and all the uncles and cousins who died in various ways, in a certain period in Germany that is known to everyone. And now she's holding hands with our father, may he rest in peace, and God has gathered them all to his breast. You *can* believe

that, Sam, if you wish, or you can believe that the earth of the
land of our forefathers is now mingled with the earth of England
whose worms are in there doing their business and her face
beneath the gauze mask is eaten away and the dead flesh that was
her brain is food not for thought but for whatever microbes can
devour it. Because that's what death is, Sam. Which version do
you prefer? You tell me.

Joseph

By working out at the gym regularly, I'm starting to meet people socially. Last night I went to dinner with the Rebicks. The brother and sister, Sam and Alix, have just lost their mother. I had looked in at the *shiva* the previous week to pay my respects: it was packed, a revelation to me, an insight into a world I knew absolutely nothing about. When I was growing up in Chicago, the England they taught us about in school and which I saw at the movies was stately homes and castles, Shakespeare and kings and queens, Laurence Olivier and Alec Guinness. At home, you might say that everyone *came* from Europe but no one had actually *been* there, not even my father who during the war was itching to get to France or the Pacific but, rated 4R because of his eyesight, sat out the entire conflict behind a desk in Washington doing the paperwork for the Normandy landings. By the time I reached my teens I'd had to retool that impression because now, to me, England had turned into the land of the Beatles, of 'She Loves You'. Pretty quickly we were a gang of stoned kids lying around my parents' garage scanning the *Sgt Pepper* album cover, fighting over who these weird people were, once we'd quickly identified Bob Dylan and Marilyn Monroe, and my father coming in and saying, 'Well, that's W. C. Fields.' I remember when I was in the army we used to sit on the half-track and sing 'Yellow Submarine' and when we took turns to guard our prisoners, they sang it also, the Beatles songs everyone knew, even our enemies. We sang 'All You Need Is Love' and laughed ourselves silly because if we were sure of anything, in the army, it was that you needed much more than love, a lot more. Just to start with you needed a new helmet and a gun that didn't jam when you tried to fire it, and better rations and better lieutenants and better generals. On the battlefield you could do very easily without love but you couldn't do without at least one individual who had some kind of functioning plan to get you out of there alive.

But what I had never expected in England, and certainly not in Liverpool, were Jews. The apartment in the Albert Dock was full of them, these old people sitting under framed prints of Hockney and Pollock and Rothko, all eating and urging the bereaved to eat. I asked my grandfather once, after my great-aunt Minnie, his sister, died, why do people bring so much food to a *shiva* house? He'd gotten very little at that point, he must have been over ninety, and he leaned towards me with his rye-bread breath and said, 'I dunno, Joe. Maybe it's because after a death, you have no choice but to keep your strength up to show God that you are still alive and he should not be tempted to take you too, in his mysterious wisdom.' These old Jews were standing at the window treading cake crumbs into the rugs and watching the river, looking at the shipyards, listening to the white seagulls

screaming in the estuary and asking (with exactly the same rye-
bread odour as my *zaidie*, which made me think of him for the
first time in years), 'How much does a place like this go for,
nowadays?' And when they heard the reply, I saw how they
looked at each other, amazed. 'When Sam said to me he was
buying one of these places,' someone was saying, 'I told him that
he was out of his mind. Who would pay to live in a flat in an
abandoned dock in the centre of town where they'll knife you
when you set one foot out the door? You're making a terrible
investment, I said that right to his face.'

After I'd shaken hands with the Rebicks and Sam's three
kids, two girls and a boy, all in their twenties now, I sat down in
a really uncomfortable chair next to this old guy, Baruch
Neslen. He reminded me in looks of my uncle Willie, my
mother's brother-in-law, the Philadelphia judge who got the
cowboy bug when he was a kid watching Hopalong Cassidy
movies, and sits in court in a Stetson hat and bootstring tie,
which is pretty incongruous for a little fat Jew with short legs
and a goatee. When the Marlboro man died of lung cancer, my
uncle Willie said, 'If you don't have to provide your own horse,
I'm ready to step up and take that job right away.' I said, 'Uncle
Willie, you smoke Camels.' He said, 'Don't worry, I'm not brand
loyal.'

I was in for an earful. Neslen had my uncle Willie's girth but
lacked his humour. He told me he had made his money from selling toys, then diversified into arcade games. 'Listen,' he said,
'you would be surprised what a living can be made out of child-
ishness. Now, their father,' he pointed at Sam, 'everyone will tell
you was a very smart man and it's true, he could have set up on
Rodney Street and had the cream of society for his patients, he
could have specialised, but no, no, he was stubborn, he opens up
on Upper Parliament Street back in the forties when the
schvartzes from the African ships were already living there, in

those big houses they pulled down in the seventies. They used to be gentlemen's mansions and what did the *schvartzes* make of them? Slums. Tenements. You should have seen those houses in my day, in the twenties, beautiful they were, built in Queen Victoria's time for men with wealth, men who worked in the insurance offices and kept a carriage in the back, the mews, they called them, the stables before the motor-car. I see houses like that in London go for a million pound. Here, they had to pull them down because the halls stank of things you don't even want to know about. If we'd had houses like that to live in when we got off the boat from Russia do you know what we would have made of them? *Palaces*, because the women were *balabatish*, they knew how to keep a home clean and a kitchen always full of food and the children turned out like princes and princesses, or as far as you could manage on the wage you got in those days, when your father didn't speak English but everyone, *everyone* helped out with what he could. I was lathering faces in a barber shop when I was six years old so we would go for nothing. Not like the Irish who spent their money on drink and came home schickered up every night and the *schvartzes* played their banjos like there was no tomorrow. That's what Rebick gave his life to, a smart man, supposedly. You call that smart? Bringing their babies into the world instead of telling them, "You don't want babies? Then keep your *putz* to yourself." And why did he waste his time? Because he was a Communist, a red. He should see Soviet Russia now.'

Before I came here I thought the English were supposed to be reserved but these people are so loquacious! It's a very talkative city.

Neslen was helping himself to cake from a plate offered by the brother's wife, Melanie. She is what my mother would have called 'a homely girl', but she keeps herself in shape; there can't be an ounce of fat on her, and the dress she was wearing, a little black thing in some kind of silky stuff, did her justice. She looked particularly good from the back, when she was bending over with the honey cake, though for myself I prefer a figure that is a little more *zahftig*, short and squeezy.

'I'll tell you about the reds. The reds destroyed this city. Liverpool is finished. The North West is finished. And why? Because of the greed of the dockers who wanted a hundred pound a week to sit on their backsides doing bugger all while I sweated blood in my business, watching every second of the day while they robbed me blind and stole the stock and fiddled the books. Not a single one ever wanted to do an honest day's graft and you know why? Because they were all counting on one thing, that one day they'd win the pools and they'd retire and live the life of Reilly. That's the workers for you, Saul Rebick's precious workers.'

An old lady with an awful lot of coral lipstick on her teeth, sitting a few old people down, shouted, 'Oh, shut up, Baruch. Behave yourself, you're at a *shiva* house. Have some respect.'

'Her,' said the old man, pointing across the room at the sister. 'She was the only smart one. The people with brains got out while the going was good. I'd have got out myself if it hadn't been too late. For myself I left it too long, but if you're born here now you should crawl on your hands and knees out of your mother's belly to get away from this place. The drug-dealers and the gangsters alone will eat you alive.' He had a soft little red mouth and button eyes and, with a glass of lemon tea at his lips, he turned and asked me a question at last, the one I'd been waiting all evening to answer: 'So, what are you doing here?'

'I see a business opportunity,' I told him.

'What line of work are you in?'

'I'm an architect. I build hotels.'

'You're building a hotel *here*?' He turned to the old lady and tapped his finger against his forehead. 'He's brought his own *mishegoss* to Liverpool with him, like we didn't have enough already.' Two hands were raised palm up to his audience, the fingers right up the knuckles stained with nicotine.

'Certainly here, not even a quarter of a mile away, just a few minutes' walk.'

'Now I know you're crazy.'

'Not at all. I see tremendous potential along the waterfront. Your city officials tell me that the future is going to be tourism and I agree. All your existing hotels are at maximum occupancy at weekends. The city's advertising campaign in America has been very successful. Of course, when people come to England they want to see Big Ben and Stratford-upon-Avon and guys in Edinburgh in skirts – the usual tourist crap – but nine million future Americans left the old world from this city, they set sail from right here, where we're sitting. That's a piece of nearly every American's family history and not only do you have that but you also have your culture, you have the Beatles and every American knows who *they* are. I'm extremely optimistic about the future of this place.'

'So what kind of hotel are you planning to build?' Neslen asked me. *Now* he was interested. The little red mouth was wet and his voice hoarse. 'We already have a Holiday Inn, a Crowne Plaza. Beautiful places.'

'I build art hotels. I've—'

'You build *what?*'

'Art hotels. I have five in five different cities.' I ticked them off. 'San Francisco, my first, then Toronto, Frankfurt, Prague, Madrid. I build in industrial areas often using derelict building stock, conversions, though here I'm starting from scratch. In each hotel there is a range of art, always modern, nothing that's before 1980, and all from the city I'm building in. I do deals with local painters and sculptors – they get a wonderful showcase for their work and the design is up to me. I go to Italy and Germany and I talk to designers and I commission them to do exactly what I want. I love German design – everything functional, every detail exact and with a style that's submerged, not at all obvious or flashy. I have fabulous taste, Mr Neslen – that is why people stay in my hotels, because they see something in them and what they see is me, my taste.'

'These are five-star hotels?'

'No. Four-star. With five-star you get unnecessary luxuries. I don't put in restaurants, just little coffee shops and room service, because they're in big cities where you can already eat in great restaurants. I don't put in pools either . . .'

He slumped back in his chair, tired, old and cranky. The motor of whatever energy he had left was running down and he was losing interest. A cookie hung from his fingers, sprinkling nuts on the floor.

'You're wasting your time,' he said. 'This city is finished, the drug-dealers have taken it over, the reds, the extortion rackets . . .'

Sam, the brother, came over and squatted on the floor next to him, rocking on his heels. The wife, Melanie, filled up Neslen's glass with whisky. 'The thing you've got to understand about Merseyside, Joseph,' Sam said, 'is this. We're not like everyone else. Other people have harmless daydreams. They take up *feng shui* or they tattoo Celtic rings round their arms or they think they've been abducted by aliens or sacrificed as babies in satanic cults. Liverpool went one better. We decided to do what the miners couldn't do and the steel workers couldn't do – take on the government single-handed, now that's a real fantasy. We fell for one of the one-day wonders that strut the streets, who told us the capitalists could go fuck themselves, excuse me, Ida, because Liverpool was going to be a capitalist-free zone.'

'You see?' Neslen cried. 'What did I tell you?'

Another elderly man was approaching; he didn't look in any way Jewish, his belly carried in front of him like a rice bowl. His hands had lost their flesh and he held his fingers crooked so the gold signet rings on them didn't fall off and clatter to the floor. 'Can I join you for a minute, get the weight off my feet?'

'Certainly,' Sam said to him, and turning to me, 'Joseph, have you met Kevin Wong?'

'I hear you're building a hotel, Mr Shields.'

'Now, how do you know that?'

'He knows everything,' Sam said.

'You're a newspaperman?'

'Me? Ha ha, very funny, I'm a solicitor.'

'So you know all the villains, the gangsters? '

'Please. I have nothing to do with criminal law. I deal in contracts, industrial-injury cases, disputes, that kind of thing.'

'Kevin, Sam said, 'drew up the first contract between Brian Epstein and the Beatles.'

'Yes. And Gerry and the Pacemakers and Cilla Black, all the Liverpool groups before Mr Epstein went away to London, a wonderful woman, his mother, Queenie. I never believed he was a fruit. I told Queenie, "In London he'll find a girl, trust me," but sadly, he died far too young, a big shame.'

'So you *knew* the Beatles?'

'Oh, yes, very much so, they all came to me when they were in trouble over whatever.'

'Like what?'

'I can't go into any of that, client confidentiality, but there were scrapes, Mr Shields, plenty of scrapes. It was Brian, though, that I gave my loyalty to. I thought to myself, This pop-singing combo, a nine-day wonder, but Brian, he'll get other singers, that's where the business is, managing them. Even when he had his Rolls-Royce we never lost touch. Through him I was invited to the London Palladium the time the Beatles played their Royal

Command Performance in front of the Queen. Another time I
had the privilege of personally shaking hands with Benny Hill. I
have the autographs of all the Beverley Sisters.'

'Wow,' I said, politely.

'All framed on my office wall.'

There was a crowd round us now. The sister had appeared
from the kitchen holding a bottle of whisky to refill the glasses
and another platter of cookies; a tall woman in a black trouser
suit, she had three or four inches on her brother, a model's figure
gone in the middle. I think she might have been a dish in her
day but she has that drawn, haggard look that surgeons in
America fix for ten thousand dollars, or so Erica tells me. And I
said to her, years ago, 'Please, never touch your face.' She refilled
Neslen's glass and gave one to me, which I took, because this is
what you drink at a *shiva* house, not Chardonnay. That's not a
tradition one can break with. It must have been schnapps in the
old country.

'You want to hear a joke?' I asked them, looking round, smiling. There was no reason for me to discuss my business in the
middle of a gloomfest about the city's future. They were wrong,
I was right and would prove them so. They were just going to
have to wait. My hotel will open in January 2001. The company
I build for already has advance bookings.

'Why do ninety-eight per cent of American Jews approve of
Janet Reno's hijacking of Elian Gonzales?' They turned to each
other and smiled. They could sense a good one. 'Because they
know what it's like to be trapped in Miami with relatives.'

I looked around to see how it had gone down. Sam had
thrown back his head and was slapping his hand on the thigh of
his pants. Wong was smiling, Neslen was nodding, 'Very good,
very good.' The old lady was saying, 'What? what? I didn't hear
the punchline, tell me again.'

Melanie nudged the sister. 'Alix, tell the one you told me.'

'Okay. But it's not a belly-laugh joke. Why don't Jews drink?'
Neslen raised his glass. 'Except on sad occasions.'
'Because alcohol dulls the pain.'
'That reminds me,' said Neslen, 'of the definition of a Jewish
telegram: start worrying, details to follow.'
'You know,' I said to Alix, 'when I met your brother in the
gym and he told me he was Jewish and that there was a Jewish
community here I thought, Are you kidding? And if there *are*
Jews they're not *real* Jews, like the people I grew up with in
Chicago – really, I didn't know what to expect. But obviously I
was wrong. You truly are real Jews. I'll e-mail that one to my
wife.' I saw something flicker in her eyes and recognised whatever it was from some of Erica's divorcée friends, the bitter
women who come round to our house and sit with her over
coffee talking about what assholes men are, the disappointment
of the single woman who has to strike yet another possibility off
the list.
But I meant it, it was a great joke.
'Do you live here in Liverpool?' I asked her. 'Or are you visiting for your mother's funeral?'
'I live in France but I travel a lot. Listen, pay no attention to
any of them. They don't know what they're talking about.
Personally, I like the sound of what you're doing, you build your
hotel, and when you've built it, they'll be the first to put their
heads in and look around and in twenty years they'll still be
saying, "No one thought it could be done, but it was a Jew who
built this place, did you know that?" You'll be claimed, you'll be
an honorary citizen of the city. They'll make you forget you ever
came from Chicago.'
'How about you? Are you an honorary citizen?'
'Absolutely not. My brother is, he's the greatest thing we've
produced since Brian Epstein, a local hero like my father. Sam
defended the Toxteth rioters, there were profiles of him in the

national papers, the media still ring him when they want to
know what's going on here. You have to understand, we're a
famous family in Liverpool.'

'What do you do for a living?'

'I engage in an unAmerican activity.'

'What? You're a professional Communist agitator? No, wait,
you're a terrorist, you bomb apple-pie factories on Mother's Day.'

'I have nothing against mothers.'

'Oh, God, I'm sorry, what an awful . . .'

But she was laughing, her wide, red-lipsticked mouth showing
long teeth, a flash of gold crown, a narrow tongue. 'No, listen, all
I meant was that I am wholly involved in the past and you really
can't get much more unAmerican than that.'

'You're an historian?'

'No, I used to be an academic. I worked at a university but I
didn't get tenure.'

'What happened?'

'Another time, maybe. Now I work for a foundation that is
trying to recover the lost Jewish communities of the world.'

'You're shipping people back there?'

'God forbid, no. We locate synagogues and renovate them. I'm
involved in the fundraising arm of it, so my work really begins at
the earliest stage, when we've located some sort of ruin or a
building that has been put to another use and I have to find out
the history of it and of the community that worshipped there and
what happened to them, which more often than not is flight,
exile or deportation, and then I sit down with the architects
who explain to me what they'll need to do to get the place back
on its feet again. Once I have all this information it's like I'm
some kind of biographer, I have to re-create the place for the
people we send out our mailshots to. And, of course, one of the
big problems is that they usually ask the same question: well, it
was a tragedy and a horror that the building has been defiled and

the people dispersed and murdered, but why not just forget about it, who needs a museum in the middle of nowhere that the minute you turn your back some ignorant little fuck will come along with his aerosol can and spray a swastika on it?'

Exactly these thoughts had been going through my own mind. 'So what do you say?'

'I say, I really don't care about them as museums, I don't care one way or another whether or not they are visited. My concern is that in those places the people who live there need to know that once there were Jews among them and that they built something and that it endured for hundreds of years until it was destroyed by hatred and fanaticism and racism. So I see it as a warning to them, a warning to their own hearts. What I save and restore is a symbol.'

'Of what?'

'That we will always return.'

'Jews?'

'No. I mean people who aren't like *you*. Which, you know, is why every fascist idea always fails. It can't contain what life is, which essentially is chaos. Different beliefs, nonsense lots of them, different ways of life, many abhorrent to me personally, and in some ways I'm a classic liberal though in other ways not at all. But what we Jews are is a symbol of the outsiders that people hate, so all I'm saying here is, let's rub their noses in it. Make them walk past that symbol every day on their way to work or school or to go shopping. Make them understand that there's no exclusive purity either of race or culture or religion.' She smiled. 'I find a lot of Americans really like the idea of making a fuck-you gesture.'

I have to say, I was enormously impressed by her. Not many women talk like this, have that kind of mental toughness. My wife certainly doesn't. But I just said, 'Count me in for a thousand dollars.'

'Well, you're a push-over,' she replied, smiling at me.

'You mean normally it takes longer?'

'Oh, yes. I have a pile of other arguments if they don't swallow this one.'

'Such as?'

'I can get your name on the letterhead, you want to be a vice-president?'

'And that works?'

'Every time.'

'I bet, knowing Americans. Listen, am I still invited to dinner?'

'Yes, we'll sort something out next week when all this is over. You must understand, we're not callous, but she's been a long time dying.'

'And you'll still be around?'

'Yes, I think so.'

'Good.' Later I thought that sounded like a come-on, but I *had* told her I was married. I had that clear at least, even though it was, as I have been forced to accept, a lie.

I watched her from across the room, standing with a glass of wine, towering over the old bubbas, her jacket straining a little around her upper back where a lot of women seem to thicken in middle age. She had that wild, curly Jewish hair, a big mop of it in a good rich shade of dark auburn, no grey. It stood out like she'd had an electric shock and more like pubic hair than the hair you have on your head. Perhaps it was the hair that gave me the idea that there was some kind of wildness in her, something witchy and savage that made me feel uncomfortable, except that now she was laughing again, her horse face, like Sarah Jessica Parker, thrown back and great lines etched round her eyes, and she caught *my* eye and did something women rarely do: she winked. And I thought, My God, this woman could let out a wolf-whistle if she wanted to, she could stop trucks with that red-lipsticked mouth, she could embarrass construction workers. I couldn't for a minute imagine what kind of man would take her on – she would be one hell of a handful. There is a cuteness I adore in women that makes me want to cuddle them like I cuddled my kids until they got too big and broke free of my arms, embarrassed by me. The voluptuousness of Marilyn Monroe will give any man in his right mind a hard-on, but the women I like in the movies are the Michelle Pfeiffer types, or Meg Ryan. You really could not call this Alix cute, not at all.

Ten minutes later, when I went to get my coat in the bedroom, I found Sam sitting on the edge of the bed in the darkness, his face wet.

'Hey, man, are you okay?'

He'd loosened his tie, his shoes were half off. It must have been a hell of a day for him: twenty-four hours ago his mother was still alive. I didn't really know at that stage what kind of state she had been in or what was wrong with her. I'd thought it must be cancer. He'd told me at the gym that he looked in on her every day and that she was going to die but they couldn't say when, and I understood that he was living a suspended life, like my own after Erica had told me she was leaving but she was still there, sleeping in Gil's room. He looked up and smiled, rubbed a hand over his eyes. 'You know what? I was thinking about my mother straightening my tie on my first day at big school. What a thing to remember.'

My mother tried to comb my hair for me my first day in high school and I wriggled away from her, shouting, '*Mom*, for Godsake.' When I talked to her a couple of days ago she said she and Dad hadn't left the house for two weeks. The winter is killing them. They really should move somewhere warmer: I truly believe that a good climate prolongs life.

'Give me a minute,' Sam said to me, putting his shoes back on, leather penny loafers, like my own.

'Take your time. Both my parents are still living. I can't imagine what it would be like to lose my mother.'

'And with us,' he said, 'there are complications. Which I will tell you about some other time.'

'Listen, I gotta ask. Who the hell was that Kevin Wong character?'

'Kev? My dad's old sparring partner. We've known him for yonks. All our lives. They used to meet up at lunchtime at Rigby's and argue about politics. Dad was left, Kevin was a Conservative.'

'What kind of law does he practise?'

'Well, supposing you go down the boozer Sunday night and you can't hold your ale, you get into a scuffle, you turn up at work the next morning with a black eye and, lo and behold, what should be in your way but a bit of baling rope somebody has been careless enough to leave lying around and, oops, you've tripped over it, flat on your kisser. What do you do? You go to your shop steward and he gives Kev a ring and the next thing you know, he's got you a hundred pounds' compensation for industrial injury. One time we had the highest rate of accidents caused by uneven paving stones in the country. People were going out at night with crowbars, pulling them up at the corners, back again next morning, down you go. Kevin! Get me a cheque. Don't smile, this is what we've been reduced to. It's a crying shame, it really is, and you, you are part of the plan to put us back where we were, on top of the world.'

The Rebicks live in the same building as me in the dockland section, which was refurbished for residential and commercial use in the eighties. I have a short-term let, which the city administration fixed up. It has everything I need, a doorman, underground parking, and there's the gym right next door. In the morning from my window I can see joggers running along the paved path between the cobblestones. All day long tourists are milling around the dock and I look at them and see potential customers. Knowing no one here, their conversations, which I eavesdrop on, are about my only social interaction some days, the only discussions that are not to do with me screaming at contractors about late starts and shoddy work. Next week the meetings begin with the artists, a whole schedule of them in my diary. When I first went into this business I thought that my dealings with the artists would be the pleasurable part of the job, but I had by no means factored into my considerations how neurotic these people can be.

So it was a relief when I met Sam Rebick at the gym and began to piece together who he was in relation to the city – not really from what he told me himself, at first, but what I heard from others. The largest criminal law firm in Merseyside built up over twenty-five years and the big break coming back in the early eighties during the race riots in Toxteth, the weekend Charles and Di got married. The first couple of nights were pretty ferocious, apparently, and the police had taken a real beating so the third night they came back with a vengeance, drove trucks into the crowd, someone was killed. Sam had gone on national television and said straight out that the police had declared war on Toxteth, that they were using illegal tactics. He took on the police chief, a man who by this stage in his career was, Sam would later tell me, 'intelligent, drunk, cynical and destroyed'. It was a huge coup for the black kids in that terrible burnt-out neighbourhood because the Rebick family was famous, the city's good guys, the father a kind of saint, from what I'd picked up from my contacts in the planning department. And when Sam finally opened up to me, I heard that he'd been involved in an amazing ballistics case.

'The Toxteth riots was the first time CS gas was used in

mainland Britain,' he said one day, as we sipped our mineral water after our work-out. 'They'd used it over the water, in Northern Ireland, but not here. But, you see, the type of gas they'd got hold of wasn't the kind that was supposed to be used in crowd control, it was for barricade penetration, designed to be fired into buildings. I got hold of an empty box from the manufacturers in the States and it said right on the label that it shouldn't be used in this way. What happened was that there was a local character, known as Dog Anderson, and this thing hit him and exploded in his groin, a truly horrible injury, he was in hospital fighting for his life. A few months later, he's out and he's arrested on the grounds that he's been identified as one of the ones who instigated the riots. Now, I was a very idealistic young guy at that point. Melanie and I had done our thing for a few months on a commune in San Francisco, we'd smoked a lot of dope in our time in America, when we were still in our early twenties, before we had to come back because we couldn't get any work permits. When I set up on my own I even put a marijuana leaf on my letterhead because I saw myself doing legal-aid work for hippies who'd been arrested on drug busts.

'As far as the CS gas was concerned, the police claimed they only shot it at a traffic-control junction box and that it must have ricocheted off and that's how it hit Dog. But I got a firearms expert from America to do the same thing, and every time he hit the box, the canister exploded into twenty or thirty fragments and the police were trying to tell us that all these fragments had flown off in exactly the same direction and every single one of them had entered Dog's body at exactly the same moment. The first time it went to court the jury couldn't agree but by the time there was a retrial I'd learned a huge amount about ballistics and the police really didn't have a defence to offer. So from then on, they all came to me and when I drive round town in my Merc now, no one stops me to ask if they can buy crack because everyone knows that I'm the guy you go to when you get *busted* for buying crack.'

'Do you still smoke dope?'

'Nah. In the early years after Toxteth I realised I had to keep my hands clean. There was too much at stake, given that there was no love lost between me and the police. By the time they couldn't touch me, I'd got out of the habit. You?'

'Me neither. There was nowhere safe to smoke it without the kids seeing. I'd had to hide my stash from my parents and then I had to learn to hide it all over again from my children.'

At dinner last night the sister, Alix, cooked. It was a wonderful meal. I got there on time, rang the bell, Melanie answered. I looked at her ass again as I followed her in. Emptied of all the old people, the place is a wow, much bigger than my apartment, with stairs leading to a whole other floor. The ceilings up here are double height and the windows give on to the waterfront, not just the sliver I can see from my bathroom. Sam was lying in a Corbusier recliner, watching the news. Some refugees were driving down a road from somewhere to nowhere. The item finished and he punched off the remote control.

'How are you feeling?' I asked him.

'Better.'

The sister came out of the kitchen, wiping her hands on a paper towel. I think the black trouser suit she was wearing wasn't the same one, or maybe it was the shirt she had on underneath, which showed more of her breasts. She smiled at me and I was startled again at what it brought out in her: that wildness I had noticed the first time we met at the *shiva* house now seemed like a really carnal sexuality, which I found unnerving in a woman who was not young and whom I didn't find particularly attractive.

We stood at the window with our drinks, Melanie handed round bowls of olives and pistachios and I began to warm up for the first time since I had been in the city, not physically because the heating works well in the apartment although it's been raw outside, and I have a down jacket with me. It was some kind of internal thawing that I felt, a lessening of the numbness that set in when Erica and I sat down at the kitchen table eight months ago and she told me why she wanted our marriage to end after twenty-three years, twenty-three years of work, not just *having* a family because anyone can pop out kids, but building it, each stage another brick in this house I was trying to construct, which I thought was going to last us the rest of our lives. And I only screamed at her once, that whole night: '*How could you just quit like this?*' And apologised. But I felt like she was asking me to walk out of a movie I was totally engrossed in for no reason, no reason at all.

'You see those joggers?' Sam was saying, pointing out the window. 'Years ago, dockers used to haul bales of raw sugarcane off the ships that had sailed from the West Indies on to lorries to be sent up to Tate and Lyle where more poor, illiterate Micks like themselves would process the stuff into sugar. And then even more poor illiterate Micks could put it in their tea and get the strength to do *even more* back-breaking labour designed for the illiterates who were the pack animals of the empire. Now every-thing's changed, everyone's on a permanent diet, sugar terrifies the life out of us like it's poison. We put Sweet 'N Low in our tea and pound a treadmill so people like me can sit in an office all day and try to figure out some use for the all the descendants of the illiterate Micks who are hanging about Halewood and Kirkby, waiting for someone to tell them what they're there for, and where they should go and what they should do for another seventy-odd years while they are in transit between a five-minute fuck and a doctor saying to you, "Shall we finish it?"'

'Sam,' Melanie said, behind us.

'Yeah? What?'

She ran her hand across her face, a zipping motion.

'She thinks I'm talking too much, she thinks I'm boring you. Okay, let's eat.'

We sat down and the meal was exquisite, beautifully cooked and presented: some kind of grilled Middle Eastern cheese with a dressing of lime and capers, then a pasta dish followed by a salad and, finally, a berry tart with cream. Everything was delicious. I have to say I love to eat. When I zip up my pants every morning I wish I didn't.

But even with his mouth full, there was no shutting up Sam. He talked over dinner about the Jews of Liverpool, how everyone lived around a street called Brownlow Hill and everyone had a house with a shop so they could make a living: 'The first building was the workhouse, no record of there ever being a Jewish inmate, then the surgery of Dr Hurd who was married to Rebecca Shapiro, and opposite, Harriman's the chemist, then Dickinfield Street where my dad always talked about Osher Blackstone, the tough guy of the Hill, the *shtarker* who hit you first and asked questions later, Narefsky's sweet shop, Kantarowitz the Hebrew booksellers, Tessie Connor who sold home-made ice-cream and next to her was Hughes's pawn shop owned by Owen Hughes who came to Liverpool from North Wales, then Shannon Street and Selig Dover who kept his dairy cows there . . . and I could go on for hours but I want you to have a flavour of what it was like back then, Joseph, the Irish and the Welsh and the Jews all mixed up together, some of them studying hard like my dad, others, like Osher, heading for the boxing gyms.'

'And when was all this?'

'I'm talking about the twenties, when our parents were kids, mine and Alix's, and Melanie's.'

'So how do you know so much about it? It was long before your time.'

'Because I schlepped round all the old people and got them to tell me and I wrote it down. Because it's part of the history of this city. Maybe in fifty years' time there'll be no more Jews here, but somebody will be able to say, "There *used* to be Jews and this is how they lived and where they lived." We're part of the fabric of this place, it's an immigrants' town, Joseph, everyone in transit, and the Mersey was the lifeline to those other worlds, this is where you took off from if you had any imagination.'

'I can tell you love it,' I said.

'And you?' I turned to Alix, who was leaning across the table to wipe a smear of cream from the surface with her napkin and whose neck smelt of a musky perfume that I didn't like, preferring fresh scents, something of citrus or, better still, nothing at all.

'She couldn't get out of here quick enough,' her brother replied.

'Liverpool was always too little to hold Alix,' Melanie said.

'Is this true?' I turned to her, she was sitting next to me. She was so much taller than her brother and sister-in-law, who are small people. Standing, I had only an inch or so on her and I am five-eleven. Erica comes to my shoulder.

'I took off one time, when I was fifteen or sixteen, got a bus to the start of the East Lancs Road, put my thumb out and hitch-hiked down to London and I got lifts from lorry drivers and, for one stretch, a guy in an E-type Jag, who said he worked in the record industry and was on his way back from Liverpool where he had been signing up a group. This was the very first time I'd heard anyone spin a line like that, but you know what? It was actually true. There was a picture of him with these local tear-aways in the paper the following week.'

'They were called the Bluejays and the lead singer drives a black cab round Liverpool these days,' Sam interrupted, pointing at me with his fork. 'I've seen him a few times on the rank at Lime Street station. They had a couple of hits, spent the lot, never made a penny even out of the royalties because of the lousy contract they signed. They should have gone with Brian.'

'How do you know this?' Melanie asked him, turning neatly in her seat. Pearl earrings shone through her hair like emphatic dots of milky light.

'Because Dad was his mam's doctor, she told him everything. They lived near the Dingle.'

'Anyway, that's got nothing to do with it. I ask this guy to put me out on the Kings Road and he did. I walked up and down, fifteen, sixteen, had the figure everyone wanted in those days, the beginning of the model style, the Shrimp look.'

'It's true she had the look, all that was missing was the straight hair. You remember you had to have these curtains down each side of your face? We could never manage it, me and Alix, we were *cursed* with curly hair . . .'

'And had to iron it before we went out . . .'

'You could smell the split ends singeing . . .'

'Though that was better than the stench of the hair lacquer they used a few years before us, spraying it on your beehive hairdo to hold it in place . . .'

'Like a helmet, and if you touched it, it made your hands all sticky. Once a girl was kissing me at a party and one of her false eyelashes came off and fell down the front of my shirt. I found it when I got undressed that night.'

'What girl? Who?'

'How the hell should I remember? This was thirty-five years ago, for Godsake.'

'So I'm standing on the Kings Road, and it's true, my hair is standing out like it's an Afro, except this is *before* the Afro is fashionable so to me, when I look in the mirror, all I see is hideous, and someone wanders over, he's wearing the tightest turquoise shot-silk pants you've ever seen and his legs are like pipe cleaners, and he says to me, with this cut-glass accent that

I'd only ever heard on TV, "Do you want to score?" I didn't know what the hell he was talking about, but we go down to his flat at World's End where a crowd of them are living, the walls painted with eyes – eyes of every colour – and he puts on the *Sgt Pepper* album, the first time I'd ever heard it, and rolls a joint. His name was Nick Siddon-James. That I remember. And I thought, Wow! So *this* is the big wide world.'

'And you never came back?'

'Are you kidding? She rang us from a phone box and said she'd run away to live with hippies in London and Dad got in his car, he had a Rover in those days, and drove down to London and tore the place apart until he found her.'

'London's a big city. How did that happen?'

'Because *he*,' Alix said, jerking a finger at her brother, 'said, "Well, Dad, I think if she's in London, she will have gone to Chelsea and if she's in Chelsea she's probably on the Kings Road," so he made straight for Sloane Square and found me about two hours after he arrived.'

'How long did you last in London?'

'A day and a half.'

And we were all laughing, not just at her but at our young selves. Everything was shining: the silverware was lit up with the reflection of candlelight and silver candlesticks and the dining-table was a sheet of glassy grey marble resting on oak trestles and the brick walls had been washed with some kind of varnish so they let off a slippery red glow. The floors were waxed to a high polish and our faces were radiating all this light, as if we were giving it out ourselves, and I looked around at the four of us, all around the same age, about to hit fifty or sliding past it and I thought, 'but just see us, now, we could be twenty again: every line is filled in and our faces smoothed out, and yet we're not twenty, we're thirty years older than that, with all the things that have happened to us in between, to my country and to theirs. I saw Erica at twenty-two sitting at a table in a café drinking a glass of tea with mint leaves in it, her hair long to her shoulders, in blue jeans and a white blouse gathered with a string above her breasts, her plump arms tanned, her face rosy, reading *Mother Jones*. What that sight awoke in me! All the longings that were expressed, for her wholesomeness, the tangled blonde hair as if she'd just got out of bed, the nappy surface of her skin like the bloom on peaches. What a smile she had, looking up and seeing me, putting down her magazine and raising her glass to her lips, without taking her eyes away from my face. The sweetness of it all, that you could walk into a café in a time of war and terror and catch sight of a girl, and twenty-seven years later, go on loving and desiring her. And knowing also that the café is *still there* on Allenby Street, with the same tall woman behind the hissing pump, her raven hair as artificially black as ever, still laying slices of cheese on bagels with gold-and-ruby-ringed hands and warming the bourekis, the little cheese-filled pastries that Erica used to love, raising them to her lips, her mouth shining with grease. I could walk in all over again and find her there, and fall in love all over again, and if death never intervened we could spend centuries just falling in love.

'You should see the plans for Joseph's hotel,' Sam was saying. 'I'd love to live in a place like that, let alone stay there.'

'I'm a Modernist, not a post-Modernist,' I told them, wrenching myself back to *here* and *now*. 'I can't stand all the classical allusion that's been fashionable since the eighties. I have no idea why British architecture is so terrible. Why don't you people know how to build any more? Where's the imagination gone?'

'The British love the old, the past, heritage,' Alix told me. 'We preserve, preserve, preserve.'

'People who preserve something half assed when they could build something fantastic from scratch,' I said, heating up, 'should be taken out and shot.'

And when they all stopped laughing I felt that Alix could not stop looking at me, and didn't stop looking at me until after we had had our coffee and it was past midnight, and I got my jacket and thanked them for the evening, and I stood in the hallway shaking their hands. Even when I turned and walked towards the elevator, I felt her eyes in my back.

Last night I spoke to Erica, a conversation I had been planning for several days, but at the end of an hour I had not improved my position. For her part she was only prepared to discuss the continuing difficulties with our youngest kid, Michael, his poor grades, his general lacklustre approach to existence, his choice of music and clothes, and when we'd done with that she moved on to the problem with a crack in the glass on the coffee table where she'd accidentally put down a hot dish, startled by the door.

Six months ago I stood in the lobby of her building for two and three-quarter hours waiting for her to get home from work. She said, 'You stood there all that time? Never once sat?'

'Nope, I never once sat, ask the doorman.'

'That's true. He didn't lean, he didn't slouch,' the doorman told her.

'Stood like a soldier, I bet.'

'Yes, pretty upright, but no soldier stands with a bunch of red flowers in his hand.'

'He'd feel a fool,' she agreed.

'I didn't think he looked no fool.'

'He just felt foolish,' I replied.

'Sir, don't say that.'

'Joe, I'm not going to invite you up.'

'For a minute?'

'No.'

And she leaned across me, her arm brushing my chest, and punched the button for the elevator, whose doors opened behind her, she stepped in, smiled and was gone in her green wool coat, round and comely, ripe as figs and grapes. And for a moment I thought of the Shulammite's words to Solomon: 'Comfort me with apples for I am sick with love.'

'What a bitch,' the doorman said. '*She* ain't worth it.'

'That's my wife.'

'You could do better.'

'I don't want to, I want her.'

'Let it go.'

'We have been married many years and I don't intend to give up just like that.'

He shrugged his shoulders inside his doorman's uniform. He had a badge on his chest that said 'Paul'. He was about forty years of age and I didn't see why I should take advice on women from someone who had advanced no further in his life than to stand behind a desk receiving packages and nodding good morning or good evening in a professional manner.

'*Were* you in the military?' he asked me.

'Yes, I was.'

'Overseas?'

'Yes.'

'Lucky you.'

I smiled as I left, thinking how I might be envied for many things, pitied for others, but for the ability to stand up straight in a draughty lobby holding a bunch of red roses, I could be awarded a medal in endurance, and granted the status of patriot and hero, as if I had gone to war for America, for things that, however hazily, that doorman thought he believed in and I didn't. To my wife, however, my time in the army was the thing that gnawed at her, her insistence that it made me unknowable, that I *must* as a consequence keep in reserve a secret part of myself. But what I would not share with her was nothing that she needed any information about, of that I was quite clear. I know women.

Because of what she regarded as this failure of mine to be 'completely open' with her, she was always interrogating people who knew me before I went into combat. 'Tell me about Joe when he was a kid, tell me about Joe when he was in high school, how was he in college?' It had been her ambition, for years, to get me to write down an account of what happened to me, one minute because it would be cathartic, and when that failed she said, 'Okay, then, write it down for the kids.' Like they care. When I got back to America after the amnesty, I was determined to avoid the situation that many of my contemporaries encountered when they returned home from Vietnam, and figured that if they talked about their experiences to family or friends, they would find a sympathetic, understanding ear. I don't know what problems other people had. I don't know why they found it hard trying to square with themselves what it was that they had been through. I don't know why they felt the necessity to talk to other people. For myself, I understood very clearly what I had done and what had been done to me, and why should I walk into an emotional ambush by getting into a discussion with somebody who believes that all war is brutality, carried out by men who have been brainwashed into sub-humanity? That we soldiers are all Lieutenant Calleys or GI Joe fascists holding our Zippo lighters up to the straw roof of a thatched hut, igniting the home of a family of innocent peasants. These are vegetarian principles held by people to whom nothing of any significance has ever happened. Frankly, I don't give a shit what they think. Their views are pointless and uninteresting.

So I would argue back to Erica, why should I agonise about what happened to me and what I did? I'm not psychotic, I wasn't traumatised emotionally. 'Listen,' I would tell her, 'there are plenty of people who have been scarred by their experiences, but I'm not one of those, war has not visited me as a curse.' Nor am I one of the types for whom their time in combat was the zenith of their existence, the shining moment, the *defining* moment, and everything that came afterwards for the rest of their lives has been a complete emptiness and nothingness – those guys who sit in Joe's Bar in their sixties and seventies and talk about the Normandy invasion. And there are people who are even worse off, who are severely psychologically damaged by all they went through and can't hold down a job and can't make a relationship work and have been more or less neutralised as human beings. 'But *as you know*, Erica,' I told her, 'I don't fall into any of those categories.' I have spent years trying to convince my wife that out of all of that horror and all of the sadness and the misery that war is, came the strength I have been trying to use for the past twenty-three years to hold our family together and to resist it being torn apart by whim or boredom or a sudden dash for a new fashion in relationships between men and women, which demands submission to some half-baked, men-are-from-Mars-women-are-from-Venus values cooked up by a guy who knows he can make a fortune gulling a public that pays attention to what's on the *New York Times* best-seller list.

And yet there is this perception that Erica has been driving away at for virtually the whole of our marriage. 'There's a coldness in you, Joe,' she said. She said it after we'd been dating for only a couple of weeks and she said it many times again throughout the course of our life together. I don't see it as coldness but as a rationality, a hard logic that you can bring to bear on almost anything, including solving the problems that two people meet when they plan to live together for a long time, and if I got anything from the army, this is it.

Erica is right, the army did change me, but as far as I was concerned, for the better. I learned from it that everything which isn't working the way you want it to can be regarded as a problem, and any problem almost certainly has a solution. When I run into a roadblock in my work I don't, as Erica would have it, think as my first thought, How do I feel about this? Here comes the enemy with a gun in his hand, how do I feel? Oh, my, shit scared, I'm paralysed to the spot. Like *that*'s going to help. You fight back or you retreat, those are your only two options. Perhaps in the end I will find out that I've been defeated in my battle to put our marriage back together, but at the moment there is still plenty I can do, even if it turns out to be a war of attrition, and I just wear her down in the end.

'Joe,' Erica said, when she sat down at the kitchen table eight months ago to end our marriage, me sniffing the milk in the carton, suspicious of a certain sour odour coming from some- where, turning to take the toast from the toaster as she spoke, 'this doesn't work for me any more. It isn't that you aren't what I want, it's that I've passed through the part of my life which is about living with someone. I want to be on my own, wake up on my own, read the paper on my own. I want to be able to hear my own voice inside my own head. I want to find out who I am when I'm not Mrs Erica Shields.'

And I sat with my mouth open, the toast in my hand, and finally I said to her, 'Erica, how could you come out with such fucking *banalities*?'

But the time apart from my wife has succeeded in one thing: answering that question she has nagged away at for so long. How did the army take *me* – a boy who two months before had lain down on a piece of grass under the Californian sun and tried not to cry as he understood what was happening to him, his prin- cipled recognition that the war in Vietnam was wrong and immoral and a disgrace, that he could not be a part of it, and that the consequence of this was his need to find another country to live in until the insanity came to an end, even if, ironically, becoming a soldier in another army was a necessary part of that exile – how did it turn that frightened, incoherent (usually stoned) kid into someone with goals and objectives and a total confidence that he would know what to do to achieve those aims?

For many years I thought about this hardly at all. Who had the time, with a business to run and three kids to raise? I was and am a busy man. Yet the breakdown of my marriage leads me to address a question that would never have occurred to me before, that would lead me down a path of introspection that is some-what alien to my nature. Life sped along on quick rails, it was enough for me to try to capture the moment as it passed. But now I set myself a task: to figure out whether there was any con-nection, as Erica speculated, between my period of military service and the man I had become. Sitting alone and unvisited in this apartment here in Liverpool I have been going back over those days, and they come back as clear to me as if I were there last week. It seems that the past remains inside us, like a stack of Russian dolls, and that the Joseph Shields who one day obeyed his call-up papers and reported for duty is still here, like a little fresh-faced homunculus.

When I knew I wasn't going to go to Vietnam, it was clear that there were only two possible places of refuge for me: one was Canada where I knew no one, the other was Israel. I chose Israel. Not from any Zionist conviction but because my dad suggested it, and in the battle between us over my rejection of the war this seemed like the one compromise I could make, the one thing I could do with my life that would make him (and my mom) happy, when they had stood together in the fall of 1947, hand in hand, their faces illuminated with joy, hearing the news come through on the radio that the United Nations had voted to give the Jews our own country, like the UN had handed a nation its birth certificate. ('So, Dad,' I said to him, a couple of years ago during one of our periodic rows about Israel, 'how did you think this would go down with the Palestinians?' 'Joe, I have to say we never gave them a second's thought. Why should we, after what we'd just been through?' 'Yeah, but . . .') Anyway, I knew I'd have to do army service but it never entered my mind (or my father's) that at some point I was going to have to fight. That was all done with, three years ago, back in 1967 when we fought what we thought then was the last war.

I remember us standing in a courtyard in the induction centre, the smell of sweating men and Mediterranean flowers in my nose. I was pushing back the hairs on my hand, raising them like iron filings in my nervousness and apprehension, shifting my toes in my new boots, which, more than anything else I was wearing, defined me as no longer a hippie but as a marching, shooting person. All of a sudden two huge Leyland army lorries backed in, brakes hissing, belching diesel fumes, trucks that were supposed to transport heavy objects not human beings, and the tailgates of these lorries folded down, and we were all ordered to get in. The tailgates and canvas sides closed down on us and we were like cattle inside that thing. The stink of sweat was overpowering and perhaps it was then that my sense of smell began to recede a little: the body gives a limited number of favours if the mind asks it to. There was a high yellow moon over Jerusalem, and opposite me a fat Canadian guy was trying to eat crackers as quietly as he could. I remember an Italian began to sing, under his breath, the words of 'Maggie's Farm', and a couple of us joined in, more whispering than singing. The air outside was colder now, the smell was of a drier, sandier earth because we were no longer climbing to the city on the hill but had passed it and were moving on, into the Judean hills towards the occupied territory. The me in Berkeley who was rebelling against the war, that was a closed chapter now. Defending America against the Communist menace half-way across the other side of the world really takes some doing to get your head around but the notion of defending Israel against a bunch of surrounding countries that don't even want it to exist isn't a very difficult concept to grasp.

The next morning we received two huge shocks. The first:

breakfast! I sat down to porridge, a slice of bread, a hard-boiled egg and a cup of industrial coffee, not coffee do-you-want-milk, coffee with-or-without, this was black and tasted like water that had drained from the radiator of one of the trucks that had brought us there. After a few of days of this, when a couple of guys really started to moan to the sergeants about the quality of the food, still not having realised that there is no point in the army in complaining about anything, we were informed that the breakfast menu had been put together by army nutritionists and every one of those components contained something essential that *you* needed. I'm telling you, it was like breakfast in one of Stalin's gulags and this was supposed to be the army defending a nation for whom eating is the centrality of our existence. The people who were particularly aggrieved were the Frenchmen. They just couldn't get over it.

The second big surprise was when we found out that where we were was the basic training centre for the army demolition corps and we were going to qualify as demolition experts. We were going to be trained in the use of explosives.

A barrack-like room with a plywood wall running down the middle and pairs of holes drilled through it every couple of feet, and in front of each pair of holes there is a chair where a soldier sits and pokes his arms through and finds on the other side a weapon. First of all he has to feel it to identify what kind of weapon it is and then he has to take it apart and put it back together. When we have mastered this they bring in different kinds of grenades and land-mines, or land-mines that have been booby-trapped. In the classroom we learn about all types of explosives and how they function, not only our stuff but stuff the other side was using, which in those days was invariably Russian, Chinese or Czech, but what is really important is the time we spend learning how to take them apart and put them back together again. By the time we're finished we can, with our eyes closed, pick something up and know exactly what it is and what you have to turn, or unscrew, to make it safe. It was the most tactile thing I have ever done. It trained you to fuse those synapses that make connections between your fingertips and your brain, you had to trust your feelings, and trust them implicitly. You had to believe that what you felt was reality.

And one of the reasons I cannot communicate to Erica what she wants to know about my time in the army is that I would have had to tell her that the hands that embrace her body, that stroke her breasts or hotly seek out the little hard bud of her clitoris, only really began to learn how to feel during three years of picking out with exquisite accuracy the provenance of a hand grenade. These are where my feelings still lie, in my fingers. I didn't understand what Erica meant by coldness. Am I not an affectionate husband and father? I hug my kids, I compliment my wife, whom I love so much that I feel my guts have been torn out by this bizarre insistence of hers that our marriage is over. But she said that I didn't know how to nurture or comfort, that she was better off alone, and I said, 'If you want sympathy, go to your girlfriends, if you want solutions to problems, come to me.'

I read a magazine article on a plane recently that asked, What's the difference between men and women? I decided to give that some thought for once in my life, what else do I have to do? And maybe it will help me understand Erica, not to mention my own daughter. I remember in the army that what I missed about women then was their completely different way of thinking, their insistence on deviating from what characterises everything about military life. In the army even in the evening you still talk about army stuff. What else is there to talk about? We have no other life. You cook up scams to get pieces of kit you're missing: it's like *The Phil Silvers Show*. Somebody has lost his helmet so everybody gets together and figures out some kind of Phil Silvers-like scam to get this guy a new helmet by tomorrow morning so that at roll-call the officer doesn't know that his helmet is missing. What doesn't go on is all these guys sitting there discussing how to resolve somebody's bad relationship with his girlfriend. Maybe somebody comes in and says, 'I've got the clap, who could I have picked this up from?' and then it's all laughed off in a quick succession of jokes and it's on to the next thing. Conversation in the army is like reading from a manual but at the weekend when you're sitting in a coffee-house having a conversation with a girl it's anything but! It meanders, it's impulsively suggestive, it's spontaneous. When you sit down to talk to a woman while you're on leave the conversation isn't utilitarian, it isn't diagrammatic, it isn't structured as a series of components. The reason why I'm not prepared to talk to Erica about the war is that I wholeheartedly believe women should stay away from the things that mark men out as different from them, just as we don't want to hear about their periods and, though we have learned to endure it, we really don't want to be around when they are giving birth.

Once Erica had said to me, 'Apart from the obvious, why do men need women in their lives at all?' A good question. Because not everything is logical, I suppose. Why do you fall in love with this person, not that one? A sexual attraction must be there, of course. Melanie Rebick – if she put on a few pounds and gave her hips a chance – would have the kind of sexiness I like, despite the plainness of her face. Alix Rebick does not, though she is an interesting and funny woman and humour is something I cherish in anyone; I'd go a long way to find that. But beyond the erotic itch there is always something else, which drives deep down into your nature, a thumping, pounding drill penetrating the bedrock of the planet that is you.

I first saw Erica in the spring of 1974. She looked up, she smiled, I thought, Dimples! And I was lost to her. Dimples, what the hell is that all about? What do they tell you about a person, other than that the genes have ordered a particular fold in the flesh? Yet my future wife, sitting in that café reading *Mother Jones*, was radiating like a nuclear power plant a warmth, a sunniness of disposition, which was incredibly hard to resist after seven months of deactivating land-mines in the desert.

I know that it was an absurd passion that made me decide to build a hotel here, that if I was any kind of military commander I would have thought of myself as a perfect fool for investing in such an uncertain prospect, but just as I had seen Erica that time in the café, and was smitten, so it was with this hotel. One day sitting in another café, in Frankfurt in the fall of 1997, I had read an article in the *Herald Tribune* about the urban regeneration of Liverpool and I thought, Hey! The city of the Beatles, and just like that I jumped on a plane.

I don't know what I was expecting, but what I found was this tough old town that had been really knocked about by life and deserved better, but that is true of plenty of places. Everything I knew about Liverpool inevitably had been subject to various kinds of long-range distortion, and the city of my imagination was a 'Strawberry Fields' fantasy. The people looked like hillbillies, they reminded me of the mountain folk of Kentucky, lost and forgotten in the hollows, the poor white trash of America no one cares about. You couldn't see what use there could be for them except to fight wars on foreign soil and only then if you could teach them to read and write well enough to follow the instruction manual on the complicated, computer-controlled weapons that are what wars are fought with these days. They'd be good for one of the little wars we have in Europe now, they'd be fine in a militia ethnically cleansing their neighbours, but that was about it.

The very first morning, as I stepped out of my hotel a girl was screaming at her boyfriend in the street, 'You arsehole.'

'Don't swear at me.'

'Arsehole isn't swearing, it's what you've got in your body.'

'Shut yer face.'

'I'll get you.'

'You and whose army?'

'You stupid Irish twat, you've picked a fight with the wrong family this time.'

And sitting next to them, on a bus-stop bench, immune to all this violence, an old man in a brown corduroy cap, polished shoes and warm tweed overcoat looked up from reading the *Morning Star*, a Communist Party newspaper apparently, and said to me, 'Don't pay any attention, it's all bravado.'

Over a heavy lunch at the Athenaeum Club, under paintings of dead guys in wigs, I listened to the history lectures the city officials gave me, but I didn't really care about their sob stories or their civic pride. If I decided to develop here, the prospectus for the finance package would cover all these details and someone in my office in Chicago would write everything up in the all fine words that would make the city happy, and they would thank themselves for their good work and never guess that nothing *they* had said made me want to invest.

The tourists were there, there was no doubt of that. In the Atlantic Towers Hotel where I was staying I could hear accents from every part of the United States and to some extent was reassured, but the presence of visitors standing in line waiting to enter a museum called The Beatles Story was not enough. When I build a hotel I have to be certain. I have to believe totally in the project if I'm going to sink my money and time into it because I don't have particularly deep pockets. There needs to be a passion. The passion the city officials were trying to instil in me was this: that on these very cobblestone streets my own grandparents had undoubtedly walked. It was true, they probably had. They sat me down and showed me the migration maps: the Russians and Poles went overland to Hamburg, took

the boat to Hull, made their way across the Pennines to
Liverpool and set sail for the New World. 'Look,' they said,
'here's a picture of someone very like one of your own grandparents, Al Jolson, who as Asa Yoelson, from Lithuania, at the
age of eight emigrated to America on the SS *Umbria* departing
from Liverpool with his mother and brother and two sisters. For
all you know,' they said, 'they might have been on the same
boat.' My father's parents, the Shifrins, who changed their
name to Shields, also came from Lithuania, so yes, it was plau-
sible that they could have sailed across to Ellis Island with the
child Yoelson, and experienced something of what I had done,
when, walking along a mocked-up turn-of-the-century street
in the Maritime Museum, I had seen the peeling advertisements on the fibreglass wall for this or that vessel sailing to
America and learned about the various crooks who made their
living from fleecing these impoverished emigrants who had
already handed over everything they had to a shipping clerk for
a scabrous passage to America in steerage. An entire industry
had built itself up in Liverpool around stripping the emigrants
bare – flop-houses where they stole your money while you slept,
carters who took your luggage down to the ship and were never
seen or heard of again, provision merchants who sold you
mouldy bread and diseased meat. When you also took into
account the various iniquities of the slave trade, you could say
that Liverpool had had it coming. That whatever state it was in
now might be a kind of punishment for the sins of the past.
They read me the original words of a young Irish girl after the
potato famine, 'The scourge of God fell down on Ireland'.

Well, the scourge of God had certainly fallen on Liverpool.

As soon as I saw the Liver Building I knew exactly what it
was. Not elegant, not refined, it was over-decorated, and horribly
sentimental. The two towers are totally unnecessary and seem to
be there for no other reason than to house a pair of gigantic

clocks. It's the kind of place you build when you have too much money – the Trump Tower of the early years of the century – in other words, a *nouveau-riche* construction where the boss wants everything he's ever seen somewhere else and the architect is too scared not to indulge him. And what he gets is a mishmash of some Hellenistic temple and a fairly obvious rip-off of Richardson who built the Marshall Field department store in my own home town. I often think of the men who constructed Solomon's temple and of the meetings they must have had with their boss, who demanded that the forests of Lebanon be put to the chop, stones hewed with primitive axes, gold quarried from wherever they quarried gold in those days. And whatever structure was in their minds, these Biblical architects and craftsmen, the king decreed that it be smothered in cherubs and carved palm trees and flowers and real jewels, an over-decorated mess that took seven years to complete. But at least God was supposed to be pleased.

The best thing you could say about the Liver Building is that it has become, over the years, lovable, it's a landmark and that should be enough. But I know that, although the place looks solid, it's one of the first really large-scale reinforced concrete buildings in the world, certainly the first here in Britain. This awkward, graceless thing on the Mersey shoreline did something that Trump's Tower never did – it started a revolution, the beginning of a system of construction that, along with the development of the steel frame, led to *the* symbol of twentieth-century architecture: skyscrapers! Before the Empire State Building, before the Chrysler Building, this monstrosity had been here already twenty years, like one of those intermediate life forms such as the lungfish, which is interesting because in it you can examine the transition from one stage of evolution to another.

So I enjoyed the Liver Building and it gave me my first insights into where I was, but that wasn't enough to make me build my hotel. What did it was a real *farbrente* moment, a couple of days after I arrived, one of those incidents when you get lit up from inside, when someone pours something flammable over your heart and applies a match to it.

I was walking along Water Street, on its eastern side, looking at the buildings. The dock was monumental, breathtaking, nothing less than an earthquake would shift it. Visually, I'd decided, much of Liverpool was interesting, a cast-iron city interrupted by the weird red sandstone I've seen nowhere else, but the whole place seemed deserted, depopulated: every time someone moved it was like a film director had cried out, 'Action,' and a single figure crosses a vast empty plateau. It was also a quiet city, not noisy as I'd expected, not like a Fellini movie. Some force of circumstance had turned it in on itself, made it introspective when this was not, I believed, its natural characteristic, which was to face outwards to the ocean pathways. And this was what was running through my head when, turning my eyes to the left, I saw something that caused me nearly to jump out of my skin, crossing the street, no – running across it, accelerating around the back side of a white car, sworn at by the driver, because of my urgency to see if there had been some deception in my eyes when I looked at the plate that was affixed to the side of it bearing the date.

An office building. Which I now think may be one of the most important in the world.

A main façade, which is a honeycomb of plate-glass oriel windows held together by a skeleton frame of stone designed to look like cast iron, and these windows give back to the street the reflection of a building next to it, a hive of windows reflecting another hive. I pushed my way along the alley at the side to examine a courtyard elevation of plain, undecorated windows cantilevered out around two and a half feet from the H stanchion frame. And went back out and looked at the date again. It was very hard to get my mind to process the figure.

My heart lurched in my chest; I was trying not to cry. How can

Erica say that I am cold when I can be moved to tears as suddenly as this? How could we have been married as long we have for her not to know me at all, or say that I'm not knowable, and when I say, 'You know everything,' she replies that if this is true (and not once is she prepared to admit that it might be) then my problem is that either I have buried my traumas so deep inside me that I can't even reach them myself, or – and this she really does not want to contemplate – I must be shallow.

But if that's correct, how is it that every day now my thoughts are with a man I never met, who lived before I was born, who built something so astounding that cognitively it is hard to engage with it? Who was he? What was it like to be *him*? To have your mind wired up in a completely different way from everyone around you, to be born out of your own time, thinking thoughts so alien that you must have felt like a . . . (and here, perhaps, Erica is right, because I don't have enough empathy to contemplate what that must have felt like, as a son born into a family whose parents loved him and tried always to do the right thing, who grew up and never fully felt alone. As Shakespeare put it in a play I studied in high school, 'To be beloved is all I need, and those I love, I love indeed'). In the middle of an era when they were designing houses and offices to look like medieval cathedrals, this man had figured out all on his own the first principle of Modernism, which old Louis Sullivan summed up in what I still think is the doctrine we should be following, even if that makes me severely out of fashion. Everything under the sun follows the same rule: '*Form ever follows function, and this is the law.*'

I handed that out on a sheet of paper when I first met with the team from the city, sitting in municipal chambers under pictures of dignitaries unknown to me. After they'd fussily poured coffee and fought for the best cookies, the chocolate ones, and stirred their cups and wiped their fingers, I said, 'I don't know anything about the history of this place, I don't know about your troubles, I don't care. A guy named Peter Ellis, who lived about a hundred and fifty years ago, designed two fantastic buildings here in Liverpool. One of them was Oriel Chambers and the other is on Cook Street. Behind it, if you buzz the entry bell and someone lets you in, you'll see an amazing thing, this outrageously modern cast-iron staircase with no central support; it's cantilevered from each floor level and the whole thing is glassed in. It's totally impossible that it could have been here in Liverpool in the middle of the nineteenth century, absolutely preposterous, so I go and get out my architectural history books, thinking, Did this Ellis copy it from somewhere, and if so, where? Probably Chicago, where I am from, because that's where Modernism started. And when I start looking things up I find out that, no, Ellis didn't copy from Chicago, Chicago copied him. The precursor of American Modernism was someone called Root and it turns out that during the Civil War his parents sent him to England to escape the hardship at home and all that time was spent in Liverpool. This kid stands on Cook Street and watches Ellis's building being put up. He goes back to Chicago after the war and always in his mind is a crazy glassed-in spiral staircase he's seen in Liverpool. He grows up and becomes an architect, became the man who laid out the ground plan for twentieth-century Chicago. He died young, but you know who his partner was? A man named Daniel Burnham. And do you know the name of his most famous construction? It was the Flatiron Building in New York, the world's first skyscraper.

'I don't know how to tell you what I feel about this discovery. I know I'm not the first. But the emotion that it comes with, that's something else. I'm thinking about Ellis, who was he? I can't find anything out, except that his work was derided, condemned, he was hounded out of the business. This fucking genius, as far as we know, only ever built two things, both here. When he died, he wasn't even down as an architect, just an engineer. He was flattened, annihilated. Now I'm no genius. I'm a jobbing architect who is lucky enough to be able to build pretty much what he wants. My aim is to have fun and be true to myself. I'm never going to be in any history books. There aren't going to be exhibitions about what I can do. I am severely limited. Who doesn't want to be a genius? But I'm not, I have a wife, and three kids to bring up, and that's enough. I plan to build a hotel here as an act of – homage? I suppose that's the word, though it's such a cliché, but when I'm retired I want to look back and say, "I built a hotel in Liverpool, this totally discarded, forgotten, abused city where something once happened that was a miracle." And after I'm gone that hotel will still be here, God willing. Not for ever, nothing lasts that long, but if it's still around in a century that will be enough for me because I intend to construct it in a way that it isn't going to fall down. You'll have to blow it up. I don't even care if it's not always a hotel. Whatever the use that it's put to is okay with me. Everything changes, the city isn't what it was and it isn't yet what it might be. For myself, I'm going to build you a beautiful hotel, which—'

And Watts said, 'Have you considered a Beatles theme? You could have pictures on the wall of when they were on *The Ed Sullivan Show*. Anything to make the Yanks feel at home.'

Everything has to go through him. Without his say-so, nothing happens. This is a boss-politics city and Watts is astride everything, a thin, oldish man who looks like you could crack him between your fingers and he sits there in meetings, in his cheap suit, chewing that gum people use when they're trying to quit smoking, and every so often he comes out with something crushingly banal yet everyone jumps to attention. The best I can say about him is that he is a cutter of red tape because he wants things to happen, he's interventionist. But not even he can prevent everything being dragged down into this pit of bureaucracy in which every tiny item has to be considered by a committee and a sub-committee and a sub-committee of the sub-committee and every single one of these consists in its entirety of morons.

Every day I go to the site and I'm a different person. Down by the river, whether it's sunny or cold, wet or dry, every day we're there, making something out of nothing, which still amazes me that such a thing is possible after spending a portion of my life blowing things up. I'm in my work clothes, my jeans, my boots, my cambray shirts, my hard hat. I like engines a lot. I love big machines, the guts of them, the power they possess under a heavy man's arm. I like the sight of cranes lifting rods and plates and beams. Diggers, JCBs. I like to see my men working, I don't care if they're crude or sweat or swear as long as they get the job done. I adore their humour, their sarcasm. Occasionally I hang out with them for an hour after we close up, trying to drink the same beer they drink, in pubs that don't seem to have changed since the thirties, little holes in the wall with destroyed women behind the bar with terrible root problems in their hair and their teeth, who would give you nightmares if you looked at them for more than a split second when you were ordering.

But always I go home at night and I shower and change and I'm dreaming my hotel. I'm thinking, What would Ellis have done if he were in my shoes? I'm trying to picture him. Muttonchop whiskers appear in my mind, maybe a top hat, I don't know how they dressed in that period. He's with me everywhere I walk, by my side. You can talk to the dead, I do it all the time. For many years I have talked to Saidi, a man to whom I never opened my heart when he was alive, that coarse, funny Tunisian who first showed me how to hold a cigarette so it's concealed, sitting on the half-track on crates of plastique explosive, more crates of plastique slung over the side and in all kinds of drawers there were blasting devices . . . a mobile demolition factory. We were sitting on a powder keg literally, but Saidi taught me a way of smoking that he was convinced was a hundred per cent safe and completely officer proof and that was to take your helmet off, light your cigarette and put the helmet over your face and toke into the helmet – you could flip your ashes inside it so you could enjoy a whole cigarette and when you're finished dump the contents of the helmet over the side. This was the beginning of my first really serious nicotine habit, which took a further fifteen years to overcome completely.

The dead Saidi I talk to now is running a garage in Bat Yam, cursing in the Arabic he learned as a kid in Tunis when he doesn't want his customers to know how he plans to cheat them, and I say to him, Saidi, here are a bunch of deadbeats, cretins, bureaucrats, what do I do? And he says, Yossef, use your imagination. The one thing they haven't got.

Night after night Peter Ellis and I talk about how I'm going to build my hotel. I have consulted him on everything. Erica wants to know how come I can talk to the dead about my visions but I cannot sit down with her and discuss the problems in our marriage. But talking about something isn't going to fix it, it might make you feel better which is why women engage in conversation as a palliative because they make some sort of equation with feeling better about the situation and it actually being resolved . . . They think that if you feel good about the problem it's *as good* as resolving it. When Erica poured out her heart to me and told me about the sense of waste that was inside her, I listened. She cried, she dried her eyes, she felt she had moved on. But to where? What had changed? There simply isn't any reason for the marriage to end, I said. Nothing you have told me is without some kind of cure. And she cried out, 'Joe, don't you get it? Relationships aren't the same as a burnt-out tank engine. You see everything as a problem that has a solution and sometimes it isn't a problem at all but a situation. The two are not the same.'

'Erica,' I replied, 'I really have no idea what you're talking about.'

Last week I met Alix Rebick in the lobby of our building. We walked along to the Tate art museum and had coffee. She ordered an espresso and drank it in small sips, her mouth leaving a brilliant red mark on the cup. Her face is capable of great ranges of expression; looking at her is a series of vivid sympathetic moments. Some people when they smile, their mouth moves and nothing else, this little mouth bobbing up and down on an expressionless plate, like a clam opening and closing. With her everything is in motion: the eyebrows rise and fall, the cheeks push up, the nostrils flare. It must be exhausting.

'How's your hotel going?'

'Every hotel I build there is a different problem,' I told her. 'In every place, it is something different. Here, theft. The contractors can't seem to keep any equipment on the site. Everything disappears, the bricks, the cement, the hammers, the nails. Yesterday morning when I turned up at the site office it looked like someone had tried to steal a crane. For fuck's sake, how do you steal a *crane*? And where would you keep it? Who could you sell that kind of thing to?'

'Who do you have doing your security?'

'I can't even remember, I've changed companies so often. They all promise you the earth and deliver nothing. One firm, nobody ever showed up. I went past the site one night and it was deserted.'

'And how did you handle it?'

'I fired them, of course. I'd paid for security and they delivered nothing. The chutzpah, unbelievable!'

'How long did you employ them?'

'Three weeks.'

'And during that time was anything stolen?'

'By a sheer miracle, no, not a thing.'

'A miracle. You are a believer?'

'No. I used to talk to God but he never talked to me.'

'He doesn't write, he doesn't phone.'

'That's *right*.'

'Joseph,' she said to me, 'the firm you used doesn't need any actual bodies: they just put up a sign saying who they are and nobody will touch them. They're not so much in the business of security as a protection racket. If anything goes missing they send their thugs out to ask around and nobody is going to deny them the information they need, and when they find out who it is, they pull their heads off. Don't you know how things operate here? Has Chicago become so tame you don't understand how to run a business any more?'

I was crushed. 'I never thought of that.'

'You're a baby. Your backside is wet. Someone needs to look after you.'

She took a cigarette from her purse and lit it. Her mouth stained the tip. Her mouth affected everything it touched. I noticed she had a couple of chopsticks holding back her hair from her face.

'I see you carry your own eating tools around with you.'

She laughed, the red of her lips was all over the café now. The nails on her hands were crimson too. She was larger than life, no one had any business taking up so much space in the world. I don't know how she managed it. Leaning over she touched my sleeve lightly with one finger. 'I eat people for breakfast.'

'I don't doubt it for a moment.'

I thought it was a shame she was alone but it looked to me as if life had made her too strong for her own good. She understood too much, and being without dreams and illusions, harmless fantasies, is not an attractive quality in anyone. Many men came out of the army like that and their prospects in life were not great. She was a single woman and I suspected that she was interested in me, perhaps for no other reason than I was on my own here. But in no way was I interested in her, I mean in the way she wanted.

Alix

'People who preserve something half assed when they could build something fantastic from scratch should be taken out and shot,' he had said. It was the *coup de foudre. At last.*

When Joseph Shields walked into Sam's flat on the night of the *shiva*, I saw a paunchy man my own height, or a little taller. He swung his arms when he walked like he was marching with a band, arms that were too long and loose by his sides. The wire-wool hair the colour of rust was thinning out and at the sides it was mostly grey – like our King David of old, he was one of the red-haired Jews. On his freckled wrist he wore an Omega watch with a brown leather strap, which was a good watch but not flashy, it wasn't a Rolex or a Pathek Philippe so obviously he didn't throw his money around, or not on himself; his wife, perhaps, was another matter. His big feet were shod in shoes the

Americans call penny loafers, with tassels. There was a high mottled colour in his face and his eyes were brown. Thick Jewish lips over flossed, scaled, polished teeth. He needed to clip his nose hairs; that was my only criticism of his grooming and I am fussy that way. I like a masculine man, but he does have to be clean. He wasn't handsome, not at all, he was no movie star, no George Clooney. There was something of Michael Douglas there, without the jaw tucks obviously, but more, perhaps, of Walter Matthau. In other words he was a middle-aged, well-to-do American male with all the external symptoms of middle-class prosperity, but invited to dinner came informally in jeans, sneakers, T-shirt and leather jacket, just like Sam, in the uniform of guys of our generation, placing him exactly as a child of the sixties and seventies, the same as us.

Now I had reached the age of forty-nine without ever having been married – had in one case (the nature-loving American) closed the deal but backed out of it – had lived with three different boyfriends (one for as long as five years) and until my early forties had never once been short of prospective partners, had assumed that sex whenever I wanted it was my God-given right, earned as a battle-hardened survivor of the sexual revolution. So what had gone wrong? Why, now, was I alone?

The unexpected appearance of Joseph Shields at this very late stage required careful thought. In the bathroom after he had left, brushing my own crooked British teeth, I had thought, But surely that's the man I should have met fifteen years ago and married! Who could a tough Jew like me live with but a Jew even tougher than herself? *This* had been my mistake, I could see it now. Maybe all my previous boyfriends had been chosen as an act of rebellion against my family: I'd wanted men who were the exact opposite of my father and brother, strong, silent types as we used to call them. If you come from a home where you fought to get a word in edgeways, wouldn't you be charmed by reticence and reserve? I had to go and find men for whom argument was a waste of their very precious breath, men who had a thing about the conserving of oxygen. I wound up with boyfriends who would answer every question monosyllabically until I would scream, 'Speak, for God's sake! Talk to me!'

Of course there had been other disasters . . . you do not reach my age without there having been pain. I had done more than choose badly: once I had chosen disastrously, someone who could not love . . . Enough.

For nearly a decade I had been in the wilderness. At forty I was in my prime. I was the toast of the stacking-chair convention centres of Prague, Dubrovnik, Krakow, San Diego, Sydney, Delhi and Jerusalem while at home, after years of red-eyed toil in libraries, I was beginning to be dismissed as a populist who had defiled her resumé with a low trade, journalism – that is, I wrote an occasional article for the *Guardian*, and once I was even syndicated in the *New York Times*. I spoke my mind on Radio Four and *Newsnight*, where for a couple of years in the eighties I was the hot academic babe, the minx with the fiery hennaed hair, the lips painted Chanel pillar-box red, the long legs, the voluptuous tits, the Jean-Paul Gaultier jackets, the La Croix bustier. Back in real life I was a senior lecturer in the sociology department at a Midlands university. My subject was crime. The questions that engaged me were less to do with motivation or the sociological or psychological circumstances that made someone run amok in a school with a machine-gun, or bash in a widow's head for enough dosh to score a few hits of smack; rather, what interested me was how justice could be done. The Christians urge us to forgive our enemies but what, I asked, was the point when your enemy didn't even know he'd done anything wrong? Punishment for the sake of it, I felt, was merely another branch of sadism. Redemption I had nothing to say about, that was in God's hands, not mine. Rehabilitation I left to the probation service.

My interest right from the beginning, since even before I was an undergraduate, was the trial. At home in Liverpool aged ten in 1961, when other children played with dolls or sat devouring buttered toast and *Swallows and Amazons*, my father had made us rush our breakfast in the kitchen so we could gather formally each morning round the bare walnut dining-table and be read aloud to from the newspaper transcript of the Eichmann hearings. Though he was in normal circumstances immune to the past, the kidnapping by Mossad agents of the Nazi war criminal (the architect of the Holocaust) from his hide-out in Argentina, the trial held not in the country where the crimes had taken place but in the one belonging to the victims of the atrocities, the eventual death sentence for genocide in a state that, in all other circumstances, had no capital punishment, seemed to him to be an exemplary exercise in the carrying out of justice, at once both pragmatic and philosophical. The trial fired the imaginations of my father's two children. While the kids of the neighbourhood roamed with dirty faces and Davy Crockett hats or raised their arms high and stiff, ack-acking nettles and dandelions in those years when the war still cast a big shadow over our lives, Sam stood under the elm tree in the garden addressing devastating courtroom indictments at the enemies of the Jews, for the moment in the person of his little sister, my wrists tied with a ball of string. But I sat in school and watched blonde-haired Marilyn Shaw at show-and-tell, when we were supposed to display neat embroidery or collections of glass horses or pressed flowers or unusual leaves and other useless stuff like that, hold up a copy of the *Manchester Guardian*, where a photograph clearly showed her aunt in Jerusalem sitting in court with a stern and attentive professional demeanour, a notebook on her lap. Marilyn Shaw's aunt an official stenographer at the Eichmann trial! Only a secretary, yes, but she was there. She recorded everything, every corrupt, lying, stinking word of his. *And* the testimonies of the survivors. At night at home, lying stomach-down on my bed under my ballet pictures, in a blue-backed spiral-bound notebook I bought for the purpose, I developed my own form of speedwriting just in case *I* would be called up to document such history. Watched over by Margot Fonteyn in a snow-white tutu, ten-year-old Alix prayed for another Nazi. Oh, Lord, leave just one more fascist for me.

Years later I came to see villainy as a form of poison. It has its toxicity and what began to interest me was the way in which the world could set itself again to rights, to restore a moral balance that had been wrecked by the crime. This, I believed, was the main purpose of justice and the trial itself was the means by which a just society exposed to the public gaze two things: the first was as much as one could possibly know of the hidden suffering of the victim; the second was the exploration of the nature of right and of wrong. I regarded the trial as a necessary rite in the cleansing of the sullied order. Obviously, I wanted it televised. I wanted jury duty to be mandatory, twice in everyone's lifetime. It was *seeing* justice being done, and playing one's own part in it, that made it just.

This business of justice had already got me into trouble with my students before the final affair with the Myra Hindley essay, which is what eventually did me in. A few months before it, a girl had written a paper comparing the transport of live calves in cattle trucks to the Continent for export with the transport of the Jews across Europe, also in cattle trucks. Except the Jews could imagine what awaited them at the other end, I pointed out, and the calves could not. 'How do you know that?' she demanded. Look, I'm not cut out for the training of young minds: it demands too much patience, too much tolerance of stupidity.

The concept of justice was what I couldn't get those students to understand, the kids who listened to Hindley's whiny nonsense, who talk of redemption and forgiveness. I typed it out for them and distributed it, 'Read this,' I said. 'It's something a rabbi once wrote – Leo Baeck, chief rabbi of Berlin, deported to Theresienstadt ghetto in 1942 and who therefore had plenty of time to think on these things.'

> As there shall be a search for the guilty, so there shall be a search for the innocent, who, if he be in need, shall be given help. The hand which metes out justice and punishment shall also be the hand that succours; because only thus does justice become a whole. The hand which succours shall also be the hand which metes out justice and punishes; because only then does help become a whole. Both together then form the totality of rectitude.

Such ideas, the moral traction of them when expressed not by a theologian with dandruff on his collar but by a beautiful and sexy criminologist, would have had me on TV twice a week if I'd had the time. So all in all my career was progressing well and it was only the day-to-day teaching that presented me with difficulties, and turned out to be the source of my failure to get tenure and the humiliation that followed, drummed out of academia, virtually, for 'intellectually abusing' my students, for my outrageous behaviour (which made the national papers) over that girl's undergraduate thesis, the one that was trying to reclaim as a feminist heroine the child murderer Myra Hindley.

Until this watershed, the job required of me no more than that I commute from London three days a week; the rest of the time was my own, to write conference papers, to go to parties, to meet people who interested me, to travel, to learn to scuba dive in the Red Sea with my former college room-mate Marsha Goode. I spent a lot of time in Moscow at one point, studying the show-trials of the thirties (an example of the trial without a crime) and had two affairs there, playing one off against the other until my visa was abruptly revoked for transgressions concerned with bringing proletarian morality into disrepute on which story I believed I could dine out indefinitely.

In those days I was living in a flat in Swiss Cottage. My energy and zest were boundless. Some mornings I was so restless I would walk into town: across Primrose Hill, down Baker Street, Hyde Park, Green Park, St James's Park, Kensington Gardens. Bandstands. Heels clicking on asphalt. Tea kiosks. Deck-chairs. The parks sparkling, the streets scintillating. The perfection of the day. Intoxicating London!

Meeting Mamma for shopping, coffee scalding on the tongue, her perfume, mine. Arm in arm on Bond Street. 'Where are hemlines this season, darling?' 'Wherever *you* want them to be, Mamma. Why be dictated to by fashion?' A ruby dress cut on the bias, ruched shoulders, 'Crying out to be tried on, not *me*, darling, *you*, my figure is too petite for this.' And a necklace of emeralds on a black velvet neck. 'My God, it must cost thousands.' 'Let's go in and try it on anyway, just for fun.' Not the wife of a provincial doctor now. Imperious in Asprey's. 'Show me this, now that.' 'But you know, darling, while we are here, my little business is in healthy profit. I would like to buy you a small diamond for round your neck.' 'Oh, diamonds aren't me.' 'Wait until a man gives you a diamond ring for your finger. Then you will whistle another tune.' The ruby dress. A leather coat. High-heeled black shoes. Black suede gloves. An Hermès scarf. 'All my pleasure, my darling.'

Lunch at Fortnum and Mason. Mamma picking the flesh from a Dover sole. Resting in the afternoon at her hotel, 'No, Alix, I will not stay with you, thank you, I do not wish to leave the West End. Too many bad memories.' In the evening a show. *Cats.* My lipstick on her powdered face, bending my head to hers. 'So tall, darling.' Then a key in my handbag, a taxi south of the river, letting myself in, 'What's that you're wearing? Here, let's take it off.'

Dress unzipped, my breasts in lilac lace, pants wet, his mouth feeding on me.

I was one of those fashionably urban single women whose work both contents and stimulates her, who has no need of 'hobbies', whose time is not required to tend the needs of others and who can, if she is not careful, fall into absurdity, self-indulgence and hence endanger herself if she doesn't watch out, and does not guard her tongue and ensure she makes no enemies.

At the very height of my fame there was that interview in *Vogue* magazine. They wanted me because I was on TV, because I was a babe, because they had found out to their own astonishment that the haughty, arrogant moralist was the daughter of the woman who made that amazing cleansing cream with the quaint name ('Lotte's Cream! How sweet'), which everyone who was anyone, from film stars to It Girls, used. Why did I agree to that? Oh, why the hell not? I said to myself. I was warned against it. Marsha Goode said, 'Knowing how *they* think, you'll be guilty of trivialising and bringing into disrepute the practice of criminology. At best, you'll come across as an air-head, at worst you'll get the backs up of a lot of people in the department.' But I was headstrong, self-willed, narcissistic.

Vogue promised to send a makeup artist, which was enough, alone, to tempt me. While she was applying the under-eye concealer and recommending various tricks with brushes, I was holding forth to the reporter on my theory of the four levels of shopping. The first, I told her, isn't shopping at all, it comes under the heading of housework, that's the weekly supermarket trip, which is such a chore, making sure the kitchen is stocked with food and cleaning products, a never-ending task that will go on for the rest of your life and which allows you to feel that something has been accomplished, but without pleasure or any real sense of acquisition. The second level is shopping for things you need, indeed have needed for a while, like sheets or towels or maybe a new microwave oven. You feel good when you have them. You're going to have them for a long while to come. You've refreshed your house and refreshed yourself. The third level takes you reluctantly out to buy anything that has either wheels or a screen and keyboard and this stuff I always try to leave to a man because I regard that type of purchase with dread. I know that the moment I leave the shop, they're all laughing at me because I've been sold a lemon. The fourth level, the one that women enjoy and men hate, is the shopping that's associated with pure pleasure, pure desire. For example, suppose you get it into your head that you want a pair of suede ankle boots, because you've seen some in a magazine. First step will be touring every single shoe shop in the whole of Bond Street and Brompton Road, looking at boots, pricing them, even trying on one or two pairs. You get home from these trips and stand in front of your wardrobe looking at your trousers, concentrating hard, and if your husband asks you what you are doing, you reply, 'Visualising.' 'Visualising what?' 'How the boots are going to look with my trousers.' Finally, you go back out again, return to maybe three shops you have selected and start trying on in earnest. Maybe you try on twenty or thirty pairs of boots, involving not only the shoe-shop saleswoman but everybody else who happens to be in there at the time, all consulted. Finally, in triumph, you bring home a bag with a box in it and parade up and down in your new boots and say to your husband, 'Well, what do you think?' He looks at the boots and says, in some doubt, 'Are they waterproof?' And if they were not brand new you would be ready to throw one at his head because that, it should be obvious, is not the point.

When the *Vogue* article appeared, this exegesis formed the bulk of the text. Almost nothing about my theories of justice. As Marsha had warned, it did not do my reputation any good at all among the faculty. I was simultaneously a bimbo, a lightweight and, because of my unfashionable views on crime, I was also a censorious moral absolutist in an age of post-modern relativism. Marsha was correct: I was headed towards disaster. Six months later, sitting in the office of my department head, with five undergraduates whining about compassion and rehabilitation and redemption, I said, 'Look, the woman is a psychotic, and I don't use that as a term of abuse but as an exact medical description of her mental state. She is incapable of empathy, and nor do I mean that as a warm fuzzy I-really-hear-what-you're-saying word. I mean her mind is wired up in a particular way so that she lacks the imagination to be someone *other* than Myra Hindley. When she says she knows God has forgiven her, she means that she has forgiven herself because she has finally registered, in a fog-bound realisation, that, dimly understood, there has been a violation of some kind. But that's as far as it goes.' And the girl with the red hair, the uncompromising combat pants and the Doc Martens whose undergraduate thesis I had failed (more than failed: my comments, apparently, had destroyed her 'self-esteem', hence the presence in the office of her support group, which had held a small demonstration on her behalf the previous week), said, 'You're just using words.' To which I replied, 'What else would I use, you fucking idiot?' Thus was I undone.

It so happened that I lost my job at the same time as I started to lose my looks. At twenty, at Oxford, I had vowed to take up as much space as I could in the world – in fact that was who I was planning to be, a taker of space – and had succeeded beyond my dreams. Whatever I assaulted, I grabbed. I was a greedy lover, I had big appetites for sex and other forms of sensuous pleasure. I remember Marsha and me in our second year sitting freezing in our flat off the unfashionable Botley Road, blowing on our fingers, drinking cheap white wine at fifty pence a bottle. Marsha in sepia velvet and frayed lace. Our eyes rimmed with kohl;

smelling of joss-sticks. The single glowing red bar of the electric fire fading with the click of the empty meter. When it was working we pushed cigarettes against the element to light them, holding our cold faces to it, drawing the heat of the flame into our mouths. 'I want,' I said, 'to be like Anaïs Nin, to leave a man while he's asleep, to just get up and go. I want to screw without attachment or sentimentality or possessiveness or jealousy.' Marsha coming back from London with shopping, holding in her hands, waving above her head – 'Come and see, Ally, come and see what I've got' – a bag from Liberty, a packet of emerald green tights, another pair in purple for me.

Our girlhood slipped by, young men passed through, dozens of them, met at breakfast, discarded, swapped: 'Try him, he's not bad.' 'Big?' 'So-so.' The smell of them on our sheets, heaving bags to the launderette and, cleansed, starting afresh. How many men? Perhaps ten or fifteen in those student years alone. And now, nothing. How could it come to nothing? *What happened?*

Marsha Goode and I (Marsha with lemon-coloured hair, like a glassy waterfall down her back, and heavy jowls) walk into a restaurant, wait for the maître d' and no one sees us, we aren't there. No one asks, 'What gives them the right . . . ?' We are no longer appraised, checked out, eyed-up. We are looked through, as if we were windows, a transparent surface between the viewer and the more interesting features of the room. In the mirror I saw my own ageing and, with all the best creams in the world, had nothing in my means to prevent it. For the first time I found myself unwillingly alone, without a boyfriend. The source of my power had been always to deny them access when I valued my autonomy and needed to be by myself. 'I want to be alone!' But one Saturday night, insomniac, waking at two a.m. after an evening at home reading a biography of Albert Speer, I had to be held. My flesh burned with the need for it. And thinking of whom I could call, which man I had temporarily rejected who could now be re-summoned, found there was no one. It had been eight months since I had last had sex. A conference in Geneva. He was married. And the one before that was married too. Since the ending of my relationship with Alan and the dissolution of our household after five years when I discovered the affair – over for six months already, he said, but so what? I don't like being betrayed and belittled – I could not find any man who was *not* married. Their marriages collapsed all the time, but only because they were ended by an affair, usually with their students. I slept with married men because there were no single ones to sleep with and wrenching them away from their wives was the gamble any woman had to take who wanted a relationship.

My single friends (and believe me, I'm not the only one, there are scores of us) have various solutions to the problem. Marsha, for example, said, six months ago when we had lunch at Nicole's beneath the bevelled mirrors among a hundred other women identically dressed in pastel cashmere, 'Alix, you really don't understand what paying for sex is all about. Frankly, you are mired in an outdated female consciousness, you're still stuck in the fifties. Why can't you regard it as a transaction, a service rendered?' 'Yes, but suppose I'm okay with it, what's going to turn him on? If there are boys who get off on older women, why aren't they actually dating me, free, for nothing?' 'Oh, for God's sake, there are pills they take to make them stiff, and exercises. I suppose they must have some male-whore secrets they pass around among themselves. Anyway, why so hung up on fucking? Fucking is *passé*. Try a mouthful of this lamb.' I opened my mouth and indeed it was tender. 'What are you saying?' 'In my view, we've got to learn from the gays. When the Aids catastrophe hit them they were inventive, they found all kinds of solutions. Have you tried the whole power/submission thing, which is very big these days?' 'Marsha,' I said, 'surprisingly, I have no perversity, I am perhaps the most boring person on the planet where sex is concerned, a little sucking, a little fucking, a finger here and there but that's it. No one's going to tie me up.' 'Then why can't you do the tying?' 'No, thanks. Listen, Marsha, I want a relationship of powerful equals, is that too much to ask?' 'Oh, well,' she replied in disgust, gesturing for the bill, 'now you're just being romantic.'

Something was lacking in us. Youth. We'd had it, we didn't have it any more. The loss cannot be revoked. At forty-nine I seemed to have turned into the kind of woman whom in my twenties I would have felt sorry for.

I *am* romantic, I suppose. Lying in bed in Sam's flat in the Albert Dock I succumb to a favourite sexual fantasy. Staring at the ceiling, my eyes half closed, I remember what my brother has said about the place that encloses me, how stone, brick and iron are the materials from which the dock was built and nothing combustible was used in its construction. The roof is a series of sheet-metal plates manufactured by shipbuilders. Invisible from the outside are the hollow iron pillars that support the barrel-vaulted brick ceilings of the warehouses, spanned with inverted Y-beams, which themselves are pre-tensioned with wrought-iron rods. Enclosed within the dock's walls is a rectangular pool surrounded by a colonnade of cast-iron columns painted the colour of coral or salmon, depending on the light. With every tide the level of the water rises and falls one and a half inches. When the dock was first opened in 1845 nothing in the whole of England could compare to it in size and splendour, the monumental mass that loomed so large upon the river, the western gateway of the empire.

I don't know what Jesse Hartley, the architect of the dock, looked like but I imagine he was stamped out by the same metal-pressing machine that produced Isambard Kingdom Brunel. Recently I have come to adore that famous photograph of him, who – with his cigar and stovepipe hat, his hands in the pockets of his trousers, one knee bent forward slightly, leaning against and dwarfed by a wall of gigantic launching chains for a ship he built called the *Great Eastern* – typifies the ferocious energy of the Victorian era. The dishevelled elegance of the man! The arrogance and swagger of his posture! He worked eighteen hours a day, built bridges, tunnels, ships, pumping stations, state-of-the-art locomotives that could run at sixty miles an hour, and in his spare time, according to a biography I found on the shelf in the flat, performed magic tricks involving the swallowing of coins (one of which got stuck in his throat and nearly killed him) accompanied by his friend Felix Mendelssohn on the piano. He never went on holiday unless his doctor forced him to, and he spent his honeymoon on a three-day excursion to the opening of the Liverpool–Manchester railway. He is my pin-up, he turns me on, though he was only five foot four, apparently, and very bald under the hat. In Joseph Shields, the demolisher of antiquity, I feel that there might be a glowing cinder of Brunel's vigour and domination.

My Issie. The forward thrust of the knee, the suggestive placing of the hands in his trouser pockets, the lips flexing their muscles round the cigar – I wanted him to bury his Victorian cock inside me. I'd fuck him in a heartbeat, lying down on that bed of chains. No masseur or personal trainer or tennis coach has what turns me on, which is what Issie has, I mean the explosive force that can stand up to me. Only the man who engineered the nineteenth century in steel and iron could meet on an equal footing a woman who tried to face down a department of feminists determined to rehabilitate Myra Hindley.

Issie got into difficulties. The building of the *Great Eastern* was a fiasco. His imagination pushed far beyond the available technologies of his era, the mid-nineteenth century; the damned engines just didn't give him the power he needed. Then the company foisted a collaborator on him, a man named Russell. What artist does not want to kill his contractor? It was a joke – bad management, intrigue, rumour, financial problems, poor quality control and in the end it was only because of Issie's colossal energy that the ship was launched at all. Chains snapped on capstans, men died, a public-relations disaster, and it killed him. He was only fifty-three. He comes to me in the night and I hold him, my short, cigar-smoking engineer, dead since 1859. I take off his hat, put his cigar in the ashtray, remove his coat, unlace his boots, ease the stovepipe trousers off his tired legs. Exhaustion overcomes him and he falls asleep for a minute, and while he is dreaming I take his cock, run my finger along the length of the long dark vein. Still sleeping, he reaches for my breast and he is waking into arousal, his eyes opening on my face and we kiss. Then I suck him and then he fucks me. His bald head, sweating, is on my shoulder, his teeth clench on my neck. We each come in our own time (he waits for me) and then we lie back in my late-twentieth-century sheets and I pass him an ashtray and a lighter and he reclines, smoking his cigar, silent, thinking of Tarmac roads, viaducts, aqueducts, engines that replace horse-power, and I say, 'Issie, listen, you want to know how to build a machine that flies?' I tell him about houses veined with invisible wires, electricity coursing through the brick body, the whole place lit up, humming, radiating power. Heat and light are the properties of the new age he's going to miss. 'It's all about energy, Issie,' I tell him. 'The world is running quicker and quicker, we overreach ourselves and come, if you have the energy, fuck me again.'

Dressing after the shower, after I had come so forcefully, as I always do when in my imagination I make love to Issie, I looked at myself in the mirror and saw the outline of a tall, ageing woman whose hips were too wide and whose arms had the familiar batwing flap of flesh beneath them and I thought, Oh, come on, who are you kidding? I sometimes fill myself with revulsion, never mind anyone else. My breasts are veined, the aureoles puckered. A few hairs grow from round each nipple. My pubic hairs are greying. Last year I menstruated a total of seven times. Oestrogen is draining out of my body, abandoning it like waters from a floodplain, leaving me high and dry, empty and arid. My vagina is drying out, the walls are papery. The collagen withers in my skin and I am deluding myself if I think that Joseph Shields, who could have a woman half my age, is going to want me.

There is a decent thing to do, according to some of my friends, which is to embrace celibacy. To end the pact I made at twenty, that I would reward myself with nothing less than my own pleasure, this is what they are proposing. How can they ask it of me?

I had vowed to meet no sexual demands other than my own. I would give no more and no less than I took, and I had planned to take plenty. I would never mortify my flesh, neither by abstinence nor by the modish compulsion of whips and handcuffs. 'The whole business is overrated,' some of my friends said. Not to me. Sex was always sublime, I came easily and still do. I never went to an orgasm workshop, or bothered with junky books like *The Joy of Sex*. I knew exactly what sex was, it was natural right from the beginning, and in my twenty-first year, never having heard the word fellatio, without even experiencing what became, later, the familiar pressure on the back of the head, it occurred to me to wonder what the cock might feel like if it was embraced in another damp place. The tongue was almost without limitations. From then on I saw the bodies of the men I loved as an erogenous zone entirely: the crook of the arm, the heel, the pleasures of the nape of the neck (which when my own was touched drove me to distraction, as if a divine creator – in which I don't, of course, believe – had put its finger on the origin of the world), the anus, the cleft in the chin, the tender skin the tongue can reach just beneath the fingernails. But with a rent-boy? And a girl was out of the question. What draws me to men is my love of their cocks inside me. I am a very vaginal woman. I don't deny that the idea of breasts is capable of exciting me and that a woman's shape can be beguiling but, to be honest, when I look at a woman I am not seeing the outline of her body but, rather, am examining her clothes, her makeup, her hair, and thinking, Could I wear that colour lipstick? Or, Look at her neck, mine will go that way too, soon enough.

In Sam's flat, sitting with the newspaper on my lap by the open window, I felt cold breezes blow off the water: rain was coming in from the Irish Sea. I was thinking about Italy, about a hotel I once stayed at on Capri, drinking *prosecco* and reading for the first time Ovid's *Metamorphoses*, of the Thracian women who in revenge for attacking Orpheus were turned by Bacchus into oaks: their toes thrust down into the earth, their arms became branches and their hair leaves. I was trapped also in this veined, woody body.

I was forty-nine, I had plenty of money, I had everything of everything except the column of fire inside me that was ignited by sexual passion, which had smoked and blazed through my life, scattering cinders and ashes, since I was seventeen. I was afraid of who I was without it. And this is what they want me to transcend in exchange for yoga, multi-vitamins, homeopathy, acupuncture, Reiki, meditation, peace of mind and even Nirvana? I might as well be dead.

Now, Joseph Shields. Melanie was right, as he made very clear over dinner: he is totally married. His wife is called Erica. They live in Chicago. Back home he drives a 1997 Chevrolet Corvette 'because that car's a classic, the best car the American automotive industry ever produced and you know why? Because the company allowed the engineers to control it, they wouldn't let the sales and marketing people into the meetings. From a design point of view it's just beautiful. Inside it was all leather at a time when American cars had plastic upholstery you could wipe with a sponge and plastic panels that snapped on with those plastic snappy things. It didn't rattle when you drove down the road and if you're going to drive an American car, this has got to be it. My wife, on the other hand, says the car is just an extension of my cock and I'm still trying to figure out what her BMW says about her and if any of you have any information' (here he looked at me, detecting the feminist, I suppose) 'I'd be glad to hear it.'

They have three children, aged twenty-two, nineteen and sixteen, two boys and a girl, the eldest just graduated in film studies from Berkeley, his dad's old school; the next one down at Boston 'with no idea at all what her major will be' and the 'baby' wearing 'his pants half-way down his ass and breathing and sleeping and dreaming the skate scene, which is skateboarding to you and me. I like to hope he isn't smoking dope yet, but my wife says, why wouldn't he be? At his age, I was. Which is okay, but I worry because the grass they get nowadays is a lot stronger than when we were kids and there are all these other drugs like Ecstasy that I don't know much about.' Erica is a lawyer. She is employed part-time for a firm that specialises in class action suits and did a lot of work on the Dow Corning breast implant 'that caused some deaths a few years back, and her job is what's left today of the combined sum of what used to be our political activism'.

The morning after I met Joseph Shields, waking in my white room in Sam's flat and considering the impression that I made on him, I had to ask myself, Was I sarcastic, overbearing, argumentative, talkative, emphatic, opinionated, loud? I didn't know how I seemed that night over dinner or at the *shiva* house. Since I had come back to Liverpool I had felt muted, apart from my outburst on the edge of the muddy river. Grief and sadness muffled me, and also the relatives, with the endless question: 'So when will I dance at your wedding?'

Then, some days after that coffee we'd shared at the Tate, walking past his site office, I saw him coming towards me, his head bent against the metal wind blowing in from the sea.

'Hey,' I said, 'what's up?'

'It's what's not up, that's the problem. Someone broke in and vandalised the place last night. You know, I really am tearing my hair out here.'

'What's left of it.' And could have cut out my tongue as I said it: you don't make those kinds of remarks to men you want to attract. They don't like that sort of thing, no one does.

But he continued without apparent offence, not seeming to notice, he was too enraged. 'I really don't know what's with you people. I don't mean you, I mean the kind of punks that would pull this kind of stunt. You want progress or you want a sewer? You should make your goddam minds up. I've got a hell of a lot of my own money sunk into this and I'm not doing it out of the goodness of my heart, I'm not a philanthropist. I want to see this city back on its feet, but not at any price, not if it's me that gets screwed. Believe me, I have my own problems.'

'What's the situation at the moment?'

'One way or another I'm three months behind schedule and every delay costs me bucks. I don't know what to think, whether I should reconsider, cut my losses, get out.'

This alarmed me. 'No, no, don't be disheartened . . .'

'I am *not* disheartened, as you put it. I'm a businessman. I have to take hard-headed decisions.'

'Whatever. I was going to say that you simply need to see things in the context of how we operate here. Why don't you show me what you've been up to? I'll see if there's anything I can do to help, and I'll ask Sam what he thinks.'

'You mean you want to come and look at the site?'

'Yes. I would love to.'

'I don't have a lot for you to see at this stage.'

'That's okay.'

'You'll have to climb ladders.'

'I can do that.'

'You'll have to wear a hard hat.'

'I am prepared to wear a hard hat.'

'Boots would be a good idea too.'

'I have boots.'

'Work-boots?'

'No, not work-boots.'

'I don't want you to slip and fall because I do have insurance but I don't relish the idea of my hotel opening with all the attendant publicity about how it killed off one of the city's leading daughters before it ever received one guest.'

'Yes, I get you. I promise I will dress sensibly. Now my rules.'

'I have never met a woman who does not have rules.'

'This is as it should be. You don't patronise me by telling your crew to treat me like a lady. I am not incapable of putting up with whistles and crude remarks.'

'I'll bet. You know, you remind me of my old sergeant.'

'Your what?'

'Nothing, never mind.'

I thought he said sergeant, which didn't make any sense because you couldn't imagine a guy like him serving in the army. It didn't fit at all. Or not with my idea of the military, which is guys with poker-straight backs who went to Sandhurst and are married to women who'd rather fuck their horse.

After I reported this meeting to my sister-in-law Melanie over dinner that night, she replied, 'Don't you need to be anywhere?'

'What do you mean?'

'What's going on with the Romania project?'

'I've got all the paperwork with me, I'm working on it.'

'Aren't you due a visit there?'

'No. Not just yet. The field trip is months away.'

'Because I wouldn't want to think you were hanging around here doing nothing waiting for Joseph to make a move.'

'Why? Do you think he won't?'

'Will, won't. What difference does it make? He's a married man.'

'You can be hard, Melanie.'

'What, me? I don't know what you're talking about.'

Melanie – who let Sam and me rant and rave and hold forth on all the ills of the world while quietly looking at maps of the Lake District where she and her rambling club went for weekend walks in muddy boots and shapeless anoraks, and missed the garden of their old house where she had planted plum and pear trees and not seen them come to fruit – had a moral code that was Mosaic.

While Mamma was dying we were thrown together, as we had not been since our teens when we both went to the Jewish youth club and I, the bratty, clever, younger sister of her boyfriend, had to be schmoozed and made nice to and allowed to borrow her peach-coloured Woolworth's lipstick – who found such lines excitingly tawdry as the child of a mother who only wore Elizabeth Arden and Helena Rubinstein. Now, between bedside vigils, I had dragged Melanie to Manchester to shop for clothes, told her the big-shouldered, long-line eighties black suit she would wear for the funeral was out of the question, she needed updating, a new image, she should look at Armani, she could afford it. And what about a manicure? Those nails! But she couldn't stand spending her husband's money, even though the Rebicks were rolling in wealth. She had made Sam donate fifty thousand pounds to a hatful of charities she selected, all carefully chosen because then they could demonstrate *practically* that they had a cast-iron track record of doing good. She demanded results, case histories; if food was sent to a war-torn land she needed proof that it had not been stolen or squandered or sold by a corrupt dictatorship in exchange for guns. She particularly liked a charity that helped the victims of torture and was wary of the ones that trumpeted windily their commitment to human rights.

'Why her, Sam?' I had asked, when it became obvious that my brother was determined to 'throw himself away' on Melanie Harris, to sample no other girl from the moment he laid eyes on her at sixteen, and they were so indissoluble a couple that he gave up the boyhood dream of America, failed to fulfil the plan that had been in operation since he was born, when marriage to Melanie had made him refuse to go illegal, to bring up kids on the run from the authorities without the right papers or the right stamps on them.

'I don't know,' Sam had told me. 'She's got something.'

Not charm, not obvious sex appeal, but that biting intelligence of hers. 'Listen, Alix,' she said to me, years later, 'if Sam hadn't married me I don't know if anybody else would have done. Nobody was interested. I wasn't popular. Nobody was lining up to beg me for dates. I was the one who the pretty girl made her friend so she would look good by comparison. A few years on none of it would have mattered. I would have stayed on at school and gone to university but you didn't do that in those days. Boys did, not girls unless they had parents like yours. No one encouraged me. I didn't encourage myself. As far as my father was concerned to get married was enough, and to marry Saul Rebick's son! You've no idea. It was an honour.'

Saul Rebick's son, who like his father could have 'had anyone', it was universally agreed, had 'wasted himself' on Manny Harris's daughter, a nobody whose mother bought her clothes off a stall at Garston market, and who lived in a two-up two-down off Smithdown Road that smelt of stale cooking oil. This was the Melanie Harris who had stood behind the chemist's counter helping the pharmacist until my brother asked her out, brought her home and made dead certain that from that day forward she commanded nothing but respect. 'Listen, Alix,' he said to me, when they got engaged, 'Mel didn't go to a fancy school like you did but in her own way she's smarter than any of us will ever be. Get it?' 'Okay.' They had been married for nearly thirty years, since they were babies, hardly into their twenties when Sam led her up the aisle in 1970, while he was still a law student. 'Do you still have sex?' I asked her, one day over coffee before the hairdresser's when I was trying to talk her into some amendment to the style she had stuck with since before the kids were born.

'Yes, we still do it, not as often and maybe there are problems I won't go into, but we get up to things, we fool around.'

'But he's attracted to you, he can still get it up for you?'

'I wouldn't go so far as to say up, not up exactly, not all the time.'

When we were kids Sam and I had experimentally kissed each other, long, tongue, French kisses. At thirteen, three of his front teeth were knocked out when he fell from his bike and my mother ran screaming, just *screaming*, into the street, when she saw him, blood smothering his face like a shroud. It wasn't serious but from then on he had worn a plate (later an expensive bridge) and so we tried our kisses with teeth and without. I had tingled in my brother's arms, felt something hard against me, seen him pull away, his face white, and heard him slam the bedroom door. My brother, at sixteen, was a potent sexual being, and I at fourteen was the same. We were rushing towards the sexual revolution, we were practising for it. And I was washed up at forty-nine, and at fifty-two, I was now hearing, utterly shocked, my brother was a Viagra case.

'So what does that mean for you?'

'What are you saying?'

'Would you turn down an affair if it was offered to you on a plate?'

'Who with?'

'I don't know. I'm speaking hypothetically.'

'I might.'

'So what's the difference?'

'The difference between me and you is that I've been married for the whole of my adult life. I'm not looking to fall in love.'

'Who's talking about love? Cheap sex would do it for me.'

'You wouldn't be able to help yourself.'

'Not necessarily.'

'I can see why you're attracted to Joseph, I don't deny that he is someone you would be very susceptible to. But you have no idea about his circumstances and I think you should leave him alone. In fact, you should go back to France.'

'No. Why would I?'

'For your own good. I don't want to see you get hurt, you're vulnerable enough already since your mother died. Do you really want a bad affair on top of all that?'

'I can take care of myself. And I'm not going anywhere until I've at least seen his hotel.'

Used to getting her own way by stealth, she cooked up another plan to get me out of Liverpool, with the unwitting aid of my brother, because men can be very stupid that way.

'So what exactly would we do,' I said to Sam, the next morning as I was signing the probate documents for my mother's will, 'with an industrial building on the outskirts of Dresden, were we able to establish ownership of it with the German authorities?'

'We could sell it. Maybe the land is worth something, make a killing.'

'I see. The Jews return to Germany in their traditional guise, the bloated capitalist, the money-grubbing, money-bags Jew.'

'Donate it to charity, turn it into an orphanage, a hospital, an old people's home, an asylum, a school.'

'How do you know it isn't any of those things right now?'

'No one knows. This is why we must find out.'

'Why should we obey the dying wish of a senile woman? If she was in her right mind, do you think she would have given us this burden?'

'We don't know that either, we only know she did.'

'And who will reclaim the factory?'

'I will do the legal work, you will go and negotiate with the authorities.'

'Why me?'

'Why not you? You're used to those eastern European types, you know their racket.'

'Why not leave it where it is? Why dig up the past?'

'*You* ask me that? It's your whole line of work.'

'This is personal. And also unnecessary. It's a waste of everybody's time.'

'We have an obligation.'

'I disagree.'

'"Honour thy father and thy mother that thy days may be long upon the land which the Lord thy God giveth to thee."'

'"And if a man sell his daughter to be a maidservant she shall not go out as the menservants do." I can out-Scripture you any day, Sam. That fucking book is a manual of hatred, misogyny and racism. The god of our forefathers is a bigot and the Jews are arse-lickers for praying to him.'

'True. But a stopped clock is right twice a day. What happened there in that room, Alix? Why, when every site in her brain had failed, when speech was finished, movement finished, when there was nothing left but the breath in her body, did she speak? How can you explain it? The doctor can't. We know it wasn't a miracle, but can't you take it as a sign?'

'Of what?'

'I have no idea. Maybe the point is that we'll find out once we know what happened to the factory.'

'A *sign*, Sam?'

We had grown up in a family committed to progress, specifically to the curing of diseases by medicines tested in laboratories with success rates established by clinical trials. We scorned herbal remedies, homeopathy, astrology. The words 'ancient' and 'natural' held no allure for us. We demanded proofs. We had sat stony-faced through every film about the Shoah. Watched the newsreels of the camps dry-eyed. It was justice we were interested in, not empathy with the victims, we didn't need to feel their pain. We had its example before us every day of our childhood. Prosecute the war criminals, harry them to the end of their days, make old men with arthritic joints sit in court day after day, force them to listen, half deaf, to fifty-year-old testimony, visit shame upon their sons and daughters. This was the kind of thing I used to say on TV, to howls of protests from the do-gooders of this world. A student once wrote in her essay on the Nuremberg trials, 'Instead of fighting a world war we should have bombed Germany with love.' She was surprised to get a D. 'Well, this is my opinion, and I'm entitled to it,' she told the department head, when she appealed. 'Not if her opinion is mentally retarded,' I said, in my defence. Another black mark against me. A further sheet in my thickening file of atrocities against my students.

So who cared about a pile of bricks? The factory in Dresden

was, to me, a myth, a fairy story. It constituted the oral history of our family, virtually fiction, its power was only in the story. Not to Sam, though. Melanie knew him through and through. I don't know what she said to him, when they sat up in bed talking and I heard the low murmur of their voices in the bedroom next to mine, but she had made it her mission to get me to Germany, well away from the temptation of breaking up, or at least damaging, someone else's marriage. And Sam, of course, had swallowed it. He was now determined that I was to be the instrument of the factory's return to Rebick custody.

As for me, I believed that our mother's dying wish, to 'get the factory back', was merely one last throw of the dice by Mamma, a final attempt to make us understand that we would never be free of our parents, that they would always thwart our yearning for autonomy, forcing us to address the truth: that though we were the children of immigrants and had the right to be anyone we wanted, we had no capacity to be reborn and that, in fact, reinvention was out of the question. And the joke was that the only reason I could live in France or do my job for token pay restoring synagogues, or that Sam could afford to buy the Albert Dock flat, cash down, or that Melanie could urge him to give so much money to charity, was because of the legacy they had left us. As the papers I was signing confirmed, it consisted of a house in Cressington Park, also near the river, some jewellery, which would need a valuation, a very small Lucian Freud painting my father had bought in the early fifties through a cabinet maker he knew in London from his time in the 43 Group. And a business, which had its roots in a German city near the Polish border, which, like our own town, had managed to survive when it shouldn't.

When I recalled all my mother had lost before the age of fourteen – her parents, who loved her; her brother with untidy brown hair, who taught her how to ride her first bicycle, and his young wife, who gave her her own childhood album of traced outlines of woodland animals and a paintbox to colour them in; her friends, with whom she played games with dolls and stuffed animals in the nursery on the top floor of the house from whose windows you could watch the river Elbe flow through the flood-plains of Saxony; her childhood home, with its dear, familiar objects; her country and its culture, whose writers and composers she had been taught to consider hers also; and her language, in which she spoke only to herself and the small number of German refugees in Liverpool who held little musical evenings – I could not understand why it should be the factory that grieved her mind with its memory. Yet the rage that soured her, the oaths curdling in her mouth, her sense of dispossession all revolved around the memory that *once* she had been the daughter of a doctor and a businessman.

She was a child in Dresden, a city stuffed full of art and arte-facts, *fabulous* paintings, apparently, Raphael, Titian, Correggio, Giorgione, Veronese and Tintoretto representing the Italian Renaissance, and Dürer, Holbein and Cranach among the Germans. Gorgeous buildings as well, but she never once returned there after the war. 'Why not, Mummy?' 'Because if my parents had not been so attached, had not been oh-so-loyal Germans, with obedient little German hearts, we would never have stayed, we would have left in 1933, the *minute* Hitler came to power. But no, no, my parents were proud to be Dresdeners, they thought it was marvellous that they could step out on Saturday afternoon and visit the Zwinger and admire the paint-ings and think of themselves as cultivated people.'

She seemed to me to be the moon, a smaller orb that reflected the light of that great blazing star, my father, who calmed and soothed her and urged her to think rationally about her griev-ances. And what, he pointed out, did she do on her twice-yearly visits to London? It was not solely for the pursuit of pleasure that she made these excursions but (despite what she said about her parents) to satisfy in herself a hunger to be German once more. German at a concert at the Wigmore Hall. German standing in front of a Dürer at the National Gallery. German in the consumption of Black Forest gateau in a tea shop in the Cromwell Road years before it had become a cliché of the dessert trolley and still carried with it associations from her childhood of fairy tales. Woodland creatures clambered on the counterpane of her bed while she slept, only to be vanquished by turning on the goose nightlight, which glowed with a fat yellow radiance on the familiar things of her room, and her father would come in and say, 'Lotte, did you have a bad dream? Maybe tomorrow we will have a cake with cream and cherries but only if you go back to sleep.'

When my father told me, in my childhood, that she had 'lost' her mother and father back in Germany he was speaking metaphorically. They were alive into the early part of my life, though not well, victim to a host of ailments, some hypochondriacal, others all too obvious, such as my grandmother's crusted eyes and the clenched veins on my grandfather's head, an external manifestation of the clot that was making its way to his brain and would kill him as he bent over to pick up the milk from the step one morning in May 1957. He was only sixty-eight. Back in the twenties, in Germany, as part of the general post-war liberation of young women, my grandmother the young bride had cautiously begun to wear rouge, powder, lipstick and even sometimes kohl to outline her eyes. Soap, she found, did not adequately remove these cosmetics. Near the Altmarkt, one afternoon, she bought a jar of cleansing cream from a pharmacist who displayed on his counter a pyramid of specimens, bluntly called 'Washing Cream'. The results, she found, later that night, were dramatic. Never before had she felt her face to be so clean, yet the skin was not drawn and tight but soft to the touch and had a translucent glow, which she admired in front of the mirror. On her recommendation, her friends flocked to the Altmarkt to buy exactly the same product and the pharmacist was hard pressed to supply his growing trade. From three or four jars a week, he was now selling nine or ten a day. My grandfather was a doctor but he also had a sharp head for business. Recognising an opportunity, he proposed that he himself come up with the capital to manufacture the cream on a wider scale and sell it in department stores in Dresden and Leipzig under the name *Violette Schimmer*, or Violet Lustre, having added a tint to the mixture to make it look less chemical. Soon, with absolutely no advertising, just word of mouth, it was all the rage among the women of Germany and was stocked as far away as Hamburg and Munich. Together they had done a roaring trade and at the same time as my grandfather's medical practice had dwindled under fascism and the boycott of Jewish businesses caused the virtual closure of the pharmacy, the factory had thrived, for even Nazi *fräuleins* liked a lovely complexion and were not too fussy where it came from. Listen, there was all kinds of co-operation between middle-class Jews and the Reich that no one talks about if they can help it; there were corners, there were cracks where a Jew could carry on a business if the Nazis preferred production to continue without interruption or unnecessary restriction. That's why they stayed so long – far longer than necessary. My grand-parents were already in negotiation for exit permits for themselves, Ernst and Dora when they put my mother on the train to England. The formula for the face cream in exchange for their lives, that was the deal they were making. The Germans got the factory, Herr *und* Frau Dorf, *der Juden*, got exile in West Hampstead.

The linoleum on the stairs of their house was a pattern of brown flowers, *brown*. The warm milk they gave me in a smeared glass was sour like the smile on my mother's face. The poppyseed biscuits were weeks old and the butter in them as rancid as the curses my mother uttered on the way home. 'That they put me on the train alone, of course I can forgive, everyone was doing the same, but that when they arrived in London *only a few months later*, they did not come to rescue me, that they allowed me to stay on with the Schwartzes, they never again made a home for me, that my childhood was destroyed by those people . . .' That everything, every penny in charity they received, every half-crown someone gave her father for carrying out a little operation on the foot, went to the pursuit of getting her brother Ernst and sister-in-law Dora a visa for America, and sending money to them every month when they got to New York – this my mother could not stand. 'He sits on a stool and tends to the stinking feet of those high and mighty Jews who think they are doing him a favour because he's on his uppers now, he *literally* stoops to this little profession, chiropody, so my brother in America gets the best of everything, and I received nothing from them, they left me to rot, to clean steps and polish silver, when I should have been eating from silver . . .' 'Lotte, calm yourself, you want for nothing now.' 'Yes, Saul, I have everything, it's true, but why did my parents allow the humiliation of their own flesh and blood? How could do they do this to me?'

A few weeks after Kristallnacht she had stood on the platform at the railway station in a crowd of Jewish children. The boys were in tweed suits, which their parents, studying old copies of magazines, had assumed was the correct form of dress for the English, winter and summer. One boy had a deerstalker hat, taken from an illustration of a Sherlock Holmes story. My mother aged fourteen wore a green woollen dress and a woollen cape, edged in emerald braid. Her hair was in plaits. She waved goodbye to her parents as the engine pulled away from the station, accelerating towards to the west, through a land in colour, not newsreel black and white, through green forests and brown plains and brick-red cities where women walked wearing spring outfits in pastel shades with cream and blue handbags, lilac hats, nut brown shoes, past red and black swastika flags, and crossed the border to the Hook of Holland. She marched up the gang-plank on to a ship bound for Harwich. At the far end of her journey was the person who had responded to this advertise-ment in the classified pages of the *Jewish Chronicle*:

> Which family can give a home to a young Jewish girl, speaks German, French, some English, very well educated. Very urgent case. Communicate with Dr SL, 116 Mare Street, London E8.

Who turned out to be in need of an unpaid maidservant for a family of five, where she stayed for the duration of the war while her parents lived in their West Hampstead bedsit and sent the money they saved to their son, who had made it all the way to America.

I knew bile rose in her throat because she caught herself occa-sionally, muttering in German, and stopped herself, reapplying colour to her straight lips as a means of telling her mouth she was in other circumstances now. Every dish she washed in the scullery in Stamford Hill, the maid's uniform they forced her to wear (itself a hand-me-down from their previous girl who had gone to work in a munitions factory), each framed family pho-tograph she dusted, the piano she could polish but was not allowed to play – every aspect of her life in London took her on a downward course, slipping rung by rung down the class system.

And whether it still stood or had been demolished decades ago, the factory was maybe the only permanent structure in a century's worth of flight. The house where my father had been born, for example, into which my grandparents moved when

they stepped off the boat in 1906, had been torn down during
that post-war period known to everyone in the city as the time
when 'the corporation did more damage to Liverpool than the
Luftwaffe'. What did we care about where we'd come from? Our
condition, the one we had inherited from our father's Polish
stock, was that of non-attachment to the dismal, flat agrarian
plains of the east where – as I saw with my own eyes when I was
taken by the Rosen Foundation to have a look at the restored
synagogue in Tkochin – men still moved about the roads bearing
heavy loads on carts pulled by dray-horses. 'Primitive,' my father
said, when I asked him about the Rebick *hame*. 'What more do
you need to know?' While the Rebicks were ragamuffins who
never had quite enough to eat and, skilled in no trade, were
sometimes forced into beggary, the Dorfs had no need of an exit
door to the New World. When my mother looked back she saw
a golden, lost realm of affluence and status, of Bohemian crystal
wine glasses and Irish linen tablecloths, her brother Ernst in
starched collars, herself in a russet velvet party dress with two
types of petticoat beneath it and an embroidered bodice over
which a seamstress had laboured, her needle threaded with silver
and gold strands. In her mind, the factory was the substance of
everything that had been brutally eradicated by racial theory.
Something of the past could, through a lengthy judicial process,
be restored. This was the difference between my parents. 'The
future!' my father cried. He saw us passing down the radiant
way to tomorrow. 'All that I have lost,' my mother murmured,
heartsick.

So I suppose the factory had been there in her mind all the
time we were growing up, a two-storey brick rectangle in a
suburb of Dresden with its workforce of thirty girls in starched
white coats and sturdy laced shoes standing at benches, their hair
pinned back from their young German faces, bent over filling
glass jars, talking of the things young girls talk about: boyfriends,

fashion, film stars. During their break, my grandmother would sometimes come round with trays of cake to keep them happy and my mother remembered the girls – 'die hübschen jungen deutschen Mädchen' – laughing with cream and crumbs around their mouths. She remembered particularly the overseer, a tall young woman in a navy suit, always with a sparkling white blouse beneath it, who controlled with a firm will every aspect of production including the design of the labels and their portrait of a racily modern, sporty girl with shingle-cut hair, marcel-waved, holding her hands to her flawless face. This manageress, whose name was Marianne, always took great trouble to be most cordial to my mother and to examine her complexion and pronounce it lovely, while my grandmother stood a little way apart, aloof. And presents sometimes came from Marianne too, on my mother's birthday. A doll or a book or a small bouquet of pansies fashioned from velvet.

Mamma's mother had put her on the train with six jars of *Violette Schimmer* in a separate suitcase, wrapped securely in brown paper, and instructions that under no circumstances was she to begin its use until her sixteenth birthday. ('Not a day before, not a day later.' '*Why?*' 'Because now you have the skin of a child and the process of ageing has not begun. But the *moment* it starts . . . Until then, only soap and water.') On the morning of my own sixteenth birthday Mamma took me into the bathroom, dim under overcast October skies, filled the basin, holding her little finger under the tap to test the temperature, and at once the walls' blue tiles swimming with red and turquoise fish misted with steam. She handed me the jar. 'Darling,' she said, 'dip your hand in and spread a little over your face.' This was not the first time I had got inside the glass jar, not at all. Ever since my fingers were big enough to stretch themselves straining around the lid and grasp it with enough strength to untwist and open it, I had been examining my mother's most precious possession, after her children and husband – more valuable to her than the diamanté clips she wore on her ears or the pearls with a small diamond clasp, or her Waring and Gillow furniture or a whole wardrobe full of smart suits and day dresses and cocktail dresses. What she gave me wasn't white, it wasn't even cream. I suppose one could call it an unguent – a sticky, greenery-yallery colour, like myrrh (the violet tint had not been added), the texture of slightly grainy egg yolks, with an odour like the tube of Vicks vapour that was inserted into children's nostrils when they had colds, a menthol smell. But that was as much as I could identify. The exact chemical composition of the special cream was a mystery known only to my parents, the industrial chemist who made it up and, many years into the future, to the research labs at Rose Rosen who bought us out, renamed it 'Clean Finish' and financed my interment in France with the geraniums.

Once the cream was on my face, covering all its surfaces, my mother showed me how to perform a massage, which consisted of pressing my fingers first against my eyebrows, moving inch by inch across the raised arc of bone; next, to spread the fingers and press them against my cheeks in a vertical movement down the face to the jaw; and then the same transition above the lips until I reached the outer limits of my face, and then I was to start in tiny motions along the length of each side of my neck, below the ears. The point of this exercise, my mother explained, was to release 'toxins' and drain the lymphatic system of unnecessary material that would make my face puffy and my skin murky. This was not the end of the business, by any means. After the massage, my mother dipped a white cotton flannel into the sink, wrung it out, gave it to me, and told me to hold it against my face for exactly fifteen seconds while breathing deeply. I was encased in a dark steamy menthol mask, the flannel drawing in around my nostrils, puffing out again, so you knew I was still alive, breathing. The last step, she showed me, was to scrub away the final remnants of the cream and lay the flannel on one more time, now rinsed and wrung out in cold water. It is the purpose of mothers to initiate their daughters into the mysteries of femininity, of womanhood. My mother succeeded in this triumphantly, even though when she was sixteen, my grandmother had snatched from her four jars of the cream for her own use with the result that they were barely speaking to each other.

Seeing her for the first time, in a little blue dress with a Peter Pan collar, playing cards in Maccabi House with a group of refugee girls, I believe that what my father noticed in Lotte Dorf, now aged twenty-two, was a fragile state of both physical and mental health that he believed he could nurse back to a bloom. She had not been a competent maidservant and, after a rudimentary night-school class in shorthand, typing and double-entry book-keeping at the war's end, had been released to find work in the offices of a refugee charity, where she did translation and interpretation. She lived alone in a bedsit in Golders Green only rarely visiting her mother and father in West Hampstead. During their short courtship, my mother told my father the story of the Dresden factory, and showed him the empty jars of cleansing cream, which she had made last as long as she could by using it once a week instead of every night. It ran out early in 1945. He took the jars from her and gave them to an industrial chemist, who during evenings and weekends was one of the 'fucking hardcase Yids' who gave the resurgent post-war fascists a thrashing. He scraped out the hardened oily vestiges, analysed the contents and wrote down the formula. This he sent off to a pal at ICI, who made up a fresh batch.

Of her childhood nothing remained. The house was buried now as far as she knew beneath the concrete foundations of workers' flats, and Dresden itself, away to the east, inaccessible behind the GDF frontier, was not recognisable as the city in which she had walked to school holding her mother's hand.

Everything that had been left behind in pre-war Germany, the world before my mother became a servant, before my grandfather was reduced to chiropody and before my uncle was given the key out of the prison of Europe, everything that preceded her bitterness, her lifetime grudge – all that was concentrated in a glass jar. Years later I finally understood what it meant, what that dying request was all about. From beyond the grave she wanted to say, *We are property owners in Germany*. What had happened to the original factory (and the thirty German girls who sometimes had cream and crumbs on their faces) was unknown.

It was she who had built it into a business, she who at first gave her sisters-in-law a sample of the cream, and their friends and then friends of friends, until (renamed by my father in her honour 'Lotte's Cream') the little advertisements in the classified pages of women's magazines in the late fifties, then in the sixties the first department store orders: from Henderson's in Liverpool, Kendal Milne in Manchester, Derry and Toms in London. Finally, the counter at Harrods and the saleswomen in their white uniforms with emerald green sashes around their waists, tutoring the customers exactly the way Mamma had tutored me. But all my memories are of the time when we were children, in short socks and short trousers, when she was still writing the labels by hand in her educated script, me and Sam and her together in the tea-time hours after school pasting the labels on to the glass with brushes and sticky glue. All of us sending Lotte's Cream out into the world to make it beautiful. From the landing behind the banisters I saw her sit up late with her books, thrilled to watch her little empire grow, the cheques banked in the special account that provided the family opulence for a household that made its primary living from attending to the health of the poorest of the Liverpool poor. And this is how I remember Mamma. And this is who she was to me. The smell of eucalyptus oil. Her head bent over her labels. Refilling the blue ink in her fountain pen. A kiss on my hair, for *nothing*. 'Because I am a good girl?' 'I would kiss you even if you were a bad girl.' 'Can I have a cuddle?' 'Of course, come here.' 'Don't tickle me like you did last time.' 'No? Where's your tummy? Here it is, tickle tickle tickle. See, you're screaming with laughter.' 'Stop!' 'Give *me* a kiss.' 'Mmm.'

Love was the iron law of our house. Mamma sitting by my bed and watching me sleeping. Her hand touching my face and waking me up. 'What, Mamma?' 'Darling, I couldn't resist. Give me a kiss.' Reaching up and putting my lips to her cheeks. 'Cuddle me, Mamma.' 'Kisses and cuddles,' says my father, standing at the door in his pyjamas, 'that is what the whole of life should be made of.' 'Goodnight, darling, go back to sleep now.' 'Goodnight, Mamma, goodnight, Daddy.' 'Goodnight, darling.' 'Is Sam getting kisses too?' 'Yes, yes, of course, everyone gets kisses in this house.'

'Oh, my beautiful princess,' Mamma said. 'You will grow up too soon and break the hearts of all the boys.' 'Will I?' 'Without a doubt. Just you wait and see.'

'Speak your mind, Alix,' my daddy said, 'give them what for. Never be afraid to stand up and fight for what you believe in. Follow that and you can't go wrong, the only person who can let you down is yourself.'

My mother butted in, 'Saul, she's a little girl not a man. What are you filling her head with? Do you think she will find a husband this way, the kind of person you are turning her into?'

And behind closed doors, 'You cannot bring up a daughter on these principles. It is a disaster. It will not turn out well.'

'So this is why you paint her face with all those cosmetics?'

'I do not see that you are averse to a painted face, Saul.'

'Let's not bring that up again.'

'You know, I fear for her future.'

'Don't. It's not necessary. She'll be fine.'

'Who is going to marry a girl like her?'

'Any man in his right mind would marry her.'

'She is not feminine.'

'She's a tomboy still, she'll grow out of it.'

'I hope you are right.'

'Plenty of time yet for her to be interested in boys and make herself pretty for them.'

'We'll see.'

They didn't get it, either of them. I was always interested in boys, from the word go. I wanted to marry my father, who wouldn't? To my regret it was my mother he worshipped, a girl so far above his station, himself the child of eastern European *luftmenschen*, beggars who lived on air. He deferred to her on everything to do with the house – well, most men do, but my father allowed her to make a showcase of his home, and the friends and family who came there were taken on a guided tour of each room, with an inventory of its antique contents, hunted out by my mother in forays into the surrounding towns of Cheshire. Her taste, her pedigree, her charm, her manners were what he married, and her vulnerability, the damage caused by her ruptured childhood, her resentment that her own parents had abandoned her, her nightmares and assorted fears and neuroses were what he, Dr Saul, thought he could cure with love.

'You know something?' Melanie was tidying cupboards in the kitchen, two feet up a stepladder taking down old, out-of-date food products from a shelf, her hips cased tight in jeans and her T-shirt straining round her shoulders, with this sexiness that women who never fully developed have. There is the bovine Jewish gene, the fleshy cows of the Polish plains grazing for centuries on black bread and *kasha*, and there are these tight little characters, another Jewish type, maybe descended from the kids who were the runts in the first place, too feeble to survive what was going to be thrown at the Jews, whom they kept hidden away in a back room and grew like forced bulbs in the dark, raised on Talmud and white chicken flesh.

'We know everything,' Sam said. 'What?'

'You know what they used to say about your mother behind her back?'

'Who said?'

'The *yentas*. They called her "that German bitch". They said, "All the Germans are the same, they're all as bad as each other." Your mother was dropped down from the sky and spattered all over Liverpool, God help her. She listened to Mendelssohn, *they* listened to Al Jolson. She bought seats to Chekhov at the Playhouse, *they* went to *The Sound of Music* at the Empire. She didn't say a word about Jolson or *The Sound of Music*, she never ran them down, she didn't have to – the day she refused to buy a ticket for a JNF tombola where you won that picture of the Chinese woman with the green face and she opened her bag and took out a ten-shilling note and gave it as a donation, as long as she didn't have any chance of being presented with this garish daub, which she might have had to hang on a wall in her house somewhere, then she was finished in Liverpool.'

'Come off it,' I interrupted. 'You know all the men adored her. Levy was bending my ear about her the day I got back.'

'Oh, yes, the *men* did because she had class, they thought of her the way they thought of a film star they could never have had in the first place, but you can only fantasise about, but the women couldn't stand her. My mum, who grew up on Brownlow Hill and left school at fourteen and went to work in a dress factory pinning sleeves, you think she knew what to say to her? As far as she was concerned, Lotte Rebick was no Jew because she didn't have a pedigree, she hadn't come over on the boat from Poland with the Braslavkys and the Rosenblatts and the Ginsbergs. Who was she? Who knew? Who had sat next to her at school in Hope Place? Who had she played with in the yard in Devon Street? Whose air-raid shelter was she in in 1941? Who did her brothers marry or her sisters? No one knew a thing about her. You know as well as I do that our parents' generation were ashamed of the Holocaust, they didn't even have a name for it, didn't want to talk about it, didn't want to know. Talk about Israel, talk about how you'd been on holiday to Eilat, talk about our brave soldiers in the Sinai, talk about anything but *that*. And then one day someone who has had a direct experience of *that* turns up in Liverpool with the very feller that everyone wanted, Saul Rebick, the doctor, who, it turned out, thought he was too good for Liverpool girls.'

Melanie, I sometimes thought, had been wasted on Sam, wasted on bringing up three children so they might leave Liverpool the minute they could and go to London, leaving our dying community. I don't know what she was still doing here. I couldn't understand why she hadn't found the means to live a life on which she could expend some of that wrathful insistence on the truth.

'Don't you understand?' she went on, as I opened my mouth. 'She was in exile, always in exile. Your father kept telling her that they were going to America and all the time he never had any intention of leaving Liverpool because by now he'd discovered the working class for whom nothing was too good and he was going to cure the evils of Liverpool on the NHS. So she was neither one thing nor the other, your mother. God help her if she tried to be German, they'd eat her alive, she knew that. But how could she be *from* Liverpool when she never knew who was related to who and couldn't make any sense of the seating plan at a wedding or a bar mitzvah. Didn't know a word of Yiddish, didn't know what they said about her behind her back. The cruelty, Sam, the viciousness of those women, much of it jealousy that she'd got Saul Rebick, not them. And all the time she has this stubborn stupid idea in her head that *one* day they'll get on a ship and sail for New York and there she can be like everyone else. In other words, she can be an immigrant not a refugee.'

'How do you know all this?' I demanded.

'Because she told me. The week we came back from honeymoon and I go round to your house when your father's out at work and find her crying her eyes out, listening to Beethoven. She screams when she hears me because she doesn't even want people to know she's listening to this Kraut composer, so bad is the hatred they have for everything German. That Mont Blanc fountain pen she bought you when you went to university, Sam, she sent away to Germany for it and the first time you take it out it's all over Liverpool, Lotte Rebick buys German goods. She's heard a woman in Coopers, while she's buying coffee because she has to have real ground coffee not Camp, not instant, she has to make it from scratch, and she overhears a woman at the fish counter say, "How do we know she's even Jewish?" And she told me everything that morning. "I AM GERMAN!" She shouted it. She couldn't get the German out of herself, didn't want to, why should she? Of course she wanted the factory back, she needed to own something that was part of Germany, she wanted to reclaim that part of herself she had to suppress all those years, the German that was in hiding in her.'

And she just walked back into the kitchen, mounted once again the ladder and began once again to throw out bags of flour, blown cans of tomatoes, rancid coconut, dried-up bottles of vanilla essence bought for cakes she never baked.

'Did you know any of this, Sam?'

'Some of it.'

'And you never said.'

'When? You'd left home already when I found out.'

Why had my mother done nothing on her own behalf in her lifetime to restore to her what she felt was her rightful claim to

Germany? The factory was out of the question, locked behind the Iron Curtain, but there were reparations, she was entitled to those. One evening, when my father found her, a cigarette between her lips, pecking the keys of the typewriter composing a letter, not to one of her satisfied customers regarding her cleansing cream order but to Bonn, he sat down next to her, took that right hand away from the machine, held it in his and said, 'Lotte, look at this.' Two photos he showed her, each of a child. 'This one, taken in 1931, is of William Smedley, aged seven, in the yard of his parents' back-to-back on Scotland Road, and what's wrong with his legs is that he's got rickets because of the diet he's been fed, with no calcium, no vitamin D, and you can't see it in this picture but he also has conjunctivitis, which he would have called pink-eye, and that's because he's wiped his face on some kind of contaminated material, probably a dirty rag because the standards of hygiene in the home would have been atrocious. Now here he is again, this is taken last year in his house in Halewood, brand new three-bedroom semi, with a garden, and the boy he's standing behind is his son, born in 1952, which makes him also seven years of age, the same as his father in the other picture, but just look at him. He is literally a picture of health, nearly up to his father's shoulder, he'll tower over him one day. He's had free milk at school, orange juice when he was a baby, he's grown up with fresh air and proper sanitation, and when he leaves school there'll be a good job for him on the Ford's assembly line. So you have to think, Lotte, whether you want to expend one iota of energy writing letters to Bonn about reparations when we have all the money we need, you have two beautiful children and there is so much work still to be done in the field of public health. Here, Lotte, look at these pictures again.'

'There is nothing left in Germany for you, Lotte,' he kept telling Mamma, time and time over.

'Saul,' she replied, 'as usual you are right.'

'As usual you are right' were not words I had ever said to Sam.
You had to break my bones to make me agree he was right about
anything. We had that way of arguing for the sake of it. My
father would terrify my teenage boyfriends when they came to
our house: 'Let's have an argument,' he would say, 'pick a subject,
anything you like.'

So this row went on for a few more hours until Sam said, 'The
person to talk to about dealing with the Germans over buildings
is Joseph Shields. He's built two hotels in Germany. Find out
what he thinks.'

And Melanie looked up at me sharply over her reading glasses.
'As I keep reminding you, Alix, he's married, so don't get any
ideas.'

Twelve feet of silt was removed from the pool in the centre of the Albert Dock in 1984 to allow the river to enter it again. In the middle of the pool there is now a green-painted balsawood map of Britain, and each morning the weatherman from Granada Television (housed in what used to be the Dock Traffic office) stands on it to deliver his report, watched by a national audience optimistic that one day he might fall in. From the window of my brother's flat you can still see the dredger that removed the silt, the *Mersey Mariner*, labouring up and down the estuary, skirting the sandbars. To understand what lies beneath the waters is a subtle science, or perhaps it is a philosophy. We are here on the banks of the Mersey, because in the Pennines a river began in an area of heavy rainfall, ran towards the sea and by the time it approached the coast it had swollen and was flowing hard and wide, thrusting itself out, broadening its shoulders until its banks were three miles apart, then huddling closer, narrowed to only a mile. Near the seashore below a wooded red sandstone ridge it was joined by a stream, which formed a large tidal pool and this was our first harbour.

The Liverpool tides rise high and fast, and for centuries we were a dangerous anchorage yet the river grew dense with coastal and sea shipping, coal boats from Glasgow and Newcastle, schooners from Norway, Holland, Denmark, Flanders, Spain, Portugal, the Baltic, Hamburg, and also the ocean-going three-masters, which traded with Virginia, Maryland, New England, Pennsylvania and the other English colonies of the New World. Georgian Liverpool was an immense place upon the waters. Riches overflowing, a great community, a vast empire. Power.

Self-confidence. Sea-bathing. Horse-racing. Tobacco. Cotton. Slave-ships. The first ship to sail without the aid of wind or sails. The first passenger railway in the world. Thirty-one miles of double track. Bridges. Embankments. Tunnels cut through the rock. Black sailors brought their music to Liverpool. In the twentieth century they carried over Bessie Smith, Bo Diddley, Muddy Waters, John Lee Hooker, Big Bill Broonzey. They sold the records for cash on the dock road and on Upper Parly and Granby Street where the seamen from Nigeria and the Gold Coast got themselves wives and settled. John Lennon bought these records and took them back to his suburban home and the Delta Blues rose as a loud, clanging voice above the city, and we sold it back to America as the Liverpool Sound. Which is where I came in, as a teenager who danced the Cavern Stomp to Gerry and the Pacemakers, Billy J. Kramer and the Dakotas, the Merseybeats, the Swinging Blue Jeans, the Searchers, and the Fourmost, and queued up overnight in a sleeping-bag at Epstein's record shop to buy the very first pressing of *With The Beatles*.

The docks are separated from the town by a dual carriageway called the Strand, which runs on to Bootle or veers off to the right to enter the Mersey Tunnel and, after a ten-minute drive, re-emerges above ground at one of several points on the Wirral in the county of Cheshire, which has almost nothing to do with us here in Liverpool. Bootle, on the other hand, is a very, very rough place. You don't go there unless you know how to look after yourself. This is a matriarchs' town from the time when the men were away at sea for months on end and the wives and mothers ruled the roost at home, but they had their areas of weakness and here the Rebick family comes in. Three days a week, my sister-in-law Melanie drove to Bootle and sat in the women's centre talking, cajoling, wheedling the girls into using the Pill or a diaphragm or an IUD, anything to raise the average age of child-bearing from the teens to the twenties. She knew every excuse. She heard what the priest would say – or, more importantly, how their mothers would go berserk, which was more frightening if they went against the Vatican, and she marvelled at the century's end that the word of the old man in Rome was still worth so much when hardly any other aspect of Catholic morality meant anything at all. They might violate every one of the Ten Commandments, might steal and murder and covet and worship all kinds of false gods as displayed on TV or in the windows of Dixons, but when it came to the Pope and the Pill, *this* they would still listen to. 'They sit there and tell me that they're going to go to hell and I say, "If you have this baby – because you *will* have a baby if you don't use something – you're going to find out what hell is like long before you're dead." And they reply, "Oh, Mrs Rebick, you can't fall the first time you do it and Kevin promised that after that he'll pull out." And I tell them, "*Or so he says.*"'

On the waterfront itself are the Three Graces, the Liver Building, the Cunard Building and the Mersey Docks and Harbour Board, and behind both of those is St Nicholas Parish Church, the four together forming the instantly recognisable twentieth-century waterfront of Liverpool. Until the thirties there was also an overhead railway, the dockers' umbrella, which took people to work to and from the river and I believe there is only one other overhead railway, the El, which is in Chicago, and when Sam pointed this out to Joseph Shields, he sat there with his mouth open, looking stunned. Of the other important overhead structures there is the conveyor belt, which links Tate and Lyle's raw sugarcane store to the Huskisson Dock across the other side of the road. It was always a harsh landscape, high brick walls separated the pedestrians from the warehouses to protect the cargoes from theft, and no wood anywhere in order to prevent a stray match turning the bales of tobacco and cotton into a fireball. Nothing on the Liverpool waterfront gave itself to beauty or to grace. There was Palladian architecture, but that was inland and, even then, built on a massive, bullying scale. Everything was about power and money and brutality and dominance, and it was across the street from all this destroyed, uncompromising grandeur that Joseph was trying to put up a work of the artistic imagination. The city was full of it. There was only one question to which everyone wanted the answer: is this going to be good for Liverpool or is he going to make a show of us?

Chavasse Park is a broad, landscaped stretch of grass across the other side of the Strand. For some time no one had known what to do with the site and it had become no more than a short-cut into town, so when the hoardings went up and everyone knew that there was going to be a hotel, and that the hotel was being built by a Yank who had come all the way from Chicago, Illinois (which was a place specifically named in the musical *Oklahoma* and also associated in our minds with Al Capone), there was huge excitement and curiosity. Normally, on the side of the boards, along with all the credits, the names of the developers and the architects and any government money that's been put in, there is an artist's impression of what the thing is going to look like. Now, Shields had the board with the names on it but nothing else, and whatever he was up to was left to our own imaginations. In a town like this, where too many people have nothing to do in the way of work and spend an awful lot of time in public houses trying to find out the latest jangle, inevitably rumours grew up quickly about what was going on. The planning department had been sworn to secrecy, Shields had put this into the contract, and the officials had maintained a blanket silence where normally they would have been leaking articles to the *Echo* and fostering rival developers' bids, but all they would say is, 'I've seen the drawings, it's going to be something else, I'm telling you. Giuliani over in New York has seen the pictures too, and he was raving about them.' Liverpool is twinned with New

York. A few months ago we held millennium-night celebrations with giant screens in Times Square so they could see us partying and giant screens in the city centre so we could see them getting legless too. In the pubs where navvies drink, the chippies and the sparks and the hod-carriers were hotly canvassed for their views since they were the ones who were actually building the place and ought to have a fair idea of what was going on, but all they could say was that there was to be a moat, which gave rise to the claim that the Yank was building some kind of castle and it was a short step from this to the artists of the city being up in arms about having a vulgar, Disneyfied pastiche put up in which no work of theirs would ever be permitted to hang.

But beneath it all there was enormous excitement. The appearance of the American could mean only one thing: that Liverpool was back on the map. 'Look at it this way,' Sam had pointed out, to some of the naysayers. 'A representative of a country that is in no way interested in the past, only the future, is suddenly interested in us. And what do you think it means other than at long last we once again have *got* a future? As far as I'm concerned, Joseph Shields's hotel is the best thing that's happened to the city in years and I'm putting all my weight behind making sure it goes ahead. So shut the fuck up, will you?'

Painfully, with many setbacks, the hotel had advanced from being just a hole in the ground, nothing more than a set of foundations, to acquiring a discernible structure, which was beginning to be visible above the unusually high hoardings. Every time I had passed by I had craned my neck but could see only scaffolding and a concrete shell and sometimes a glint of piercing light. Dressed in jeans, a black cotton shirt and a pair of Timberland boots I'd run out and bought from Wade Smith, I presented myself at the gate where a security guy, who had my name on his clipboard, gave me a high five and waved me through.

On the other side of the wooden door the air smelt of wood dust, cement, sweat. In front of me there was a rectangular trench, about fifteen feet across. A row of planks lay over it like a draw-bridge so you could see where the moat rumour had come from. Across it something that was definitely on its way to becoming a building rose five storeys into the sky. The inner fabric was con-crete but windows were cut in and deeply recessed to create large balconies. Over this body a glass wall fell like a curtain but it was not uniform, the plates were uneven in size and overlapped each other like giant fish-scales. Stainless-steel staples held them together. The uneven surface of the glass engaged the eye.

I walked gingerly across the dry trench and came to a doorway. Joseph, in jeans and a blue polo shirt, was having an argument with a guy dressed in a suit, whose red ponytail was the only sign left of that rare breed in the Liverpool of the seventies, the peace-and-love hippie. Who had a ponytail in Liverpool? Only one kid.

'Vince?'

'Alix! I haven't seen you in years. Come here, give us a kiss.'

I leaned over and pecked him on the cheek, where red stubble poked through his pink skin. 'Still not cut your hair.'

'No way.'

'What are you doing here?'

'Building his hotel for him.'

'You're the contractor?'

'That I am. How do you know Joseph?'

'Through Sam. They go to the same gym.'

'I was awfully sorry to hear about your mother, I read about it in the *Echo*. I should have sent a card.'

'There was no need.'

'And how do you two know each other?' Joseph asked.

'I was at school with his sister Marie.'

'Very clever girl, our Marie.'

'She still in Liverpool?'

'No way, she moved down south to go to university and never came back.'

'Didn't she get that graduate traineeship at Marks?'

'That's right. She's done fantastically well for herself. She's getting close to being on the board.'

'Oh, I'm made up for her.'

'Thanks. If she gets it, Mam will put a banner up across our street.'

'Is she still living in the Holylands?'

'Of course. I wanted to buy her a bungalow over the water but she wouldn't budge.'

'She lives in Israel?' Joseph asked.

'Why do Americans say Isr-e-al, with the E before the A, when it's not spelt like that?' I asked him.

'I don't know. I never thought about it.'

'Mam has been to Israel, as it happens, our church organised a trip a few years ago, a whole coachload of them went. She brought me back a boxed set, with an olivewood cross in it and a bottle of holy water from the Sea of Galilee. We have to remember to put it out on the mantelpiece every time she comes round. She was dead proud of that when she gave it to us. She said she bought it from a feller on a stall near the Garden of Gethsemane. Carmen, that's my wife, has to keep the Cellophane dusted. But the answer to your question is that the Holylands are a bunch of streets round the Dingle. They've all got names out of the Bible. We grew up on Isaac Street.'

'Those houses were always immaculate, inside and out.'

'But you should have seen Alix's place, Joseph. It was like Buckingham fucking Palace. I went there a couple of times with my dad to pick up Marie when she'd gone there after school. We got invited in and they had these posh chocolate biscuits and we watched the tea-time cartoons on a colour telly. Never forgot that.'

'I thought you went into hairdressing.'

'No, not me, that was our kid. You still teach at college?'

'No. Okay, Vince, what do you think of this place? Be honest now.'

'It's going to be a stunner.'

'You hear that, Joseph?'

'He doesn't have to tell me.'

'No false modesty, then.'

'No. I don't believe in it. That's the British disease, and another thing, you're so fair-minded, always wanting to listen to both sides of the story.'

'Are you going to stand there and let him get away with that, Alix?' Vince said, smirking, hoping to see the Yank demolished by the mouthy bitch he had observed pelting her parents with opinions, defying her father, arguing, rowing, and no one prepared to give an inch.

But I couldn't help smiling at Joseph, feeling the full force of him coming at me and wanting to be flattened myself, literally on my back, by his confidence.

'You see? She agrees with me.' I took out a cigarette from my bag. He snatched it from me. 'Are you nuts?'

'No smoking?'

'Absolutely not. There's a hell of a lot of flammable stuff round here.'

I winked at Vince. 'No Jewish lightning on this site.'

'No, we've got enough trouble as it is.'

'So I heard.'

'You wanna see round or not?'

'Yes, yes, show me.'

We walked inside, across the concrete floor, and passed almost at once below a roofless atrium and in front of us was another rectangular trench from which glass fish-scale walls also rose. 'The whole place is going to be enclosed eventually,' Joseph said. 'With more glass.'

'What are these holes in the ground?'

'Pools. For water. When I first saw the Albert Dock I had this idea that I'd make a reference to it, so the centre of my hotel will be a square lake, which is going to reflect the glass walls and the glass walls are going to reflect the water. And the approach to the hotel on all four sides will also be by water.'

'Ah, the moat.'

'Exactly. If everyone in this town came here from the sea or set off from here across the sea, that's what my hotel is going to be about. Water.'

'Amazing. Yes.'

He took me up the unrailed concrete steps to the second floor.

'Someone came last night with a sledgehammer and tore up the next flight of steps. Look.'

The stairway had been partially demolished. Blocks of concrete had fallen down what was going to be the lift shaft. The sledgehammer had been taken to several of the rectangular glass fish-scales and they had diagonal cracks across them.

'This must break your heart,' I said, turning to him.

'It does.'

'But listen, you'll beat it, you know. You mustn't give up, absolutely not, because this thing is a wow. It's a wow now and it's going to be wonderful when you've finished.'

'You think?'

'Absolutely.'

We came down the concrete steps together; he took my arm for a moment as we skirted a piece of vandalised debris. I felt a light finger on my back as I walked across the planks.

'No ladders,' I said.

'Not today.'

'I was ready for ladders.'

'Oh, you, you're ready for anything.' He turned to me.

'What do you mean?'

'Nothing.'

We walked back into the site office. His gym bag was on the desk next to a stack of plastic files, the whole place like the headquarters of a military command post, with maps and plans on clipboards, and the only untidiness was Vince leaning against the wall drinking tea.

'You work out often?' I asked Joseph.

'Only three times a week, I'm not that fit, it's something you grit your teeth and do. What about yourself, do you play any sports?'

'Bit of tennis. In France I play every weekend in Bergerac. I can't stand gyms, they're too monotonous. I like thwack games.'

'Are you good?'

'I used to be. When I was a teenager I was school champion one year.'

'Is that a big deal?'

'It is when you're fifteen. Do you play?'

'Yeah, a bit, just to fool around. I learned a few years back on vacation. You want a game some time?'

'Yes, I'd like that.'

'Where do you play round here?'

'Sefton Park.'

'Is Saturday afternoon okay?'

'Fine. I'll book a court.'

'May the best man win.'

'Indeed.'

'This should be interesting,' said Vince.

'I never played tennis when it was raining before,' he said.

'A bit of rain won't hurt you, it'll stop sooner or later. It's only drizzle.'

'I didn't say it bothered me, just that it's unusual.'

'If you waited for the sun to shine you'd play twice a year.'

'True. I've become addicted to your weather forecasts. I never knew there were so many words for rain.'

'What's the weather in Chicago?'

'It's got two gears. Hot and cold, like taps.'

'And no shades of grey.'

'Absolutely not.'

'That's what I like about Americans.'

'What?'

'No shades of grey. I find it refreshing. The British are too on-the-one-hand-but-there-again-on-the-other-hand for my taste.'

'You're telling me. This is not your style, then?'

'Not exactly.'

'I kind of picked that up. I really like your family, you're very different from your usual Brit.'

'You can say that again. If you think Sam's bad you should have met my father.'

'I would have liked to. He sounds like something else. You ready?'

'Yep.'

The smell of wet grasses in the verge on the edge of the courts. Misted air. Muted birdsong in the trees. Yellow-brick mansions on the horizon, circling the city's verdant heart. Scaffolding on the Palm House. 'Who are those statues? Real people?'

'Maritime explorers. That one's Magellan. And there's your guy, Columbus.'

'*Really?*'

I lift my arm and stretch my right hand and my racquet high. My breasts rise. My hair is held back from my face by a white band. My left hand bounces the ball against the mesh and takes it across the net with an accurate smash, right inside the line. Pleased with myself, I still have good technique.

And watch him thump across the court towards it, legs pounding on the shaking ground, his arm rise and the racquet

come towards the ball and return it with such speed and feroc-
ity that—

'*Holy shit*, are you okay?'

'Yeah, give me a minute, I'm just winded.'

'My God, I didn't mean to knock you out.'

'I Iooooo.'

'Let me help you up. Oh, man. Your knee's cut.'

'Just a scratch. I thought you said you only patted the ball
around?'

'Yeah, we don't really keep score. But apparently I have a
strong arm.'

'That ball must have been going about ninety miles an hour.
What do you think you're doing?'

'I really am sorry. I was forgetting I was playing against a
woman.'

'You *what*?'

'Aw, come on. I'm sure you're a far better player than me but
I'm pretty strong. I can lift a lot of weight in the gym.'

'Now you have enraged me.'

'So I see.'

'Get back your side of the court right now, we'll see who's
going to thrash who.'

'Okay.'

'Stop laughing.'

'See? I'm wiping the smile right off my face.'

'Fine. Here it comes.'

I *could* make him run. I *could* send my shots all over the court,
watch him miss, stumble, trip over, pound after a ball he was
never going to catch because he truly was an atrocious player but
anything he managed to return was terrifying. His serve!
Ungainly, his feet huge in his tennis shoes, he lumbered about,
and with each return he sent something through the air like a
cruise missile into my guts.

The rain stopped and a small crowd of dog-walkers gathered to watch.

'Who's winning?'

'I am,' we both shouted back.

After an hour both of us were done in. We were dripping with sweat and rain.

'What's the score?' he said.

'I don't remember.'

'Loser.'

'Ha!'

'The feller's winning,' a kid piped up.

'Hey! Is that right? I never beat a school champion before.'

'Did you used to be a school champion, missus?'

'Apparently.'

'He's no good, but he's a feller so he'll always beat you because fellers always do. Anyway, he's American and they're the best. We're rubbish.'

'Will you piss off?'

'Ha ha. The kid's right.'

'Give it a rest.'

'Should we call it a day?'

'Okay.'

We got into his car. The windows steamed up. Turning, before he started up the ignition, he smiled and clutched my upper arm. 'No hard feelings?'

'Nah.'

'You,' he said, 'I like. Get it?'

Back at Sam and Melanie's my sister-in-law said, 'How did it go?'

'The bastard annihilated me.'

'Is he good?'

'No, useless, but he has a very heavy, fast return and a hefty serve.'

'Well, Alix, I know you hate to lose so is that the end of that? Are you finished with him now?'

'On the contrary, Mel.'

'It's stupid trying to compete with men.'

'Who's trying to compete?'

A knock on the door. His skin still flushed. Beads of sweat still breaking out on his neck. Arm like a bough raised on the door handle. Leather of his watch strap. Hairs curling over it.

'Hi, Melanie, how are you? Good, I hope. Is Alix around?'

'She's—'

'Yes, I'm right here. Back for a rematch?'

'Maybe tennis isn't our thing. I was thinking, how about a hike someplace tomorrow?'

'Hike? With crampons and ropes?'

'No, no, no, no. I just mean, like a walk.'

'Oh. I always thought hiking was more energetic than that, you needed boots. If you mean a walk why don't you say a walk?'

'Because I'm a dumb American?'

'Yeah. That's right. Anyway, we'll go to Ainsdale.'

'What's there?'

'Something unexpected.'

'I like surprises.'

'I wash my hands of this,' Melanie said, when he'd gone.

'Good. What have you got in the fridge? I'm going to make dinner. Suddenly, I have a huge appetite.'

To collect my thoughts: was it a harmless illusion to believe that my lumbering new tennis partner had actually succumbed to my abrasive charm or was I doing serious damage in deluding myself? On the other hand, might it really mean the closing days of the unshared bed and the solitary activities that go on there? *Where is my man?* I had cried and now it was possible that he had turned up, hopelessly late but at least he had arrived.

It was always at this stage that I felt most fiercely the limitations of my sex. Who makes the first move? The man, I always say, they just can't stand being pursued. Maybe with kids it's different, maybe my nephew Simon thinks otherwise on this matter, brought up by a mother who told him, 'Don't ever believe, just because you are the oldest, that you are one iota better than your sisters or that because you've got a putz instead of a fanny this gives you the right to rule the world. Are you listening to me?' 'Yeah.' 'I want that girlie magazine out of my house, do you hear, and don't get any ideas into your head that this is because I'm a prude or an old fuddy-duddy. What I won't put up with is the degrading of women, turning them into objects that . . .'

I like to think that Simon took something away from these lectures, and for the next generation things really have taken a progressive step forward, but for mine, everything is the same. And everything we learned as modern women too (all the stuff that men like Sam and Joseph Shields profess to admire) – to be forthright, to speak our minds, never to resort to those low, girlish tricks of manipulation, flattery, passivity and acquiescence – it all has to be temporarily forgotten. Because in the early stages of a relationship it is men who must be in control. We wait, as we have always done since its invention, for the phone to ring. You have no idea how much this galls me, how I hate the passivity.

We came here on Sunday afternoons when we were children. The sky opened out above the wind. The sea was in front of us and behind it the sand ranges, the scrubby dunes clotted with coarse tufted grass, hills we climbed or tumbled down, rolled up like conjurors' balls. The light this morning was extraordinary: a great bowl of sky above us, scored with long clouds like freeways. Gulls like jets, taxiing and banking, turning on the winds to come in for a landing. It was low tide and the beach stretched down towards Ireland, interrupted by drilling platforms on the horizon. A P&O ferry was setting sail from the Pierhead to Dublin. Close up, brown waves boiling with sand slammed on the shore where red flags waved in the strong warm breeze. Tracks of dogs and seabirds led into the dunes. Shattered sea shells, twigs, bark underfoot. Sand insects burrowed and re-emerged, emerald noses and bronze wings folded over to form a back. Birds sauntered, black tails, grey bodies, white necks, red beaks and legs. Long grasses like palm fronds with ears of seeds that pulled back with a squeak from their tight green sheaves. Weird red prehistoric flowers with snails climbing their stems. Toads, lizards. Salt on my lips. The sea's tang.

He *was* surprised. Did not speak for several minutes, looked around him as though he was seeing something that wasn't here in this landscape, visible only to him. 'And where are we again?' he asked, more than once.

'Ainsdale.'

'So close to the city.'

'Yes.' The Lancashire coast is even more unseen and forgotten than Liverpool. Away from home, I often believe that I am the only person in the world who knows about it, that only in my imagination does this tiny desert wilderness roll down to the Irish Sea.

'It was sandier in my childhood, drier. Now the dunes are grassing over because the rabbits died, the rabbits that eat the grass. They all died in the myxomatosis epidemic in the fifties. Or most of them did.'

Then he started to talk about my family, asked about my parents, about Melanie's. How did we come to be here, in this godforsaken place? What had thwarted us in the national flight of our people to America? The explanation was an easy one: my Rebick grandparents had bought a fraudulent ticket to the Promised Land. After the discovery ('This is not New York? We are not in America? But look at the fine buildings, surely we can't have . . .'), they might have regrouped, saved up a second time, bought another set of vouchers, but the initial surge of energy ebbed away, they collapsed, the heart went out of them. Watching the waves ease themselves round our shoes, I thought of how that continent must have seemed, standing on the very edge of Europe and looking longingly across the Atlantic Ocean to the country glimmering faintly in the western light, immense and unattainable.

'I want to know about you,' he said, turning to me. 'I want to know where you get your guts.'

'I come from a tough city and I had a father who taught me when I was growing up to be a tough little girl.'

We were sitting on a ridge of sand, high above the water's edge, the ground beneath us slipping away as we moved, the wind very fresh now and the sun burning through some thin brown clouds.

'Now tell me something else. Vince Tobin said you know a hell of a lot about murder. Why is that?'

'Because it's what I used to do – studying it, I mean, trying to force my imagination to come to terms with it. By training I'm

a sociologist. I did my MA in criminology at the London School
of Economics in the mid-seventies back when feminism was
starting to enter academic life and people were beginning to
look at women who kill. All the thought then was that female
murderers were almost always responding to abusive relationships. There were no female serial killers, no women going out
on a shooting spree. They killed, on the whole, in self-defence or
to defend their kids and the courts utterly failed to understand
this. There was a huge body of work developing, most of it quite
correct as far as I could tell, yet we couldn't account for these
isolated examples, the Myra Hindleys who did what almost no
other women did, kill strangers. When we investigated further
we saw that in nearly every case these women did not act alone,
there was always a guy they were teamed up with – Bonnie and
Clyde, Myra and Ian – so the thought began to grow up that
women *naturally* were not killers, that they did so only when
men tore them away from their instincts. What followed was a
radical feminist leap: that women who did kill in cold blood
were persecuted because they denied what the world regarded as
the essential biological female nature of women as nurturers and
protectors. From then on it was just a short step to saying that
they were in fact feminist heroines. And I didn't agree with a
word of it. To cut a long story short, by this time I was working
as a lecturer and there was a run-in with a student. I was pick-
eted, demonstrated against, I became a cause and that finished
me as an academic. Though my own big mouth may possibly
have contributed to my problems.'

Four-wheel drives were racing on the beach, children in
bathing costumes running into the sea. A man with binoculars
inspected the drilling rigs. I put my hand to a frond of grass and
pulled it, but it was hard rooted in the unstable sand.

'Some story. Wow.' He put his arm around me and tightened it
for a moment. I turned my face towards him, smiling. In response

he leaned forward and kissed me on the lips, parted them, his tongue in my mouth, the smell of him, the feel of reddish skin on my olive skin, his bare arms under his shirt sleeves, the rust hair, the meaty muscle, this middle-aged man with me sitting next to him, everything about the picture wrong wrong wrong because how can there be sex in the air when round his waist, under the denim shirt, there is a discernible swelling, a slow deposit of fat that no amount of jogging has shifted? And as for me, it's not bags that have settled under my eyes but what looks, sitting despairingly in front of the mirror lit by a cold grey northern light, like Louis Vuitton luggage – the whole matching set. I am expecting someone to grab me and drag me out of the way because of the sheer incongruity of my presence in this otherwise photogenic image of two soon-to-be lovers sitting on a beach.

Imagine me on that sand dune. That carnal self *erupting*. And I was exploding inside: years of banked-up frustration had detonated and sparks and fragments of my hot desire were flaming across the dunes, burning shells, seaweed, pebbles. Full of surges of desire for him, so long becalmed, so long unplugged from the sexual current, my pants wet with it, trembling, my nipples tensing. And my lust, my filthy thoughts of what I wanted him to do to me, his fingers with my smell on them, my mouth full of his cock, his mouth full of my breasts, his weight on top of me, the hundred and eighty pounds I needed to keep me from hollowing out and so, light with my own thoughts and sorrows, disintegrate. *Fuck me, Joseph*. Stop me from turning to thin air. So despite everything I knew I could not let this moment escape me, by waiting, by wanting to be sure, by playing by a set of rules someone made up to keep women like me in our place, so I said it.

'Should we do it here, like teenagers?'

'I'm sorry?'

'The sex.'

Silence.

Then, 'Oh, Alix, you know I'd really rather be your friend than your lover. I like you a lot but I don't want to be your boyfriend.'

'I'd rather you were my lover than my friend as I have plenty of those, more than enough. As for boyfriends, I have none.' But I realised as I spoke that it was hopeless, you can't argue someone into fucking you.

'You know I'm married, I haven't concealed that.'

'So what was with the kiss?'

'I wanted to.'

'Why?'

'I don't know, I just did.'

'And you meant nothing sexual by it?'

'No, not really.'

'Then why did you do it?'

'Oh, I don't know, for the hell of it. Please understand, I think you're a fantastic woman, I've not met many like you, not at all, a woman who has the capacity to think like a man. I find it exhilarating, listening to you talk, but I really have no interest at this stage in my life in having an affair, with you or anyone else for that matter.'

'I see.'

'So I'm very sorry if I gave you the wrong impression. It was just a light-hearted thing, a moment of . . .'

It was my own fault. I blamed myself. Everything misread and misunderstood. The wrong interpretation, totally the wrong idea I had got. I nodded, got up, climbed the sandy mountains, tears stinging my face, my mascara running, applied that morning – forty minutes in front of the mirror for *this* – walked down towards the car-park, fumbled in my bag for the keys to my car and drove off, leaving him by the shore, hoping a ship would take him and carry him off back to America, to his fucking wife and the three fucking kids and the Corvette and the house and all the other paraphernalia.

Joseph

I seemed to have insulted her in some way. She had got hold of the idea that I had brought her out there on a kind of date, like we were young things, and that when I kissed her on the beach I meant for it to be a down-payment on something else altogether, that I was inaugurating an affair. But a kiss doesn't mean all that much. There was definitely a spark of attraction, seeing her on the building site, dressed down, in her jeans and boots and shirt, the way she looked at my creation and got it, absolutely loved it. She's a wonderful woman, I've not met many like her; she talks about stuff I don't know much about and whatever she has to say is interesting. I like the way that horse face is always animated, that the smiles come easily to it, and laughter too, but behind the eyes you can see a mind is working. And, man, did she give ever me the run-around on the tennis court!

The way she stood up to her full height and you could see her breasts were damp under her shirt and the muscle on her arm, like an Amazon warrior, the kind of character you'd find in one of the comic books I had when I was a kid, big chicks who would make you hard just to look at them going *pow* at one of the superheroes. Yeah, she really did have that comic-book quality. And it makes me smile now to think about her: she really did light up my life for a couple of weeks.

I had coffee with Sam and asked him what had gone wrong, and he shrugged and said I should forget about it. 'I long ago stopped being surprised at anything Alix does and says. By the way, she told me about the problems you've been having on the site and I've made some phone calls.'

Apparently the land I'd leased, when you got past all the company names, was owned by a character called Brian Humphreys.

'Who's he and where do I find him?'

'In Longlartin maximum security prison. He's serving two consecutive life sentences. When our Brian went down last year he was the single largest importer of drugs into Europe. For a period of time in the mid-nineties, every dose of smack that went up an arm in Britain was bought in by him and most of it sailed into the port of Liverpool.'

'How did he get into the big-time from Liverpool? I hadn't realised there was room for that kind of operation here.'

'There is, believe me. He started off in a small way when he was a teenager, ram-raiding back in the early eighties.'

'What's that?'

'Say a bunch of scallies steal a BMW or a Rover, anything heavy, what they want with it is to drive it through the window of a jeweller's and grab what they can. Before they set out they load up the front with bricks, broken paving slabs, golf balls – you name it – and chuck the stuff through the sunroof at anyone who's chasing them. Back when they were in their teens it was okay but there wasn't that much money in it, and what you have to understand about Brian is that he has a bit of everything in him, bit of Welsh, bit of Maltese, bit of Senegalese. It gives him a very distinctive look, dead white skin, woolly hair, poached-egg eyes, a type you see a lot of in Liverpool. Now, the drugs trade has always been what your friends on the council would call a multicultural enterprise. Once you get into the premier league, they're all foreigners – the Colombians, the Triads, the Mafia, the Turks. And Humphreys thought this was exactly where he belonged, among these exotic, ruthless men who all sprang up from poverty, from the poorest places in the world, and came to have private jets, wealth the rest of us can only dream of. This may be the city of the Beatles, but to men like Brian it might as well be the Sicilian badlands, and whether or not you get on in life depends on what family you're from, what parish you belong to, who's your priest and who owes you a favour.'

'And this is what I'm supposed to deal with? Fuck.'

'Don't despair, I've got a theory. I think that since Brian has been in jail one of his lieutenants who is running the business for him made a stupid mistake. He agreed to a lease being granted for the building of your hotel when Brian had already done a deal with a rival developer but he hadn't had time to tell anyone this because he had stuff on his plate that concentrated his mind in another direction for a period of time.'

'It gets worse. I need this like a hole in the head. What's he planning to put up instead?'

'A training school for hairdressers, but never mind that. Listen, I am very keen on your hotel going ahead. I've put my weight behind it and not just because of my personal friendship with you. This is about the future of Liverpool, Mersey pride, and I think I can get Brian to see that too so I'll try to pull in a favour. Our father was Brian's mother's doctor.'

'You people are tied into everything, aren't you?'

'Yes. We are.' He picked up the paper. 'Listen to this,' and he read out an item from the local crime pages about a drugs bust. 'A simple little thing on the surface, but behind it, a whole cast of characters. This kid they've arrested, my client, Paul James Roberts, his father was a right *shtarker* back in the early sixties, a real hard case, tattoos up one arm and down the other. He'd been at sea, got all the way to Hong Kong at one point and worked for one of the early drug-dealers, McLaren, who was bringing in heroin before there was any real taste for the stuff, when the most anyone wanted was good-quality hash and a bit of speed. A pioneer. He's in Walton on a twenty-year sentence. Roberts went down with him. The boy, just a petty pusher. A nobody. Selling crack to schoolchildren, peddling guns in Toxteth and Speke and Garston. A toe-rag. And very typical of the way things are here, these days. Another case I'm doing at the moment, a bunch of guys hired a truck and went round the posh houses in Woolton stealing top-soil, which they then sold in Kirkby. They took the shrubs as well, but not the flowers, they were too much bother, they died before they could get them unloaded. If you live in West Kirkby, you can have an instant garden now – mature bushes – for a hundred quid. People mount posts into the ground and set them in cement and chain their garden furniture to them but if you have bolt cutters that isn't going to stop you.'

So, everywhere I look now, I notice the gangsters and their wives. You can spot them a mile away, absolutely no class. The women are either pasty blondes or have a kind of Spanish appearance, that very sleek dark-haired look with these terrible sunbed tans, and either way they never wear enough clothes however cold it is; the men are no better, stinking of stuff you buy in Duty Free, and covered from head to toe in labels, Prada, DKNY, Calvin Klein, and weighed down by a ton of jewellery – they have everything except taste. The town is full of cut-price

jewellers' stores hawking gold and every single Saturday afternoon they are all packed. I guess in a place as run-down as this
was, the way you show your wealth is round your neck, like back
in the Old Country where the women walked out with their
dowry on display.

None of this has lowered my resolve: it's stiffened it. I said to
Vince over coffee in the site office, 'You know, I don't accept that
the future of this place has to be drugs and guns. There's nothing
preordained about it. There are choices you can make.'

And he said, 'I know, boss, that's why I'm working for you.'

'I'm not going to give up on this thing. As far as I'm concerned, my hotel is going to be Liverpool's own Statue of
Liberty.'

Next day, a little souvenir Statue of Liberty appeared on my
desk, the kind that tourists bring home from New York. The day
after that I arrived to find an American flag draped over the
hoarding and a sign lettered next to it – THE COLOURS IN THIS FLAG
DON'T RUN.

'Is this the irony thing I keep hearing about?' I asked him.
'Which we Yanks supposedly don't have?'

'Not necessarily. Let's try and do this the American way.'

'Which is what?'

'We're all going to stop carping and just get on with it.'

'You mean the American work ethic?'

'If that's what you want to call it.'

'What do the crew think of the flag?'

'As long as they don't have to drink weak, watery American
beer at the end of their shift, they're happy. Oh, and I told them
that Julie Roberts was coming over from Hollywood to cut the
ribbon and they were all invited, put a bit of lead in the pencil if
you get my drift.'

'And they swallowed it?'

'They're not sure. But it gives them something to natter about, and by tomorrow morning it will be God's honest truth as far as Liverpool is concerned so you'd better get hold of her.'

'Are you out of you—'

'Boss, I'm only winding you up. How did your tennis go?'

'Let's call it a dead heat.'

When Alix left me on the beach I was reminded of the last time I was stranded, which was the result of what I considered to be a very poor practical joke known as a navigation exercise.

The army had bundled us into helicopters and dropped us in the middle of nowhere. Our orders were that we had forty-eight hours to get from here to there, the *there* being an X on the map. The *here* that they had left us in was a place that was completely featureless: anywhere you turned to look everything was exactly the same. How the hell were we supposed to get to that *there* from this *here* when the two seemed to be identical? In our case, we never found out, because we got hopelessly lost, and by the end of the third day we were running out of food and water and, generally speaking, in a pretty bad way. Now, obviously this was controlled deprivation, because there was no way the army was going to forget about or abandon us; they knew exactly where we were because while the mothers of Israel understand that their sons may have to die for their country, there was no way that they would contemplate them being cold and hungry in the middle of the Sinai for the sake of a training exercise. But the army wants you to suffer the results of your mistakes and your inadequacies, so at the time you aren't aware that actually everything is under control. There were twelve of us in the unit, with an officer who had a radio (this was the concession to the mothers of Israel), which unknown to us was putting out a kind of *ping* that we couldn't hear but the *ping* was how headquarters could tell whereabouts we were. Back at the base there was a big map on the wall and a string of yellow lights going across it, which showed where Avi and his twelve lost boys were. And, man, were we lost. We knew we weren't where we were supposed to be because when you got there, there would be somebody with a clipboard, so we understood that we'd blown the exercise and the problem now was how we were going to get the fuck out of the desert. Avi got on the radio and phoned in, declaring, as the officer in command, that the exercise was over and could they please come and get us. But this didn't go to plan either because it turned out that unluckily there were no helicopters available just then and they were going to have to collect us by truck, which might be several hours – in fact, maybe it would be a day or so before they could get through. They told us, stay there, don't do something clever like move, because where you are now is where we're sending the trucks. We wound up spending another thirty-six hours baking under the sun, shivering during the evening and freezing at night.

But, you know, I was very impressed with the desert. I felt whoever built this place really was somebody I wanted to meet. It was just astounding. Kids today would say, 'This is awesome,' and that is exactly what it is: the ultimate exercise in minimalism and optical illusion. Our eyes are trained to judge distances by registering certain features in the foreground, mid-ground and far away, that is we are engaging in an act of neural relativism. But in the desert there is a here and there is a there and nothing much in between. As city dwellers we use our ears to judge and assess danger – for example, when we cross the street we're attuned to how close is the sound of that engine and when a horn beeps we know to turn around and look, but in the desert there's no sound. There's nothing to hear, there's nothing to look at, it's just big and empty and absolutely stunning and monochromatic. When you look out of the window in a city you see any number of colours; in the desert there are two or three – brown, green and I suppose what you'd call sand, a dirty yellow. When you first encounter the desert as an outsider, it's a completely hostile place. You stand there and you know that with every passing minute your life is ebbing away because you can't survive unless you bring an artificial world with you, usually in the form of a truckload of supplies. If you stand by yourself, your time is finite. Yet the paradox of the desert is that there is no sense of time, it's absolutely timeless. In our world there are two kinds of signpost, night and day, but after a while I was to discover that you could change the rhythm of your life so that daytime and night-time became indistinguishable, they were simply different states of the same time. You could have a whole life in the dark in the desert as well as a life in the sunlight and those two lives were completely interchangeable: they didn't mean the same things as they do in the city.

So eye and ear were annihilated by the desert. As for the nose, the only smell that was ever apparent to me was the smell of carrion, of death. The smells that I associate with the desert are those that came to me much later, during the war: of cordite, the propellant in gunpowder, diesel fumes, rotting flesh.

I spent a couple of nights wondering exactly what I had done to so upset Alix. Erica would have known but I didn't particularly want to call her up and explain to her why I'd suddenly felt like kissing this woman, and I suppose you could say that I messed up that business with Alix just like we totally failed the training exercise in the Sinai because I didn't have a plan. I didn't think it through. This is what I'm always telling Erica, if you want a relationship to work you have to be clear about where you want it to go and what it means to you. If it's not important, why get involved in it? If it is, why is it? If Erica would only use her head she would understand that *this* is how the army changed me. If my number hadn't come up in the US draft lottery, and I'd stayed at home, graduated from college, hung around for years on end figuring out what I wanted to do with my life, apart from smoking dope and going on demonstrations against the war, I would be very different today. I would not have been exposed to a kind of thinking for which there are all kinds of terms now: risk analysis, crisis management, how to confront a situation by examining it, taking it apart, understanding the consequences, putting it back together to give a plan of action to arrive at a goal. That's called military science, and you can apply it to anything. For a relationship to survive is hard work and you have to have an objective in front of you. What's the goal? The goal is, I want this relationship to work well, because on that depends our collective happiness, and both of us *will* be happy if the relationship works. It's the same way you plan to seize a missile base. Though when I first suggested this to Erica, she said, 'Are you *nuts?*'

What I have learned, living with her all these years, being married, raising three children, is that perhaps the analogy is not so exact. Although happiness is the goal, the brutal fact of the matter is that I no longer think there is a truly happy relationship. Some people are happier than others but by the very nature of relationships it's impossible ever to hit the target and that's the difference between marriages and the army. In the battlefield if you don't hit the bullseye it's a disaster but in a marriage if you're not one hundred per cent happy that's okay because the very best you can ever do is come close. You're dealing with a set of parameters called emotions, which you can't handle the way you handle battlefield logistics where you can get rid of something that's in the way by blowing it up. In a marriage if something is in the way you can go around it or climb over it but it's still going to be there; it will be there when you're going towards it and when you're climbing over it, or going around it. And if you turn around it's still always going to be there – I mean some irreconcilable conflict between you. In our case (and this is a minor example), Erica likes to be in a house full of people and I don't. I hate the doorbell ringing all the time and people turning up unannounced, dropping by just as we're sitting down to dinner. What do you do? That is a solid piece of concrete sitting right there in the middle of the floor. You're locked into this relationship, you're travelling together, there's nothing you can do to remove it, short of one of you promising to dramatically alter your own personality when in my experience that rarely if ever happens.

But if I learned all this from Erica, how come it was her not me who decided to end our marriage because she no longer believed that she could be happy in it? I had accepted that happiness was only partially attainable. Erica had decided that her whole state of existence, being married to me, came under the heading of Not Happy. Yet I could never pin her down on what she meant by that.

If there had been affairs . . . but there had been no infidelity she had ever been aware of. It's true, I have not been entirely monogamous in the twenty-seven years since I first met her but sex is not the same thing as an affair. There have been women with whom it's understood that what you are doing takes place out of time, it's not a part of anything. You fuck each other because one or both of you is away from home and lonely, or you are suddenly ravaged by erotic desire which your wife isn't there to help you with and you want more from life than your own right hand and a porn channel on a Holiday Inn TV console. These encounters are about nothing at all but pleasure, momentary ecstasy, which you look back on with a faint, fond memory, sometimes not even able to remember the woman's name or her face. Six or seven times it's happened, always when I have been abroad building hotels. I've never told anyone. Who would I tell and what for? There's nothing to discuss. There was no connection with anything else that was going on in my life, they represented no dissatisfaction with my marriage, or with Erica's face or her body, which still drives me wild when I think about it, even now, sitting in this little apartment on the wrong side of the Atlantic, thousands of miles from Chicago.

I see her only last year sitting at our dining-room table, working late at night on her law papers, the reading glasses she needs to wear now down on her nose. She's in a light-coloured sweater that feels soft when you touch it and it pulls a little across her breasts, which I find incredibly sexy but she looks at herself as she's getting undressed and says, 'I'm fat.' I see her at thirty holding both our children in her arms, one feeding at her breast, the other resting his head on her shoulder, sleeping, and the thought of this now makes me want to cry and it seems that in fact I am crying, a tear running down my left cheek, soaking the collar of my polo shirt. She looked so beautiful and everything I had been through in the war was fading out, because in spite of all the slaughter, all the death, the killing, I had survived it – whether because of luck or my own good soldiering, I don't know – but it was a miracle to me that I was still here, still alive, with a beautiful wife and two babies (soon three babies), a wife I had fallen in love with the moment I saw her in that café, in her white embroidered peasant blouse. And what are these meaningless little fucks I have had compared to that life-defining, all-encompassing moment when I walked through the door of a café in a time of death and of terror such as we thought had passed us by for ever, nearly thirty years before, and thought, Who's *she*?

That was the question, all right. Who was she? Not who I thought when I first laid eyes on her. Not, for example, the Jewish college kid whose parents sent her on a graduation trip to Israel, to hang out on a kibbutz and visit museums and imbibe a little culture before coming home and getting married.

Just to start with she was Canadian. She grew up in one of those white-bread towns in the interior of British Columbia, a region along the border called the Okanagan where they grow fruit and the burghs have names like Kamloops, Salmon Arm and Peachland. The Erica sitting in the café was only a few years away from being a farm girl, dwelling among her father's orchards of apples, acres of land blooming green and red, and on Sunday they went to their Mennonite church.

'You know why Mennonites don't approve of fucking standing up?'

'You tell me.'

'Because it might lead to dancing.' Eighteen years of her life in the middle of nowhere and yet she had a sense of humour!

'And this is how you were brought up?'

'Yes.'

'What about your mother?'

'My mother picked apples and washed apples and baked apples into pies and sold them at the farmer's market in Penticton. She smelt of apples. That was her perfume. Is. She's still back there in the Okanagan, baking.'

'So how did you get away?'

'I was a God-fearing girl all right and I expected I was going to marry one of the boys at school, another fruit farmer like my dad, it really never occurred to me that that wouldn't happen, but you see I have an older brother called Everitt and something appalling happened to him when he was sixteen. One day when he was walking across the yard carrying a bucket of water to sluice down the stable – we had horses too – it suddenly popped into his head that he didn't believe in God. He was so scared that he just dropped the bucket. It fell right out of his hands. Of course he didn't say anything to anyone, in our house the Bible was the whole of our conversation. I remember one time a Jehovah's Witness came to the door and my dad invited him in. Well, the Scriptures were flying all over the place, they weren't just hurling verses at each other but whole chapters. In the end my dad showed him to the door and said, "You go ahead and worship God in your way and I'll worship Him in His." Anyway, Everitt hung around until he graduated from high school and then he moved away, to Vancouver, he became a postal worker. He was a mailman first, what we call a letter-carrier, then he went to work in the sorting office and rose to be a big-shot in the union. It broke my father's heart but what could he do? At least there was still my baby brother to take over the farm. I went to Vancouver one time telling my folks I was visiting with a girlfriend in Osoyoos. In fact, I stayed with Everitt and met his friends, some of them were these scary big-time labour-union feminists who drank at the beer parlours on Granville Street and they persuaded me I should go to college.'

'You talked your parents into that?'

'Yes. But on one condition. That when I graduated I would take a trip to the Holy Land, and here I am.'

Here she was. She was sitting, drinking a glass of mint tea, I was coming towards her cursing my gun, the FN 30 calibre rifle I had to carry round everywhere when I was on leave when what I'd really wanted was an Uzi. Actually the FN packs a stronger punch than an Uzi, has a longer range and is a much more powerful weapon, but it wasn't sexy. The Uzi is what you pick up girls with, and guys like me, schlepping these Belgian FNs around, man, we were dorks. First of all when you walked into a café with one of these things, you invariably caught it on the door going in, which was exactly what happened that day I first saw Erica, just as I was trying to think of what I was going to say to her and if there was any chance of getting a date. And the other thing about the FN, it's really heavy, and it was hot and I knew I was sweating, which made my heart sink even further when I thought of this girl looking up and trying to assess if she'd want to get it together with me. Of course if I'd known the situation, I'd never have even approached her.

She'd come to Israel to do what she promised her parents, to look for Jesus, but as it would turn out she didn't find him.

What a cataclysm that marriage was for both sets of folks. I really don't think her parents understood who their daughter was or what she had become in the three years away from the farm at college. She seemed to have sloughed off altogether an entire upbringing, like the minute she hit the campus she was reborn. Together with her brother she got involved in all kinds of anti-war politics and was a member of a Church group that found places to live and jobs for the anti-war resistance movement, a kind of underground railroad for people like me. She helped out too in a law centre that advised draft-dodgers on their immigration rights and it became clear to her by the time she was graduating with a major in Political Science that the law was where she was heading.

'I wouldn't say I have totally lost all faith in God,' she told me. 'I wasn't entirely discounting some kind of divine revelation when I came here, but it didn't happen. This just seems to be a country of stones and people who, one way or another, worship stones. I felt more comfortable on the kibbutz helping out with the grapefruit harvest, at least there I knew what I was doing. The conditions for growing apples and grapefruit are very different, but it's all still fruit when you get down to it.'

She held fruit like no one else I've ever seen. Held each piece like it was a baby in her hand, running the pad of a finger across the flesh, holding it to her nose and smelling it with big gulps of breath. Like a wine expert she could detect with each inhalation all kinds of scents, and talk about the odours of the soil it grew in and their mineral and chemical content. I had never met a woman so sensual, or at least in such an unusual way.

Our marriage killed her father. Or so Erica believes. Let's just say he had a heart-attack one early morning hour in the fall while on top of a ladder appraising his harvest. He fell to the ground and lay there, dying alone among the fruit of the garden of Eden. I never met him. Her mother is on the farm still, with Lloyd, the youngest, and his wife and their five kids. Erica calls her once a month. I always keep out of the room during those conversations. Once a year she makes the trip to Canada and she stays a week but, again, I have no idea what she and her mother discuss. I don't ask, I don't want to know.

As for my parents . . .

Here's the joke. Erica, who came to Israel to look for Jesus in order to pacify her folks, wound up converting to Judaism to pacify someone else's. I say converting, we went through the motions and only then because there was no way round it. I fought to marry Erica. For the second time in my life (the first was over the war) I faced down my father and it tore my heart out to do it. It was horrible, I never want to go through anything like that again as long as I live, and if they did come round in the end it was only because Erica herself won them over, and partly because of her own erudition. She knew the Good Book like the back of her hand and she sat in my father's study while they talked about Job and Jonah, Jeremiah and Isaiah, she knew them all. I looked in on them and saw her sitting in a hard chair by his side while he read to her from one of the papers he was writing for a scholarly journal of Hebrew studies. It was difficult to square the attentive solemn face, the hair tied back from it, the sober dress she'd bought for the occasion, with the hot babe I knew from our sessions in bed. But maybe that's what Canadians are, neither one thing nor the other, forever capable of becoming something else.

She sailed through the conversion. I told her she didn't have to if she didn't want to, I'd marry her anyway, but she said, 'No, it's not like a lot of this stuff is new to me. I'm sure I'll pick it up.' And she did.

Apart from little stresses on certain vowels in her speech you'd

never know she was not an American, native born. Until the
announcement of our break-up it had not occurred to me to
wonder about the rupture that she had made with her own
family, it seemed natural to me that she would want to escape
from a life like that, growing up in the middle of nowhere with
only God and your parents and two brothers for company and no
intellectual stimulation, no movies or plays or anything to read
except the Bible. No questing and questioning and travel. No
engagement with your government, pushing away at what
democracy is supposed to be. Everything I had grown up taking
for granted she lacked. What she did have, land, acreage, earth,
farm animals, dogs, I saw no value in and never questioned the
haste with which she abandoned them, keeping her links to the
farm only out of duty and affection for her mother and her
nephews and nieces. She had reinvented herself as an American,
as a citizen of the great city of Chicago, had reinvented herself as
a kind of Jew. But I never questioned anything because that is
what becoming an American is all about: whatever baggage you
bring with you to the New World, you have to leave it behind
you at the dock as my grandparents, arriving at Ellis Island in
1906, swore never to set foot again in the land of their birth, nor
did they, and nor did their children retrace their parents' foot-
steps. It's only my generation that has secured our world enough
to risk the return, through exactly the kinds of projects that Alix
Rebick is involved in.

So should I have been so shocked when Erica told me she was
leaving? She'd done it once, now she'd done it twice. The only
past she'd ever been interested in was my time in the army and
this was because she could not decide from the little I had told
her whether or not I had killed in cold blood. At heart she was
a pacifist and the thought of war repelled her. But there again,
growing up among the apple trees, what did she know from
enemies?

Perhaps I had been careless with Alix Rebick. She might once, when she was younger, have been a woman with whom I could have had sex out of time, but not any longer. There are single women of her age whom men will fuck because they believe that they will be grateful for anything, that they can't expect any more than what they're offered. To those guys, Alix would fit right into that category. But she's too good for that kind of treatment. She deserves better, though I don't know how she'll get it. Her problem is that she's just not the kind of woman most men are interested in having a relationship with, she doesn't look the kind of woman anyone would marry. Though it is odd how my thoughts keep coming back to her, throughout the day, standing on the roof of my hotel, looking out across the city with that great bush of hair around her horse face, something going on in her head that I didn't get at all, even if apparently, according to Sam, she's gone to London and has no plans to return, so that, I would say, is the end of that.

One night, a couple of weeks after the beach incident, Erica rang me and asked me to come back to Chicago for a few days because she had got to the end of her rope trying to figure out what to do with our wayward teenager, Michael, who at sixteen was flunking all his grades and who was showing no evidence whatsoever of either aptitude or interest in any course of study available to him, apart from doing 'tricks' on his skateboard in a series of concrete walkways down by the lakeshore in the company of a crowd somewhat older than himself; roughnecks and dropouts, my father would have called them when I was Michael's age. And that's exactly how they seemed to me now, except they didn't have enough drive to be hooligans. They listened to hip-hop, scored dope and a bit of Ecstasy (if they had some get-up-and-go, even sold it), dressed like gangsters from the ghetto and believed in nothing. They were transparent vessels for whatever capitalism could fill them with, fish-like, swimming about the city with an attention span seconds long. And my son had got himself drawn into this life of inertia. His reports were awful, just terrible, there was no indication that he could do better if he tried, there was barely a sign of life at all, yet nothing the matter with him, mentally, not one thing. We'd dragged him round every educational quack in Chicago, had him tested, measured, invited him to express his feelings and everything was normal. Good IQ, no sign of dyslexia, no problems with his eyesight, no psychological problems that anyone could discern. He answered all their questions politely, no rage, no sudden upsurge of violence in him, no sign of repression either. He was normal. And then they asked him what was his problem with school, was he picked on, did he feel the teachers had a down on him, did one of them represent some repressed feelings he had about his mother or his father? He said, no, school was fine, the teachers were fine, he just wasn't interested in education, didn't care to learn, it wasn't his thing. '*Not your thing?*' I screamed. 'How can education not be somebody's thing? Education is what stands between you and the trailer park. I don't notice that when we go on vacation you're averse to staying in a fancy hotel with a pool. When we go to a sports store to buy you new shoes I don't hear you saying, "It's fine, Dad, the cheapest pair will do." On the contrary, you'd skin us alive for the price of what you put on your feet. You don't tell us, hey, we could do without this expensive sound system and the big TV and the computer we got for you. Well, where do you think it comes from? How do you think we earn the money to pay for it? You think you'd have all that stuff if your father worked as a security guard or a janitor or in a convenience store?' 'Actually,' the little fucker said, 'Adam's dad works in a convenience store and he's got pretty much the same stuff as we've got.'

Years of demonstrating against the Vietnam war has come to this. Where are the values, the ideas? Where's the confidence we had (misplaced, admittedly) that it was possible to change the world? How could my own son turn out so vacuous?

This was what Erica wanted me to address, urgently, when I picked up the phone on a Sunday evening, the sun setting on the river after a warm day and the red brick of the dock flaming under the light as the ferry passed across the Mersey to the Cheshire hills on the other side, a place I still hadn't been to yet, and when I'd asked Alix what was there, she'd said, 'Shipyards. Suburbia. And the worst beach resort you've ever seen in your life.'

I said to Erica:

'Your voice sounds weird.'

'What do you mean?'

'I don't know, different, muffled, thick.'

'It's probably just the line. When can you get back?'

'I'll have to talk to my site manager but it should be within the next few days.'

'Have you met a Beatle yet?'

'There are a number of plastic models of them in their mop-top days, but apart from that, no.' On my second day I'd visited the museum called The Beatles Story and later asked Alix if she had gone herself. 'No', she said, 'or at least only in real life.' It was odd, she said, to have your own past served up to you as a theme park. I tried to imagine her at thirteen or fourteen, this lanky Jewish teenager, there at the very birth of sixties rock and roll while I was in Chicago listening to the dregs of the fifties, pallid, manufactured talent like Paul Anka and Fabian.

'Another thing,' Erica was saying, 'have you spoken to your mom lately?'

'Yeah, at the weekend, why?'

'I bumped into her at the market a couple of weeks ago and she looked very shaky, such a shame, I always loved your mom right from the word go. Your father with his big mind was another thing, I felt like anything I said made me sound like such an ass.'

'Come on, you gave as good as you got, the two of you hurling those Scriptures around. You really had him when you got on to the New Testament, you drew a complete blank there, I've never seen him stymied before.' It made me laugh to think about this kid from Canada spouting stuff about the Epistles and my father powerless to respond.

'I can still see him looking at me over his glasses, that moustache, so black it was on his face, bristling. But, Joe, honey, they're not that way now. How old is your mother? Nearly eighty, something like that, and your father a couple of years older? We went for coffee and she really poured her heart out, about how hard things have been getting lately, your father's osteoarthritis is getting worse and worse, he can hardly get out of his chair, he can't hold a pen any more. You know, she told me not to tell you, but he can only just about peck at the keys of the Mac you bought him. She says his mind's the same as ever, just as sharp, but he can't really write, it tires him out just to type a paragraph. And she has to do everything, help him to the bathroom, wash him, even clean his teeth, she's exhausted all the time. I went over there, the place was a mess, there's a smell in there, sour, like they don't open the windows ever, and when I asked her, she said, no, they didn't, your father can't stand draughts. I found the kitchen stuff and I began to clean because I couldn't bear to see the house the way it was, there's crud all over the place. A cat got in and lived in the cellar all winter, she left food out for it and when I went down there it was full of its shit. I vacuumed and washed down the kitchen and opened the window in the bedroom to air out while they were eating dinner, and gladly I'd do that for them, but not as regularly as they need it.'

'Do you think it's time for a retirement community of some kind?'

'I think so, but I raised it with her and she said, "Well, I'd love it, but not him, never, he'll never go."'

True. I could not imagine my father playing cards, taking part in art classes, going on trips in a bus with a bunch of other old people, unless in Chicago there's some home for retired rabbinical intellectuals where they can spend all day hair-splitting about the Mishnah. Which would drive my mom round the bend.

We talked for another half-hour; everything seemed to be softening in her, that hard implacability which I had confronted when she told me she was moving out was giving way, returning to the old Erica, my wife. There had always been something *round* about her, not just her figure, which she moaned about and I loved, but her whole personality had no edges. She didn't confront situations, she just walked away from them, like she'd walked away from the farm and from her parents, and when she did fight me it was by stealth. But someone in a marriage, someone in a country, needs to take on life's shit and that had to be me. I was the one who took out the garbage, and not just literally. I saw off the kid in high school who'd threatened Gil with a knife and never even told Erica. I left work early and waited for him and rammed the little pisser up against a wall and told him I was a crazy fucked-up war veteran and if he ever so much as looked at my son again I'd slit his throat. And instead of reporting me to the school authorities, as I'd figured, he never said another word and walked past Gil with averted eyes. I didn't want Erica to know because I didn't want her to develop the hardness she would need to confront this kind of crap – who wants to come home to that? And the price I'd paid for not exposing her to horror was keeping the war locked up inside me, like there is an iron chest behind my ribs which sometimes lurches and knocks against my heart.

So I was on my way home, sitting in a plane, thinking about the freedom I had had in the past few months, pretending to live as a single guy and kiss women. What a playact that had been. Real life was here, in Chicago, with all the bonds you can never rid yourself of, nor should you want to. And I remembered Alix Rebick and thought of how strange it must be, to be her, someone alone, unaffected, disengaged, free to tackle the big questions to which my dad had devoted himself, but without the support of someone like my mother who listened attentively to what he said and sometimes added a thought but who found herself not in the life of the mind but bringing up two kids in fifties America and doing a little painting on the side – abstract pictures, untrained, unsophisticated, which none the less expressed something of the serenity of her personality in their choice of colour and the balance of their composition. We have one in our house; I'd forgotten to look at it for years but now I wanted to again, more than anything else in the world.

It wasn't Erica who met me at the airport but Michael, standing there with a big smile on his face and his thumb raised when he saw me. I dropped my bags and grabbed him and held him tight. How do you tell a kid who drives you insane and you're at each other's throats what you feel for him, and that nothing of all that nullifies the love which is in your bones – that's how hard it would be to extract it from you? I knew deep down that this phase we were going through was a big zero compared to all the years of memories I had of us doing stuff together, playing zap-'em-up games on his computer, when his mom was out of the house, for example; and even further back than that when we stood together in the bathroom and I first showed him how to hold his penis when he peed and shake off the stray drops and put the seat back down out of consideration for the women in the house. I remember him pulling up his little pants with the elastic waist and asking when he could have pants with a zipper like me, and I said, 'Okay, let's go out and buy some.'

We walked out to the parking lot and then I got a shock that jolted me.

This little boy in my absence had learned to drive and got his permit and was now reasonably competently steering my Corvette along the freeway. *My car. My fucking car!* This sixteen-year-old pot-head behind the wheel of thirty-five thousand dollars' worth of automobile.

'You know what, Michael?' I told him, when I'd recovered. 'If you don't buck up your ideas and improve your grades and get to college, you'll be taking buses the rest of your life or buying beat-up old wrecks that break down every twenty miles. Enjoy every minute of my Corvette because you'll never have another chance to drive anything like it.' His chubby arm was poking out of the window, a heavy-set boy who had inherited Erica's looks and build, her easy nature, everything, even down to the dimples. There didn't seem to be a cell of my DNA in him.

'Oh, lighten up, Dad. Grandpa told me that when you were in college you were real big on that anti-materialism shit. He said you walked around with the ends of your jeans all in threads.'

'Sure we did. It was the *fashion*.' You got a girlfriend to pick out the stitches on the hem then fray the ends of the fabric with scissors. God knows why. 'How's your mom? When will she be home from the office?'

'Didn't she tell you? She's gone out of town, back next week.'

'What?' I was so surprised I turned to look at him.

'Yeah, it's a shame, you'll probably miss her completely.'

'So. She's left you on your own, all by yourself in the house, filling it with pot-heads, having parties, because I'll tell you, that's what I'd have done if my parents had gone away and why should I expect you to be any different?'

'No. I'm not at home at the moment.'

'You're staying with one of your deadbeat friends?'

'With Grandma and Grandpa. I'm looking after them. I come home from school and do all Grandma's chores for her, wash the dishes, vacuum, clean the bathroom. I don't mind, I enjoy it, they're relaxing people to be with.'

'Frankly, I'm surprised. Why would a teenage boy want to hang around with old people?'

'I like them.'

'Let me see, you can't stand school, hate learning, have no interest in it and yet you want to hang out with an old man who's been nailed to a chair with his glasses on since he came out of the army in 1945, writing studies of the thoughts of another guy who's been dead eight hundred years. How does that work?'

'I'm not bothered. They leave me alone, they don't nag me. Grandma's baking again, she made that strudel thing with the apple and the raisins we always had when we went over there when I was little.'

'Mom hasn't baked for years.'

'She did yesterday. It was amazing the way she rolled out the dough so thin you could see through it . . .'

'. . . on the kitchen table with the edges going down over the side, and she said it was like working with dress fabric.'

'Yeah, she said the same thing to me.'

The city of my birth and childhood was being eaten under the wheels of my son's direction, driving along the lakeshore, cold and vast, and all of England could be swallowed beneath it, and all the people I had met in the past few months, like a dream. What an incredible place it is; I never get over the sight of it, the hard outlines rising into the sky, this concrete statement on the edge of an inland sea. A truly fucked-up city, where my parents live in a dwindling enclave of old-school, middle-class Jewish suburban values like thrift and prudence and education and political liberalism and taking a high moral tone. They could hardly bring themselves to vote for the Daleys, 'Corrupt men,' said my father. 'Democracy and theft don't go together.' Yet Chicago just goes on putting up these amazing buildings, constructions often of astounding elegance; it's everything Liverpool isn't, where life continues at a pace, instead of having ground to a full stop. I always feel, when my plane touches down and I'm pushing my cart along the curvaceous moving walkway of the United Airlines terminal, how lucky I was to have been born here, to have been exposed visually to maybe the most all-American city there is. Lucky that my grandparents got off the boat and went over to a window where a guy was handing out flyers about how there was work in the prairies for new immigrants, and schlepped their asses a thousand miles across the country instead of walking off into the Lower East Side and staying put.

We pulled into the drive. The same grey paint on the house,

the same dimensions to the yard bounded by the same fence, the same big sycamore tree growing in it and the treehouse that my uncle Gideon built me and Evie when I was eleven years old and she was eight, where we climbed up every day in the summer and fought and played and imposed our own cruel rules, banishing the other when our own friends came over. From our treehouse you could see over the rooftops of our neighbourhood and I told Evie that when, if ever, she reached my height, she would be able to take in the vista of the whole of Illinois, except each new inch wouldn't quite do it, until she reached fourteen and realised at last I'd been teasing her. The quiet of our house, always peaceful, my dad at home all day studying, the radio muted in the kitchen while my mom prepared our meals, tuned to the classical station on public-service radio, and me upstairs, frustrated, because I could not play rock and roll in case I disturbed him. So once again Uncle Gideon, the practical one of the three brothers, came over and cleared out the basement for us and soundproofed it, so we could get up to anything we liked, Evie and me, and it was here, at fifteen, that I lost my virginity with Gloria Marcus, told her I loved her, which was not strictly true.

I have always been a dutiful son, I have always tried to obey the wishes of that patriarch my father, who in his solitude none the less cast upon me the eyes of love. Sometimes at night he lifted his head and found me standing at the door of his study in my pyjamas, watching the fountain pen in his hands pass across the sheets of yellow legal paper, writing in the language I was learning to decipher but did not yet understand and which he spoke into the telephone after it had been brought back from the dead. His moustache, his reading glasses, his pipe, his tweed jacket, all seemed like the plastic things you pressed into Mr Potato and were not of him, because beneath these insignificant expressions of a purely superficial identity was *my dad*, who looked at me and saw who I was, saw pain confusion guilt happiness shame remorse generosity, and stamped himself on each feeling to raise me from them so I could see into the minds of those creatures who stand between us and God, the living beings who orbit in unending circle powered by perfect knowledge of the divine. I was the rabbi's son, the son of the reb who had no congregation and no *shul*, who was a scholar, who wrote commentaries on the thoughts of the man whose name we Jews affectionately abbreviate to Rambam – Rabbi Moshe Ben Maimon, also called Moses Maimonides, the physician and philosopher who united Aristotle and the Torah. 'From Moses to Moses there was none like Moses,' the folk-saying went.

I came back to America in the fall of 1974 after the Ford amnesty when you got to return if you took a public-service job for a couple of years. I did my stint teaching in the public-school system while Erica enrolled in law school, and as soon as my gig was up I began my training as an architect. They were tough times, the two of us not getting careers begun until we were in our late twenties having started a family as soon as we could. My folks were a huge help: looking after the babies while we studied, guaranteeing loans for us against their own home, but it was Erica who was the rock; she was what made it work. She never complained, the farm-girl stock in her really came out, her stoicism, her cheerfulness, she knew how to make ends meet, in ways that some of the spoilt girls I knew when I was growing up never dreamed of. Our kids for years went to school in home-made clothes and ate vegetables that she grew in the garden she made in the yard of this house we lived in then, more of a clapboard shack than a house. But under its roof we had the most incredibly hot sex, however tired we both were, man, we couldn't stop. Having taken on both sets of parents we felt we could now take on the whole world, together we were invincible, we could accomplish absolutely anything, and the only thing we really lost in that time was the political activism that had marked our early years. We were just too tired to go on demonstrations. Sex or politics, that was the choice for the few hours we had undisturbed together. It wasn't hard to decide.

When I first told my dad that I wanted to be an architect, I was worried that he was going to be disappointed in me, that I hadn't become a thinker like him. But then our greatest commentator on God was also a practical man, as my father was fond of telling me: 'No bread, no Torah; no Torah, no bread' – that is, without physical sustenance we cannot study, but without study we are not really nourished. Other kids learned of Robin Hood and Davy Crockett, me, I got the early life and times of the medieval rebbe: the birth in Cordoba in the era of Moorish Spain; the precocity of his childhood intellect; the persecution by the fanatical Almohad sect; the flight from Iberia; the family's exile in North Africa, disguised as Muslims; the final settlement in Cairo. Then the formative years supported by his brother David, the pearl merchant, and the catastrophe of his death in a shipwreck in the Indian Ocean; the need for Moshe to find a career to support himself. So he did what any good Jewish boy does: knuckled down and became a doctor, specialising in gastroenterology and preventive medicine based on proper diet and basic hygiene. Rambam rose to be the court physician to the Sultan as well as the leader of the whole of the Jewish community in twelfth-century Egypt. In his last years, when he was very successful, he retired from public life and from philosophy, and started a charity clinic, ran himself ragged combining his medical practice, community leadership, scholarship, teaching, fatherhood, and an international correspondence, and all without the postal service, let alone the Internet.

Imitatio Dei. 'What the angels are, humans desire to become,' and our end is the *summum bonum*, to know God. But how? For us Jews, my father taught me, it's discovering what acts you need to perform and how to perform them properly, the basis for the 613 *mitzvoth*. A man must try to do as many *mitzvoth* as he can, even if it is only to say his *Shema* and give charity and attend a funeral. If the Ten Commandments mostly tell you what you can't do, the *mitzvoth* are a list of what, if at all possible, you *should* do, including making a parapet upon a flat roof to make sure no one falls off (truly, it is written); not keeping a dangerous dog in the house; and decimating the descendants of Amalek – a difficult one, the rabbis advise us, because we don't know who they are and won't know until Elijah the prophet comes back and tells us, but when he does, believe you me, *then* we will wipe out all remembrance of the evil Amalek from under heaven. I used to wonder what the Amalekites had done to piss us off so much until I found out that they used to creep up on the Children of Israel when we were wandering in the desert after the flight from Egypt and pick off the stragglers who were usually the old and the weak. What a bunch of *mamzers*. Personally I think the descendants of Amalek are all around us, a secret society who since Biblical times have said to each other, under their breath, 'Listen, we're descended from a guy named Amalek, but whatever you do, *don't tell the Jews*.'

Mitzvah No. 42 lays down as a positive commandment to have a reverent fear of one's father and mother and here the instructions are specific. You can't sit or stand in your dad's place (so no hunkering down in his favourite TV chair from where he watched Alistair Cook presenting *Masterpiece Theatre* and Jacob Bronowski's *Ascent of Man* on PBS and, if he thought no one was around, Marx Brothers movies). You can't contradict him or express a deciding opinion about his words, and if that weren't enough you can't even call him Dad but 'my father, my master', like that Italian movie, *Padre Padrone*. On the other hand, if a father is willing to forgo his honour then everything's okay and you can argue with him until you're blue in the face, which is exactly what I used to do, particularly when I got into my teens, and later over the Vietnam war and what to do about it. (I never told him about my copious inhalation of marijuana or my two acid trips or the speed I used to finish up my term papers. That would just have been stupid.)

For all the memories I have of him as a scholar, his stillness, his concentration, the sincerity with which he approached his work and, indeed, his reverence for the study of all philosophy, the way he restrained the expression of his pleasure when each new book arrived from the printers . . . what is burned into my brain is the look on his face when I passed out, as a soldier in the Israeli army, my parents seeing their first-born wearing the military uniform of the Jewish people.

Man, that was a cinematic moment, not Jewish at all but Gothic, almost pagan. The Parachute Regiment, the élite of the élite whom I would see in operation during the war, get to do their ceremony at Masada but for the Engineering Corps it's some other hill on the West Bank whose significance eludes me completely; in fact, I'm not even sure there is one. They took us up at night and we found the whole place ringed by pith torches, with stands built for the invited guests, mostly parents. The whole unit was standing there, all lined up and at attention, dressed as combatants but significantly minus the rifle because they'd been collected at the ceremony, and there was a long table arranged in front of us at which were standing all the brass: the chief of staff, the brigade commander, the unit commanders. They called us up one by one, and in our left hand they put a Bible and in the right our gun. All around us the torches were burning and the flags were flapping in the wind and the moment overwhelmed me completely, the symbolism of the Bible and the rifle just knocked me out, it really did, I was deeply, deeply moved. I felt that this was the moment at which I was called to defend the Jews. It was amazing, haunting. There was a seriousness about it, a finality.

The people back in Berkeley, the pacifists I knew then, would never have been able to fathom what it was all about. And I can still see it now, to this day. On one side of the table were people who had no idea what they were getting into and on the other were people who knew full well what this all meant, because they'd been through it, because they had a grasp of the reality of living stripped of all the rhetoric and the cant and the sham and the posturing. I'd made it, I'd come this far entirely on my own. I saw myself as the logical successor to everything that my father had dedicated himself to, the chain of survival of Jewish life. I was a Jew with a gun. I was twenty-two and saying to myself, 'I'm the first Shields [Shapiro, really] to defend the Jews.'

Dad came up to me afterwards and hugged me, his head was against my cheek and that was the moment when I realised I was taller than him – all the time I'd been in college I'd still been growing. Taller than Dad! It couldn't be. My mom was crying, my sister was looking around at all the cool Jewish guys in tight uniforms and I said, 'What would Rambam think, Dad?' And there and then, under the flaming torches on the West Bank hillside, he launched into an exegesis about Maimonides' ideas on the repair of the body politic, how Moshe believed that while even a rudimentary human society is impossible without the pro-hibition of murder, idolatry is worse because it is exceptionless, no wriggle room at all. That the commandment of the Jews was to adopt a purely spiritual form of worship consisting solely of the adoration of the transcendent God, which is why we could not become Christians because of their division of Yahweh into three and his manifestation in a form the imagination could supply and even reproduce through art. And that what he saw in the ceremony troubled him because it was creating a new idol for the Jewish people, the image of the soldier, and that we would have to take great care that this picture did not come to blot out the idea of God himself. 'We are here to pursue truth,' he told me, his face hardly discernible now, as the torches burned low and the people were filing out, leaving behind their debris, orange peel, newspapers, film canisters, 'which is to be conducted in the created order, including the communities we live in from day to day. Accept the truth, Maimonides told us, whatever its source. Even if we find it in the words and deeds of our enemies. I want you to remember that, Joe.'

Then they left, and I went back to my unit and my parents and sister went on to Jerusalem, where Evie, schlepping round a museum of archaeological artefacts with my parents one day, met an equally bored American kid with *his* parents and they started dating and in the end she married him, and stayed married for fifteen years until she ran off with Rivki Solomon and they now run a women's restaurant in the Mission in San Francisco. A city whose name my mom curses to this day for the ideas it put into the heads of her two children. As for me, the swearing-in ceremony marked the end of basic training, when you're assigned to your unit and absorbed into the regular army. Because we had been trained as a demolition team we were assigned to a battalion in the engineering corps, which meant we sat at a former British army base in a place called Beit Lid, inland between Haifa and Tel Aviv.

In the kitchen my mother looked up as we walked in and the smile she gave me split her face in two and my heart was breaking to look at her because she had a spot of dried toothpaste on her chin and had not noticed because she was old and no longer vain enough to look in the mirror, or maybe she feared what she would see there. And coffee stains were on her white cotton sweater, my mom whom I remember in those fifties dresses with the stiff skirts underneath to make them stick out, showing off a clinched-in waist highlighted by a shiny patent belt; she was even slim enough to get away with those short pants that stopped at the calf, even when she was in her thirties and I was about ten years old. She was a stylish woman, my mother, always wore lipstick and powder even when she ran out to the store. Now this. Yet the strudel was on a platter, coffee cups were stacked up beside it, four plates, a knife, pastry forks, and her best creamer, decorated with blue and white Dutchmen dancing in clogs in front of a blue windmill. She got up and tried to run across the room to me and I came towards her and she reached up and held me in her arms. I smelt the traces of shampoo in her hair, the old medicinally scented one she always used, never varying the brands of anything she bought because that was how her generation was, they found a product and stuck to it, nothing in them was susceptible to advertising, only to usefulness. Behind me Michael was already spooning coffee into the electric filter machine I bought them as a fortieth wedding anniversary present and before I could ask where my father was he said, 'I'll get Grandpa.' We heard the study door opening upstairs. I heard scuffling on the stairs, my father's voice, 'No, thank you, Michael, I can manage.' My mother's little scream, her hand in front of her mouth, then, 'I should trust Michael, he manages very well, a strong boy.'

Here was my father. Back, hands, legs, arms, twisted like a sugar stick. The glasses whose dusty black-rimmed frames he hadn't changed since 1980, were drooping down his nose and Michael reaching up to push them back. The moustache still there but now also a beard, white, stained. ('It's hard for him to shave any more.') He dropped into a chair and I squatted by his side and held him. 'Dad.'

'Joseph.' The voice came out of this grotesque figure clear and commanding, the disease that had not touched his brain had passed over his vocal cords too.

'Dad.' My heart full.

We discussed Gil and Allison, both in college, whom I talk to when I can get hold of them, their answering-machines usually on and the message tapes full of the usual garbage college kids that age receive, organising their social lives, and I'm too smart a dad to call them up on their cellphones and embarrass them when they're in the middle of something. When I was Gil's age I was still in basic training, going into the city on weekend passes, meeting girls who were in the country on vacation, and once or twice women a little older than me from the press corps, or secretaries at the US embassy, and having affairs that would last for a couple of weeks or a couple of months and then they'd be over. It was by no means certain that I would be off every weekend and I understood quickly that there's no point in forming a relationship with a soldier and there's no point a soldier trying to form a relationship. So I had this series of short-lived flings, which suited me fine, until I walked into the café and saw Erica, which was the start of the phase that became known to me as my life.

'And this young man,' my mother was saying, 'what a help he is.'

'Very good, but what about school?'

'Dad, don't start.'

'Has Erica told you about his grades, how worried we are?'

'No,' my mother said. 'What's this, Michael?'

He flushed up to his hair. His hands moved to his mouth and his teeth began work on his fingernails. One foot was kicking the table leg, like a child, and in that moment – *for* a moment – I couldn't stand the sight of him, irrational loathing rose in me. Photographs of all my kids when they were tiny babies, a week or two after they were born, are on the dresser at home as well as all the usual pictures, because each baby seemed unbelievable to me, that one day they were part of Erica, and the next, part of the world, with personalities defined the minute they were born. I used to subscribe to the nurture-not-nature argument until I actually had kids myself. Gil asleep at fourteen days, his head to one side, his arms raised behind him and look of such concentration, a serious, intense little sleeper. Now he's a hundred-and- seventy-pound man, yet I could still look at that infant for hours, driving myself crazy wondering what was going on inside his mind, what he could have been dreaming about. And Allison, different altogether, the picture of her wide awake, gurgling, her fingers in her mouth, a mischief in her even though she could hardly be aware of anything other than Erica's face and breasts. Then Michael. A flaccid baby, he ate so little that at seven weeks he slipped under his birthweight for a few days (though he's made up for it now, gorging himself on junk food). He's in my arms in the photo and he looks as if he's retarded, nothing there in his face, as if he'd have preferred a few more weeks or even months in the womb. It took me a long time to like him and I did, eventually, when he began to chub out, and I looked up one morning and saw him in the yard, having crawled out on to the grass, and pointing at a worm, turning to us, squealing with pleasure and delight. But I couldn't keep that image in my head now because bile was rising up inside me. I wanted to reach out and take his head and bang it against the table, I wanted to knock his brains out and put them back in again but right this time. He enraged me, because there was nothing I could do about him, I was powerless, felled by this sixteen-year-old kid, his obstinacy, his refusal to engage with the reality of what his future existence was going to be, the slackness of him, his limp attitude to what went on around him. It was rage at his passivity that boiled up inside my chest, passive in his lack of resistance to everything but his parents' demands that he engage himself with a world independent of what the marketing guys wanted to do to him, to mould him, to make him theirs. I was in a war and my enemies this time were not the Egyptians in the south and the Syrians in the north but the manufacturers of running shoes and whoever it was who ran MTV and some crack-heads in South Central to whom the record industry gave millions in order to indoctrinate *my* son with the idea that women were bitches and it was fun to pack a weapon and kill people. Except to have behaved like any of those hip-hop stars would have required an energy he didn't even seem to possess. I couldn't think of a single thing that would arouse him out of lethargy. This was how he defied me – not with argument, passionate argument, or how I had defied my father when one day I went into the yard and shouted up to the window of his study, 'Look, Dad, I'm burning my draft card,' the sparks and ashes flying up towards him, past him, over the roof of our house, over the highest leaves of the tree of my childhood treehouse until the fire in them was extinguished.

'I don't wanna stay in school. Why can't I leave now?'

'You know why.'

'I read in the Bible that it says, "Of making many books there is no end and much study is a weariness of the flesh." Isn't that right, Grandpa?'

I was so infuriated with him I felt a pain in my chest. I stood up and shoved him, took him by the shoulders and dragged him through the door into the yard. 'Stay there, just stay there until I'm finished here. Don't move.'

'Fine.'

He lay down on the lawn under the morello cherry tree (it was Erica, of course, who first told us what kind of cherries they were) and closed his eyes, but his chest was heaving and his arm went up and a fist wiped away a tear. Standing over him, I had the desire to deliver a kick to his fat ass but you don't hit your kids, that's not me at all. In our family, there was plenty of intellectual violence but real violence we left to other people, the kind we didn't want to know.

'Can you believe that?' I asked, coming back into the kitchen. 'He quotes the fucking Bible at me.'

There was silence, which my mother broke, saying, 'Let me refresh your coffee cup, Joseph.'

My breath was coming back, we sat for a few moments and no one spoke. I looked out of the window and he was still there, still lying with his eyes closed. 'Thinks it's time for a nap,' I said. My parents said nothing. I knew what this kind of silence meant. Extreme disapproval, and it was being directed at me.

'What?'

'Some psychology,' my father said.

'You think I'm handling this badly, well, you tell me, what am I supposed to do?'

'Keep your temper.'

'We've tried reason, we've tried your way, it doesn't work, he doesn't listen. You're having an argument with thin air.'

'Another time for this,' said my mom. 'Meanwhile we have the pleasure of you and let's not spoil it with fights.'

'Some advice I forgot to give you, Joe,' my father added. 'Never raise your hands to your children, it leaves your groin unprotected.'

The timbers of the house creaked, the leaves rustled in the trees in the yard, we ate our fill of strudel and wiped our mouths on fancy red patterned paper napkins until it was time to talk about their health and their future in this house, my childhood home, from which my parents dared not move any more, not only because of their own age and infirmity but because of what they were surrounded by. A world they could not comprehend for a moment, had no desire to understand. You know in the *mitzvoth*, there are various injunctions about how we Jews can't tattoo our flesh or scarify it or shave the sides of our heads or wear our hair in a crest, and these glances, from the corner of the eye, tell us about the idol worshippers, the heathens, the barbarians that the Jews chose to set themselves apart from. Now the barbarians were at the gates, or just a couple of miles away, a few streets' distance from this old man and woman who married after the war and thought the future could only be improvable and improving.

This was the marriage I had always sought to emulate. When I stood under the *chupa* with Erica, slammed my foot down on the wine glass wrapped in a linen cloth and it shattered into a thousand pieces to symbolise the destruction of the Temple, it was in my mind that my old life as a single man was what I was really breaking, that what lay ahead of me was the building of a new temple, which was to be a family, very much like the one my parents had made. And my anger with Erica was that she had deprived me of the lifelong project I had committed myself to all those years ago. What right had she to rob me of that ambition? Who the hell was she suddenly to throw in the towel just because she felt like it?

'Mom, have you thought about having some help round the house?'

'You mean a maid?'

'Nah, someone to come in every day or every couple of days to give you a hand with the heavy work, the laundry, the floors, that kind of thing.'

'Joseph, I don't want a stranger in my house.'

'That I understand, but these days you go to an agency, you ask for references, you don't like one, you get another, you don't even have to talk to her if you don't want to, or maybe you'd prefer a guy who could also do the yard.' I knew enough about my father's finances. One book, written in his late forties, had been a best-seller – I don't mean the *New York Times* kind of best-seller, but it was still in print, a study of ethics that you can find on all kinds of required reading lists on college courses in theology and philosophy today. That was his income, a royalty cheque every six months from his publisher, plus my mother's inheritance, which my uncle Amos had invested for her in AT&T stock at the beginning of the fifties. They were not impoverished but they were at an age where the future was a fear. 'And of course I'll take care of the bills,' I said.

'I don't know,' my mother answered, 'we're doing okay at the moment, aren't we, Leo, with Michael coming after school?'

He was at the window, had come right up to it. 'Dad, why pay for a stranger to come here? I could quit school and look after them.'

I treated that statement as it did not exist. As far as I was concerned the next step would be to research retirement communities, to find the kind both my dad and my mom would feel comfortable in.

My father had been silent. He had little small-talk and matters that concerned the running of the house he left to his wife and to her brothers. He had no dignity as far as any of that was concerned. I make him sound like a remote, uncaring dad but nothing could be further from the truth. He was a very loving man, the one to whom I came to speak of troubles, of *tsores*, I gave him problems and he gave me back answers. He was a man who touched his children and only demanded from them that during certain set hours he must be understood to be not there, as if he was away at the office, but at five thirty his study door would open and he would come out and shout, 'Who's home?' And whoever replied, he would run down the stairs and say, 'Okay, what's up?' Maybe we went into the yard and threw a ball around between us (he had had some minor athletic triumphs before he went to the *yeshiva*), or we played chess, or he would climb up into the treehouse and I would show him my secret world. Among the trees, above the house, my father seemed most like himself, the young man ardent for learning, flushed and excited by it, telling me tales of Jewish heroes like the Maccabees and how they were more than fighters, but symbols of a set of ideas about the eternal truth. He never obfuscated, never showed off his erudition, but wrote in an easy prose style that anyone could understand even though it was formal and precise, which is why his book on ethics was such a success.

Honour thy father and thy mother, says the fifth commandment. They made it so easy for me.

He sat in his chair, strudel dough stuck to his gums, waiting
politely for the conversation to turn to something that could
include him, for he would never venture an opinion about any
matter concerned with what he considered, in his old pre-
feminist mindset, to be my mother's domain.

My mother reached across and refilled his cup. I noticed
Michael was now standing by the door, he had disobeyed his
banishment and silently moved back into the house. I was hardly
aware of his presence in the room, he bent down and gently
took my father's hands and placed them round the cup, both of
them, so he could lift it to his mouth. Dad drank, messily, and
before my mother could reach for her napkin, my son had wiped
away the dribbles from his grandfather's chin. Dad pulled
Michael's head towards him and kissed him on the cheek, and
Michael did not recoil but bent down and kissed my father's
head.

'Grandma, do you want me to do the dishes?'

'Thank you, Michael, yes.'

My son stood at my mom's sink, the big old one that came
with the house when they built it in 1949 and which she would
never replace for something else, something newer, because she
liked the idea of the unity of the building, that the whole con-
ception fitted, that someone's mind had thought up a home and
put it together, each in its constituent part. 'Why a new kitchen?'
she asked me, bewildered. 'What's wrong with the one I have?
Everything works just like it should, and, if it breaks down we
can always get it repaired.' Ha! Just wait until she tries.

Michael was washing the knife that had cut the strudel, a
knife my mother had used to slice her baked goods ever since I
could remember, perhaps even before I was born, never mind my
own children, and it struck me how these little things you don't

notice around your house are what really make your home: the cup my mom used solely to measure out flour and sugar for those baked goods, the old blue-painted stool she sat on in the kitchen when she talked on the phone to her girlfriends, my dad's collection of fountain pens stuck in an old chipped mug on his desk, the towels in the bathroom that we'd had as long as I could remember, with a pattern of fishes on them. This is what makes a house, not the chrome Italian kettles that go out of style or all the *chatchkies* you buy when you're hanging around an airport somewhere in Europe and have nothing else to do. When the dishes were stacked Michael turned to his grandfather and said, 'Ready to go back up now?' My father nodded. The two slowly ascended the stairs, me behind them, and in my father's study, overlooking the yard and my treehouse, he sat him in his chair wedged in among cushions and I pulled up another chair next to my father and we held each other.

'Much pain, Dad?' I whispered.

'To hell with it,' he replied, trying to smile. 'I'm trying my best to be philosophical, to remember what the Preacher said: "But if a man live many years and rejoice in them all yet let him remember the days of darkness. All that cometh is vanity.' I had good health when I was young, and now the days of darkness are surely on me.'

'I'll come back tomorrow. Are you knocking any sense into Michael's head?' If my father could not imbibe in him a love of learning, who could?

'God grants different kinds of wisdom, Joe.'

'He isn't backward, I mean mentally.'

'No, I understand that. I used to love a fight, I don't mean boxing, that's sadism, a leftover from the gladiators. I mean a good argument. Now, I get tired very quickly, tire of people's voices. Your mother's lonely, she wants to talk, she misses company and she can't get out as much as she did. There's a problem

between us we'll have to confront one day. A retirement community she wants. It's not for me. Michael knows how to be
quiet, it's not a very Jewish quality, he must get it from his
mother's folks. He doesn't have much to say so he doesn't say
much. I like his calm. It eases me.'

'I see.' I had never thought of Michael's slackerdom as an
advantage. I didn't believe it for a minute.

The sun was setting, I was very tired. It was around three in the
morning on European time and I gestured to Michael; we got in
the car and I started it up and took off to drive us home, back to
the house I built for us in 1990, which won me an award and you
can find pictures of it occasionally in architectural magazines, my
own uncompromising gesture towards my father's idea of the
eternal. It's built of glass and steel, in the manner of Mies van der
Rohe, but his interior minimalism I have considerably softened
to suit the needs of a family and the hand of my wife is freely
seen in the homeliness and sensuality of the things she's chosen:
the colours umber, dark green and red are here in the velvet of
the fabric of the couches and the lacquered wood of the furniture. She has created something that almost seems voluptuous,
encased in the hard steel skeleton that protects us from a hostile
world. But I insisted on light, no drapes, not in any room, and
only the sides of the house are metal elevations permitting pri-
vacy from our neighbours' prying eyes.

'Dad,' Michael said, 'you frightened me today.'

'Because I lost my temper?'

'Yeah, like I know you were in the army and you must have
killed people, so I mean, you could kill me if you really got out of
control.'

This sentence came as a thunderbolt. My kids thought I might
throttle them, that potentially I was a murderer! I stopped the
car and pulled in to the side of the road. 'Michael, how could you

say that? I'm aghast, is that how you see me?' I *couldn't* have driven any further, my hands were shaking.

'Occasionally.'

'But don't you understand that there's all the difference in the world between going to war, being a soldier where you have to do certain things in certain situations, and what normal life is? I never hit you kids when you were growing up, you know that.'

'I know what I see on TV, about the Vietnam vets who are so fucked up and all the craziness going on in the world right now.'

'Yeah, but you know *me*.'

'Maybe. I know you as a dad but I don't know anything about what you did when you were a soldier.'

'I don't want to talk about it.'

'That's what Mom said you'd say.'

'You asked her?'

'Yeah, and she said she didn't know, because you never have talked about it, even though she met you when you were in the army. She said you never talked about it then either.'

'Okay, what do you want to know?'

'What's it like to kill someone?'

'I'm not answering that.'

'Why not?'

'It's a private thing, and you wouldn't understand.'

'Okay, so what would I understand?'

'Oh, hardly any of it. Listen, Michael, I don't want to inflict on you something you don't *need* to know. My job as a father is never to expose you to evil.'

'Did something evil happen to you?'

'No, nothing, not at all.' I grabbed his head and pulled it to me and kissed him. 'I'm gonna give you a hug now, okay? You won't set up a wail?'

'No.'

So we sat there for a few moments, holding each other, hard.

Now it was dark. I started the engine and turned on the headlights. Michael said, 'Dad, you're tired. Let me drive.'

I opened the door and we switched places. We drove home talking of sports while my mind was working, trying to figure out what to do about him, how to get him to see things from my point of view. I was trying to imagine him and I wasn't succeeding, he bore no resemblance to my teenage self, no girls hanging around, no porno magazines hidden under his bed. He was a cipher to me, I couldn't get my head round him at all. Yet here he was in command of my Corvette, driving confidently through the darkening suburban streets soaked in the day's heat, towards our home, which I had left for too long and which now awaited me, empty, without my wife. And I was filled with gusts of sorrow, like I had myself been abandoned in the desert, one of the wrecks we left behind when the fighting really began. How could I tell him about war, what they don't show you on those computer games we used to play zap-zap-zap the baddies? That's not what war is: war is more like life itself, full of sadness and tragedy, moments of elation, hours of boredom. How do you explain that to a sixteen-year-old? How do you explain a marriage?

I was exhausted. We pulled up to my house and I thought at first that it might have been a trick, this business of Erica being away, because the lights were on and inside there were people moving. But it was Gil and Allison, home for a surprise family reunion, to see their old dad again. Man, was I ever glad to lay eyes on them, because talking on the phone really is no substitute for holding your kids in your arms and hugging them and looking to see how they have grown and hearing all the news that they're prepared to tell you, knowing of course that there's a degree of censorship going on there, because I sure didn't tell my parents everything when I was their age.

Allison opened a bottle of wine and laid out some olives in a bowl and we sat together as a family should. My heart was aching with love for them, and I couldn't wait to get the Liverpool project finished so I could come back home where I belonged. Maybe they would, maybe they wouldn't return to Chicago one day, but at least in America here they were just a couple of time zones away, not five or eight. As for Michael, he needed me. He needed a father. And when Erica saw that, she would understand that she had to subordinate her ideas about how she wanted to live her life for something more important than any of that, the Family. *Our* family. The house that Joseph built. And, as I always tell my clients, I build to last.

Before I went to bed I remembered that I had a bag full of Beatles stuff and I handed it out and everyone seemed pleased with what they had got. Alix Rebick had helped me choose it, after I met her for coffee in the Tate. I wondered how she was doing, then I fell asleep.

Alix

Apart from the house in France, I have a flat in London that I bought in the late eighties when Alan and I split up. It is on the sixth floor of Highpoint, a block of apartments built in the 1930s by the German-Jewish refugee genius Berthold Lubetkin. It was constructed in the Modernist style and painted white so that it stands out like a sore thumb next to the red-brick houses that surround it. My heart always gives a lurch when I return here after a long absence. The severity of its form is not offputting to me, and those who consider it a monstrosity could never be my friends. In my childhood I grew up in a house near the river, a four-square late-Victorian red-brick villa with two bay windows on either side of the door, surrounded by black-painted railings like swords and an old-fashioned lamp-post in front whose lantern, when my father first walked down here as a young man in the early fifties, amazed by the grandeur and elegance of the gated estate, was still lit by a gas mantle. The four of us spread ourselves about the place, occupying it with books and music and my father's medical journals and left-wing magazines and my mother's reparations papers locked away in iron boxes. In my flat the rooms are a series of white cubes and each is very tidy. I do not have a garden but from the windows you can see the whole of the city – the dome of St Paul's, the Lloyds building, the blinking tower of Canary Wharf – so why would I need one? The sense of space and light is incomparable, as if I were in a plane in the moments at which it begins its descent and the clouds are penetrated and London lies below, limpid in the morning air, and you gaze and gaze and gaze and, so transfixed, think you might not mind if your death was going to be now.

Having fled from Liverpool the morning after the débâcle on the beach, I turned the key and let myself in. In France I had bought everything from scratch, down to the last teacup. I hate to admit it but I had even agreed to have the place *feng-shui*ed, all in my attempt to achieve, by the force of my will, this peace of mind that everyone tells me is such a necessary component of existence. Here, set out in front of me in the Highgate flat, was the chronology of my life. A gold-framed picture of a bowl of plums, executed in the little squares of pigment from a child's painting box, had been done by my niece Sasha when she was nine and signed and given to me with pink pride when I asked if I could have it. Photos of my family were on the piano (my parents were of the generation that believed every Jewish child should play a musical instrument, Mamma would have preferred me to learn the harp). In the kitchen there was a photograph of me when I was twenty-two and my hair was at its most uncontrollable. In this picture I am wearing an outlandish garment: a Thea Porter – well, what would you call it? A sort of hip-length frilled shirt with an enormous collar and batwing sleeves. The fabric is printed in a design of peacocks and the whole thing is belted at the waist and worn over velvet knickerbockers tucked into Cossack boots. A matching scarf is tied around my head, one hand jutting from my waist, and no doubt to myself I appeared the epitome of hippie chic, bold and romantic, and to my mother, 'something out of the circus, good God, are you going out like that?'

I turned on the TV, sat down and watched a documentary about a war I had missed when I was in France – the whole thing, beginning, middle, refugee exodus, ceasefire and exile of the defeated leaders – then I put clean sheets on my bed and by ten thirty I was asleep. Numb, inert, dreamless slumber came, the sleep of my mother in her pine box with a handful of the earth of the Promised Land by her body and her worn-out face beneath its mask of gauze. The rictus of death was on her when they came to close her eyes, her mouth half open, still greedy for its last breath. Deep in the earth of Liverpool she is buried beneath stone teeth.

The next day I woke quite late and rang Marsha.

'It was more than embarrassing,' I said, 'it was humiliating. And added to that I ran off and left him there with no way of getting home.'

'I don't know what to say.'

'There is nothing *to* say. It was a stupid mistake on my part.'

'Why did you misread his signals?'

'I've no idea. A man suddenly grabs a woman and kisses her. What's that supposed to mean? What could it mean? I only have one explanation, that there's a sexual attraction, yet he says there isn't.'

'But he only said he didn't want to have an affair with you, that's not quite the same thing. Remember, he'd already told you he was married. What it looks like to me is that something irrepressible happened – he finds that he's kissing you without being able to help it. He *is* drawn, he *is* attracted. He didn't mean to kiss you but he couldn't stop himself. And your interest in him is what? What are you expecting?'

'I don't know.'

'Did you think he was going to leave his wife for you?'

'I honestly hadn't got that far, I'm not a teenager fantasising about her wedding dress. I just met him and I thought, This is it. He's for me.'

'So you wanted more than an affair?'

'It would have done in the absence of anything else. What I'm after is something rather than nothing.'

'Do you suppose that this might still be possible?'

'How can it be? He made his feelings quite clear.'

'Perhaps he needs some persuading, maybe you need to work on him instead of running off like an adolescent with a broken heart. You can be quite childish at times, do you realise that? You *could* have been gracious, you know, you *could* have seen him again, worked on him, worn down his resistance. Because this is what a man would have done. Instead you behaved like a school-girl with a crush.'

'This is true.'

'Well, think about it. Anyway, you never know, someone else might come along.'

'I doubt it. Apparently the ideal age for a woman is half the age of a man plus seven years, which makes me exactly the right age for Saul Bellow.'

'How old is he?'

'Eighty-four.'

'You're too old for Lucian Freud, then.'

'Yeah, he's still in his seventies.'

'What are your plans?'

'I don't know.'

'When does the next project start?'

'It has started. I do a couple of hours a day, mostly back-reading at this stage, filling myself in on the local history. But, really, there isn't more than two hours in it, that and a few faxes. We won't start organising any field trips until later in the summer.'

'How do you propose to fill your time?'

'I had a call asking me if I wanted to contribute to a book of essays on the Bulger trial.'

'What did you say?'

'I said maybe, but in fact I think it's going to be no. I'm finished with that part of my life.'

'Nothing else at all?'

'I was thinking on the train about the possibility of writing a paper on the amnesty hearings in South Africa but it would require a long visit and I have unfinished business in Liverpool to do with my mother's affairs. A matter of some property in Dresden that my brother wants me to take care of and I have been trying to get out of. It's to do with finding out what happened to the factory my mother's parents owned, which originally made the cleanser.'

'That sounds like a good idea.'

'I'm glad you think so. There's a dire shortage of Communist beauty products. I'm sure they'll go like crazy at Harrods and Bloomingdales. Kiss my ass, Estée Lauder, we offer a *real* revolution in face-care.'

'Have you ever thought of psychotherapy?'

'I don't think it's for me.'

'Why is this?'

'I'm not going to spend fifty quid a week laying the sins of the world let alone my own, at Mummy and Daddy's door. I am intensely proud of my parents. All in all, given what they overcame, one way or another I think they were quite magnificent people. My mother certainly could be difficult but I don't begrudge her a few neuroses and I refuse to spend two years denouncing her and accusing my father of abusing me. Apart from that, what else is there to discuss? I don't have an eating disorder, I don't have an addictive personality.'

'Yes. And equally this is the source of your arrogance. Your problem, as I see it, is that you have an overload of self-esteem married to a critical sense of reality and you were like that when you were eighteen. You have no comfortable illusions about yourself while I, on the other hand, maintain several. It's an excellent form of self-protection. And whatever I don't like, I choose to ignore. No wonder you're in trouble, you worry away at life like a rabid dog.'

'What am I to do?'

'My shrink has a weekend workshop coming up. Why not try it? It isn't one to one. Just give it a go.'

'Not on your life. I can't stand that stuff, really I can't. It's not me. Forget it. Let's change the subject. Have you seen Helena lately?'

'Oh, my God, don't you know? She's got the Big C.'

'Where?'

'Ovaries.'

'No!'

I felt rage and fear. The women's cancers have felled a number of my friends. Breasts, ovaries and cervix all have a tendency to become diseased. A melon-like cyst grew in Marsha's womb and the whole bag of tricks was surgically removed last year. We're terrified of our bodies and the unfathomable things that are going on in there, the bleeding and the withering, the tendency of tumours to grow right inside our sexual selves. A few months ago at a private hospital on Marylebone Road I had had a mammogram. On the film they showed me how the tissue was thickening and small benign cysts dimpled the flesh, 'typical of the hormonal changes happening at your time of life.' This is the beginning of the Grand Climacteric which I was not looking forward to. Two years ago Marsha had run from her house in the middle of the night and the heat that came off her melted a pool of snow where she stood. I am already neurotic enough about my health without *this*.

My loving father was intolerant of illness in his children, diseases did not particularly interest him; nor did the miniature world at the far end of a microscope, with its writhing, passionless creatures, hold him in awe. 'Daddy! I am *sick*.' 'Here, let me look at you.' He held open my eyelids, made me expose my large red tongue. 'An infection. Eat a bowl of clear soup.' '*Daddy*! My head is splitting, my vision is blurry. Am I going to die?' 'Flu. Eat nothing.' '*Daddy*! I am fainting with pain, I have agonising cramps, Sam says I'm white as a sheet.' 'Periods. Go and talk to your mother.' I did not present a public-health case and my condition could not be improved by inside sanitation, adequate heating and ventilation, a damp course, regular bathing, or a well-balanced diet rich in calcium and vitamin C, since all of these were the normal condition of my existence in the house in Cressington Park with the yucca plant in the garden. A home in which I had my own bedroom, climbed into bed and was benighted only by fears that goblins inhabited the toy box that stood under the window. Using the state of my health as a strategy to get my father's attention inevitably turned in later life into a permanent state of hypochondria. At forty-nine I suffered from a multitude of symptoms that never cohered into an ailment that could be assaulted by a cure. 'Doctor, I've found a lump in my neck, here.' 'Alix, it's the lymph node that drains the tonsils.' 'Doctor, I feel drowsy all the time.' 'How high do you keep your central heating?' My mother's disease, which fell under a number of potential headings but wasn't quite any of them, developed after the death of my father and might also have been a response to the sudden withdrawal of his affection. He, on the other hand, didn't require any ploys to draw others to him. He was never a planet, always a sun.

'You could,' Marsha argued, 'come to that weekend workshop to study your hypochondria. You have to agree that's a full-blown neurosis.'

'I suppose.'

I arrived, a few days later, at a creaking houseboat moored at Little Venice. Deprived of our shoes, ordered to dress 'comfortably' (I wore a Jil Sander trouser suit and gold bracelets), we painfully sat cross-legged on the floor, shifting from one buttock to the other, and after a short period of deep breathing and visualisation we were ordered to announce to the group the single most important quality each of us would want the others to know about ourselves. I went last. The eleven preceding participants said, 'Well, it's very important to me that I'm a really *caring* person.' 'Me too!' 'And I would say the same.'

When it was my turn, I began with: 'When I think of myself, caring isn't the first word that comes to mind . . .' What I wanted to tell them was that I was tough. I came from a tough family and a tough city. I was exactly how my father had wanted his children to turn out: I was one hell of a tough Jew in a world where knowing how to look after yourself, how to survive, was as important as your nose being able to breathe in oxygen and your throat being able to swallow food. We, the Jews, were the century's first and foremost poster boys, the *ur*-victim, and all of us born after the war had been taught the same simple truth: that our blood was going to have to secrete a ferrous substance, so that our bones would be clad in iron.

But before I could move on to this exposition one of the women in the group, a blonde cow of a girl in a baby blue tracksuit and glasses with matching powder-blue rims, which magnified her blonde lashes and the powdery skin beneath her eyes, burst into tears. 'I feel very put down by what you've just said,' she announced, as tears rolled quickly and professionally down her cheeks. 'I feel that you have attacked my self-esteem.'

At this the axis of the group's attention shifted like the pointer in a magnet. Tissues rained from heaven. Ten other caring women comforted her and, as it turned out, I never did get to say what my 'quality' was and I understood, from a small triumphant smile I caught on her lardy face at lunchtime, that in a land where the victims were the kings, I was very soon going to find myself the sole member of a flattened subject race.

'Well, that didn't work,' I told Marsha.

'I admit from what you told me it was a bad start. What about a one-on-one? Please? For me?'

'Oh, all right.'

Veronica Losse, highly recommended by Marsha, sat opposite me on the edge of her navy sofa, neatly dressed in biscuit-coloured suede, her face unreadable – and that alone really gets on my nerves, people who don't let on, who see the absence of expression or passion as a means not just of self-control but of controlling *you*. My hands move while I talk, apparently, and I was pointing my finger at her.

'Do you even *know* the difference between "I feel" and "I think"?' I demanded, as she sat there. 'Is this analysis? Because if it is, you *analyse*, and to analyse you use your brain, mental processes, ever heard of those? How do I feel about not having had sex for two years and no prospect of any? How the fuck do you think I feel? What kind of a question is that? It's puerile. It's not worth answering. Explore my feelings? Why? They're not a foreign country, unmapped, unvisited. They are there, all the time. Rage. Yes. Tears, yes. Hurt, yes, there is pain. What is there to explore? Are you stupid?'

By mutual agreement, we decided not to continue.

Though one insight I did take away from that session was her assertion that my hypochondria was indeed a very obvious form of neurosis, a flowing of sexual energy back inwards towards the body it sprang from. The libido, if it could find no object to which it could attach itself, manifested in various forms, she explained, and in my case it was an eruption of aches, pains, menstrual cramps, a kind of dense, woody feeling in the skull, eczema on the hands and feet, bleeding gums, cold sores. Yet if anyone said, 'How are you, Alix?' I replied, automatically, 'Fine.' For I only feared myself to be ill and my repeated visits to the doctor were always to demand proofs that I was not.

'Did you tell her about the pregnancy?' Marsha asked.

'No.'

'Why not?'

'I don't know.'

Me, at thirty-six, the unknown baby growing in the wrong site, not in the expansive space of my womb but the narrow passage that leads to it, the Fallopian tube. Terminating far too early its journey from the ovaries, stubbornly, stupidly, fatally embedding itself somewhere where it cannot remain. The fertilised egg is hell-bent on its own metamorphosis, can't and won't stop, changes shape, acquires a head and vestigial limbs, curled like a comma, growing and growing until there's no more room and the walls of its long chamber expand until they can stretch no further and burst, ripping along the whole length, tearing into the ovary from where the child came, the child dying inside me, realising too late what it has done, that it has stopped short of the hospitable place, is never going to make it to the Promised Land. I feel a sharp pain, grow cold, icy sweat on my face. Can't stand, breathing shallow. On a trolley outside the theatre. The anaesthetist says, 'I'm going to press your neck then I want you to count to three.' The clock says 7.10 p.m. One, two, thr . . . Dreams rushing back into blackness like time reversed, of tall buildings, cities, powerlines, freeways. Cold. Incredibly cold. 'She's coming round.' 'Her blood pressure is still falling.' 'Put a blanket on her.' Panic in the voices. Someone is dying. Eyes opening. The clock says 8.50 p.m. 'Get a drip.' 'Can you raise your arm, dear?' 'Yes.' Under the mask on my face the word is soundless. Watch myself lift the tip of one finger, then it falls back. 'Pain.' Needle goes in. Morphine settles in my bloodstream. Maybe I'm going to die, I think. Too bad. And sleep. The nurse. 'Shall I ring your husband?' 'There is no husband.' He comes, finally, on the sixth day. 'What took you so long?' 'You don't need me. You've got your witches' coven.' I turn my head away because I don't want him to see me crying. 'Would you have had it?' 'No.' 'That's what I thought. Probably for the best in the long run.' 'I nearly died!' 'Yeah? We've all got to go some time.' I didn't see him again for six months. On St Martin's Lane by the opera house, I punched him, he stumbled, slipped and fell on his knees in the gutter while I slammed my briefcase round his head.

'Eat,' Marsha had said. 'Eat. Nourish yourself.'

I did, and lost my figure.

'*Who?*'

'He's Ernst and Dora's son, from America, our only cousin.'

'I never knew they had a son.'

'Neither did I.'

'Mamma never mentioned it, do you think *she* knew?'

'She had to, the guy's nearly sixty years old. He would have been born when she was working for that family in Stoke Newington, our grandparents would have told her.'

'What's he like?'

'Absolute pain in the arse. He's with his wife, she's no laughing matter either, younger than him, second marriage, I think. I've had enough of them bending my ear on the phone. Twice this morning already.'

'What happens now?'

'They're coming to Liverpool for a show-down, he wanted me to schlep up to London and meet them in their hotel but I said, "To hell with that. If you think you have a case, it's up to you to make it. I'm not dropping everything because you've got an idea in your head that you're owed something." They're flying up on Tuesday, you'd better get back here.'

'I really don't want to.'

'Because of Joseph Shields? Ignore it. He asked after you the other day. I'm sure the two of you could get on perfectly pleasantly if you run into each other.'

'He asked after me? What did he say?'

'Oh, I don't know. How are you, what are you up to, that kind of thing.'

'Did you talk to him?'

'What about?'

'For fuck's sake, Sam.'

'Oh, that. No. Why? What's there to say?'

'Well, to start with you could have said, "Why did you deceive my sister?"'

'Deceive, what kind of word is this?'

'Okay, you tell me, what do *you* make of his behaviour?'

'Alix, I've no idea. I'm not a mind-reader.'

'Exactly. Which is why you talk to someone, to find out what they're thinking.'

'Listen to me, do you think in all the time I've been married I haven't kissed another woman, not a woman I'm going to start an affair with but because you can't help yourself for a moment? You do it, and you know and she knows there's nothing more in it, it's like a form of flirtation.'

'Who? Who have you kissed? Does Melanie know?'

'I'm going now, I've got a waiting room full of druggies. Are you coming back or not?'

'I'll answer that if you tell me who you kissed. Do I know her?'

'I'll tell you who if you get yourself on a train.'

'I'll get on a train if you talk to Joseph Shields about what happened.'

'Come on, this is serious, will you stop playing games? Your personal life is none of my business. I don't care. You're behaving like a baby, grow up. What is it with women that you can't focus on what's important?'

Unbelievably, we kept this up for a further fifteen minutes until I agreed to get the next train to Liverpool and Sam agreed to talk to Joseph Shields the next time he saw him at the gym.

The night before the Dorfs arrived Sam said his strategy would be to keep talking. I had spent far too long in France watering geraniums while he stood in the magistrates' court day after day, arguing the toss, because as long as he was still on his feet, still speaking, the trial wasn't over and he might yet win the case. 'And afterwards the soft lads will mumble something because they have some dim idea they should say thank you, and their mams, who've come to court in their best shell-suit because it's an *occasion*, will turn to them and say, "I told you. Mr Rebick, he's the best. I remember him after the Toxteth riots, before you were born, when he was in the paper every day for what he did for Liverpool, standing up for the working class. But you see he takes after his dad, he was another wonderful feller." And then their lad is back home to watch telly for a couple of days until he can think up some other equally witless scam.' Sam walked through the city streets and people came up and shook him by the hand, as if he were a film star or an Everton striker or someone who had given the Beatles their first break. And that was true even of the ones who were sent down because no matter how long or hard he talked, nobody could get them off if they'd left their fingerprints everywhere and fenced the stuff they'd stolen to an off-duty policeman. But it didn't matter, he was Sam Rebick, the solicitor, a Yid, true, but neither Catholic nor Protestant; he was immune to the tribal battles that had choked the city and could be trusted to be fair to all comers, like Brian Epstein, another Yid who put Liverpool on the map.

This was who confronted the couple, sitting on his excruciating chairs in the Albert Dock flat, venting their sense of aggrievement, conscious that they had not only been unscrupulously robbed of a fortune but had been forced to endure since they had been in Liverpool what they considered to be spectacularly low levels of service from our hotel trade. Staying at the Atlantic Towers, she, for example, had asked at Reception if there was a gym where she could continue her exercise regime, which her trainer back home had told her should never be interrupted for more than two days and had given her a stack of clippings explaining the risks to her health if she ignored the warning. No, the desk clerk had told her, 'But you can run up and down the stairs if you like, it's free of charge.'

Our cousin Peter, tall, white-fleshed, fishy, was jabbing his finger at Sam. 'Your lawyers made no attempt to trace us.'

'Why should they? We didn't even know you existed. You expect me to put a notice in every paper in the whole of America saying, "Hey, anyone got any long-lost cousins in England? If so, give us a bell, there's a pile of money waiting for you"?'

'You're going to have to prove you didn't know about us when this thing gets to court. I was informed that you are yourself an attorney. They may take your licence away. Do you realise that?'

Lauren, the wife, was nodding hard. She was years younger than her husband, reddish curls, leather pants, snakeskin boots. It turned out that it was she who in the hairdresser's had read a magazine article about the new Rose Rosen cleansing cream and its fascinating history. Why should she not recognise the family Dorf? It was her own married name. Friends started to ring her and enquire, 'Is this you?'

'How did you trace us?' I asked.

'From the telephone directory. My dad said he had a sister in England who married a guy called Rebick from Liverpool, a town I recognised when I was growing up because of the Beatles, so as a name it stuck in my memory, though I was too old for that kind of music. I preferred the Everly Brothers and Buddy Holly, which came a little earlier. There were a lot of Rebicks but directory assistance gave me all of them and I started with Rebick, Abraham, and his widow answered the phone and I told her I was looking for a Lotte Rebick and she gave me your number immediately. It wasn't hard at all.'

'Two transatlantic calls,' Lauren interrupted. 'That's an expense we'll be claiming.'

'Sounds like you're short of a bob or two,' Sam said, looking at the diamond ring on her finger. He knew how to get at people where it hurt. Peter and Lauren lived in a town called Hartford, in Connecticut, where Ernst, after a long struggle, had re-established his doll factory (selling out far too soon to Mattel to have made serious money) and Peter had been brought up there and gone into early mainframe computer design.

'I can support my family,' Peter said, his pale skin flushing. 'This is a matter of rights.'

'So you're asking for a three-way split?'

'Absolutely not. Fifty-fifty. You and your sister can share your half. And, of course, we'll also need substantial compensation from the profits you made on the product before you sold out to Rose Rosen.'

'Listen, my father created something from nothing. There was an empty glass jar with a hardened smear of cream around the screw lines. He had it analysed, he had it made up. Our grand-mother never gave your father a jar of that stuff . . .'

'That's not true. In fact, she gave some to my mother before they left Germany in 1939.'

'And what did she do with it?'

'She used it up and threw out the jar, what do you think she would have done with it? But none of that is important because what we are talking about here is a matter of intellectual prop-erty theft.'

'Rubbish. If anyone had any rights over the formula of the cream after 1939 it was the Nazis. Our grandparents *sold* it to them in exchange for their own lives and those of your parents as well. I've no idea what happened to the production of it after the war but Rose Rosen couldn't find a trace. The lawyers went back to look for the original pharmacist who invented it, found the guy – that is, found the record of his death in Bergen-Belsen and every other member of his family. And, by the way, have *you* talked to the Rosen lawyers?'

'Not yet, but we will.'

'Bluff,' Sam said later, when they'd gone. 'The Rosen people would crucify him, they'd eat him alive.'

'How can you be so certain, Sam?' Melanie asked him, clearing away the coffee cups and the uneaten fruit cake and scones she'd bought. 'You don't know anything about this kind of law.'

'I know that they don't have the money they would need to pursue the type of lawsuit they're talking about. If they'd turned up earlier when we were still in negotiations we would have been dropped like hot coals. But the position they're in now is that they have to establish that Rose Rosen acquired the company unlawfully without having taken proper steps to find out whether who they were buying it from had the right to sell. I don't think they're going to get all that far. Rose Rosen has thrown a huge marketing budget at this thing and they're not going to have its image sullied by allegations of fraud.'

'Do they have rights?' I asked.

'I don't think so. Who owns the formula? We were the ones who took out a patent on it, back in the fifties. I mean, Dad did.'

'What about the factory?'

'That's another matter. To that they are indeed entitled to the same compensation as we are.'

'What do we do?'

'Convince them that they have no case worth pursuing on the Rose Rosen sell-out, but that if they join forces with us on the restitution claim, they have a chance of actually getting somewhere. I bet they don't even know about the factory – at least, they never mentioned it.'

'What do we think of them, as people I mean?' Melanie asked. 'How do you feel, confronted by your own relatives?'

'More relatives. We're swamped with them already on Dad's side,' I said.

'He's awful. She's quite cute.'

'Cute?'

'Yeah, in that kittenish way some women have – don't worry, Mel, I'm only winding you up.'

Our parents looked down at us in frames from the walls. What would they have made of this new twist in our family fortunes? I know what Dad would say and now it's time to talk about my father, Saul Rebick, about who he was and what he came from and why his legacy attached us to the city of our birth and refused to release us.

How my parents met, what a story that was: it goes back deep into their opposite childhoods. What could have brought them together, one the offspring of settled, cultured, contented affluence, the other of *shtetl* pond-life? What was my father doing in Maccabi House in West Hampstead one evening, where he saw the pretty young refugee from Germany and she told him her story and six months later they were married?

'Your father, you have to understand,' my watery-eyed uncles and aunts told me in their old age, 'was the baby, and that meant everything, *everything*.' He was the pampered, clever, argumentative kid – the One, the chosen child for whom nothing was too good because the fate of the Rebicks rested on him. Were they one day going to be big-shots or stay where they were, moderately getting by? My father was a flaming torch they were throwing into the future, he was supposed to light up the way forward and burn down every obstacle in the path of those who came after him. In his infancy, during and just after the First World War, the Rebicks were suffering from an accelerating attrition rate. Two girls had died together, wrapped in each other's arms, in the world-wide influenza epidemic of 1919 and a six-year-old son had been killed when a dog barked at a brewery wagon on Leece Street, and the horse plunged into the pavement trampling four children on their way to school. Their bloody, battered bodies were carried home in the arms of screaming, sobbing Irish and Jewish women and laid out on cold horsehair sofas in bitter front parlours, which no one ever went into because your breath froze the moment you stepped inside. After these catastrophes, the oldest boys (Wolf, Ike, Hersch, Abie) became the *de facto* heads of the family, charged with translating my grandparents' anguished laments to the various English-speaking authorities. The old people (though the father was only in his fifties and the mother a little younger than I am now) were simply crushed. They had left Poland knowing they would never again see their own parents, because nothing was there for them on the banks of the river Bug but heartbreak and suffering, violence and more violence. 'What you needed in Poland was a gun,' said my uncle Wolf, who remembered from his childhood shots in the night, a fire, his mother's stifled scream. 'But how could a Jew get a gun? Impossible.' Now *in America*, none of these tragedies, these terrible, unnecessary deaths, would have happened, which my grandparents knew because they both had brothers in New York, who wrote and told them nothing about foetid tenements and sweatshops and strikes and going from door to door looking for work, but only of the wonders of the Flatiron Building and Coney Island ice-cream and nephews studying science at City College.

They were tailors and cutters, at first, the brothers. Then they schlepped handcarts or sold buttons or peddled chamois leather from door to door. Eventually they got a market stall, then came a shop, a little business that made enough money if you worked all hours God sent, and they did work, worked their fingers to the bone, Bessie and Ruthie, the sisters, included, so that when Saul won the scholarship – up against a hundred other boys and still he beat them hollow – he would have everything on the list that the school required for its new pupils: the blazer with the crest on it, the cap, the tie, the flannel shorts, the grey socks, the initialled handkerchiefs. Not to mention the satchel, the pencils, the rulers, the compass – the whole geometry set – and, above all, the fountain pen to which six separate people contributed for his bar mitzvah present. The fountain pen! It had a silver nib. It came in its own leather presentation box, lying on a cushion of imitation silk. And because so much was invested in the future of Saul Rebick, upon whom so many of the community's hopes and dreams and aspirations rested, an extra ninepence was wrung out of their pockets to pay for his initials to be engraved on the side of the barrel.

Top marks, for Saul. Top marks in everything. What was the alternative? To come home with a report from his teachers saying, could try harder, could do better? No, top marks were the only marks he could bring into the house. Where did stupidity get you? It got you to Liverpool when you thought you were on your way to New York. At eighteen he was accepted at university to study medicine. The first Rebick ever to have an education, the first Rebick to shoot off to the stars, the first Rebick to light a match to the rocket of professional ambition. All through the thirties my father was passing examinations, every single one with merit or distinction or honours, until by 1940 there were no more exams to take and he was fully qualified as a doctor and a member of a reserved occupation. Then, for the first time in his obedient, studious, disciplined life, Saul Rebick let his family down. When he came home on the day there was nothing left to achieve, having that morning joined the army as an enlisted man, they screamed at him, they wailed. Herschel threatened to go down himself and tell the army to tear the papers up. Bessie wept. Ruthie slammed the door and went out. Ike, the TB case, the reasonable brother, lost his temper. Private Rebick! He could have been an officer! But no, my father wouldn't give in, he wanted to 'do his bit'. He didn't want to sit on his backside and give orders or join the intelligence service or serve as an army doctor, stitching people up. He wanted to march with a gun, and when he got within firing range of Nazis, kill them.

Years of study had suppressed the yearnings for action that seethed inside the twenty-five-year-old hot-head he was now. A good boy all his life, the war had given him the chance to unleash the aggression that surged in him when he sat, night after night, studying, learning, cramming his head full of facts, while his brothers looked at the reflection of their brilliantined heads in the mirror before putting on their hats and going out to dancehalls where they did the Charleston and met girls and took them home and kissed them. But Saul barely knew the city he lived in. He walked a narrow corridor between his parents' house off Brownlow Hill to the Jewish school on Hope Place, then to the Institute, on Myrtle Street, then the university, none of them more than a few minutes away. He didn't need so much as to get on a tram. Kids were running down to the dock road and getting taken on the ships in their trade: barber, baker, cook. They saw the world, came back speaking of the Orinoco, of the Gold Coast, of Vancouver and Shanghai. He'd seen nothing, been nowhere. This was my father at the outbreak of the war. About to hurl himself at Hitler, ready to march on Berlin, with or without permission, he was coming, ready or not.

Having disembarked in Southampton in January 1946 five years later, my father sent a telegram to his mother (his father had died of fright during an air raid in the May blitz of 1941; that is, his heart had stopped at the precise moment the heavy thump of a land-mine shook the shelter at the bottom of the yard), saying that he wanted a week to see the sights of London before he came back to talk to the brothers about the arrangements for finally going to America. And this is how close it gets to me being an American-born woman, a citizen of the New World instead of a subject of a dying empire, that is, an individual for whom anything would be possible. What happened? A well-brought-up young Jewish man arrives in London, the capital of the country he has lived in his whole life except for three humid years in the Burmese jungle. He goes to the Tower of London, to the British Museum, to the National Gallery. He stands outside Buckingham Palace waiting for a glimpse of the lovely young princesses. He rides a red bus because he may be a war veteran but, still, he's a kid at heart. He's staying in Clapton, sleeping in the spare room of an army pal, Joe Silver, who is back at home living with his parents. In the evenings they go to Maccabi House and sit around drinking tea and ignoring the noise from the next room where the teenagers are hanging around in their zoot suits fed up with being told to pipe down by the old men who have come back from the war.

The political situation is difficult. Europe is full of refugees, the government is trying to keep the Jewish DPs out of Palestine, and there's plenty of anti-Semitism at home. Colin Brooks, one-time secretary to Lord Rothermere, the press baron, writes an article urging Jews to quit Britain (for where?) and hand over their homes to returning ex-servicemen. One day, my father is drinking a cup of coffee when Gerry Flamberg, Alec Carson and Len Sherman come back from a ruck in Hampstead. They've broken up a fascist meeting, not defended themselves but gone on the offensive. Up at Jack Straw's Castle, having a pint, they've heard Jeffrey Hamm, the Mosley sidekick, ranting about 'the aliens in our midst, the black-marketeers who'd made money out of the war', and they've waded in and given him a kicking. Because, believe it or not, and this is news to most people, the war has only been over five minutes and the Nazis are organising again. A couple of weeks later, my father sat in Maccabi House, one of thirty-eight men and five women, and became a founder member of the 43 Group, which during the next three years would stop post-war fascism dead in its tracks.

What was America to this? Who would sail to America when you could go out on a Saturday morning (part of a commando force) and grab handfuls of some anti-Semitic rag on street corners and trample it into the gutter? When, hearing through the grapevine that Hamm ('whose name told you everything you need to know about him, as far as the Yidden are concerned') was holding another of his festivals of blackshirt propaganda, you could break up the meeting by rushing the platform and sending it and Hamm flying, and when the thugs came at you with knives and knuckle-dusters, feel the weight of thirty or forty stone of Jewish muscle pushing behind you, screaming, 'Let's give them a good hiding, lads,' and 'This will shut your filthy mouth, you toe-rag.' They had blond-haired, blue-eyed Jews who infiltrated headquarters and tipped off the boys back at Maccabi House when the next meeting was going to be, so the Group was always there to break it up. Middle-class boys from Kensington, public-school types – or actors who could make themselves sound like Leslie Howard, if they wanted – were *agents provocateurs*, who got inside the Mosleyite discussion groups, genteel occasions where, over coffee and biscuits, after the Wagner and the Mozart (*bona fide* Aryan composers), they would artlessly remark, 'I must say this, and I hope it doesn't offend any of you here, but I'm rather glad Mosley has started up again and if he puts Britain first and gets rid of the Jews, I, for one, would seriously consider joining him, wouldn't you?' Then go back to Maccabi House with the names of those who had enthusiastically taken up their comments and gone much, much further.

My father was always in demand to bandage head-wounds

and set broken arms and filch splints from the surgery in Swiss Cottage where he was in temporary work as a locum, but he resisted every effort to make him the Group's official doctor. He was a commando, he was a fighter, he was the scourge of every street-corner Hitler from Brondesbury to Bethnal Green. Saul Rebick, the good boy, the passer of exams with honours, distinctions and merits, had turned himself into one of the 'fucking hard-case Yids' who never stopped beating up fascists until he met my mother and brought her back home to Liverpool, and was still there, forty years later, when he died in his sleep one night aged seventy, from lung cancer, because they'd never get him when he was awake. Awake, he always had a plan.

Liverpool made me. My father's city was mine too. Be tough, survive. The message came in two voices, from the mouth of the Mersey and the mouth of Saul Rebick, who returned there in August 1947, a red-hot socialist (politics he picked up in the East End and from the Jewish Communists who did not control the 43 Group but who wanted to recruit from it) and seasoned anti-fascist street fighter, together with his young wife, a damaged girl who got on the train at Euston station believing she was being taken away from barbarism to civilisation, in other words, she thought she was going from austerity Britain to the fabulous shores of America where people were starting to drive cars the size of ocean-going liners. He *was* taking her there, he had every intention, but there was unfinished business, a plea from his brother Abie who wrote to tell him of some local disturbances:

You should see the streets, broken glass everywhere, all the Jewish shops with their windows smashed, though everyone will tell you it's mostly just a load of hooligans on the grab and looting is the real name of the game. They're sending the kids in to pick up as many pots and pans and schmattes as they can carry and on one level,

you can't blame them. If they can't get what they want on
the ration they'll get it another way but there's a story
going round about how the goyim are saying, get the Jews,
get the stuff and get into the shops. The community is
terrified. They think the police are going to take care of
everything and they're too frightened to make a fuss when
they don't. Come back, Saul. You can sail to America
from Liverpool. Just come back for a few days to help us
sort things out.

So my father came home and began organising. He got
together a defence committee, ruled them along the same lines
as he had learned in the 43 Group, sent them out across the city
to Jewish shops and businesses, showed them what to do. And
by the time the trouble had died down two things were in the
process of being born, my brother Sam safe in my mother's
womb, and in London, in Parliament, the National Health
Service, free medicine for anyone who wanted it. To miss this?
No way. 'Darling,' my father said, 'how can we make a start in
America when we have a little tiny baby, with no one to help
you, when here there's my sisters, all of them with children of
their own, and there, I'd have to support my family on what?
Five years in the army and a year or two as a locum? It doesn't
add up to much. But if I hang around for a few months and I
help this great enterprise get on to its feet, then we're talking.
This is the kind of opportunity that comes along once in a lifetime, to do good, to make something of yourself as a man, a
human being, a *mensch*. Listen, Lotte, we're going to America,
have no doubt of that, but we're young, we have the whole of
our lives ahead of us, and sometimes you have to do what's
necessary, so one day you can stand up straight before God and
look him in the eye and say, "Here's my record, this is what I
did."'

On Upper Parliament Street he opened his surgery. They came in with rickets and pink-eye and cancer and blighted lungs, they sat in his waiting room, the scum of the city, poorest of the poor, and he went to their houses and saw damp running down the walls, saw outside privies, six kids in a bed, two families in a room, cured their bodies with penicillin, but more than that, he went to the corporation with them, stood by them and spoke for them, said, 'How can you keep people in these conditions? Rehouse them, do it now.'

He wasn't the only one, there were other heroes like him, but it was in the sixties that he rose as a god in the hearts of the women of Liverpool and they blessed him, silently. You know why my father was St Saul of Liverpool 8? What it came down to was this: he wasn't a Catholic. You went to your GP and he told you, 'I can't sign the form, I'm afraid, I won't have it on my conscience. You can cope, Mary, talk to your priest, you'll manage, a big strong girl like you, you're made for babies, your mother will help you, a fine family she's brought up, all of you in work, no troublemakers.' 'If you won't sign, I'll go to the clinic. Dr Rebick gives permission.' 'Dr Rebick is not of our faith, he doesn't know the true Lord.' 'Everyone says he's a good man.' 'So he is, but led astray. This is murder, do you realise that?' The local Catholic paper did an editorial on him once: 'Dr Saul Rebick understands in his heart the sufferings of the people of Liverpool but he does not know the suffering of Our Lord Jesus Christ on the cross.'

Had Lotte and Saul gone to America, would my mother have healed the breach between herself and Ernst? Probably. Separated from her parents, from her resentment of their abandonment of her, perhaps the two of them would have got along; she always liked her sister-in-law Dora back in Dresden, who was kind and gave her dolls and other pretty presents. But Liverpool held her, it would not let her go. And now her two children were left to deal with what remained, the unfinished business that was still here to torment us.

'Do you think I should get rid of the grey in my hair?' Melanie said, when Sam had gone to bed and she had set up the ironing board in front of the TV.

'How can you ask me that? I've been telling you for years you should do something about it. Why ask now?'

'Lauren said something to me.'

'She what?'

'When I showed her where the bathroom was, she said to me, "You could be a gorgeous woman if you'd do something about your hair."'

'How dare she?'

'Well, it gets worse. She practically ordered me into the bedroom and wanted to take a look at my makeup. She was picking everything up and telling me the colours were out of date or they were the wrong shade.'

'That fucking bitch.'

'Well, I felt that way myself but actually, after a while, I think she was just trying to be helpful, I'm not sure that there was any malice in it. She offered to come back and give me a makeover.'

'What did you answer to that?'

'That I'd think about it.'

'What else did she say?'

'Nothing much, asked about the kids, I asked her if she had any and she said no. Probably doesn't want to lose her figure.'

'Yes, that's exactly the type she is. But she does have a point about your hair.'

'When do you have yours done?'

'Every four weeks.'

'As often as that? It must cost a fortune.'

'Yes, and it's time-consuming, but if you don't want the roots
to show, that's the price you have to pay.'

'My hairdresser said he'd put in some blonde highlights
because it would be easier to maintain.'

'Not a bad idea at all.'

'It's not me, though. Somehow I can't see myself as a blonde.'

'I understand what you're saying but why not give it a go?'

'In truth I'd rather *let myself* go.'

'What do you mean?'

'Sometimes I see myself in a house on the edge of Lake
Windermere with a garden and a boat, maybe a little business of
some kind that I could run from home.'

'What kind of business?'

'I've no idea.'

'Sam would never go for it.'

'No, I know he wouldn't. Not in a million years.'

'You could buy somewhere and have it for the weekends.'

'I'd like that.'

'What would you do all day?'

'Read, walk, grow flowers.'

'You'd be bored. I was.'

'That's because you're fundamentally discontented and I'm
not.'

'You mean there's nothing missing from your life?'

'Not really.'

'So why are you thinking of going blonde?'

'I'm not, it was something my hairdresser said.'

Do you know what she did, between bringing up three children and working for the family-planning clinic? She was a
member of the Chevra Kaddisha, she was one of the women
who volunteered to do the *tahara*, to wash and dress the bodies of
the dead and prepare them for the grave. 'How can you?' her
children asked her. 'Because,' she answered, 'it is a *mitzvah*.' A

good deed. And who will give you thanks for it? The stiff? The family? No, it was enough to do it for the act itself. It was Melanie who wrapped my mother in linen and laid her in her pine box in the earth. A boyfriend of mine once left me for another woman. 'What's she got that I haven't?' I demanded. A still centre, apparently, which usually means that they are stupid. You could be deluded into thinking that Melanie, who did not talk and argue and interrupt, as Sam and I did, possessed this inner stillness but it was not that at all. There was a core of moral seriousness inside her – I thought about justice, she felt it intuitively, she knew without recourse to books or rabbis what was the difference between right and wrong. At times she came across as spiky, with her pronouncements on adultery, but that wasn't her at all. She just took a ground zero approach to ethics.

So I knew what was coming next.

'You learned your lesson with Joseph Shields?'

'Yes. I learned my lesson.'

'Good. I agree with Sam, by the way, I think you should take on that business with the factory. It's exactly the kind of thing you excel at. You have every necessary skill for this. I wouldn't know where to start.'

'*Agree*? You put him up to it.'

'What makes you think that?'

'I'm not daft. You wanted to get me out of the way.'

'Yes, and you ignored what I told you and look how it turned out. A disaster. You wound up hurt and angry, nothing was accomplished. A rejection you needed like a hole in the head. You did yourself no good. Didn't I warn you?'

'Yes.'

'So, the factory?'

'We're turning into a money magnet, our family.'

'I know, and I can't think of anything to do with it all.'

'You could buy the cottage.'

'Not really. It's Sam's money not mine.'

'He wouldn't begrudge you.'

'Of course not, but he'd never go there.'

'He wouldn't mind if you went.'

'Maybe not, but that's not how you keep a marriage together, leading separate lives.'

'Isn't it? I don't know. Perhaps you each need some kind of autonomy.'

'I wouldn't buy a place in the Lake District just for me. I'd be worried that I'd never come back.'

I sat in front of the mirror by the light that comes from across the Atlantic, which even in summer is strong and cold, and saw my face with pouches of darkly pigmented skin beneath my eyes, little spiders weaving their Gothic webs around my mouth. Tiny red thread-veins are crawling over my nose. Every single day, after I cleanse and tone and exfoliate and moisturise, I spend twenty minutes concealing all the damage I have accrued simply by being alive and exposed for forty-nine years. A man's dermis is thicker than a woman's. Even without the protective barrier of expensive creams they age more slowly than us. The presentation of a woman's beauty is an arduous activity. You're arresting disaster and death and this takes time and money. Male or female, if you're poor and unattractive no one's going to love you even if you have a heart of gold. A woman who had been a babe at twenty, with a bad marriage and a hard menopause, can look like Norman Mailer at sixty; what a reward for a lifetime's struggle, not to give us the power of men but to make us look like them.

Assembled in front of me, set out neatly on a table, were powders of various colours, creams of different consistencies and brushes of a number of sizes, my *batterie de maquillage*, and I started to make up my face. First a tube of flesh-coloured liquid out of which I squeezed a few drops on to my palms where I warmed them for a few moments, gently patting my hands together. Then I pressed the liquid on to my cheeks, smoothed it across my nose and forehead, opened my mouth wide as if I was going to scream, to take the foundation down below the line of my jaw. It was a mask at this very early stage, cheeks, forehead, chin, lips and eyes were the same pale beige, but there was a lot more to be done. A small palette contained a denser cream of a darker shade and I took a tiny amount of foundation and poured it on to the surface. I picked up a brush with a pointed tip, dipped it into the concealer and mixed the two substances together to make it creamier and easier to apply. Then I painted this concoction over the dark circles under my eyes and blended the edges, using a small sponge to pat it into the skin, so all looks as natural as possible. Next I turned my attention to my eyelids. I opened a square black lacquered box and in it were four shades of eye-shadow ranging from ivory to dark brown. With another brush, I applied a sheer layer of the ivory powder across the whole of the eyelid. Then I put that brush away and picked up a third and I adhered as much of the taupe power to it as I could, and ran it lightly across the soft lower lid, below the bone. A brush with the finest tip of all I put into my mouth to wet, and I rubbed it over the surface of the dark brown powder and with great care, and thirty-five years' experience, I drew a straight line just above the lashes. Next the mascara, perhaps the most difficult of all the aspects of makeup to apply: to separate the lashes, make them darker and longer without clumps and clogs is an art with which few people ever get to grips, though I am one of them, because I understand the necessary precaution of always *wiping the wand on a tissue first*, which wastes a considerable amount of product but ensures the best and most even application, a tip I picked up when I was seventeen after the demise of the old block mascara, which required wetting with your own spittle, a habit, as we have seen, which I have never quite broken. My spit is an essential part of my kit.

To the brows. Stepping out of the bath or shower I always look in the magnifying mirror and if there are any stray hairs I pluck them with tweezers (manufactured as precision instruments in Switzerland) while the pores are open. This causes me exquisite, eye-watering, sneezing pain but I do it anyway.

Eyebrows are the frame of the face. In order to make two perfect dark arches the next step was to take yet another brush, the size and shape of a toothbrush but with a narrower row of bristles, and I pressed this on to the surface of the same brown shade of powder and took it through the brows. Finally, I applied a little gel with my fingers and finished them off by setting every hair straight and flat with a tiny comb. And now my attention could be turned elsewhere, to magic! A gold wand. The cap removed reveals a brush and if you push a button at the end of the barrel a small amount of a pearly cream emerges on to the bristles. This is what you call a miracle product, it goes on every part of the face where shadows collect: the deep creases beneath the wings of the nostrils, the cleft of the chin and the curved place between chin and lower lip. A dab next to each eye widens and brightens the face. Another spot, on the frown line between the brows, relaxes the forehead. The face was now ready for its final decoration, having been prepared for colour. The penultimate step is blusher, cream or powder, and I have always used the latter, a box of dusty rose pink, the fattest of my brushes dabbed on to it and a swoop across the cheekbones, nothing too intense, we don't want to look like a Dutch doll. Which leaves the lips, my fat full Jewish gob. A thin pencil draws the outline. The last and final brush paints in the interior in brilliant red, a true Chanel red, what in a child's paintbox might be called 'Crimson Lake'. I took a paper tissue and placed it on my mouth, pressed my lips on to it so the outer layer of lipstick was rubbed away leaving a scarlet stain, which is driven deep into the pores. Next a very fine dusting of powder (almost all of which is brushed away but a few motes are left to give a second application of lipstick something to adhere to) and these stages were repeated a total of three times. A touch of sticky lip-gloss applied to the centre of the upper and lower lips gives a Bardot-esque pout and I was finished.

This is the face the world sees, not the one revealed after I have used my mother's cleansing cream. My basic techniques, improved on by the *Vogue* stylist, were bequeathed to me by Mamma, sitting at her own dressing-table while I watched and learned what it was to be female, to subdue the toughness that my father taught his children, to soften it beneath a layer of artifice. At university I had rebelled against these black arts, but that was at twenty when a face can afford to be as it pleases. The white terry-towelling band was unwrapped from my hairline, a spray of Van Cleef & Arpels Birmaine on my neck and wrists and in my hair, and I was ready to get dressed. Since my teens I had worn black lace bras but black lace now made me look like a middle-aged whore leaning against a wall. White was virginal, red out of the question, flesh-coloured fabric resembles anything but flesh. This left brown, chocolate brown, which was hard to find but not impossible. I wore chocolate brown bras and chocolate brown panties and my chocolate brown pubic hair curled around the edges. I stepped into a black linen shift dress and fastened red suede sandals across my manicured toes, varnished in a shade to match my lipstick, and I was dressed.

I had come out that morning first for a manicure, then to have what was bound to be a difficult, taxing lunch with Peter Dorf in which my aim was to charm and woo him. An initial writ had been issued to us, Sam and me, and to the Rose Rosen corporation, which had met it with an assault so deadly and terrible, so ferocious in its legal firepower, that the couple seemed dazed, shattered by the response. A phone call I had received from corporate headquarters' legal department indicated that they considered the buy-out closed, *finito*. It had been up to the Dorfs themselves to come forward at the appropriate moment and establish a claim. If they had failed to do so out of ignorance of their inheritance, that was their problem. *Goodbye.* I brought up the business of the Dresden factory. Rose Rosen said that was nothing to do with them. If it could be reclaimed, then the story would be interesting for publicity purposes, but as far as they were concerned, they wished us well and we were on our own. Sam and I had divided the two of them between us: I took on Peter, he dealt with Lauren. Such was their crushing legal humiliation, they needed building up again. 'Make them feel part of the family,' Sam advised me. 'Schmooze him, Alix.' I can do that, if necessary, though anyone who knew me in the slightest would observe, 'Of course, it's all an act.'

Starbucks opened up last year right by the town hall, just along from the law courts – we're really on the map now. Early, I stepped in for a coffee and a nosh and Joseph Shields was sitting there reading the paper, his hard hat on the chair next to him, a big hand extended to scratch his big back, a bagel half-way to his mouth with the other hand. I would have run off down the street but a woman with a push-chair was coming out and I had to hold the door open for her so he looked up and saw me, and beckoned me in.

Sam hadn't talked to him, despite repeated nagging and nudging, no, 'What de fuck you do to my sister?' 'It's beyond him,' Melanie said. 'Go and knock your head against a brick wall, you'll have more luck. He isn't built that way, he isn't made for male buddy-buddying. You should face facts, Alix, he's a guy and they're not like us and it's stupid to try to get them to be any other way, which you would understand if you'd ever been married or lived with someone long enough.'

Sam said to me, 'You know, you can bet he's forgotten all about it. Pretend nothing happened. Because at the end of the day, Alix, *nothing did.*'

I bought coffee and a bagel and sat down. 'So,' I said, 'how is the hotel going?'

He seemed not in the slightest bit discomforted or embarrassed by my presence; there appeared to be no self-consciousness. 'I've replaced the cracked glass sections that you saw and the roof is going on.'

'Any more vandalism?'

'I finally have that meeting with Humphreys' lieutenant in a few days' time.'

'Did Sam arrange it?'

'Yes, we're going together. I want to fix this thing once and for all.'

'So what you been doing lately?'

'As it happens, I've been back in Chicago seeing my family.'

'Very nice. How's your wife?'

'She's . . . fine.' What's this? A hesitation in his voice?

'I went to Chicago, years ago.'

'You know America well?'

'Yeah, pretty well, I travelled after I left university, worked on a fairground in Maryland for a few months as a ride operator, pulling levers on the bumper cars, that kind of thing, then I hitched to California, up over the top, the high line, the truckers called it, across Montana and North Dakota, and back again to New York.'

'If my daughter wanted to do that I'd tie her wrists together, I'd lock her in the house before she did anything so crazy.'

'I can't say I blame you, with hindsight.'

'Did you run into any trouble?'

'A bit, yes.'

'What was the worst you ever got into?'

'That's easy. Once, in southern California, I got a ride from a Mexican. I was trying to get from LA to San Francisco. We were on the freeway, talking about this and that, I think Nixon, maybe, because this was during Watergate, and suddenly right out of the blue he pulled a knife and drove off on to a road that led into the desert, one hand on the wheel, the other hand with the blade bobbing up and down on my neck and all the time raving about *el gringo* and what we've done to the Hispanics, our racism. I sat there thinking, I don't believe this. I don't believe that I'm twenty-one and I'm going to die in the desert, my throat cut by a maniac. It wasn't possible.'

'My God, what happened?'

'I kept talking. I knew there was no way at all that I could defeat him physically, so I thought I could calm him down, just outwit him psychologically, and I suppose that's what happened. After a few miles he stopped the car and let me out.'

'And you went on hitchhiking after that?'

'Sure. What were my options? I didn't have any credit cards in those days. I had a book of traveller's cheques and that was it, all I had.'

'Could you have called your parents?'

'I suppose, but it wasn't part of my purpose.'

'Which was what?'

'A freedom.'

'From your family?'

'Exactly.' From the suffocation of it, of being a Rebick and of being a Dorf. I was remembering another time, at night, somewhere in Nebraska where two roads forked and the driver of the truck I was in was going one way and I was going the other. He let me out and I was standing by the side of the road under a great starlit sky, the bowl of evening, and I saw for the first time the crescent moon not as a cut-out shape but as a three-dimensional object, whose face was part in shadow. And I was utterly alone, utterly anonymous, more solitary than I had known it was possible to be, out there in the middle of a nothingness I had not even imagined. In England, in the middle of nowhere, you walk a mile and you come to a village, civilisation is always moments away, but here, I knew could never walk far enough to find a refuge, that I would be dead and that maybe it would take years before anyone would find me. I understood then what America was and what I was not, that there was nothing in me that was American, nothing that understood space in this way, that I had only the faintest instinct for what it was to be of another country. That everything I knew was about history and how you were rooted and where, and that was true even of an immigrant family who could say every year, "'Once we were slaves in the land of Egypt.'"

'How long were you on the road?'

'Six months.'

'And then?'

'Then I came back and enrolled for an MA at the London School of Economics.'

'As a father I consider what you've told me a shocking story but on the other hand it exhibits a strong energy. My youngest son lacks any direction of any kind.'

'What's the matter with him?'

He told me this story about a kid who plainly had not the slightest interest in or aptitude for learning, a gentle, caring boy. I remembered those smug women in that therapy group, 'I think of myself as a *caring* person.' I supposed this Michael didn't think of himself in any way at all, just had a certain set of impulses, which reminded me of some of the better carers in the home where my mother lived her last years and died, the ones who did what I could never do in a million years, simply *be* with someone. To know how just to be is something that has always eluded me. These people possess the tranquillity that so far I have utterly failed to find in myself but I have seen them, the women and occasionally men who can sit and be a presence, without motion or enquiry, the force of them being in their selves rather than in what they do. But I'm not like that and I doubt I ever will be.

'I love him so much,' he said, 'and I just can't stand seeing him make a mess of his life. You've no idea how it hurts. Only a parent could know.'

'Well, look at it this way, maybe only a parent, who for all the right reasons is blinded by love, is exactly the kind of person who *can't* see a way out. Have you asked yourself why he has to stay at school?'

'Because he has to go to school.'

'Not necessarily. From what I understand your son is a natural-born carer of other people. There's lots of jobs that need that. Not highly paid jobs, that's certain, but there are jobs. He could be a social worker or a nurse or someone who does something with children, I don't know, but it seems to me that that's where his abilities lie.'

'Yeah? Well, even for those jobs you need plenty of qualifications, you need a college degree.'

'What's the rush? Why not pull him out of school for a couple of years, let him look after your parents, get the feel for whether this is what he wants to do with his life or not. Then when he's got some sense of direction he can go back, get his high-school diploma and apply to college to get the qualification for whatever it is he's chosen. Seems simple enough.'

He was totally silent.

'So?'

'I should have thought of that. I'm a fucking idiot.'

'Logic, Joseph.'

'I know, I know – what's more, *military* logic.'

'What?'

'Nothing.'

'You said military logic. Were you in the army?'

'Yes.'

'Vietnam?'

'No, Israeli.'

'Well!' I was stunned. A soldier! A Jewish soldier! The toughest of tough guys. Be gone with you, Issie, a new phantasm will come to me tonight.

Lunch with my cousin Peter did not go well. It seems that loquacity is a tendency inherited from the Rebick side of the family; the Dorfs, of whom my mother apparently was typical, are more reserved, more contained, more prone to harbour seething resentments. After my manicure, with vermilion nails I borrowed Melanie's Golf, picked Peter up at the Atlantic Towers and took him on the magical mystery tour we feel obliged to offer to out-of-towners. First to the suburbs, to Calderstones Park where we entered through a pair of giant stone Atlantes and strolled along tree-shaded avenues: limes, horse-chestnuts, beeches. Rhododendron flowers bloomed on bushes, deep little mauve cups. In the centre of the park, surrounded by a shallow ha-ha, was a small mansion house where, on summer afternoons as kids, Sam and I came to buy Walls or Lyons Maid ices, a cold fatty slab that came in three flavours only, white, pink or brown, eaten as a sandwich between dusty wafers (the fad for American-style ice-cream would never catch on, a vendor had told me, 'because the English aren't ice-cream minded'). And lolling on the grass under a 1960s sky felt ourselves blessed to have been born in Liverpool and to be teenagers who bought sweets, games and budget-line makeup at the Penny Lane shops and knew that Strawberry Fields was not an Elysian meadow but a sombre Salvation Army orphanage, a few minutes' walk from where we lay.

I schlepped Peter round the angel-ridden Burne-Jones windows in the Ullet Road church, directed him to the florid marble urinals in the Philharmonic pub, let him stand in the opulent gloom of our great synagogue whose three blue and gold domes, studded with stars, glittered in the light of its rose window. I took him along streets of yellow brick houses, showed him mews, carriage paths, gate-houses, palm-houses, a city of the dead beneath the Anglican cathedral: a hundred sandstone catacombs piercing the red rock, and we strolled past them along the ramps that took the funeral processions down to the sunken floor. Pointed out the sad, restless graves of pauper children in the churchyard and (cross yourself) the Metropolitan Cathedral of Christ the King – a concrete drum crowned in thorns, our Paddy's Wigwam, our Mersey Funnel, inside which psychedelic light circles the altar and Arthur Dooley's tortured iron Christs bleed iron blood on to the floor.

Over lunch between pistachio walls and dining off full silver service, he told me whom he really admired, the one European with guts and balls, who stood up to everything that was rotten here – Oh, God, no, I thought, not this, please don't let it be what I think it is. 'Your own Iron Lady, Maggie Thatcher, and Ron Reagan, what a team they were. I voted for Ron both times and for Bush.' There was more about the Lewinsky affair and Clinton, 'No morals to speak of, his wife, awful.' In a series of laconic assertions, which allowed no further discussion, he told me how Maggie and Ron had 'saved the free world, destroyed Communism and brought the economy into line. End of story.' He ate fast and without much enjoyment, pushing things away to the side of his plate.

'Have we done now?' he asked me, refusing coffee.

'Yes, I'm finished.'

'Done with this nonsense?'

'What nonsense?'

'Are you trying to humiliate me?'

'What are you talking about?'

'This show you've put on.'

'What show?'

'The little tour you just gave me, was that to demonstrate what down-home folks you and your brother are? You've ripped off your family but you're just regular people, is that it?'

'No.'

'Because you don't fool me. I know about the factory. We know.'

'Yes. And we know that you know because Sam told you himself.'

'We'll have our share.'

'As you should.'

'I'm not going to stand for any double-dealing.'

'There won't be any.'

'Then why have you put in a claim behind our backs and lied about it?'

'What claim?' I sat down again.

'You know perfectly well what I mean.'

'I sincerely do not.'

'You told us that you hadn't made a move on the factory. You were lying. You put a claim on it years ago.'

'What the hell are you talking about?'

'Our lawyers have looked into everything. They know about your claim.'

'Listen to me, I have no fucking idea of what you're saying, none of it makes sense.'

'Watch your language.'

'Oh, fuck that.'

'I don't have to sit and listen to this.'

'Me neither. And unless you spit out what it is that you have to say, I'm going. Just watch me.'

'Are you denying you've put in a claim?'

'I most certainly am.'

'Are you aware of the Claims Conference?'

'Of course. It deals with reparations.'

'Do you know how it started?'

'Absolutely. With a speech. I can recite it by heart. In 1951 Konrad Adenauer, the German chancellor, addressed his parliament and this is what he said: "Unspeakable crimes have been committed in the name of the German people, calling for moral and material indemnity, both with regard to the individual harm done to Jews and to the Jewish property for which no legitimate, individual claimants still exist. The Federal Government are prepared, jointly with representatives of Jewry and the State of Israel, to bring about a solution of the material indemnity problem, thus easing the way to the spiritual settlement of infinite suffering."'

'And what happened?'

'They put people through a lot of paperwork.'

'Your mother did this?'

'No. She gave up. My father told her it was a waste of time.'

'So you're sitting there saying that in her lifetime she made no attempt to get the factory back?'

'That's exactly what I'm saying, she was only after reparations. She couldn't do anything about the factory because it was in Dresden, behind the Iron Curtain. That was something else altogether, not under control of Adenauer's reparations programme.'

'So what happened when the Wall came down, after reunification?'

'Oh, listen, by that time she was starting to get sick. We had other things to think about.'

'So do you know you missed the deadline?'

'What deadline?'

'I'll tell you what my lawyers told me.' He got out a piece of paper and took a pair of reading glasses from an inside jacket pocket. 'Yeah, this is it.' He handed it to me. 'Read this.' I looked at it. It was a letter from his attorney outlining the situation.

After reunification the German government passed legislation for the restitution of property nationalised by the Communist government in the former East Germany.

The Claims Conference succeeded in having included in the legislation the clause that Jewish property expropriated or forcibly sold as a result of the Nazi rise to power after 1933 would be subject to return to its original owners or their heirs. We have been informed that the deadline for the filing of claims by the original owners or their heirs expired on 31 December 1992.

This came as a great relief to me. Enormous. The burden imposed on us by my mother had been lifted, her dying wish was to be thwarted. Thank God. May you rest in peace in your grave, dear Mamma, but we cannot respect your wishes, the law won't let us, and lying next to her in *his* grave, I know what my father would have said to us: 'There's nothing you can do about this. The law is against you. Stop banging your head against a brick wall. You've got better ways to spend your time.' We were unchained now, Sam and me, capable of being entities operating under free will. It was possible at long last (having reached middle age tied to our mother's apron strings) to reinvent ourselves. Maybe I would go to America. Maybe I *would* take the job with the Rose Rosen Corporation. Maybe I would devote my life to face creams and eye-shadows and lipstick. To hell with history. To hell with the Nazis. To hell with the Jews and their never-ending sorrows. *Viva* superficiality.

'. . . but when my lawyers found this out and, let me tell you, it only took one call to Frankfurt, they got the bureaucrats there to look up the files. They wanted to know exactly what had happened to the factory and it turned out that before the cut-off date someone had already put in a claim, and the file was open because under German property law if there is any likelihood of there being other heirs to an estate the whole thing is frozen until those heirs are found. What were you planning? To wait till I was dead?'

'*What?*'

I suppose I must have registered such shock and perplexity, awoken from my reverie, that he paused. His dead-white face went red. Red showed in the skin of his scalp beneath the fine white hair. The reading glasses were clenched in his left hand. Rage suffused him but none the less he had stumbled on a big fat obstacle in his relentless path of accusation: my huge astonishment.

'Okay. Here's a name for you to conjure with. Marianne Koeppen.'

'Who?'

'The name you picked to file your claim in. I dunno why you chose that one. To cover your tracks, I guess.'

The factory I had never really believed in – a fairy-tale, Mamma's fantasy, my bedtime story – suddenly, in this restaurant on Hope Street, between the two cathedrals, rose from the German soil, assembling itself brick by brick on the table between me and my cousin. It was real. In Mamma's mind, in the last few hours of her life, the factory had broken through with such force into her consciousness that in its hands it had pulled together every broken synapse, mended each cell, soldered back together sites of her brain destroyed by blood clots and forced into her mouth its message, moved her tongue to make it speak. '*I exist! Don't deny me.*' How had I diminished my own mother by my rejection of her past? I felt such shame. And, for the first time since the funeral, I cried, I laid my head down on my arms and sobbed for my dead mother, in her grave on the edge of the Atlantic Ocean, who had been born in Dresden, Germany, on 2 April 1924 and who had died alone in the night on 29 April 2000. *Mamma.*

'I'm sorry,' he was saying, 'I don't know how I've upset you.' He took a pack of paper tissues from his briefcase. 'Here.'

Mais gardez le sangfroid, they would have said in France, so I took out my powder compact and reapplied my lipstick. Thus armoured I was restored to myself, to Alix Rebick who could hold her own in any situation. Be tough, Daddy told me. Look, Daddy, see, I am. Never forget you are a woman, Mamma said. I have not forgotten, Mamma.

'Peter,' I said. 'Listen to me. You are going to have to understand that what has happened this afternoon is that you have delivered to me – to Sam and me – new information. This claim you are describing, this Marianne person you've told me about, we knew nothing whatsoever about it. Or her. I have not a clue who she is. I have not a clue who she *could* be. And that's the truth. The Rose Rosen lawyers didn't go looking for her for the simple reason that they weren't interested in the factory, their brief was intellectual property rights, they only needed to know if there was anyone left alive who had any claim to the formula, which meant they were looking for descendants of the pharmacist who invented it. They couldn't care less about real estate.

'As to this woman, the most likely explanation I can think of is that this is a fraudulent claim, that she's an impostor, which I don't understand because I would have assumed that the German authorities would have required some kind of proof of her identity, and certainly proof that she was related to our grandparents in order for her to be a lawful heir. So what we are dealing with is a mystery. Clearly this is going to have to be investigated and the best way of doing so is to pool our resources. Sam, of course, is a lawyer, but not that kind of law. He deals with crime, minor crime, mostly. We know people who do contract work, an old friend of my father's does it, Kevin Wong, but this is out of his league. My proposal is that we ask the Rose Rosen Foundation to recommend someone, I don't mean the cosmetics people, I mean Rose's son, who heads up the arm of the business which is involved in funding restoration work, the people I deal with.'

He quarrelled with the idea of using anyone recommended by Rose Rosen, he still thought of them as co-conspirators in the theft of his true inheritance, but I said, 'Listen, do you want them with us or against us?' I lied a bit, implied that maybe Rose Rosen would want to grab the factory for themselves, they sold the cream now. I posed a cynical legal argument in which they could make out the whole thing was theirs, and such is the power of the huge corporation, and the fear that the little guys like us have of them, that he caved in and we shook hands. Out of the restaurant, on the sunny street, he raised his eyes to God, first to the left, to the Catholic cathedral, then to the right, to the Anglican cathedral. 'What do you need two for?'

We walked along to the car in silence. Then suddenly he said, 'You wanna hear a joke?'

'Yes, of course.' Though I could barely imagine what kind of humour he might possess as it had been well hidden up to now.

He began a convoluted story concerning a pair of Jewish bees trying to muscle their way into a Fifth Avenue bar mitzvah where they knew there was a pile of food, dishes loaded with salmon and potato salad and slices of buttered challah and all kinds of cakes, but one of the bees tells the other that he'd better put on a *yarmulke*, 'in case they think you're a Wasp'. And he began to shout with laughter. 'What a pathetic joke,' he said, 'but it gets me every time. You know, I feel like that bee sometimes. Everyone thinks I'm a Wasp but inside I'm anything but.'

'What makes you bee-like?'

'Well, you know how a bee runs about all day picking up pollen and making it into honey? That's me. I'm a honeytrap. I just love good food and I hate that crap at inflated prices they served in there on a half-empty plate. I have a real weakness for home-style cooking.'

'You keep the weight off.'

'I know. I'm naturally skinny. Lauren hates that – she goes to the gym five times a week and I play a game of softball once a year and still I weigh the same as I did when I was twenty-five.'

'What's your favourite dish?'

'Spaghetti with meatballs, every single time.'

'When you first laid eyes on Lauren did you think of her as a dish?'

'Absolutely.'

'What cuisine?'

'The kind you know won't do you any good, but you have it anyway. Listen, I know how it appears, a guy in his fifties dumps his first wife, hooks up with a younger model. You see her as my trophy, don't you?'

'How could I not?'

'It's not the way it seems. My first wife died twelve years ago, it wasn't a quick death and it was not at all pretty. I was running through our health insurance, we were on the brink of losing our house and Lauren worked in the beauty salon where Connie went every month to have her hair done and her nails manicured. Lauren watched Connie get fat as the cortisone they used for the treatment blew her up, saw her hair fall out, and she couldn't stand seeing her decline like that when Connie had always taken such a pride in her appearance. It was Lauren who sent away for a catalogue of all the finest wigs and helped Connie choose one, and styled it for her. When Connie couldn't leave the house Lauren would come over and fix her hair and nails and face in the bathroom, and even when Connie couldn't get out of bed she still turned up every week with her bag of tricks. And did it for nothing. Wouldn't take a penny. She was still fixing my wife's hair when she was in hospital, the day before she passed on, and when she died she prepared her for the coffin. There was some kind of loving bond between them, because what Lauren did for Connie was to make her feel about as better as anything the drugs could do for her. I sure don't understand this about women, but I don't deny it. Lauren saw us get ripped off and done over by the insurance company, she doesn't like anyone taking advantage. She is a very loyal woman. I'm not in love with her, not the way I was with my Connie, and I believe she understands that, but she's had her own hard times that I won't speak of here and I think with me she has at last found some kind of peace.'

'I see. Why did you tell me that, about the bees and food?'

'I suddenly saw that my wife and I hadn't made a good impression on you. And I remembered that, after all, we're family. I have no siblings, no kids – though that's not for want of trying – my parents both dead, no uncles or aunts or cousins in America. It dawned on me, these Rebicks, it's just them, I have no one else in the world except my wife, and even my friends are starting to move to Florida in their retirement. You got kids?'

'No.'

'None to make you laugh, none to make you cry.'

'So people keep telling me.'

'I feel like I did a master's in tears. I think I dried myself out I wept so much. There can't be a lot of moisture left.'

'Grief,' I told him. 'What can anyone do?'

'I stopped laughing and I stopped eating for two years. Then I started up again. Now I eat when I can find good food and I'm trying in my retirement to build a computer that can create a joke.'

'Any luck?'

'Nah. Every one a stinker.'

The next day I sat down with a German dictionary and started to write letters to Marianne Koeppen at an address in Dresden, which I got from the Claims Conference, sent them off; no replies were received. Nothing. Silence. They went into a void. 'Someone,' Sam said, looking at me, 'needs to turn up on this woman's doorstep and see who she is and what she wants.' 'That's me, I suppose.' 'Yes, it's you.' 'And in the meantime,' said Melanie, 'the two of you could clear out your mother's house.'

To sell our childhood home was unbearable. 'Sell,' Melanie had said, three years ago when I had just moved to France. 'No,' Sam replied, vehement, not while his mother was alive. Melanie wrote to me. I wrote back and I said I would keep out of it. So she rang. 'You realise we're paying tax on an empty property and if we sell now we could give the money directly to the kids? It would give them a down-payment for their own homes.' I said, 'Melanie, we're rich. You could open your chequebook and *buy* them each a house. And if Sam wants to keep it, we keep it.' 'So you won't support me?' 'It's not a matter of taking sides. If Sam has some reason for wanting to hang on to the house then he has a reason, it's an emotional reason and I'm not going to argue with him.' 'That's your motto, isn't it, Alix?' Melanie said. 'Don't get involved.' And she hung up on me. A month later there had been a card asking for forgiveness and I wrote back saying, 'Nothing to forgive.' But Mamma was dead now, dead and in her grave two months already. 'It's immoral,' Melanie added, 'for a good property to stand empty when people are homeless. If you want to hang on to it, turn it into a hostel.' 'But it was a family house, it always had been from before us and now some other family should have it.' 'Fine, so sell.' 'We should.' 'But you'll have to clear it first, the two of you.' 'I'm not ready for this, can't it wait?' 'For what? Listen, you're never going to be ready. It's a demolition job and no one with a heart can do it.' 'I have a heart.' 'So do I. And I've bought two hundred bin bags, do you think it will be enough?'

One morning, not long after this conversation, my brother and I drove out of the underground car park, on to Mann Island and down Strand Street, along Wapping and Chaloner Street, left on to Parliament Street, up Park Road to Aigburth, and the car turned again towards the river, to our childhood home. The gas was off, the electricity was off, there was still water in the taps. Melanie, who came sometimes to see that the place was not overrun with vermin or wasps or had been squatted or used as a crack house or a needle dump, would let herself in with Sam's key, look at the dust accumulating on the furniture and think of the house where *she* had been born, and the people who lived there now, strangers moving among the rooms where she once ran in rabbit pyjamas when she heard her father's key turn in the lock at the end of the working day. And smelt again the frying of fish in the kitchen and touched the smooth, cold marble of the fireplace in the lounge and saw herself, at seventeen, her face in the mirror, her eyelashes clumped with cheap mascara, thinking of Sam Rebick who earlier in the week had slipped his hand inside her panties and put a finger in the place the blood came from. And she could speak to no one of these thoughts, but me, blushing but wanting to anyway, because she could only cry and cry for the mother *she* had lost, very suddenly, not like her mother-in-law, but of a heart-attack, which she thought was a disease of fathers not mothers, Etta Harris clutching her arm in the middle of Tesco, leaning on the trolley for support and it rolling away from her so she collapsed on her face on the floor in the paper-towel aisle and when they got her to hospital she was dead at sixty-two. Leaving Manny at sixty-five to watch TV every night with all the lights on, the football pages of the *Echo* open on his lap, 'An old man before his time because he'd never known a moment in his life without a woman to look after him. He'll go like Joe Marks after his wife died. Burns in his suits from his cigarettes and one day he fell asleep with his cigarette lit and burned the house down.'

Sam paid a man to come in once a month in the summer to mow the grass so it wouldn't run to seed and ruin the neighbours' lawns. The hydrangea bushes were flowering at the bottom of the garden, new blooms on old wood. There had been heavy rain a few days ago. The grass was overgrown and dandelions were sticking their heads up among the strangling coarse blades.

'Where shall we start?'

The house has five bedrooms. It has a long sitting room with french windows that open out on to the garden. It has an attic. It has a cellar. It has a box room. It has a big bathroom, which was modernised. And it has a kitchen, which was not.

'This is going to take days,' I said. 'Days and days.'

'Yes. And the sooner we get started the sooner we'll finish. So where?'

'In the kitchen.'

This was a room that was old-fashioned because Mamma did not really like to cook. What she loved to do was entertain and for that she did not need a *batterie de cuisine*, she needed dishes: Royal Doulton dinner services in white with a narrow green, gold-flecked rim, consisting of dinner plates, side plates and hors d'oeuvres plates with matching serving platters and gravy boats; Royal Albert tea services in floral patterns with teapot, sugar bowl, milk jug, cake plates and side plates, teacups and their matching saucers; wine glasses, sherry glasses, whisky tumblers, liqueur glasses, all cut crystal. And for each of these types of china or glassware there was a minimum of four sets because, out of respect for his sisters and brothers, my father insisted that we keep a proper kosher home with a set of plates for milk dishes and another set for meat dishes, and another two sets for Passover, both milk and meat; and yet another set solely for the meal after Yom Kippur ended, the plates on which was put the food that broke the fast.

Sam had brought boxes and newspapers. Melanie had phoned the house-clearance people. What do we want to keep, what do we want to give away? And what will go into the black plastic sacks to end up on a landfill site?

'Do you want the china, Alix?'

'No. Does Melanie want it?'

'No. And the glasses?'

'I'll keep a few. Do you want any?'

'Melanie and I can't stand this old-fashioned stuff.'

In an hour we had filled fifteen boxes. Sam said, 'I'll make a start on the food cupboards.'

Half devoured by moths where there was something moths could devour, we found: flour, baking powder, unopened packets of biscuits (Rich Tea, Digestives, cream crackers, Ryvita), cans of pineapple rings, cans of baked beans, cans of Weight Watchers soups, cans of tuna, cans of sweetcorn, vegetable oil, sugar, artificial sweetener, skimmed-milk powder, cider vinegar, salt, tea bags, instant coffee, rice, dried thyme, dried mint, a bottle of vanilla essence, three jars of cinnamon, Worcester sauce, Tabasco (some of this up to nine years beyond its use-by date), two hundred pounds in out-of-circulation five-pound notes rolled up in a rubber band inside the flour bag, and a diamond ring inside the packet of skimmed-milk powder. Sam put the ring in the watch pocket of his jeans and the ragged, moth-eaten notes with the Queen's head consumed, into the glove compartment of his car.

We were working hard, working up a sweat there in our

parents' house, dismantling thirty-nine years of our parents' marriage and the whole of our own childhood, as we threw away the
frying pan in which Mamma fried every egged and floured plaice,
sole or haddock the fishmonger ever delivered, the pot in which
she boiled the hen for soup (*shtetl* food, made for my father),
because my mother knew that cooking was one of the principal
duties of a housewife, a wife who had been saved from the jaws of
hell to arrive in a kitchen where she cooked meals and baked
cakes and loaded her dishwasher and was in every way a slave to
domestic life. 'But what a thing to be a slave to, Alix, when I
could have been a slave in a camp and they would have shot me
when I was too worn out to work any more,' is what she might
have said, but never did, for she did not utter a single word about
what-might-have-been, preferring only to reminisce about her
mother's damask tablecloths and her linen press with its ironed
linen sheets and lace-trimmed pillow-cases, and the smell of her
father's pipe.

When we'd finished the kitchen we started on our own bedrooms. I found: a tangerine-coloured lipstick from 1966, its
darkened tallow dried up and no longer viscous enough to leave
even a smear on the back of my hand; a blue Revlon eye-shadow;
a shrunken palette of eye-black. Hanging in the wardrobe were
a spotted Biba blouse with leg-o'-mutton sleeves, a purple Mary
Quant mini-dress, which I wore when the Beatles came to play
the Liverpool Empire to an audience of teenage girls howling in
their frenzy, screaming for no reason other than to add our own
throats to the uproar that drowned out the rhythm, the lead, the
bass guitars and Ringo's drums, not to mention John and Paul
silently mouthing 'A Hard Day's Night' in the collarless Mod
suits that Brian stuck them in. Teenage sexual hysteria.
Hormones bursting out of us. Acceptable to open our mouths
and scream our desires, those tiny lusts of the thirteen-year-old
girl, popping up like our little breasts suddenly popped up one

day, when we weren't looking, unnoticed until we were soaping ourselves in the bath, feeling the tenderness of nipples. The suggestion of a bump beneath our school blouses, and greeted with the same shame and excitement as the first flow of blood. Both coming with paraphernalia, the training bra, the sanitary-towel belt. A lifetime ahead of us of discreet items in our handbags, cupped in the palm on the way to the ladies' room. And popping up at the same time as those budding breasts, on the bedroom wall, the posters of baby-faced Paul, the least threatening of the Beatles, along with Ringo, the ugly feller, the big-nosed 'Jewish Beatle', the one we could imagine being our friend, confiding in him our romantic fantasies of Paul holding our hand in the moonlight.

But I had seen George once in his 'perfect leathers', driving down Mather Avenue in a green Vauxhall, and taken off my school beret and flung it in the air so that it soared like a Frisbee above the suburban skies and he honked his horn at me and rolled down his window and shouted, 'Can you catch it?' I ran across the dual carriageway in front of him, reached up and impaled it on my index finger, twirled it like a plate, this blue felt spinning school hat. And he laughed and said, 'If you want a lift, jump in.' So we drove along through Liverpool to the airport, while he asked me the usual questions: 'Alix Rebick? Is your dad that doctor in Toxteth?' 'Yes.' 'He's famous,' he said. People called out at us and my hair flew behind me. 'A magnificent bush, you've got there,' George remarked, in my innocence. 'Is it hard to comb?' 'You can't comb it, it's out of the question.' 'I'm growing mine. We all are, me and the other lads.' Then at Speke, when he got his green suitcase from the back seat, he said, 'Can you get home all right?' 'Yes. No problem. I can catch the bus from here.' 'Good. See you around. Don't lose your hat.' I stood for half an hour by his car in the car park, studying it, memorising it. I had not asked him for an iota of proof of this meeting – forgotten to get an autograph! – and now I am no longer sure if it even happened or was an embellishment or a trick of memory or a fantasy. But here, on the top shelf of the fitted wardrobe, was that blue beret, with the enamelled school badge pinned to it. My records were stacked in a wire rack. My old record player was still sitting on a table. I plugged it in, took out *Rubber Soul* from its sleeve and put it on the turntable, the stylus rose and moved itself to the spinning disc and fell again. I threw the beret in with the rest of the rubbish. After *Rubber Soul* had run its course, I unplugged the record player and entombed it in black plastic, tying a knot.

Twenty of the sacks were full when Sam, turning to open the window, found our mother's ironing-board beside it, an object so worn down with familiarity that it had become invisible and if we stared at the wall a thousand times we would not see it. It was *part* of the green wall, a raised series of vertical wooden lines, abutting from the surface. Cracked, wooden Utility equipment, purchased in 1947 in the first year of our parents' marriage, over which my mother had bent to press collars exactly the same way as she had watched the maid Frieda press her own mother's in Dresden in 1936, when Frieda said, '*Meine liebe*, always first from the inside. See?' And later to me, 'Darling, always first from the inside. Do you see?'

Holding it upright – the ironing-board on which Sam's school shirts had been pressed, and his school trousers and the Paisley Mod shirts he'd worn as a teenager to the Jacaranda, the Casbah, the Cavern and the Mardi Gras where he tapped his toe and danced the Cavern Stomp to the Beatles as well as Gerry and the Pacemakers, the Fourmost, Billy Fury – my brother looked up, his face wet, said, 'Enough. I can't stand any more of this.'

I turned. The room was empty. I found him outside on the grass by the yucca plant, sat down next to him on the damp ground. Planes were passing overhead, buzzing in the limpid summer air.

'I'm sick of it, sick of the lot of it.'

His neck is starting to age, I thought.

'I'm sick of the house, sick of everything. Sick of my own life.'

I couldn't believe my big brother, the inheritor of righteous-ness, was coming out with this claptrap. 'Don't be so babyish.'

But still he was in tears.

'Taking a whole marriage apart like that, you realise our kids will do the same to Mel and me one day? This is what it will come down to, they'll pick up our stuff and they'll think, No use for it, it's rubbish, put it in the skip. I was standing there with that ironing-board in my hand, couldn't stop myself crying, and I thought, Come on, Sam. Grow up. And that's when it hit me. I've been grown up since my bar mitzvah with barely a break, a couple of years in America and that's all. A grown-up since I went to the Picton library every day after school, study, study, study, pass your O levels, pass your A levels, get articled, pass your law exams and before you've even passed them you're married.'

'Why did you marry her?'

'I'll tell you why, because I was *aching* for a fuck. She would let me go so far, but she wouldn't let me go all the way and I figured I either go down the aisle with her or I go into town and find a prostitute. You know what I did? I got the bus one night, went down to Gambier Terrace with a tenner in my pocket, had a look, turned round and came back home again. Terrified. Scared of the clap, scared of pissing green. The next day I proposed. The minute we'd been to Boodles and got the engagement ring I was in the clear, she'd do it, and I've done it with her and no one else ever since. Don't you think it's too much to ask?'

'What about when you lived in America?'

'Oh, yeah, the commune, except it wasn't really a commune, just a shared house with brown rice. We were only in it a month, as long as we could stand it, and Mel never wanted to be there in the first place. It was all my idea, she'd have been happy in New

Jersey if that's where I'd taken her. Neither of us could put up with the mess and the disorder. We weren't raised for chaos, we were brought up to put chaos right.'

'So now you want to do what you never did at twenty. Any candidates?'

He giggled, his face lit up, his wolfish Rebick grin, my father's face. Dead leaves on his back. Grass stains on my jeans. Rose petals rotting under their bushes. 'Yeah . . . Lauren.'

'Why?'

'To be honest, I get a hard-on just looking at her. Isn't that enough?'

'Thirty years of marriage and you'd throw it away?'

'You know what? My dick doesn't have a brain. It doesn't have that much of a memory and it certainly doesn't have a conscience. You think I'm going to run away with her? Nah. She's not a woman you want to sit down and have a conversation with. She's not the mother of my children and I'm not interested in making her the mother of any future children. I'd just *love* to fuck her. She's a walking sex bomb, I want to bury my cock in her until she pulls me in after her and go the oblivion road – fancy dying of a fuck instead of for a fuck.'

'For Christ's sake, you can't talk to me like this.'

'Why not?'

'I'm your sister, I don't want to know.'

'We used to have a go, you and I, when we were kids.'

'Drop it.'

'Ally, do you know what it's been like, this past thirty years? Have you any idea, while you swanned off round the world doing your own thing? I was a father at twenty-four, I had my own firm at thirty with three solicitors working under me.'

'Don't give me that. You spent the first five years doing nothing but drugs busts and smoking dope in the evening. You were a layabout, the only solicitor in Liverpool barely making a living.'

'And maybe I could have been happy carrying on that way. I didn't want to be famous, I didn't ask for the burden of being Saul Rebick's son and, believe me, it was a burden and still is. I remember the night of the riots, Melanie and I were in bed, we were under the blankets making babies, having fun the only way you know how when you're young and you haven't got much cash, and the phone rang. It was Dad. He said, "Get down to Toxteth, the People need you." He said it so you could hear that capital P. What a load of hooey. The more I think back the more I see him for what he was, he was a gas-bag, our father, a bore. What did he know about socialism? It was all self-aggrandisement, he loved the power of it.'

I was enraged by my brother. I wanted to grab him by his thinning hair and slam his head down on the concrete path.

'How dare you? His *patients* loved him.'

'Of course they did, Saul Rebick, the abortion king of Liverpool. How many of the ones he did away with do you think were his?'

'What are you talking about?'

'He must have had a dozen women on the go at any one time. Didn't you cotton on?'

The sun went out. A cloud did not pass before it, I mean it was extinguished and darkness fell upon the land like the darkness of the firmament before God divided the heavens and the sea.

'He had affairs?'

'Not exactly affairs, more like little quickies, twenty-minute stands when the door was shut, no wonder his waiting room was always full. Mamma had to keep the bitches away from his hospital bed when he was dying. She wouldn't let a single one in, why should she? '

'I don't believe you. Why didn't I know any of this?'

'Oh, Ally, you worshipped him, you never noticed because he

made you his little princess but any other female was fair game. And the one who was beaten up in all this was Mamma. She wanted to put an ocean between her and Germany and he wouldn't let her, not because he was committed to the Cause but because he had so many women on the go he could never extricate himself from all of them. She wanted to start a new life, she wanted to go somewhere where everyone was an immigrant, and he buried her here. He wouldn't even let her apply for reparations, and you know why? If you ask me it was because he was frightened that if she had some money of her own – not just the cream, that was a family business – she'd just up and leave, she'd go to America by herself, come hell or high water. And that was not an option because not only did he have to have the affairs he also had to have the Dresden-doll wife, the beautiful refugee he'd saved.'

'I refuse to believe Daddy would behave like that, it's not the man I know.'

'Really? Now why would you say a thing like that, the way you used to flirt with him, competing with your own mother for your father's attention? It was disgusting. I used to be embarrassed for you.'

'Are you implying some kind of abuse? Because if you are you'd be dead wrong.'

'Of course not, that wasn't Dad's style, not in the slightest. He wasn't interested in little girls, he was a womaniser, and when I got married I made my decision, that the last person I was going to take after was him. I was going to be a faithful husband come hell or high water and I picked a girl I knew would be a faithful wife.'

'So what are you planning to do now? Walk out on Mel?'

'I don't know. Do I love her? Of course I do. How could I not? She's part of my life, the mother of our kids, she has everything a man like me could look for in a woman, she's tough and brave and loving and truthful and she's kept her figure, which shouldn't matter but it does. What's wrong with her? Nothing. Nothing is wrong except that I don't want to be married to the same woman for sixty years, and if I live till I'm eighty that's how long I'll have been married to her. *Now* I realise that men aren't made for decades of sexual boredom. I lie in bed every night thinking how I'd like to sell up, give Mel half of everything, maybe more, maybe two-thirds, and just vanish. I'd go to America, see all the places I've never seen, Motown, Memphis, Nashville, all of it. Be a bum.'

'How banal.'

'What?'

'It surprises me that you could be so predictable.'

'That's rich, coming from you, Ms Why Does No One Love Me.'

'Such a pattern – the middle-aged man tells his wife he's going out for a packet of cigarettes and two years later there's posters of him on the Tube. "Have you seen this man? His family are desperate to hear from him." Starting a new life, how possible do you think that is? It's a Jack Kerouac fantasy, something from *On The Road*. You're fifty-two years old and you're still daydreaming about driving a convertible on Route 66. Grow up.'

'I'm not entitled to daydreams?'

'So you admit that's all they are?'

'Possibly.'

'And what about Mel?'

'What do you mean?'

'Is she as sick of sex with you as you are of sex with her?'

'Possibly.'

'Could she have had affairs?'

'No way.'

'Why are you so sure?'

'She's too self-disciplined.'

'So you're saying you're weak.'

'Maybe I am. But aren't I entitled to some weaknesses?'

'Not when you damage other people.'

'*You*? You say that? Sniffing around Joseph Shields like a dog, trying to lick his balls.'

'Listen to me. Maybe I've made a mess of my life but I'm not going to have you hurt Melanie for some half-baked fantasy. Go and have your affair, have half a dozen if you like, but you belong here and you belong with her.'

'The reason you think I belong here is so you can belong somewhere else. One of us had to stay and you were damned sure it wasn't going to be you. Why is any of us still here in Liverpool? Give me one good reason. Nine million people passed through this place, nine million went to America and we had to stay where we were. I've had it. The city's finished, face it. It's a shell, a theme park.'

'You'll pull everything down on top of you. You'll be walking down Fifth Avenue with a rug on your head and a trophy wife on your arm. You're pathetic.'

'I'm pathetic? You've never even made a viable relationship, every one you got bored with. What was the longest you've ever lasted? Five years with Alan?'

'Oh, don't talk to me about Alan.'

'What was the matter with him?'

'The silence. I thought his monosyllables represented something deeper, some profundity that drew me to him out of sheer curiosity. It was unusual and relaxing to live with someone who never spoke. When we first met I thought it would take me a whole lifetime to plumb those depths but he was a lake frozen over. You couldn't drill a hole in the ice.'

'You looked good together.'

'I know. We did.'

'He was taller than you, a very handsome man.'

'Yeah, I could get them in those days.'

'You were eye-catching. The two of you together, I remember you had a necklace of fake diamonds and you wore them with that red slippery dress, you came into a room, the pair of you – he always wore good suits, years before anyone else did – and everyone turned their heads. You brought him back to Liverpool and you looked like film stars getting off the train at Lime Street.'

'He rang me a few years ago. We had a drink together.'

'What's he up to?'

'Jesus Christ came into his heart.'

'Jesus Christ!'

'He works with his hands doing the Lord's work.'

'Saving souls?'

'Carpentry. He makes furniture.'

We began to laugh. And could not stop. And we were rolling around on the ground, screaming with pain and laughter. If a stranger had witnessed this conversation I know what they would have thought, that things had been said that never could be retracted, that would fester into wounds that wouldn't heal, that grudges would be borne, that nothing could be the same between us ever again, but it wasn't like that with me and Sam. We dug our knives in deep and then withdrew them, but nothing we said to each other could ever do any lasting damage. Tempers flared and died down like a match applied to tissue paper. I would talk to him again about our father, I would think about everything he had said, find the flaws in the argument, challenge him, make him give a full account of his allegations. And if they were true, then everything would change, but not between Sam and me.

Neither did I believe he would leave Melanie. Or go to America. Or fuck Lauren, though one day, sooner or later, he would find someone, and he would choose her in exactly the same way as his eyes had lit on his cousin's wife, because she oozed sex appeal, because it came off her like hot breath, because you would be able to smell her hormones in the air around her skin. And Melanie would be apart and separate from this coupling, would be kept in the dark so he could end it almost as soon as it started. Because the truth was deeper than the dirty desires, the truth was his hatred of chaos, he couldn't live a life that way, wasn't built for it. I was, not him. 'When a client comes in to see me,' he once said, 'some smack-head or gangster or petty crook, I look at them and see mess. Everything is an explanation for an explanation so you can't follow it, and I go home and think about how these people live. Personally I couldn't stand it. When they leave my office I've given them something they never had before, I give them a story. It's sound. It's logical. They only have to remember it. I make sense of the chaos and if they stand up in the dock and tell that story, just as I told them to, they'll get off. But the minute they start telling the truth, the complex, complicated truth, then they're finished. I'm not persuading them to perjure themselves, I'm only pointing out that the truth will not set them free, it will get them locked up. And I know this not because I'm an expert on the law but because I'm the child of immigrants. And you know what immigrants do, don't you? They tell the authorities what they want to hear. Every immigrant who wants to get on in life does this. Every immigrant who insists on authenticity sinks.'

So that was why I knew he couldn't do it. The story he'd concocted for me, about his simple, simply urgent need for extra-marital fucks, was his attempt to get himself off in the court of the Rebicks. I don't know if he'd convinced himself, never mind the judge and jury, who would consist of me, his wife, his kids, and the whole of Liverpool.

'We'd better press on,' I said. 'Loads more to do.'

We got up, our limbs stiff from the damp ground. 'I feel like an old man,' my brother told me.

We went back to work with a vengeance. An hour later Sam came and stood in the door holding towards me a glass of water.

'You want this?'

'Yes. What you said about Dad, how much of that was true?'

'A lot of it. Most. He had loads of affairs.'

'Yet it was Mamma's hand he held when he was dying.'

'There had to be a hand to hold.'

'Who will hold yours when you are dying if you leave Melanie? Who will you know at eighty who knew you at twenty? Who will remember you when you were young?'

'Who'll hold yours?'

'That's cruel.'

'I know.'

'Then to hell with you. Go to America. Be it on your own head. Whose side do you think your kids will take?'

'They're grown-up now. They don't need me.'

'Such a family man.'

'How long should *any* man have to put up with this? A whole life? Part of it? Do I have to spend all my days gritting my teeth? When do we get our declaration of independence? When do we get our bill of rights?'

'Oh, Sam, don't you know there isn't one? I come home to an empty house and whatever I have left undone remains undone. The clock ticks. The dust settles. The silence has my voice in it alone. I have absolute authority over myself. You want this? Take it. It's yours.'

My mother's wardrobe. Sunlight with dust in it. Strange metallic scents. Perished crumbling rubber diaphragm in a blue plastic case. Pearl necklaces. Gold watch. Diamond clips for unpierced ears. Rows of skirts and blouses and dresses. A drawer full of stockings and underwear. Bras, pants, half slips. Sachets of dead lavender to scent her smalls. Shoes with wooden shoe-trees or

balled-up tissue paper stuffed into the toes. Her emerald engagement ring on my little finger. Her mink held around my
shoulders and, looking at myself in the mirror, I thought,
Mamma would kiss me and cuddle me now, seeing me like this,
dressed like this. Daddy's clothes, his suits, his sports jackets, his
ties, his shirts. Sam far away at the other end of the house. Free
for a moment to try them on, a jacket would fit me fine. What
should I wear, Mamma? What do you think would suit me?

Opening the bathroom door, behind it, hanging on a hook,
Daddy's yellow silk Paisley dressing-gown, the one my mother
brought home from the hospital with his silver Ronson lighter
and a half-finished packet of cigarettes and his leather slippers.
On his deathbed, shrunk to a hundred-pound doll, unable to
swallow, tubes down his throat, his skin yellow, a bad smell
coming off him. 'Give me a kiss, darling.' I shrank away, touched
his face lightly with my lips and my breast brushed his birdy
chest. 'Alix,' he whispered, 'don't deny me, after everything.'
'What do you want, Daddy?' 'Kisses and cuddles, my gorgeous
girl.' But I only held his hand, my fingers tight around his bones.
He closed his eyes. 'You're right,' his breath replied, 'who would
look at me like this?'

The house grew emptier, the rooms grew larger. We did not know
the space we once had. We took down the velvet curtains, folded
them and put them in the pile for the charity shops. Light
flooded the halls and landings. Our parents came here in 1954,
from a flat on Lark Lane. Finally, when we had removed from the
house all the relics of our parents' forty-three-year marriage, we
took what we didn't want to the landfill site.

And I thought then of the words of the opium eater, Thomas
de Quincey, who came to Liverpool in 1810 and witnessed the
fire that utterly destroyed the slave warehouses. At Everton he
had a vision, standing on the brow of the hill in short, springy

grass, the air blowing very fresh from the water, and invisible to his eyes because they weren't there yet, the Second World War observation point on Perch Rock and the oil-drilling platforms in the Irish Sea. This very morning in the year 2000 a pretty refugee from Albanian Kosovo, wearing a cherry red cardigan, scolds her son, dressed in red and white Liverpool away strip, who is watching a container ship coming out of the North End docks. A man smoking a pipe with his back towards the sea looks across the estuary towards Wales, observes the mountains and thinks of a cycling holiday he and his late wife had when they were young and of her sitting on her Raleigh in a buttercup cotton dress, a scarf in matching material left over from the Simplicity pattern tied round her head to protect her hair. Where the factory that cures the tobacco that the man smokes in his pipe, and the factory that spins the white and black striped sugar lumps called Everton mints, which the boy in the Liverpool strip is sucking as he watches the container ship, his mother taking out her comb and running it through his hair as he wriggles from her grasp – here de Quincey stood too and he saw this:

'Obliquely to the left lay the many-languaged town of Liverpool; obliquely to the right the multitudinous sea. The town of Liverpool represented the earth with its sorrow and its graves left behind, yet not out of sight nor wholly forgotten.'

Not *wholly* forgotten, Mamma. Not wholly forgotten.

Joseph

The phone rings, you pick it up, you think you know who it's going to be, you've got beyond excitement and expectation. The voice at the other end introduces a problem, because in my work problems are what come to me, particularly from the artists who tell me that I don't know fuck all about creativity and that their paintings can't be hung this way or that way or on this or that kind of surface and every one of them claiming to detect exactly what my plans are for my hotel and to have expressed their utter disagreement even before I've got a word out. Secrecy is a thing with me. I don't put up a picture on the side of my building site saying, 'It's going to look like this.' Let 'em wait. I intend to wow the city.

But the truth was that I no longer got as many of those calls as I did, the problems had all been receding and at last I could see the light ahead, the completion date. Alix had fixed it for me. The day after I had that conversation with her about Michael, I was drinking coffee once again in Starbucks and trying not to give in to a bagel and cream cheese, waiting for Sam to show for the meeting we had arranged with Brian Humphreys' lieutenant. Then my cellphone cheeped and it was Sam to say something had come up, he had to get to court, he couldn't make it and he would try to rearrange. At that moment I saw Alix walk past, raised my hand and beckoned her in and told her I was free, did she want to go to lunch? But even as I was speaking I had the idea: why not let her take the meeting? I mean, in all probability this kid could handle anything, it would be a delightful notion to see Alix in action against a hoodlum. At first she said no way, she didn't know that type of person any more, she would be out of her depth, but after quite a bit of pleading on my part she eventually agreed at least to tag along and we got up to go to Wood Street where my meeting, a guy named Ritchie Sylvester, had a club.

As we walked over I asked how her lunch had gone with her long-lost cousin.

'A revelation, in many ways,' she said. 'You think you know exactly who people are just by looking at them but really you understand nothing about them at all. The impressions you form are largely valueless.'

'I deal with how things look and the aim is that what you see is what you get.'

'You have no secrets, personally, I mean?'

'There may be corners.'

'Hidden pockets of neurosis?'

'I don't know about that. Are you neurotic? Most women are.'

'I'm a terrible hypochondriac.'

'You know the one about the guy who goes to his doctor and he tells him, "You got three months to live"? Then he gives him a bill for a thousand dollars. The dying man says, "I can't afford this." So the doctor says, "Okay, I'll give you another three months."'

'That's an old joke.'

'I'll try to come up with something more current next time.'

We turned off Bold Street into Concert Square and she was reminiscing, telling me how quiet it used to be here, just a block from all the smart stores where her mother once strolled in high heels in the fifties, shopping for shoes and hats and handbags, and only a step away the alleys with their small businesses: a tea-shipping company, a hairdressers' suppliers, an old clothes shop, a pub for merchant seamen who sailed out of Genoa, a Chinese kitchen-equipment store for the restaurants on Duke Street. All gone away, she said. Then the time of dereliction and emptiness, abandonment and desertion, trees growing on the upper storeys, kids kicking balls against a wall, junkies shooting up, people lost and forgotten. All gone away, too. 'For on the eighth day, after he had rested,' she said, 'God woke up with a start and accomplished the chroming of Liverpool, resurfacing an entire city so you could see your face in it or lay out a line of cocaine, and that night the angels went out clubbing.'

We got to a door with Club Seville written in shut-off neon above us and I rang a bell. 'I feel like an idiot,' I said. 'I'm twenty years too old for this place.'

'Don't flatter yourself, more like thirty.'

'As bad as that?' She really is not my or anybody else's idea of the polite Brit. I found it pretty adorable that she would say such things, it made me laugh. 'Perhaps I should learn British modesty.'

'Quite right – after all, we have a lot to be modest about.'

Still there was no reply and I began to hammer on the door with my fists.

'*Hey*. Anyone home?'

It opened.
'Yeah, me. Who are youse?'
'Jeezus, what the hell is that on your face?'
'Who the fuck are youse?'
'I have an appointment with Mr Sylvester.'
'Are you Joseph Shields?'
'Yes, I am.'
'Where's Sam Rebick?'
'I'm Alix Rebick, Sam's sister.'
'Okeydokey.'

The guy had a swastika tattooed on his cheek, a fucking *swastika*! And I thought, Where am I? What am I getting myself into? but Alix seemed unperturbed and we followed him up the stairs to an office with cases of liquor stacked against the wall, a couple of half-dressed girls in the corner, lap-dancers, I guess, with their hair scraped back from their foreheads in ponytails, sitting there applying false nails, talons with rings through them and hearts and daisies embossed in enamel. Another girl was standing up doing exercises with a couple of weights, one in each hand, with a leather exercise belt like an old-fashioned corset round her waist. Ritchie Sylvester was behind an antique desk, not rising, not putting forward a hand to greet us, his arm round the shoulder of a dog. I don't know what Alix meant when she said that people are opaque, that you cannot judge them. If you ask me, it's the exact opposite. The sorrow and the pity of it all is the way they invite you, in fact beg and plead with you even, to accept at face value what they are trying to say about themselves. Some of them are so hollowed out, have so little left in them that what are they *but* front?

People like him are everywhere, we have them in Chicago too. Just loudmouths really, dyslexic kids written off at eight, no good at schoolwork but keeping reams of numbers in their head, punks who can do sums and see an opportunity and take it, in fact take anything that isn't nailed down, and I say good luck to you, if that's the best you can manage. I can't fault you for trying. Look at him, with his fake gold Rolex, the Adidas jogging suit, the sparkling white sports shoes, the hair cut close to his head, each strand separated by gel like the sea had run through it. The baby's nose that never grew. The pea-green eyes. The slackness in the mouth. The cuts on his throat. The tattoo marks on his fingers. He badly wants me to think that there's something inside him that is deranged, that the only response is for me to be terrified out of my wits, but I know different: he's nothing, a little man with a little face.

We sat down and he lit himself a cigar and I thought, Do you really have to be so *obvious*?

'So what do you want? I'm not interested in time-wasters.'

'I want my hotel to open with no further harassment, no more vandalism, no more intimidation.'

'Aye-aye,' he said to the girls, 'Buffalo Bill's home on the range.'

They giggled.

'I have a business to run, just like you.'

'A Mickey Mouse one. And you think I'm Goofy. Hear that? Soft lad here thinks I'm Goofy.'

Bravado. I knew what he was doing, trying to act up in front of his girls like *he* was in control, that *he* ran the show, playing the crowd. A little man with little ambitions. I knew what I had to say and I knew who my audience was, not these punks, but the guy in prison. For Sam and I had agreed our strategy: we would appeal to Humphreys' *pride*, local pride. We would talk him up as a co-sponsor of something only big-shots get to have a say about – the future of a city – acting in concert with other big-shots across the Atlantic in some of the greatest cities in the world.

'Come on,' I said, 'let's cut all that crap. You're right. I'm American-born, I don't like being told any more than you that I

can't do something, that it isn't possible, I dislike negative thinking and I don't care for pessimism. Every immigrant came to
America with some kind of dream for the future and the best of
us kept alive the idea that dreams were worth having. I aspire to
a transformation of this city, not by myself, alone, but in the past
twenty or thirty years you have not put up one significant piece
of architecture, nothing to match the heritage you have here of
fabulous buildings. The city is what it is because it's gorgeous to
look at, whatever they say somewhere else, it is not a dump and
never will be as long as these places survive. You have a beautiful waterfront, you have all kinds of stunning structures. I came
here rather than anywhere else because I want to take what
Liverpool is and turn it into what Liverpool *will become*. Being
and becoming, Mr Sylvester. Now you run a club here, I believe,
I hear that kids are flying over from Barcelona to party here at the
weekends because you give them such a good time in Liverpool.
That's great, and why do they come? Because the city has an
edge, a buzz, an excitement. It's a real place. And what's more it
needs people like me, *Americans*, people who are your friends,
who want you to be part of what America is, which is the only
country in the world maybe concerned solely with the future. My
hotel is going to be more than a place with beds in it, it's a
symbol of American optimism, American can-do, and whatever
you planned to build on the site instead will never outstrip that.'

'Sounds dead good. It'd make a great write-up in the *Echo*
and the next day the whole of Liverpool will be using it to line
their budgie cages.'

Fuck *you*, jerk. Forget it. There was nothing to do here, this
guy was a total waste of time and I was wasting my own on this
ignoramus, this futile little creep, and I was turning to Alix to
tell her I was ready to go when she leaned forward and looked
Ritchie in the eye with a very weird smile I'd never seen on her
before.

'You know,' Alix said, 'I'm feeling a bit peckish, Ritchie, got any snacks? Nuts, I like. Got any walnuts?'

'You what?' It was like she'd poked him with a cattle prod. I swear his hands were shaking when he came down after that apparently innocuous question and he was blazing red on his neck.

'I love walnuts, all kinds, I like them in chocolate too. Walnut whips, they're nice. Walnut whip, what an odd name for a chocolate swirl.'

'Sounds kinky,' one of the girls said. 'How do you whip a walnut?'

'We've got some nuts down in the bar,' the minder said.

'She doesn't want any nuts,' said Ritchie, and I saw that he was addressing a corner of the room with boxes of cigarettes piled high and couldn't even look in her direction at all.

'Okay,' she said. 'Can we start again, please?'

He nodded.

'Has Brian talked to his mum lately?'

'Don't know. She's a bit soft in the head. Her and the auld feller smoke too much wacky baccy.'

'Still at it? How old would she be now, you reckon?'

'Rita? She must be knocking on, pushing sixty.'

'And Brian's how old?'

'He's forty. Same as my good self.'

'I'd like you to give her a message for me.'

'What's that, then?'

'Tell her Dr Rebick's kids would like a favour off her, for old times' sake, from her family to ours.'

'And that's it?'

'Yes, that's it.'

'Nothing else?'

'Nothing.'

'I'll pass it on.'

'Why don't you give her a bell right now?'

'Me?'

'Yeah. Go on.'

'You want me to ring Rita?'

'That's right, ring her up, tell her who's here and what the situation is.'

And to my amazement the jerk actually picks up the phone and calls the lady and she actually replies.

He says, 'Did I get you out of bed, Rita? Sorry. Late night, was it? You've got to stop staying up watching those horror videos. They'll give you nightmares. Anyway, I've got Sam Rebick's sister sitting here with a Yank who's building a hotel at Chavasse Park, the site Brian leased to that other outfit. She's saying that she wants Brian to stop messing and call off his security. She says she wants it as *a favour* to the family.'

He handed the phone over to Alix. 'She says she'd like a word.'

Alix held it. 'I know,' she was saying. 'Of course, you're right, the best thing that ever happened to you. He was. I know.'

I was going wild trying to figure out what was going on at the other end. After a few minutes of this she handed the phone back to Ritchie.

'What she say?'

'She says she's going in to see Brian next week and she'll have a word with him. Now we'll take our leave. We'll be expecting to hear from you.'

'Well, that was short and sweet,' he said. 'Just how I like it.' And winked at the girls.

We came down the stairs behind the security guy, who tapped a code into a number pad. 'Listen,' I said, 'I gotta ask, why do you have that thing on your face?' He looked at himself in the mirror beside the door.

'I dunno. I just like the shape. It's cool.'

'Cool?'

'Yeah. It's dead cool.'

'Do you know what it is?'

'No. What?'

'Are you serious?'

'It's a swastika. It's the symbol of Nazi Germany.'

'Joseph,' Alix was saying, 'let's *go*.' And she put her hand on the small of my back and pushed me out on to the street.

'Did you hear that? He—'

'I don't think he really knows what it is, I don't think he knows what Nazi Germany is. Just leave it.'

'What? Are you telling me he doesn't know what a swastika is, what it stands for?'

'Well, you've seen Ritchie, so what kind of IQ do you think his personal security might have?'

I stood and looked at her, her arm against the railing, the amusement in her. It was just delightful to me to see her in what, in a way, was her element, watching that arrogance stretch to its full reach. She really was amazing, I'd never met anyone like her, what a tough babe: the only women I could compare her to were the girl soldiers in the army, but once you got into the real war there weren't too many of them about and they sure weren't going to look at a private like me when they could hang out with one of our blond blue-eyed boys in combat units, particularly the officers. I'd have loved to have seen Alix at twenty in uniform. Give her an Uzi and see how many she'd take out.

So I just couldn't resist grabbing her arm and saying, 'You are something else, you know that? You really are.'

'That hurts.'

'Sorry . . . What went on in there?'

'It's no mystery, I have no secret powers of persuasion, just local knowledge, what men would call gossip. When Rita Humphreys was in her late twenties she had an affair. She was an absolute stunner in those days, blue-black hair, long legs. Her father came over from Malta before the war and worked at Tate and Lyle, the sugar processors. They lived round the back of Granby Street and when she was sixteen she got married to a really rowdy docker by the name of Harry Humphreys. They used to go twelve bells on a Saturday night and after a few years she was sick to death of him. Now, do you remember at my mother's *shiva* house a solicitor called Kevin Wong?'

'Sure.'

'Rita was his office cleaner. She got pregnant by him, this was in 1963, Brian was just a toddler. Kevin was married as well, with his own kids, and she was faced with catastrophe. There was no way in the world she could pass off Kevin's baby as Harry's, even if Kevin was only half Chinese. The two of them were absolutely desperate. If Rita had the baby Harry wouldn't have killed her but he'd have done her a very serious injury, there was no doubt about that, so Kevin came to my dad and asked him if he could help her.'

'How do you mean?'

'It was when abortion was illegal.'

'So he . . . ?'

'Yes.'

'I see. Wow. And you and Sam both knew this?'

'Not Sam, I did.'

'How come?'

'She brought her daughter Floris, Brian's half-sister, into Melanie's family-planning clinic and she told her and Mel told me.'

'Why didn't she tell her own husband?'

'Women's secrets are a funny thing, Joseph, we like to keep them to ourselves.'

'And what happened to Rita?'

'Eventually, when she was well into her thirties, she left Harry and went to live with a guy who ran a club for seamen from Trinidad, Floris's father. I believe they're very happy. I hope so. I see her on the street from time to time. She's still kept her looks to a certain extent.'

We were walking along, it was a warm day, and on turning to her I noticed a glow of sweat had broken out on her neck and the gold chain around her throat was sticking to her skin instead of hanging loose, a flower perfume and salt coming in waves from her, and I was sweating too, my shirt damp. There was a rain feeling in the air.

'And what about the walnuts?'

She giggled. 'You know, when you told me the name Ritchie Sylvester I was thinking about all the people Sam knows and it rang a bell but I couldn't remember anything he'd ever said. Then, suddenly, I got it. I *did* know about him but not through Sam, through my father. Years ago, when I was at Oxford but was back visiting over Christmas, my father got called out on a home visit to this family called Sylvester. They had a ten-year-old called Ritchie and he and his older brother were messing around with a bowl of unshelled nuts someone had bought. Anyway, the older lad had dared him to stick a walnut up his arse and the little idiot was so full of pep and piss that he actually did it, put a walnut up his own anus, and the thing got stuck and my dad had to remove it with forceps. He came home in a fury with his shirt covered in blood and shit, and Sam and I were wetting ourselves laughing. But after that, for years, Ritchie was always known as Walnut Whip.'

'*Jeezus.*'

'I know. The minute I remembered, I thought, I've got you.'

'And he knew you knew, I could see it in his face.'

'Listen, everything in that room, every single thing, was about face, including a retard who tattoos a swastika on his own. These people have nothing but their face. Nothing. Take that away from them and they're nobodies. As long as you understand that you can always deal with them.'

'You want to get a drink?'

'Yeah, why not?'

We walked into the bar at the Lyceum and I ordered a couple of glasses of wine. 'And bring us some nuts,' I said, winking at her.

'Actually, I hate nuts. Got any olives?'

'A successful meeting deserves a toast.'

'To your hotel,' she proposed.

'Indeed, and hell and damnation to those who try to thwart us.'

'To hell with them.' She picked up an olive and bit into it.

'I have to say, you really are something else. I've never met a woman like you in my life.'

'Thanks.'

'You think like a man, you talk like a man, you seem to have discarded all the usual nonsense that women are interested in.'

'Such as?'

'Oh, you know, do my shoes match my handbag, I can't do anything with my hair, if I buy this fantasy cream will it make me look twenty again, that kind of stuff.'

'*Fantasy* cream?' She brushed away a strand of hair from her face and her green eyes lit up with the kind of wattage they use to floodlight stadiums.

Nevertheless, I ploughed on. 'Yeah, I mean why do women plaster themselves with makeup, who do they think they're fooling! What's wrong with looking your age?'

'What's wrong? What's *wrong*? I've never heard anything so vacuous in my life.' She was leaning forward stabbing at me with the cocktail stick she had used to skewer the olive. 'First of all, when the World Congress of Men get together and they take a unanimous vote that from now they find middle-aged women with wrinkles more attractive than teenage girls without them, then maybe, just *maybe*, we'll pay attention to your little lectures about natural beauty. Okay? Second of all, do you know what paid for Sam's flat that you like so much? Do you know where the money came from to put me through my MA? Do you know how we get to give ten thousand pounds a year to human-rights charities? *Did* you ever ask yourself that? No? Okay, I'll tell you. It all comes from the sale of those so-called fantasy creams that you're complaining about, which *my* grandfather developed and which *my* mother brought all the way over from Germany with her on the *Kindertransport* and which *my* father reconstituted from the ashes of Nazi Germany. So, if you don't know what you're talking about *shut the fuck up.*'

Then she called over the waiter.

'You want another glass of wine?' she asked me, putting another olive into her mouth.

'Absolutely, whatever you say.'

One humid evening a couple of nights later, walking across the room in my underwear, I picked up a ringing phone and it was Erica and what she said was this: 'Hi. I'm coming to London. Want to meet up for a couple of days?'

Would I?

'What brings this on?'

'A whim. I'm going to go shopping.'

'Nothing new there.' All women love that kind of thing. Buy them whatever they like if you want to keep them happy, take out your credit card. Let it be your pleasure.

'I need a whole new wardrobe.'

'Whatever you say. You always look good to me.'

'I've made a reservation at the Basil Hotel in Knightsbridge. It's just behind Harrods.'

'Couldn't get any closer, huh?'

'Don't mock me.' She giggled.

'So should I call and get myself a room?'

'It's taken care of.'

'You've got me a . . .'

'Why don't you wait and see?'

'Are you teasing?'

'Yes. It's fun.'

'So does this mean—'

'Don't spoil it, Joe.'

I was so worked up I could hardly breathe.

'Okay.'

'Listen, I know you must be dying to hear about Michael. The whole thing has turned out well, very well. I must admit I was

surprised when you suggested it, it was hard for me to swallow
and I didn't really in my heart of hearts believe he would go for
it, but he did, like a shot. Your mom and dad are happy with the
arrangement, your dad particularly, life's a lot easier for both of
them now. Michael is talking about becoming a nurse, he's sent
off for all kind of catalogues. He knows he'll have to finish high
school and go to college sooner or later but he has a direction. I
suppose it was obvious all along what sort of kid we had there,
but we missed it and somehow you had this moment of real
insight. You found a solution. I was impressed.'

'To tell you the truth, it wasn't my idea. Someone put it into
my head.'

'Whoever he is, he is some smart character.'

'Yeah. She is.'

'Who's this she?'

'A woman I met here.'

'Oh?'

'No, it's not what you think. She's interesting, very bright, a
little lost in her life, attractive, but not that way, at least not to me.'

'Married?'

'No.'

'What kind of age?'

'Around fifty, maybe a little younger, not much.'

'So how attractive?'

'Striking, the kind who must have been a knock-out when she
was a kid. Tall, dresses well.'

'Good figure?'

'So-so.'

'Lines?'

'I never noticed. I suppose – just round her eyes.'

'She dyes her hair?'

'How the hell should I know? Anyway, why are we talking
about her? What about you?'

'Oh, me. You know me.'

'Yeah. I do. I miss you so much.'

'I'll be here in a week. Can you wait that long?'

'I've waited nearly a year.'

'Yes.'

'So are we back together?'

'Joe, come to London. We'll talk there. I'm different now. A year is a long time and a short time, but we all change. And I've changed. You don't know how much. I don't want to make promises on the phone.'

Changed? Thank God. Dumped that inane stuff she'd been coming out with, which she'd got from God knows where, some book she'd read, I bet, by a shyster with a few letters after his name or some fucked-up sister who wanted to export her own miseries and failures to every other woman in the world. But apparently Erica had seen through it as I knew she would in the end, it was just a phase she was going through, which if I waited long enough would pass, as obviously it had. I knew that sooner or later she would return to herself, to being a wife and mother, committed, as I was, to the *idea* of marriage, to its enduring power, which I had signed up to with no hesitation. I believe in marriage. Many of my generation don't, I do. It's hard work, that's for sure, but you can *will* it to operate properly if you only take the right attitude. One thing I was certain of was that no one was going to rob me of what was my right: the right to a marriage pretty much like the one my parents had, as good as.

What could I say to her now on the phone? Say that I was dying with excitement, say that my breath was labouring in my chest, say that I was getting a hard-on thinking of her breasts and her thighs and her silky wet cunt (having not really touched a woman's body since she walked out, apart from that careless kiss with Alix Rebick), say that I missed her, that this life was no substitute and that I wanted things back exactly where they were before, before she made her inexplicable decision to leave me. But I kept schtum and got out my diary and fixed up a date in only a few days' time. Spent those days having my hair cut, clipped the hairs in my nose and my ears, got talked into having a manicure for the first time in my life, which left my nails short and trim and buffed up, fingers I was going to push inside her, knowing how she loved to have her G-spot pressed as part of our foreplay; bought fresh white boxer shorts (the ones I had, which Erica bought for me at Marshall Fields, looked grey); bought a navy Ralph Lauren shirt and a Gucci tie; and, thinking that I might do something to surprise her, made up my mind to go to one of those stores in the Burlington Arcade and buy myself a Panama hat.

And I was feeling pretty good about myself when I turned up at Lime Street station, my cheeks as smooth as Michael's bottom when he was a newborn baby, and reeking of a new aftershave. I had a biography of Lyndon Johnson to read on my journey, a guy who really changed *my* life, without whose escalation of the Vietnam war and his careless expenditure of the lives of men of my generation, I would never have left America, never gone to Israel and never met Erica, sitting in that café in her drawstring peasant blouse with her tits bursting out from the fabric and it was all I could do not to drop my gun and run over and grab them.

But life always turns out as farce and this was a journey from hell, the train an hour late leaving, stalled past Runcorn, dumped us off at Crewe where it broke down completely, limped down to London in six hours and twenty-three minutes, instead of the two and a half it said on the schedule. I called Erica and said I would be late but she told me it was no problem, she had a lot more stores to look at, and I said, 'I bet.' She loved to shop, my wife. They all do. For me, it's a raid. You know what you want, you dive in, you find it, you're out of there. For women it's very different: it's a sport, it's a hobby, it's half their fucking lives.

All this made me smile to remember, my beautiful wife, no different from any other woman when it comes to this nonsense, and I don't understand any of it, but that's what marriage is, a lifetime's task of staring at mutual incomprehension. I know a few men who have refused the married state or have been divorced so many times you know they were never really serious about it, they weren't even serially attaching themselves. It's a desire for an existential freedom that drives them on; well, freedom is what they're getting. Free to die alone. You can keep it. Women to them are like animals in the zoo, wild creatures, another species. Erica taught me the word misogyny. At Berkeley in the late sixties there were a lot of angry young women and at first I felt defensiveness when confronted by the rage trips they were laying on us (to use phrases that haven't passed my lips for decades). According to these people we were no longer allowed to call chicks, we men were responsible for every evil in the cosmos, from the rape of Cordelia Perkins (the best friend of my then girlfriend Barbara) while walking home one night from the subway, to the rape of the whole planet by the male-dominated military-industrial complex.

Look, we were all scared of girls in our teens, you badly want what they aren't prepared to give you. They have the power, they're the ones who are holding out, not you. So to be told, a few weeks into college, that simply by being in possession of a cock instead of a fanny you're part of a race of Nazis who control the planet, and women are a slave race or a race you were committing some kind of genocide against, what with the Pill and dosing them with napalm in Vietnam, was a little difficult to swallow. But Erica taught me a subtler kind of feminism, she showed me how certain men (not all) feel a disgust for women, and a disdain. 'What I hate about porn,' she told me, 'is the way it turns women into meat, like those pictures of cows and sheep and pigs you used to see in old-fashioned butchers', with the parts sectioned off and named. I don't think that the men who run these magazines truly believe that women are fully human.' At which I thought, but didn't say, that the pictures that guys jerk off to are indeed of objects, *sex* objects, and that the trick is to know the difference between the air-brushed, pumped-up, silicone-breasted fantasy, and a living, breathing, ageing, imperfect woman who is your wife. One is solely there to come over, the other is there for everything else you need from a relationship. And the misogynists are the ones who are always surprised when a woman whom they thought was a come-dream turns into what they would call a 'bitch', in other words concerned with the needs and desires of herself as well as the guy who is essentially masturbating inside her.

These are the conversations of years ago, of our firebrand days, of the times when we had politics. Now, not so much. I watch the news, I keep up with a few columnists, I stretch my mind with a couple of magazines (finding to my discomfort and surprise that on certain subjects I'm more inclined to side with the *New Republic* against the *Nation*) and maintain subscriptions to some Middle East journals which I don't always get round to reading. Erica, as far as I can tell, confines herself to *Glamour* magazine, *Vanity Fair*, novels recommended by Oprah's reading club, and a hell of a lot of those books that are all the rage these days about people who have had terrible times in their childhood and, for some reason, feel they need to share their misery with everyone else. I've come home and found her damp-cheeked as she mourns some Irish girl dead these fifty years of poverty and I say, 'What are you weeping for? You're crying for the sake of tears!' Either that or she's with her beading.

A whole room of the house is devoted to this hobby, plus we have bead books stacked up by the bed. She makes necklaces and earrings and bracelets which she wears all the time now, and our friends and relations have to wear them too, because she makes presents for everyone. She likes very elaborate numbers called chokers which go round the neck, thousands and thousands of tiny little glass beads threaded on lines of plastic with dangles coming down off them. Beading took over from quilting. And before that, crochet shawls. All of these olde worlde American crafts are anathema to me. Plain. Keep it plain, I say. I could only hope that Erica's great change was that she had finally grown tired of such pursuits and had thrown away the clutter, the lengths of wool and scraps of fabric and the plastic bags of coloured glass that spilt out everywhere and that I was always treading on in my bare feet and yelping, finding them impaled in my soles. She would kneel down and with her fingertips pick them up and I would let on that I dropped them on purpose so I could stare at her ass up in the air while she was hunting for them but this didn't go down well. She regarded the whole *megillah* with deadly seriousness. She cannot take a joke about anything which matters to her, reminding me of what Alix said one day when I was talking about my work. 'Makes you wonder what Jewish minimalism is,' she remarked, lifting her coffee cup to her crimson mouth. 'I suppose it would be, "I want the finest minimalism money can buy and I want it *everywhere*."' Which made me laugh so hard I knocked over a bowl of sugar which emptied itself into the crotch of my pants. I like the way she dresses. Plain, good tailoring. No beads. I doubt if she has hobbies. I'd declare my views to Erica about the beading if I could, but that's not what marriage is. If you want it to work, you put up and shut up because it was her without the necklaces I was interested in, her with nothing on at all that got me going.

These thoughts got me as far as Crewe. Then, in exasperation, dumped off the train, I had to wait for an hour. There were no announcements, no customer-service people, everyone was grumbling, and we sat with soft drinks, trying to read or listening

to Walkmans or fiddling around with games consoles. A combi-
nation of the chaos and the physically heavy biography of
Johnson I was reading (it must have weighed a couple of pounds)
made me put it down and remember a conversation I had with
Michael before I left Chicago on that last trip. He had not given
up on pestering me about my 'army career' and a couple of days
after my arrival, sitting in the yard one early evening before
dinner, he suddenly came out with another question: 'Here's
one, were you in *shul* when the Yom Kippur war started? Because
Grandpa thinks you weren't.'

And now I began to laugh because he had, inadvertently, hit
on something I could tell him about, that day the war began, a
story he would, I'm sure, be able to relate to very well, stuff that
would make him giggle rather than expose him to the reality of
being a soldier, a vocation that he and my other son were never
going to have or, at least, not if I could help it. So I went into the
kitchen and got a beer and got one for him too (a travesty of
male bonding because I don't think he even likes the taste), put
my feet up on the recliner and began to tell him a tale of war
such as he'd never seen on any movie or on TV.

'No, I wasn't in *shul*. You have to remember that I had just –
like a month before – finished my three years in the army and I
was looking around for a job. I was sharing a house up in the hills
in Haifa with a bunch of other guys, this was before I met your
mom, and we were sitting on the porch having woken up late
because we'd been hitting the booze and . . . oh, what's the harm
in telling you?, there was no booze, we'd smoked a lot of dope.
Anyway, one of my room-mates, another American guy named
Steve, remarked that there seemed to be a lot of traffic for Yom
Kippur and what's more it was moving pretty fast, which was
odd, people weren't creeping along trying to make it look like
they weren't driving their car on the holiest of days, they were
really putting their foot down and in the distance we could hear

a lot of sirens. So we go back into the house and turn on the radio and there's a guy reading in a monotone a list of codewords for mobilising the reserve units – not buried in the weather bulletin, this was: "We're at war, no time to fuck around" – and after a while I hear my codeword: Hazan Barak, which means strong lightning. So I knew then that I had to get down to Jaffa. I began running around the place looking for my stuff, you know, rucksack, boots, that kind of thing, but the problem is I'm still so stoned that I can't find any of it. I'm turning the house over and there's nothing. Then Steve says, "Didn't you leave it with a guy in Tel Aviv for safekeeping before you moved up the coast?" and I remember, yeah, that's right, so this means I have to go and find it first, but the problem is, there's no time and even if I went there, he wouldn't be in, he'd be on his way to his own reserve unit.

'I ran out the house in my jeans and a T-shirt and those rubber thong sandals people wore in those days because they were so cheap, and I got on a bus. They were all going to one place: they were filled with civilians trying to get to the staging area for their reserve units. But when I eventually turned up at the staging post at Beer'sheva first of all there wasn't anyone there who knew who I was, and not only that, there wasn't anybody there who knew any of the other people I had been in the army with. You see, for reserve purposes they take a group of people who finish their active service and throw them out and wherever they land they land, so what in active service had been a tightly knit integral unit was now scattered all over the place, divided up among many different units.'

'So what happened?' Michael said, unable to visualise his father as this stoned panicky hippie, although he'd seen the photos often enough, but thought, I suppose, that some impostor had taken his father's place in front of the camera, a guy with a full head of hair and no worried look on his face.

'It's night-time now and the scene is chaotic – in fact, it looks like the HQ of the Wehrmacht with the Russian troops getting ready to enter Berlin and everybody running round trying to shred all the files. I remember thinking as I got off the bus, *this* is supposed to develop into a fighting machine that will win a war? There were tens of thousands of people milling about, drinking coffee, checking kit and duffel bags, walking around with packs of bundled blankets tied with string on their shoulders. Man, it looked like a refugee camp not a mobilising army. There were no tanks or cannons, just thousands and thousands of people milling in these huge sheds – buildings with no sides, just corrugated roofing, you could park aircraft in them, they were that big – and on the far side, behind a bunch of soldiers sitting at tables with clipboards, piled all the way up to the ceiling were shirts, pants, blankets, sleeping-bags, duffel-bags, socks, boots, mess kits. Behind each soldier with his clipboard was a mountain of *this*. And I discovered that what everyone was doing was looking around for their buddies before joining a line so they could get kitted out as buddies before going down to the Front. As for me, I'm still alone, don't see anybody I know, but I figure I'll be fucked if I'm going to go fight the Egyptians in jeans and T-shirt, so I decide to go and join one of the lines. I proceed along and I get two shirts, two pairs of pants, pair of boots, mess kit, sleeping-bag, tent, webbing. I have everything I need except when I get to the very last window where you sign up for weapons it's closed. I remember thinking, *This is not a good sign*. You're laughing, Michael, I'm glad you think it's funny, yeah, well, it was funny, but only in hindsight.'

He was sitting on the grass, his hands over his knees in his big baggy skateboard pants, with a leather thong round his neck and a bit of turquoise stone threaded through it, had taken off his shoes, which were so big they looked like alien spacecraft.

'Okay. So I knock on the window, and the guy pulls the shutter up and I say, "Could I have a gun, please?" and he says, "No." I say, "What do you mean, no?" He says, "We're all out of them, there aren't any more." I say, "I'm supposed to go off to a war without a gun?" He says, "Look, I just work here. There's nothing left, I gave them all out." At this stage I was starting to get a little bit angry. I didn't know anybody. I expected to be part of a unit that didn't exist. I'd done what I was supposed to do. As soon as I'd heard the codeword *Hazan Barak* I'd dropped everything and run off to the war. I get to the war and I find that they don't have any guns to fight with and I'm supposed to be part of the army of the regional superpower? God help the poor fucking Egyptian privates if this is what's happening to me. So I'm standing there trying to figure out what to do. It's already getting on for midnight and this joke had been going on since noon. By now the throng of tens of thousands had started to thin because as they got their kit they were moving out down to the Negev, and out of the corner of my eye I'd noticed a sergeant who looked substantially more intelligent than most of the other people. He was an Ashkenazi who had a red beard and glasses, and he looked like someone who might be a doctor or an architect in civilian life – some of the other sergeants were already sclerotic, they were miles and miles from the Front and already they were behaving like shells were falling all around them – and I walk over and explain the situation to him, starting with the morning in Haifa and ending with, "So here I am, standing in front of you, and I don't have a gun."

'He stands there for a minute and thinks and then he says, "Well, listen, the best thing I can tell you is that you've got to understand that this is what the army is about – chaos – and there isn't anything you can do about it. It's only going to get worse, not better, and here is my advice to you. You have two problems. First, you're here when you should be there, down in the desert. All these people you see around you are the dregs, people who are seven or eight hours behind the war, drivers and cooks and mechanics, people who the war can wait seven or eight hours for. The line units are there already, so that's your first problem, you gotta get to the Front. My suggestion is the next truck you see, just jump on it. As far as a gun goes, the war has been going on for a day already, there are already dead Israeli soldiers, and when you come across the first dead Israeli soldier you see, take his gun." And I thought, So this is what it comes down to. This is how I'm going to defend my country, they don't even have a gun of my own to give me.

'Now I realised this guy was talking more sense than anybody else so I turned around and hopped on to the first truck I saw. It headed out the gates and I sat there for three or four hours until it stopped in the middle of the desert in the middle of the night. The tailgate came down and standing at the bottom there was a lieutenant smoking a cigarette. I tapped him on the shoulder, told him my story and he said, "Fine, I've got a unit, if you go and stand over there, you're in it."'

'So how did you get your gun?' Michael wanted to know.

'I got my gun through some very weird circumstances. One of the guys standing "over there" was a recent development in Israeli society, these long-haired twenty-somethings that didn't feel they could kill, Israeli hippies. It was quite obvious what his strategy was, something straight out of *Catch-22*. This guy was going to convince everyone that he was crazy so he would get sent back, he was being a real *nudnick*. He would selectively target everyone in the half-track to *nudgie* them for twenty minutes so by the time he's finished annoying everyone for twenty minutes apiece, we would all vote to get rid of him. Our lieutenant worked out what his game was so he exercised his executive prerogative to discharge him on the spot and I got his gun. And that's it. How I fought the Yom Kippur war. And you know what? I guess half the guys in any army in the world could tell you a similar story.'

That was what I told my son Michael. It was true, every single word. And I don't know, can't begin to figure what it is that I'd omitted that makes it sound like a travesty to me. Every word is correct, just as it happened, yet there's something missing. And all you can think of to say is that lame thing people come up with when they've told a great story to someone else who doesn't laugh, doesn't get it: 'You had to be there.'

I have diaries that no one has ever seen, little paragraphs I wrote under fire.

I wrote this:

Was shot at again at work today. I guess only bank-tellers and airline pilots can make a claim like that these days.
A hit drilled a hole the thickness of a hot dog through a
DANGER – MINES sign that I had been standing in front of.

And this:

Chanukah in Egypt. Donuts from Beer'sheva delivered by helicopter. We made a menorah from eight brass 105mm artillery casings, filled with diesel oil. By the eighth night, the Egyptians dug in at the oasis should be thoroughly confused.

And completely unaccountably, this:

Dreamt last night I was dating Tricia Nixon.

I have no idea who wrote all that stuff. I have no idea who it happened to. I have a picture of myself, right in the middle of the war. We'd found a beach chair in the middle of the Sinai and none of us had a clue what the fuck it was doing there, but I sat down in it and someone got out an Instamatic and snapped me. My hair is much longer than it is now, there'd been no time to cut anyone's hair when the war started. My army shirt is open, my legs are stretched out in front of me, ending in huge boots, laced up tight. The sand is pocked with tank tracks, as far as the eye can see, and way in the distance, just above the horizon, there's something that might be a helicopter, or possibly just a small smudge on the negative. I don't remember that day at all, which week of the war it was, who got killed and who made it to bedtime. But looking at the photo, I realise that if I did what Erica demanded of me, unburdened myself of all my war-time secrets, I'd be telling a story not about me at all, but about that kid sitting on a beach chair in the desert who had a dream about dating Tricia Nixon and, as I see it, I don't have the right to pass off someone else's stories as my own.

I had enough on my plate, with ageing parents, a wayward wife, a problem son. The guy in the desert could look after himself. He'd survive.

Then there was an announcement. Here was our train. By nightfall if I was lucky I'd be in bed with my beloved wife, whom I'd stolen from the soldier boy. She's mine, kid, not yours. All mine.

No time to buy a Panama hat in the Burlington Arcade to impress my estranged wife. I got into a cab and went straight to the hotel. The desk clerk was expecting me, handed over a registration card to fill out, then gave me a key. I couldn't bring myself to ask him what kind of room had been assigned, if I was on my own or sharing, like I was a teenage kid on vacation with his first girlfriend. It was a dark, old hotel. In the lobby there was a women's club where ladies in town from the country could come and wash up and change their clothes and drink tea or cocktails between shopping and the theatre. Male guests were 'not permitted to enter'. Quaint. Erica's idea of a joke, no doubt, meeting me somewhere so totally at odds with my idea of comfort. Some of the rooms didn't even have their own bathrooms and you needed to creep along the hallway with your towel over your arm. But it was only a couple of minutes' walk from Harrods, you couldn't fault it on that.

I see myself striding through that hotel, a tallish, confident, middle-aged American male, out of place in his surroundings, looking as if he was about to start berating the bellhop or demanding all kinds of services he knew the place couldn't provide, but I was thinking of how I was minutes away from seeing her, and that this long inexplicable nightmare was about to come to an end, that she would be my wife again, instead of a voice at the end of the phone.

She'd got us a small suite and she wasn't there but two thousand shopping bags took her place. Maybe not that many but the room was full of bags – not just Harrods, Harvey Nichols, Selfridges, Chanel, but Issey Miyake, Bruno Magli, Emma Hope, names I'd never heard of, except maybe there was some connection between this Bruno Magli and the O.J. Simpson trial. It looked like her credit cards had turned into heat-seeking missiles. The bags were all over the place: on the floor, on the couch, on all the chairs, the bed, stacked up on the night table. In the bathroom I saw a bunch of women's cosmetics and her perfume, Rive Gauche, which was packaged in a blue, black and silver metal container, a scent she'd worn for years and years, which to her was a really sexy smell but to me nothing was sexier than what came off her own skin.

On the night table I found a note. 'Hi. Back soon. Rest.' Nothing more.

I took a few bags off the bed, lay down on it and closed my eyes. I was at total peace now because I'd reached home after a long journey. I knew we were man and wife once more. And I fell asleep.

Dreams come easily to me, even when I'm catnapping I always dream, of buildings I've seen and ones I hope to build, impossible structures that defy every law of engineering, those earthbound rules that tie you to the ground. 'Castles in the air,' Erica calls them, and that's what I design in these strange interludes between consciousness and the submerged places inside me that you get to through longer, darker stairways, though in my case not that often. Perhaps I dozed for twenty or thirty minutes, a tumescent state, my hand on my groin, my balls with the memory of Erica's tongue moving towards them. Her face. The buttercup hair, the chocolate eyes, the coffee-coloured mole behind her right ear, never seen by her, only by me, until I held up the mirror she carried in her purse and showed it to her in the reflection of another mirror. She had six moles on her back. They formed the shape of the Big Dipper, 'You starry girl,' that kid soldier said, when he saw her unclothed for the first time, tearing off his army shirt, his hands shaking as he unlaced his army boots, which she at once slipped her own feet into and paraded around in them. The room we were in with the cracked blue walls, the musty brown calico drapes, the framed photos of Ein Gedi and David Ben-Gurion: just a youth hostel on Ben-Yehuda Street. A twenty-two-year-old girl from Canada waking alone to hear the sirens in the street, terrified, a war breaking out in a foreign land. She was walking around that room stark naked now, except for my army boots, the very ones that had been issued to me in the aircraft hangar in Beer'sheva. My boots that had marched across the Sinai desert, that I'd killed in and nearly been killed, on her pretty size-seven feet with pink-painted toenails. I was ready to die of lust and ran across the room and seized her breasts and put my mouth to them, my tongue sucking on her nipples, licking and biting, and she pushed me down on the bed and took my cock in her mouth, a naked girl on top of me, giving me head still in my boots, which dropped from her feet to the floor. Then she pulled her lips away and impaled herself on me, drew my left hand up to her breast and the right she guided to her clitoris, her trigger, she called it. And in ten seconds flat I came. Closed my eyes. Saw trees scorched and blasted, wrenched whole from the earth and dumped like Pick-Up Stix down on the canal's edge, the air filled with the smell of gunpowder and burning pine needles. Opened my eyes, saw her smiling face, plump pink mouth bending to kiss me and reached my hand again for her cunt to make her come, which she did, a few minutes later, with such a howl of pleasure that I was aroused again and nearly came again.

When my pass expired two days later I went back to the army, doing my job, clearing land-mines in the desert. The Sinai is a huge place and you really begin to grasp its vastness when you're traversing it crawling on your stomach. You're working in rows, as migrant labourers on a farm walk miles and miles cutting tobacco, a dozen of us all doing it, from before sunrise until just before eleven, then knocking off and coming back at three o'clock and working until after sunset. At night we climbed into sleeping-bags, you turn the half-track around and sleep in the shadow of it, in the sand, then more of the same at daybreak. You crawl on your belly, you've got a commando knife, you move along inch by inch, probing. This is minimalist work. When you hear the metal blade hitting metal, that's a mine. So you chop up the earth, scoop it out, defuse it, carry on. You don't think about anything but what you're doing when you're defusing mines. It's a job that requires all your powers of concentration and all the time I was trying to screen out Erica's face because I *had to*: if your attention wanders and you get something wrong they're going to be picking up your body parts with tweezers. Horrible to have to ignore the pornographic picture pasted at the front of my skull of her body, the film that was playing there, round the clock, free of charge, no intermission, of that amazing, unbelievable fuck in a dingy hostel room with a girl whose body I craved like crazy and astoundingly, nearly thirty years later, still felt exactly the same way.

She was a girl not a woman. I had to stop calling her that when the feminism took hold, and when she had our children the girlishness indeed fell away from her, maturing, rounding with each pregnancy but she grew sweeter and more luscious with each pound that grew in her belly, carrying our kids. To me she was what God promised Moses, a land flowing with milk and honey, the milk in her breasts and the honey that dripped from her cunt. *Set me as a seal upon thy heart.*

These were my dreams and I woke from them to a key turned in the lock, the door opening. I opened my eyes and saw standing at the door some other woman, a stranger who had mistakenly been given the wrong key, not Erica, a little shrivelled-up thing with a birdy, bony-assed body, the type that

Tom Wolfe calls the 'social X-rays'. No hips at all. Hardly any space in the room was taken up by this person. She was trying to smile at me but her face had a mouth in the middle of it like a slot, as rigid as the eye in a needle. She could hardly move a muscle.

My hand was resting on my cock.

'Hey, Joe. What you doing with that gun in your hand?'

Our oldest joke.

'Erica?'

'Yes. It's me.'

'What have you done?'

She twirled and danced around the room in clothes of a kind I'd never seen her in before, a tiny black suit with a short skirt half-way up her thighs and a little thin silver chain round her scrawny neck. Where did the beads go? What happened to them? And the rest. A hundred and twenty pounds when I met her, around a hundred and forty-five a year ago, now what? A hundred? Ninety-five? A child got up as a middle-aged woman and the parents should be saying, 'Take that off right now.' But I didn't want her to take anything off. I had dread of what was under that suit.

'What do you think?'

'What have you *done*?'

'It's the new me.'

'I can see that. Where's the old you?'

'Gone. Dead. I killed her. Fat Erica with the saggy boobs and the saggy face is a thing of the past.'

I closed my eyes and opened them again and she was still there.

'What? You're blinking. You got a lash in your eye?'

Nothing. The apparition wouldn't budge.

'Please say something. At least tell me what you're feeling.'

Numb.

'I'll talk, then. You could say, "Well done." That would be appropriate because you know this has taken hard work, not to mention suffering and pain and endurance, all those army virtues you've always been reciting. You don't get to look like this just lying in bed and wishing for it, you make it happen.' She was trying to smile but not a mote of the old radiance was there.

'What did you do to your face?'

'I had it fixed in Denver, I got a recommendation from Bernice Fisher, you remember her?'

'No.'

'She's in my book club.'

I knew books would come into this one way or another.

'Dr Davis was my saviour, he gave me back myself.'

'That's not you. You're unrecognisable. You never looked like that in all your life.'

'I know, it's odd, isn't it? He said that he could make me look twenty-five but not me at twenty-five and I replied, "Fine". At twenty-five I could have borne some improvement.'

'And you let him do this to you?' A stranger had taken a knife to my wife and mutilated her.

'He only did what I told him.'

'You didn't think to ask me what *I* felt about it? You talked to him but not me? Why did you do it?'

She sat down on the bed, barely making a dent on the blankets, and touched my face. There were no pads left on her finger-tips, just little bags of loose skin.

'Joe, you've got to understand this was a decision I reached out of a crisis. What I'm about to tell you is not the kind of thing women ever talk about to their husbands, to their girlfriends yes, not to a man. But I don't know any other way to explain myself. For several months a couple of years ago I had a pain in my right breast . . .'

'What!'

'Hush. Listen. It was a sharp pain tormenting me at odd moments. I went to the doctor, he felt my breasts, he couldn't find anything. He sent me for a mammogram, same verdict. Nothing there at all. No lump, as far as anyone can tell, I was healthy. Yet the pain was still around. It wouldn't go away. Now a year ago I'm in Marshall Fields picking up a new bra and I hand it over at the cash desk to pay and the woman looks at it and says, "Is this for your daughter?" and I say no, it's for me, why do you ask? So she says, "This isn't your size." I say, "I've worn the same size bra for years, 36C cup." Well, she looks at my chest and she says, "I really don't think so. To me you look like a 40DD. Why don't you try one on?" I go back to the changing room and I try this other bra and I realise that she's right, for years I've been wearing the wrong size. But for the life of me I can't bring myself to buy the bra even though it is the most beautiful white lace thing with some little pearls sewn into the straps, because I am *not* a 40DD. I'm a 36C. That's who I am. Yet standing in the store I look in the mirror and I examine myself and I think, this is it. This *is* who you are, a woman coming up to fifty, bra size 40DD, who is never again going to stand at a bus stop waiting to go to Vancouver, with wings on the soles of her shoes. I go back to the till with the first bra and the sales clerk says, "What happened? It didn't fit?" I said, "Yeah, it fitted, but I just don't want to be a 40DD." And you know what she says? *"You're going to get pains in your breasts if you continue to wear the wrong cup size and you'll frighten yourself into thinking you've got cancer."* So I had to turn back and buy the bigger bra.'

'I'm sorry, but I don't get this. What has the size of your brassiere got to do with our marriage?'

"Because everywhere I go, and everything I do, the same thoughts are running in my head. I'm doing the laundry and I'm thinking, I'm driving to the store and I'm thinking, I'm at work and I'm thinking and all I can think about is one thought: is this *it*? Is it all one long freewheeling coast downhill to old age, to being your mom and my mom – old ladies, however much their kids may love them. Old lady material! Me! I couldn't believe it.'

'I still don't understand what this has to do with the size of your brassiere.'

'Size 40DD is an old lady's size. It's not the size of a young girl.'

'But you're *not* a young girl, nor am I the kid you married. We get older, so what?'

'For a man and for a woman it's not the same thing.'

'Sure it is.'

'Believe me, it isn't.'

'So *this* was your solution!'

'I wanted to make a big change in my life, *needed* to. I read all the magazines, saw what other women in my position did, paint or write or learn to play an instrument, all those frustrated desires of busy people like us in middle age. Nothing excited me. I didn't need to travel, we've been all over the world on our vacations. And yet still something was wrong. And I figured that whatever it was, was existential, deep in the soul. It needed time and space to figure it out. I genuinely believed that a whole phase in my life was coming to an end, that I had to go into hibernation and see who I was when I woke up. There was nothing wrong with our marriage, but it was a marriage, and I was fat, married Erica.'

'You weren't fat. Or if you were it didn't bother me. But even if you thought you were, why didn't you talk to me about all this?'

'You don't get it, Joe, what happens to a woman as she nears fifty. The human race doesn't need you to survive any more. My kids didn't need me, so who did?'

'Me. I needed you.'

'You? You're self-sufficient. That's what the army taught you.'

'Nothing you learn in the army has any connection with what one person needs from another person.'

'Well, you know what? I was tired of your litany of self-control, your list of what men are and what women aren't. I didn't fall out of love with you, there was no one else and nothing else on my mind except to examine what I was going to do with the rest of my life, this life that had no place for me.'

'No place for you? You are still a mother. One day you're going to be a grandmother. And your mom's still alive, you're a daughter.'

'I mean no place for who I am essentially, my essential self rather than what role I take. I felt invisible in the world. I felt like you could see through me. I was a pane of glass you didn't even notice.'

'Oh, come on, for fuck's sake, what is this nonsense?'

'You say that, it took me four months to come to the same conclusion. I saw a shrink. She took me here, there and everywhere in that search through my psyche. We tore the place apart. A whole month alone on repressions. Had I been abused by my parents or another relative or a friend of the family when I was a child? No. Had I buried the memories? No, there were no memories. Did I have a bad sex life? No, I had a great sex life. On and on this went until one day, I looked at her, Tonya Ruben her name was, in narrow black glasses, looking at me, and I started to see her through *your* eyes. I thought, what would Joe make of this woman? and, of course, I knew at once. You would have called her a charlatan, said that everything we had been doing in those sessions was garbage. And you know what? You would have been right. It was garbage. A waste of money.

'So I go home and I pull out an envelope from my purse, an old utility bill. I start to make a list on the back of it. The list is: what is wrong with my life. Find one word to sum it up. I came up with two words. Fat. Old. It was as easy as that. And when I looked at the two words on the envelope, I thought, how would Joe approach this? He'd see it as a problem and, as we know, problems have a solution.'

'You're telling me I have some responsibility for this?'

'Yes, I think I am. I said to myself, You think you're fat? So do what the doctor tells you, go on a diet. You look old? These days, this is not a burden any woman has to put up with if she has the money and the will. It's not as expensive as it seems, when you look into it. So I came at these solutions in exactly the same way you would have done as a soldier. I had a plan, I put it into action. I decided I was going to be a size six. Or maybe a four. I wanted to walk into a store and instead of always saying, "Do you have this in a larger size?" I would say, "What's the smallest you do?" I lost forty-five pounds, and it nearly killed me, I haven't let sugar pass my lips in eight months. But boy did it pay off. This trip to London, this shopping, it was my reward. The face, that was something different. I was scared, I don't say I wasn't, but I'm not the first woman in Chicago to go that route. The problem is the bruising. It takes months to die down which is why I couldn't let you see me when you came to town last month – the kids all knew of course, they've been amazing, totally supportive. When they take off the bandages after the operation at first you get a shock. You look in the mirror and you're hideous, like after a car crash, but then you kind of appear, the new you appears. You set out to accomplish something, and after all the pain and fear, it's done. So what do you think?'

'I hate it.'

'Oh come on, don't be grouchy.'

'Everything you've said has appalled me. Sitting here looking I feel like I'm watching a remake of *The Invasion of the Bodysnatchers*. And what is the worst thing of all is that you have some fucked up idea that you got this from me. Why the hell didn't you ask me what *I* thought?'

'I told you, because I wasn't doing it for you, I was doing it for me.'

'But it's *me* that you're married to.'

'Listen, you don't dictate to me what I can and can't do.'

'Not dictate, venture an opinion.'

'I assumed you'd approve.'

'Well I don't. Jeezus, Erica. I have no idea what you see when you look in the mirror. I can tell you what I see, someone who is *not my wife*.

'Don't shout.'

'If I passed you in the street I wouldn't recognise you. For one thing, you are way too thin. You look like you just came out of Belsen and someone took you to Bergdorf's to give you something to wear. The next thing is that your face doesn't move. Look at yourself, you're rigid, frozen. How much did you pay for this mutilation? You should sue the guy. You have no mobility left.'

'It's still a little numb but he says that should die down in a few months.'

'And you don't mind that?'

I was recoiling from her, in horror and distaste. It was difficult to read her reactions. Her face had a serenity that came not from peace of mind but from muscular immobility. She had cheekbones now. She never had cheekbones before. The bones sticking up in her face terrified me, disturbing an old memory that had been reburied in the sand on the edge of the Suez Canal twenty-seven years before. Whatever it was I wanted in a woman, I didn't want cheekbones. Alix Rebick's gaunt long wolfish face had them, they were not for me.

I still hadn't moved from the spot on the bed where I'd fallen asleep. I was paralysed. I thought, If I stand will I wake up? Am I dreaming this? and I kicked my legs over, got to my feet and walked to the window, shut my eyes and opened them again and still she was there and still I was there, looking at her. All of which was absurd because when you are asleep you don't know you're dreaming but when you are awake you know that this is reality.

'Listen here, Joe,' she said to me, moving across the room to a little rickety chair and crossing her matchstick legs. 'It's happened. End of story. It's done, I've moved on. I'm applying for a partnership in another law firm, I've stuck too long in the same old rut. It's a small outfit, it specialises in environmental cases and apparently I've got a good chance of getting it because of my experience of class action suits. They liked the work I did on Dow Corning.'

'So you don't mind having your face cut open but you do mind women having their chests cut open to insert bags full of chemicals?'

'It's not the same thing at all. Those procedures were unsafe.'

'You told me that you were ethically opposed to all cosmetic surgery on feminist grounds.'

'That's the kind of thing you say at twenty-five. It all looks very different when you get to fifty. Anyway, the techniques have hugely improved.'

'I just don't understand how you can be so superficial.'

'Well, honey, you know you can't have depths without surfaces.'

Which was unanswerably true.

We got ready to go out to dinner. She'd booked an Italian restaurant a few blocks away where a lot of beautiful, well-dressed people were the clientele. Princess Di used to go there, the concierge in the hotel said. Erica changed into something she called a cocktail dress, which was also black, a colour women like because apparently it makes them look slimmer and when Erica turned round to the side in this thing, she vanished. She put on high-heeled pumps, which consisted mostly of straps made of some kind of reptile skin, and the only thing that remained of our life together was the watch I bought her for her fortieth birthday, the Omega I got in Zurich. Sitting watching her get changed I could see that to her own eyes, to the eyes of women in general, she'd undergone an entirely successful transformation. A glamorous sheen had fallen on her, rubbing out the old dishevelled Erica, who at weekends wore jeans and a T-shirt and sneakers. Her butt had filled the jeans. I used to watch her bending over and my cock would stiffen at the thought of her creamy skin under the denim, because there is something sexy about seeing a woman's body in what was the uniform of the working man, the blue collar guys who built America, literally, with their own bare hands. Now that flesh had dissolved, had melted away. Where to? I'd no idea. My own body is heavier than it was when I was a kid soldier. My army shirt is still hanging in the closet in Chicago and I take it out sometimes and put it on. The side with the buttons and the side with the button holes are inches apart across my chest and stomach. It's enough for me that I run on the treadmill three times a week for half an hour and that my heart is good, my cholesterol levels kept in check. I'm not trying to look like a muscle boy from one of the gay magazines. My job isn't to be looked at but to build structures that will be looked at.

'What happened to the beading?' I asked her, as she put a silver bracelet on her wrist.

'I threw it all out.'

'You cleared your hobby room?'

'Yes.'

'So what will you take up now? Macramé?'

'We have a lot of empty rooms in the house. When Michael goes to college there'll be another one. We should move.'

This stopped me in my tracks as I was pulling on my shoes.

'Leave our house?'

'If it's too big, why stay there?'

'Because it's my house. I built it. I never had any plans for us to leave it. I wanted us to stay there until we died, or at least until we're too old to look after it ourselves.'

'Like your parents?'

'Exactly.'

'They're from another generation. No one lives that way any more. What do you think about an apartment overlooking the lake?'

'I don't live in other people's buildings. I build my own.'

'Now you're just being silly.'

She came towards me and took the tie that was lying on the bed and began to knot it for me. Her sweet breath was on my face. Her hair was radiant against my cheek and surging with longing, forgetting, I bent down and kissed it. But she looked up at me with that dead expression and her red tongue passed over her lips to moisten them and instead of seizing her mouth, I turned aside.

For the first time I saw uncertainty on her. She backed away.

'Are you seriously trying to tell me that you don't like the way I look?'

What does a man feel when his wife asks him such a question? What can he say? He has no answers. We see something we like and there's no difficulty figuring out if that like is really there or not. All too humiliatingly, it is or it is not. But when your *wife* confronts you with such a response? A few guys are married to women who really balloon, they're hitched to someone who weighs two hundred pounds and I've no idea how they deal with this. For myself, such an idea had never entered my mind because of all the changes that had taken place between us, during our years together, my physical desire for Erica was the one thing that endured. And this is why I had been so sure our marriage would survive.

Now all I could manage, looking at her, was, 'It will take some getting used to.' Which seemed to be enough, because she smiled and said, 'But you will. I know you will.' And turned away to look at herself in the mirror one last time before we left for the restaurant.

She ate virtually nothing over dinner. Wouldn't touch the pasta. Scraped the sauce from her fish. 'Are you still dieting?' I asked her, incredulous.

'You have to keep it up or the weight piles back on again.'

'Don't you think you could afford to gain a few pounds?'

'No.'

'Do you cook at home?'

'Not much.'

'So if you move back in to our house, will you cook?'

'Sure. But you know, Joe, you could cut back a little on the calories yourself.'

Which made me decide to order dessert.

I was looking at her across the table, searching her face for the ghost of my old wife. I thought, Alix is right, you don't ever really know someone. You're married to them for quarter of a century, you think you are familiar with every nook and cranny and then they surprise you. Yet why should I be surprised? Who was the Erica looking back at me? If she was not the girl I married, then I have to face the fact that neither was she the girl who grew up on the farm in Canada, who made her way to college in Vancouver, who with her church took in draft resisters. If anything was consistent in her character it was to make these great changes in herself, massive alterations to her life, colossal upheavals, and just walk away from everything she had been and everyone she had known before. That was her. That was who she was. Marrying me had been her second abandonment, the religious conversion my father had forced on her was the third. She never looked back. It was extraordinary, hers was a truly immigrant soul. When we married I never really wondered what she said to her mother and brothers, I didn't care, I'd fought my own father too hard to worry too much about hers, but what the hell could that conversation have been like? 'Hi. I'm marrying a Jew and converting to Judaism and going to live in America. This is me now. Erica the Christian girl who grew up on a farm and could recite' (because she'd done it for me once, and then later for the kids, her party piece) 'the names of a hundred varieties of apple, she doesn't exist any more. She's dead. You accept the new Erica or else.'

I never really witnessed this destruction of her old personality, it was already half gone when I met her and what there was left to accomplish I aided and abetted her in. I was her Dr Davis that time round. It was me that offered her a new life, a new beginning. I never put up with the fights, the tears the rages the sorrow that must have burdened their hearts, heavy enough to kill her father.

Between these personalities there had been a long interval, which formed most of her adult life. I had assumed that the Erica I was married to was the real, the one and only, the true Erica and that what had gone before was merely a draft version, scrapped, abandoned, thrown out, that she did not become a person, become *herself* until she met me.

This operation. Another man had been let into our relationship, the Dr Davis to whom she had handed over responsibility for remodelling her physically. I couldn't think of a worse form of adultery or a more unforgivable one – what *I* adored she had allowed *him* to destroy and she hadn't even asked me, not a word. But what if she had asked? That was something to contemplate. Because if she had what was I going to tell her? The truth? Would I have said, 'Erica, for God's sake, please don't do this to me. You have to understand that I spent three weeks seeing the most extreme forms of mutilation, of bodies blown to bits, of the medics and the stretcher-bearers having to look away because of the fucking awfulness of what they had to carry off the battlefield.'

I would have had to say, 'Erica, it was during the battle of the Chinese Farm, right on the edge of the canal that we first discovered this Egyptian secret weapon that really freaked us out because we hadn't anticipated it and didn't have any response to it. The Russians had sold them these things called Sagar missiles, which are a personal anti-tank weapon, and you give one of these to ten thousand Egyptian soldiers and tell them, "Okay, go." And they just run around in the desert looking for enemy tanks and when they see one they drop down to their knees, open up the attaché case, flip up the missile, line it up to the tank and when it fires it's got something like three kilometres worth of nylon fishing line snaking out the back. It's called a wire-guided missile and you can't miss. And they didn't. The kill rate was phenomenal and we were losing tanks left right and centre. When they gave me my gun, the one I was so pissed off about because it wasn't sexy, what I was going to do with it was to try to kill as many of these guys as I possibly could. In the wide-open desert you just see somebody scurrying along in the middle distance and anything that moves you shoot at. Sometimes you miss and sometimes you don't. I was shooting shadows in the sand because that was what these things were, shapes scurrying around in the sand, lying low, trying to find a target of opportunity, a good place to open up their attaché cases and fire the missiles. What we were doing was picking them off. And when we failed, and they hit a tank, then whoever was inside it, he fried.'

They were all over Israel, and because of Vietnam they were all over America when I got back there, young men of my age who had had their faces sewn back together after the most terrible mutilations. If the surgeon had done a good job the scars were perhaps behind the ears and they kept their hair long to disguise them. What terrified and sickened me was the thought that we were going back to the hotel sooner or later, Erica would undress, put on a fancy new nightgown, which would hopefully conceal her bony new body, and I would hold up my hand to her face and the scars would be there on her neck, behind the ears where that mole was that I showed her once in the mirror.

Maybe I was wrong never to talk to her about the war. Maybe if I had she would have known better than to pull a stunt like this. I don't know. But I was aching with sorrow and loss, sitting in that restaurant, trying not to cry over a plate of coffee dessert. And I knew also that the whole business went deeper still. For quite a time something in Erica had been held back, as I had deliberately held back what I wouldn't say about the three weeks of the war. For months, if not years, inside her a new woman had been forming, gestating, hatching and this woman was as much a stranger to me as the Jewish wife I turned her into was an alien to her own parents. A serial Pygmalion I married, God help me.

Where did our life together go? Had it all been an illusion, the picnics we had, the jokes we made, the rows, the vacations, the sitting up at night talking about our kids, worrying about them, rooting for them, turning to each other, reaching for each other with that indefinable thing that only a marriage can give and which every soulless singles-bar-hopper lacks entirely – intimacy?

No. I suppose not. It was real. But had passed away. A death.

Nothing now but grieving.

We walked back. She took my hand. It was a sticky, humid night. I felt as I had on the eve of a battle, the same fear and apprehension. I didn't know if I could love her any more and I hated her and hated myself for this terrible turn of events. Something had gone terribly wrong. I knew that I hadn't a clue how to fix it.

Alix

In New York once, I met a woman who collected antique type-writers. She had just bought one, manufactured, according to a small enamel label on the underside, in Germany in 1942. 'What do you think was written on that thing?' she asked me. 'What kind of lists? What should I do with it?'

I said, 'Put in a sheet of paper and type this: "We are still here."'

I am on a train that is taking me to Germany. The wheels spin on the iron track. There comes a time when one must cease all resistance and submit, so I am going to Germany, the child of the *émigrée* retraces her mother's steps. It is not the first time I have been to this country: there were academic confer-ences to attend, both in my past life as a sociologist and in my present work as a fundraiser for the resurrected past, but never before had I travelled by train, made my mother's journey, but in the opposite direction; I was reclaiming history in the most satisfying way possible, on a first-class ticket. In the dining car I eat a plate of meatballs and potatoes and salad, they serve me a glass of Rhine wine. I have everything I need, the countryside rolls past, hills and hedges, horses, cows, sheep, farms, peaks, valleys. The vocabulary I possess for describing the countryside is very limited in English, let alone any other tongue. I am reading my German grammar and my dictionary. I do speak the language, studied it at school, have had cause to use it since, did refresher courses at Berlitz when I began my new career. The wheels spin on the track. The more they spin, the closer they take me to Germany.

The train rocks you and rolls you and you shuttle from side to side like matches in a box, no point going against the flow, you can only brace yourself against sudden judders and gasps. Submit to the quest, to the finding of Marianne Koeppen, whoever she is and whatever she has to do with us. Submit to the truth, to the solitary life that is ahead of me, find out what are its pleasures. There is a void that I'm not in a position to fill in the way I desire. So I'm thinking about how to deal with the unknown Marianne, about who she is and what does she want and, frankly, after what I've been through since I came home to Liverpool to see my mother in the final weeks of her life, nothing would surprise me now. At the point at which your parents die, when you think there is no more unfinished business and you can get on with being yourself, all kinds of shocks are in store for you. Who turns up at the funeral? What's in the will? You can go your whole life and still be staggered by what lies in wait, near the end of it.

When I consider my parents' marriage, my brother's, my cousin's, all I can suppose is that however much we plan for it to be otherwise, whatever kind of idealism you start out with, one way or another you're going to end up in bits: damaged, flawed, hopelessly blind to yourself and to your own inadequacies, because if your eyes had sight – if for a single second you could glimpse how much you've failed in *being* yourself – you could barely survive it. You wouldn't get out of bed, let alone try to sustain a marriage. Who am I to think I'm going to be redeemed? What it comes down to is that there's nothing much for it except to get on with the business of being alive as best you can. Try this, try that. Whatever. It doesn't sound like much. It isn't. And as far as wisdom goes, this is the best I can offer. That's the biggest surprise of all, perhaps: that the secret of middle age comes down to the kind of thing they roll up inside a Christmas cracker: Please, God, give me the courage to change what I can and the wisdom to accept what I can't. We're walking clichés, all of us. How dispiriting. How *irritating*. You think any of us signed up to *that*? I know I didn't.

The Hotel Kempinski is an example of what I think is known as 'cake' architecture, a creamy baroque palace built at the beginning of the eighteenth century for his mistress by a guy called Augustus the Strong, destroyed and burnt to a blackened stump by the RAF in 1945, left there by the side of the road doing nothing for forty years by the Communists then reconstructed as a simulacrum of its former self by a western hotel chain after the Wende – which is what they call here the reunification. When I checked in, I was handed a fax, and opening it, expecting a message from Sam, I saw to my total astonishment that it was from Joseph Shields. He had a yen to leave Liverpool for a few days, what did I think of him joining me in Dresden? He had spoken to my brother who thought I wouldn't mind, but if I'd rather . . .

What?

Not a hint, not a clue as to his purpose, he had given me no help at all, there was nothing for me to do but speculate, for my thoughts to revolve on the rails of my imagination. What did he want here, and what, if anything, did he want with me? It was inexplicable and there was only one thing to do, which was to scrawl on his fax, 'Sure, come,' and have them send it back, and an hour later, having showered and unpacked and repaired my makeup, yet another fax was delivered, this one detailing the arrival time of his flight the next morning, confirming that he had booked at the same hotel, and he hoped this was not too intrusive.

I was invaded with thoughts of him. My mind was occupied and conquered.

Stepping out, I went to the art museum, to the Zwinger where my grandparents had walked among the pictures as law-abiding German citizens, given to the admiration of culture. I stopped before a Veronese, *The Marriage at Cana*, not the one in the Louvre, a different version. The guests and the bride and groom are sitting round a table in the middle of some classical masonry and the waiting staff are falling over themselves bringing out the serving platters on which there's not much food, which goes to show that Veronese didn't know an awful lot about Jewish weddings. Never mind turning water into wine, what about turning four courses into eight? The mother of the bride or groom is one hell of a woman, massive head, huge feet, which she's eased out of her shoes, short grey hair – apparently Veronese put all the big-time celebrities of his era into his pictures, wearing the latest fashions, and this old lady really must have been someone to be so monumental in her appearance and not hidden away under a sack. Jesus is seated in the centre, as usual, and in the picture's composition this is the spot that the sightline is supposed to be drawn towards except that, as usual, his is a face of such unexceptional blandness that your eyes slide across him to the left (his right) where, as if you were a guest yourself, you suddenly notice something and you wonder if anyone else has picked up on this little drama. A woman is looking at someone. Who? The groom. And he in turn is engaged in conversation with a girl to his left, obviously the bride, an exquisite creature, utterly delicate and delectable, her hair threaded with pearls, ravishing, divine, a real twenty-one-carat beauty, the Julia Roberts of her day. So back your eyes go to the first woman, who isn't that young and isn't particularly pretty, at least not compared with the babe opposite her, and the look she fixes on the now-unattainable, married groom is that of the bridesmaid, the gaze of longing and jealousy, of desire and want. When you turn back to Jesus you see that everyone is ignoring him, everyone has something else on their mind, even the waiters, one of whom apparently has the hots for the other. Who cares if water is turned to wine? It's just a conjuring trick. If Jesus really loved mankind he would transform not the beverages but the bridesmaid, make the plain lovely, liberate her from a life doomed to be unloved. Now that's what I would call a miracle.

It was late in the day. I walked across the cobbles to the hotel, ordered a meal to be sent to my room with a glass of wine and watched the news on TV. Who will be the next president of America? Surely not the idiot son? Today, I am reminded, it is three years since our princess died in the underpass. I saw her once, my taxi passing her car at midnight. The moon was full, she sat on the edge of her seat in her Bruce Oldfield gown and our eyes met and we smiled. I winked. She winked back. Aha, I thought. The goddess Diana is out hunting. *Good*. In bed read some more of the book that has accompanied me these two years: the *Metamorphoses*. I looked back at its first words: '*My purpose is to tell of bodies which have been transformed into shapes of a different kind.*' This sentence took me to the mirror. Somehow I had been transformed into the shape of a middle-aged woman against my will. The flesh hangs from the bone. There are remedies for these problems, science leaves nothing untouched. I come from a generation that thinks it was the first to stay young for ever, old age and death are out of the question, ageing is not who we are, it goes against the existential grain. Suffering and heroism were for our parents, not us. A small operation I had been considering for some time was to have a line of tiny dots tattooed round my lips, where they lose definition in middle age, and your lipstick bleeds into the wrinkles above and below your mouth. Obviously there is also botox for the frown line between your eyes and laser treatment for dark circles, but the question is: if I started where would I stop? How much would be enough? And what I doubted about the whole procedure was whether it would actually change anything. Would I still be a middle-aged woman with too sharp and ready a tongue, hypochondriac, arrogant destroyer of others' self-esteem, a fidgety hag who could not find peace of mind in a French garden even if she did have her jowls taken in?

Still, I wouldn't rule it out completely. I was tempted. I don't know a woman who could say she wasn't.

On a map of the city the concierge is circling a street that corresponds to the address of Marianne Koeppen, and I look up and a few feet away, approaching the reception desk, Joseph is carrying a leather valise. I see him stand for a moment hesitating, looking at me, feel myself smile at him with what I hope is welcome and graciousness, and hope, too, that this smile does not betray a surge of sexual appetite.

'Hey, you,' he says.

'Look at *you*,' I reply.

He comes further forward. He raises his arm then drops it. 'Are you going out?'

I gesture to the map. 'I'm finding out where this Marianne Koeppen lives.'

'Did you call her yet?'

He walks a few steps closer so it is no longer as though we are shouting to each other across a prairie wheatfield.

'No, I thought I'd just turn up.'

'Can you speak German?'

'Yeah, quite well, actually.'

He is next to me, me feeling the heat of his body, the flush of his skin.

'I never picked it up, not more than a few words.'

'You don't need it in your business, you have a *lingua franca*.'

'Are you apprehensive?'

'No. What of?'

'I don't know. I imagine it might be quite a visit.'

'I'm sure it will be, one way or another. Do you want to come with me?'

'You don't want to go on your own?'

'I'm fine going on my own. I just thought you might be interested.'

'Definitely I'm interested. You sure you want me along?'

'Why not?'

'Okay.'

And as he bends to pick up his travelling bag I am emboldened to ask, without blushing or flushing, my voice level and steady, my eyes meeting his in all sincerity, as if there could be some straightforward explanation to my enquiry, 'Why are you in Dresden?'

'A good question.'

'The answer to which is . . . ?'

'Call it perversity.'

'Okay.'

And both of us blush.

'Can you hold on half an hour while I check in and shower?'
'I'm not in a hurry.'
'Good.'
What is going on?

I am wearing a cream wool Jil Sander suit. She is Germany's most important designer. It's interesting that the best fashion – Issey Miyake, Sander, Armani – comes from the three former Axis powers, while in my view the Jews Calvin Klein, Donna Karan and Ralph Lauren make awful clothes. France is in hopeless decline as a centre of really innovative or wearable couture, and Britain can export designers but really has no industry of its own. Russia . . . Joseph had spoken often of the excellence of German and Italian design and the Japanese, of course, make the most streamlined, desirable electronics while we Brits have the brainwaves and produce ugly, clumsy prototypes. There is, perhaps, something inherently fascist about surface perfection.

He's standing by the lifts, looking at me drinking my coffee at a little table. He is next to me, saying something about the florid décor. I remind him, 'People who preserve something half assed when they can build something fabulous from scratch should be taken out and shot.'

'Who said that?'

'You did.'

'When?'

'At dinner at Sam and Melanie's.'

'Did I? I don't remember.' And he is repeating the words, considering them, no longer certain, I feel, if he believes them or not.

The circle on the map tells me that we need to take a taxi to our assignation with the mysterious Marianne Koeppen, whose street is well beyond the historic centre, about fifteen minutes from the hotel. We drive through the Altmarkt where our cleansing cream began its pre-war history, and past the cheap, bungled architecture put up in haste and pleasure, to glory in the flattening of the classes. And perhaps I should mention here that, according to the reading I have done prior to my arrival, half of those incinerated in the firestorm that came in two waves on 13 February 1945, destroying a city whose chief industries were food-processing and cigarette manufacture, were refugees, Allied prisoners-of-war, slave labourers and wounded soldiers. Because before I meet this woman, whoever she is, this thief, this confidence trickster, I have had to apprise myself of an evil that was done to her city by *my* nation, which sent rain from the sky in the form of fire and turned people into carbon.

He's sitting beside me, listening to what I'm telling him, about what we did to Dresden, and he asks me if the bones of the corpses are still there beneath the foundations of the new, concrete city, and I tell him, 'I believe so.' He nods and looks out at the paving stones like they are graves and should have the names of the entombed dead inscribed upon them. 'Around here, in the Altmarkt, the Red Cross got forks and shovelled up body parts, arms and legs and heads and hands and torsos, and poured petrol over them and set them alight. I suppose they buried the ashes. And there were other atrocities but I'll spare you the pornography of the detail.'

'Good.'

'Though you must have seen things yourself if you were in the army.'

'Yes.'

'In a war?'

'Yes.'

'Well, my mother was well out of this, even if she did have to scrub steps in Stamford Hill.'

'What?'
'Nothing.'

The street of Marianne Koeppen is near Nürnbergerplatz, by the Technical University. The taxi turns into it and we see that not all of the old city was vaporised: the houses are enormous and built in a style of architecture from the middle of the German nineteenth century with which I'm not familiar, really wild stuff, like out of a child's picture book of fairy tales where Maurice Sendak monsters might live, and witches bake lost children into loaves in fiery ovens. I find them appalling, but what would I know? Every so often there is an interruption, a modern structure stands on its lot, glassy and brash and new, and these to me offer the eye's release from over-decoration. Marianne Koeppen's garden is full of geraniums and pansies and other flowers whose names I'm not familiar with. At the gate there is a row of bells and the name Koeppen is typewritten on a card next to one of them, so the house seems to be divided into eight flats. At the end of the path the front door is standing open. It is a sweet, balmy September morning, an Indian-summer day, and there are all kinds of fragrances in the air, the street is quiet and you can't hear any traffic from the boulevard just a block away. We walk on and through the door and up the wide wooden stairs to the third floor and the name Koeppen is now inscribed in German black-letter script on the wall. The door of the flat is ajar. I can see through the hall into what seems to be a spacious room and in it a woman is sitting propped up against cushions with her eyes closed, snoring. Beside her, on a small blue wicker table covered with a white, tea-stained cloth embroidered with simple flowers of coloured thread, is a stainless-steel kidney-shaped hospital dish and in it are various brown bottles of pills and a roll of bandages, together with gold safety-pins and sticking plaster. How old can she be, a hundred? A hundred and fifty?

Do they actually *make* people this old? The arms have fallen right off the bone, they're hanging there in folds. The spotted maroon and cream blouse is twenty-four sizes too loose around the neck and pinned to the collar, sagging with its own weight, is a large cameo brooch. But the odd thing is that even though she is sitting down there's the sensation that she would be a tall woman if you could unfold her; she's worn away to almost nothing but the almost nothing is still of a good height, and now our knocking on the door has woken her, she's looking at us with blue eyes and above them the brow is all smooth until it meets the hairline of a very obvious brown wig set in a row of fifties waves and curls.

'Holla!'

'Frau Koeppen?'

'Ja.'

'Ich bin Alix Rebick.'

'Ah,' she says in English, 'what took you so long?'

But this, I soon establish after a few exploratory greetings, is *all* her English, a phrase she had memorised and rehearsed, heard once on a street corner from the lips of a British Tommy after the surrender, waiting for a pal.

'So we are here at last,' she says, thinking Joseph is either my husband or my brother or a lawyer and as the phrase 'just a friend' is greeted with such suspicion I concede that, yes, he is a lawyer, and that I will be translating everything he says, and from his pocket he takes out a notebook and makes like he's writing up the meeting with her for my benefit. We pull up ladder-backed wooden chairs with rush seats and she sends me to the small kitchen with its oilcloth-covered table and instructs me in the making of instant coffee from a jar of Maxwell House, and she takes from under the blanket that is over her knees a packet of cigarettes called West and with trembling hands tries to light one, until Joseph leans forward, gently removes the box of matches from her nervous fingers and does it for her. On the walls around us are hung landscapes in oils in gilt frames depicting cows grazing by a stream against a background of hills, a real bronze shield, a pair of real crossed swords, a glass-fronted china cabinet full of Meissen china shoes, and only the presence of a style of ceiling light produced by the millions in the Soviet Union betrays the fact that we are not living in the kind of pre-war German home into which my mother must have entered to go to children's parties – or would have done had the Jews still been invited.

'We are ready to start,' she announces, when she has tried a sip of coffee. 'My first question' (taking a piece of paper from the cushion behind her and looking at a list she had written on it) 'is why you did not reply to my letters.'

'Not reply to *yours*? Why didn't you reply to *ours*?'

'There are your letters,' she says, pointing to a neat pile held together by an elastic band on a desk by the wall, 'and next to them are the carbon copies of my responses. Kindly, you wrote in German as well as English and I replied in German. I gave them to my granddaughter to post.'

I leaned forward. 'So how do you know she posted them?'

'Oh dear.' She thinks about this for a few moments. 'This is the possible explanation. Annemarie was reluctant from the very beginning. I think she has a skinhead boyfriend in Leipzig, which her mother is furious about. She is a little Jewish herself, unfortunately, which she knows perfectly well and of course this is my fault so she is simply waiting for me to die so that the inconvenience can be forgotten. And like all young people she is totally uninterested in the past. In my view she spends far too much time fiddling with her computer. Do you know what an Internet chat room is?'

'She wants to know if I know what an Internet chat room is,' I say to Joseph.

'Oh, yeah? Maybe she talks to my dad. He has a bunch of buddies on line who natter about good and evil.'

'My subject.' And turning back, 'Yes, I know what an Internet
chat room is but, Frau Koeppen, I have no idea at all who *you*
are.'

'This is correct, now we know about the problems of postage.
You are the daughter of Lotte or Ernst?'

'Lotte.'

'Either way it is the same thing. I am your aunt.'

'I don't believe it,' I say to Joseph. 'That's all I need, more
fucking relatives.'

'What's that?' my aunt asks. 'What are you telling your
lawyer?'

'I was merely expressing my astonishment.'

'Well, of course it is surprising.' Her cigarette is a fragile coil of
ash, I move the ashtray closer to her. 'I did not expect you to
know, unless your grandfather mentioned something, perhaps
on his deathbed. He is not still alive, I suppose.'

'I believe he was born in 1888. So no.'

'That is right. If you go to the desk, my dear, you will find a
small metal box containing photographs. Bring it to me and I
will show you a photograph of him as a young man.'

Joseph is on his feet. 'This?' he says, holding up a biscuit tin
with a picture embossed on it of a Virgin Mary with a conniving
expression on her face.

'Exactly.'

He hands it to her. She removes the lid. 'Good, it is right on
top.'

And I am looking at a picture of a young man in a thick suit
with a low wide brow, his clumps of hair standing up in several
directions; he's holding the arm of a dimpled young woman,
taller than himself, who is wearing a white lab coat, standing in
a park or a garden in front of a camellia bush blooming with

white flowers and he is not obeying the orders of the photographer for his eyes are averted from the lens, he's looking sideways
at the woman.

'This is my grandfather and grandmother?'

'Not *your* grandmother, no. Mother.'

She must have been waiting half her life for this moment, for
the settling of an old score long held: something that began in
1911, in my grandfather's twenty-third year while a medical student in Berlin, was coming to its conclusion here in this flat,
during a conversation that was taking place in the first months of
a new century about people who had been born in the one before
the one before that. Marianne Koeppen, who has maintained an
upright position in her chair since she opened her blue eyes and
saw us standing in her hall, her spine never touching the pillows,
now sinks back, puts out the stub of her cigarette and folds her
hands, whose bones look like a tangle of wires, her tongue
parched and remoistened over and over again with sips of coffee,
her eyelids reddening with tired blood, her crêpey throat rising
and falling, and every so often straightening her wig, which sits
like a helmet on the head of an old warrior, and this is what she
tells us.

'My mother from a very young age held progressive ideas.
The ideas were what our former masters would have called bour-
geois because they were not particularly concerned with the
failings of the political system or the situation of the different
classes. She was interested in the individual and in particular
the question of female emancipation, which meant that she was
a great admirer of the Frenchwoman Madame Curie, and so she
set out to become a medical student at a time when this kind of
career was frowned upon. In addition, she held ideas about free
love.'

'What's this?' Joseph asks.

'Her mother was a feminist.'

'Oh, good.'

'You're not *anti*-feminist, are you?' I demand, glaring at him.

'Absolutely not. I was at college at Berkeley. '

'Continue, Frau Koeppen.'

'I wish I had known my mother in this early part of her life but unfortunately, by the time I came properly to understand her, she was bowed down by a number of responsibilities, in fact principally myself. She met my father, also a medical student, and they fell in love and *made* love, relying on what she scientifically believed was an infallible method of contraception, the insertion of a finger inside herself to feel the consistency of her vaginal juices, which supposedly indicated whether or not she was in the period of fertility. A baby was the result.'

'It came back into fashion in the seventies, we called it the feminist rhythm method. It didn't work then, either.'

'Really? I don't doubt that my father was planning to seduce and abandon my mother, but he was absolutely no match for the force of his family's disapproval. She was not a Jewish girl and furthermore she was not even a Gentile girl of a good family, for if she were, her parents would not have permitted her to enrol in medical studies where she was exposed to the animal nature of our existence, its mechanical qualities. Which had led her to the ways of harlotry.'

'You know,' I say, 'I have never given a single thought to my great-grandparents. I know absolutely nothing about them. Did you ever meet them?'

'I did not meet them, but I saw them, my mother pointed them out on the street one day, they were in a café drinking coffee and eating sachertorte, and she took my hand and said, "Marianne, see, there are your grandparents," but they only looked to me like two drab old people in out-of-date clothes and I wasn't interested. Which was absurd because it was due to their intransigence that my mother's career as a free-thinker came to an abrupt end. My father did not marry her. He did not defy his family. What he did instead was to persuade one of his friends, a Gentile, to marry my mother. I believe that a large sum of money changed hands. Some huge amount of marks gave my father his freedom from a marriage that would have been a disgrace and gave my mother's husband the means to finish his studies in comfort. I think it was a matter of paying off an accumulation of debts.'

'Did he turn out to be a good stepfather?'

'I have no idea. He was a ferocious German nationalist, he looked around and he thought, If Britain and France can have their empire, why not Germany? so he enlisted in 1915 and was killed at Verdun. Though perhaps his militarism was driven by dislike of my mother. I have no memories of him at all. Of course, my mother had been expelled from medical school and after his death a life began for her of many, many personal difficulties. I have to say, she was rather a bitter person.'

'So the Dorf family abandoned you.'

'Not exactly. You must understand that my mother and father were *wildly* in love. Papa felt a keen responsibility towards me and from the moment he qualified as a doctor he always, with total punctuality, provided an income for us and, of course, free medical treatment, that went without saying. The difficulty was that after some years he dutifully married the wife his parents approved of and she wished there to be no contact at all, but eventually he overrode her objections and I was brought to his consulting rooms once a week and we would spend an hour in play.'

'What were your games?' I ask, remembering the stooped old man, the sour milk, the rancid cookies, the little tools in a leather case, the heat of the room in summer and the pores of his face as he bent down to kiss me, the white hairs in his nose, the smell of tobacco and disinfectant. Sitting on a chair, legs dangling in white ankle socks, I listened to him talking to Mamma in German, pointing at me. We had no common language, my grandparents and I. I said, 'Guten Tag, Oma. Guten Nacht, Opa.' And they replied with nods, looking across a continent that separated me from them, which was in fact only one end of the room to the other.

'Oh, you know, he took me up in the air in his hands and twirled me about. I climbed on his back and he pretended he was a bear in the forest. The usual things. And each week there was something in his pocket for me, some toy, and once a year a special present such as a large doll. But, of course, as it turned out, the greatest gift of all that he had given me, though none of us knew it at the time, were the two names on my birth certificate of genuine pure Class A Aryans and one of these an accredited war hero, deceased and unable to make trouble. Meanwhile, when I was leaving school my father presented to my mother a proposal. It was 1930 and the factory was now becoming very successful, he and his wife had bought a new house in a most fashionable neighbourhood – Blasewitz, on the banks of the Elbe, do you know it? His idea was that I should become the manageress of the factory, that I would be in charge of the girls who worked there, which was a great responsibility for an eighteen-year-old girl but one I relished because it meant working with cosmetics.'

'Marianne . . . !' And it comes back to me, the tall young woman in the factory who was so kind to my mother, who sent presents to her and whom my grandmother shunned, the girl who was always there in the story, the extra, the non-speaking part, the one who is always overlooked for she seems to have no role in the main drama.

'And did you wear a navy suit? And white blouses?'

'Always.'

'Then my mother spoke of you. With affection.'

Marianne smiled and her hand went up to adjust her wig. 'Did she know I was her sister?'

'I don't think so. Or at least she never said.'

'I remember when they put her on the train, I can see her in my mind's eye, in her green woollen dress. The family she went to in England, were they kind to her?'

'No.'

'I'm sorry to hear that. But at least it wasn't many months before she was reunited with her parents. So there was a happy ending.'

'Yes. Absolutely. There was a happy ending. And what about you? Did *you* have a happy ending?'

'You must understand that *if I had chosen* I could have gone with them to England. Papa was quite clear about this, quite clear. He would have fought for me but it was entirely my decision to stay. My mother had remarried in 1927 and she had no wish to go. Of course, we all knew there was going to be a war any minute but my new stepfather was an insurance salesman and he was beyond the age of military service. My own situation was similar. By 1939 I was engaged to Rudolf who ran a family business printing art postcards for the Zwinger, and calendars and greetings cards. This was his family's house, you know. He wasn't a Nazi, he wasn't even an opponent of the regime, he was totally apolitical, he joined whatever he had to join, as long as he could attend the opera and play the cello in his chamber orchestra and worship God at the Frauenkirche. He was a distant cousin of *the* Koeppen, you know, Wolfgang, the novelist.'

'But they conscripted him anyway.'

'No, no. Don't make assumptions. You think he went to the Eastern Front and died there? Not at all. He had a club foot. Useless in war. There is a picture of him on my desk. Look.'

'A lovely face,' I say, and mean it. 'How old was he then?'

'It was taken in 1955, when my second daughter was born, so

he was forty-eight, I think.' A small red floret from a geranium is attached to the frame. 'I put a fresh flower from the window-box on the photograph every day.'

'Is he still alive?'

'No. He died of cancer five weeks before the Wende. He never lived to see it.'

'What a tragedy.'

'Yes.'

She sets the photograph down on her knee and with her little finger strokes the face of her dead husband, so maybe some marriages can be made to be happy. 'Oh, I loved him,' she says. 'He was a *wonderful* man.'

Out of the silence that comes after this I ask, 'What happened to the factory during the war?'

'Well, you must understand that the Gestapo had no idea at all about my relationship with my father, no idea I was a Jew. A handful of my mother's old friends knew but they were in Berlin and, very surprisingly, I was not denounced, although my mother, in the eyes of the state, had prostituted herself with a filthy Hebrew. Even so, my father was very anxious to protect me. This is what he did. During his discussions with the authorities he made something quite clear. He told them this: "I am leaving Germany with nothing, you have taken it all, everything. But in leaving behind my factory, I am making over the ownership to a pure Aryan young woman, the *Fraülein* who manages the workforce. The factory will belong to her in law, and not only this but the chemical formula for the cleansing cream I am also giving to her. She will become the factory's director. She alone, apart from myself, understands every aspect of production. As long as she is in charge, the factory will continue to turn out a first-class product. If you attempt to replace her, you will not have the formula, and even if you did, you would not understand how to manufacture it." It was at the railway station in February of 1939 – and I always remember I was wearing a red hat with a turquoise pea-cock feather and a red coat – that he put into my hands, which wore brown leather gloves lined with rabbit fur, the formula for the face cream, the *Violette Schimmer*. He took off his own glove, it was bitterly cold, and reached into the inner pocket of his overcoat and took out the envelope. "I'll tell you exactly what to do," he said to me. "Don't keep it in your office. Keep it at home, under lock and key. This is the guarantee of your future." And in front of his wife he kissed me, and held me hard in his arms, and I saw the shock and disgust on the faces of the people around us, that I contaminated myself with something unclean, *they* who went home and applied to those very faces to remove dirt the cleansing cream he made and sold to them.

'After that, things were quite quiet. I married. We moved into this house, which had been in my husband's family for sixty years. The war started and dragged on and on, but we kept up production and from time to time letters of appreciation came from quite high up in the Nazi hierarchy. I did not hear from Eva Braun herself, but Frau Speer indicated that when she visited her house, the two ladies stood together in the bathroom while Eva was instructed in how to use the cream, wetting the cloth, and they were like schoolgirls together in front of the mirror, gig-gling, and Frau Speer gave Eva her own pot to take home. It was a chilling letter, but quite funny in its own way.'

'The Nazis were fond of cleansing,' I said.

'Exactly.'

'Do you think they all used it, all those bitches?'

'Probably. The cream was very popular. The problem, how-ever, was that as the war continued the ingredients became harder and harder to obtain, not only because substances like liquid paraffin were in short supply but the cocoa butter and eucalyptus oil had to be imported and this proved totally impos-sible. So eventually we were reduced to a very short production

line and every pot we made was earmarked for a particular cus-
tomer in the highest ranks of the regime.'

High in Hitler's mountain eyrie, the women gathered, handing over their babies to the Führer to be kissed and petted by
him. Standing in the sunshine they shaded their eyes to enjoy
the view. The air was clear and pure. In the morning they rose
and, cheeks smooth, they looked in the mirror and applied rouge
and powder and lipstick to their clean skin. They talked of things
that women everywhere talk of: how to maintain your figure,
what shape of dress enhances the form, how the chemicals in different perfumes interact with the body's chemicals to unite and
produce a pleasing and idiosyncratic scent. 'Try this.' 'No, I swear
by *this*.' 'Let me see.' 'You use it with a face cloth.' 'What is it
good for?' 'I told you, cleansing and purification.'

'Better they should have had a facelift, Joseph,' I say, 'and
died under the anaesthetic.'

'And now we come to the day of the thirteenth of February
1945. The factory was shut up. We had no more materials left
for production. Every last jar had left for Berlin months ago for
that list of favoured customers and I only went in to answer the
letters that kept coming, from women begging me for any information about a store or a pharmacy that might have some
remaining supplies. I went in the evenings because during the
day I was a volunteer at the railway station where the refugees
were camped, the people fleeing the Russian advance, arriving
in rags. My husband's cousins from the Sudetenland had lost all
their luggage, they had nothing, the only nutrition they had had
on the journey was water and bread, and their child, a seven-
year-old boy, could no longer walk. Yes, I was on a tram during
the first wave of attack, it was around ten o'clock and I was very
tired. I had typed several letters, taken them to the post, and I
was thinking about a dress the colour of bluebells I had seen the
previous day in a shop window and about how long it had been

since I had had anything new to wear, and how I might raise with my husband the question of buying it. I was completely absorbed with these thoughts when I looked up because my body could feel that the tram had made an unexpected turning – you know how if you are on a journey that is familiar to you, your bones know the route as well as your eyes. We had pulled into a siding and stopped and I heard the sky full of noise. Next to me, a man said, "What a lot of planes." The raid started at ten o'clock and it finished at ten twenty-five according to the history books but, of course, I didn't look at my watch. As far as I'm concerned, it went on for hours. I don't know how to talk to you about the horror, about the hammering and shaking of the ground beneath us, the air full of explosions, the terror, the nausea in your stomach, the whole of you, every cell and every molecule, in torment.

'And when it had finished, everything was silent like the sound had been turned off in the universe. We climbed off the tram and I remember particularly walking past a women's hospital and the patients were standing outside in their nightclothes. All of them were silent in the street. I can still see them, the women. We said nothing to each other, no one asked if anyone was hurt or needed help, we walked like we were asleep, in our silence.

'I was still trying to make my way home when the second wave of bombs came and this time it was not better in my mind but worse for I did not think, I have already survived such a terror, because now there was no element of surprise, we knew what the consequences were of this horrible devastation of bombs. A group of us who had been walking from the tram ran into the cellar of a villa while the bombs exploded all around us, setting off the fires that multiplied. When the planes had flown over and we could no longer hear their engines and our house was not hit, we thought we were saved and we climbed the stairs only to find that in the dining room sparks from the street had ignited the brocade curtains and set the room ablaze and everything was burning, great hot raging flames turning into sheets of pain rolling, turning towards us, catching everything up and sparks coming from the electrical sockets, then more fire and books falling, burning, vases crashing, a carpet of fire under your feet and you knew there was no safety anywhere, not inside, so we ran out on to the street and the firestorm passed among us. I was running through an avenue of myrtle trees, which had caught alight, and I was hemmed in by two walls of fire and people were screaming, running past me like flaming torches. And then I saw something completely crazy – fiery animals abroad in the streets, fiery apes and elephants and bears, and you know, I had been brought up by my mother as a Catholic and I thought, This is the day of the Revelation, but it was only that the zoo had caught fire and the creatures in it had escaped and were running for their lives. Some of the monkeys climbed the trees of the Grosser Garten but the next day they died from drinking water poisoned by the chemicals from the incendiary bombs.

'I was demented. I was wandering the city trying to find my way home and I saw such terrible sights but they were things I don't want to talk about, women wandering, wandering because they were looking for their husbands and they could not understand why there was no husband, alive or dead, because the heat was so intense that there was nothing left, no human remains, all dissolved into atoms, or there were only pieces of skin scattered to the winds. It took me two days to reach my home, this house, and when I got here, it was flattened. Only the ground floor was left standing. Some men had come and cleared out the rubble and everything, all my possessions were gone. The metal box in which I kept the formula for the cleansing cream was gone. This was not my first concern, my first thought was, *Where is Rudolf?* But he was safe, he was with our neighbours, playing Mozart when the attack came and the house was spared.'

Fifty years later it took her a few minutes to return from that blazing inferno. I sat and watched her face and thought of the memories that are locked inside us, that this is the true mystery of others, not what you know or think you know about them, but what *they* know, what they have seen, those images that survive behind their eyes – a hundred years, some of them – of a woman in old-fashioned dress leaning over a child's bed, of a car with running boards speeding along a street, of the face of an old king or the voice of an old president. I close my own eyes and see the last tram that ran through Liverpool. I see the Cavern Club in its heyday and I see George Harrison as a young boy. If I live long enough, like the last man to serve in the trenches of the Great War, they might say of me, 'She was the last person to have ever seen the Beatles play at the Cavern.' Not much of a distinction, compared with a man I met once who saw Lenin return to Moscow from exile, speaking at the Finland station, but I can't help that. So I looked at Marianne and I thought, I am sitting in a room with the only person alive who can tell me what my great-grandparents looked like.

And I pulled my chair towards her and took her hand and her fingers held mine for a moment until she released them and she smiled at me, a few yellow teeth in her red mouth and the dusty smell of her wig in my nose, and yet I was not repelled but warmed.

'What is very curious in all this,' she said, lighting another cigarette, and the flame of the match Joseph held to her face cast a livid glow on her skin, 'is that while the factory was untouched – it was well away from the *innerstadt* – what animated the equipment, the soul of the enterprise, the formula, no longer existed.'

'Surely after all these years you must have had the formula by heart?'

'Look,' she said, energetically, 'it is not enough to put things in a vat and stir them, we're talking here about a process, about everything being at the exactly correct temperature from moment to moment. This is what I had to explain in great detail after the war to our new masters, who instructed me to continue production and I had to convince them that this was not possible. So they told me to manufacture cold cream and that is what I did. The chief ingredient is paraffin. It's a heavy white substance and it will do the job of removing dirt but unless you have very dry skin it leaves a greasy residue behind on the face.'

'I know. And that's what you've been doing all this time, making cold cream under the Communists?'

'Yes, until 1959. The two regimes were different, and what characterised the Communists was their vindictiveness. They only ever tolerated us at best, and the best was the times of *weiche Welle*, what we called the soft waves. But there were always waves coming at you, slapping you down. Because Rudolf and I were both capitalists, both factory owners, we received no rations during the worst periods after the war. The children did, and we had to watch them eat while we starved and stop ourselves grabbing the food from their mouths. My son Dieter refused to join the Freie Deutsche Jugend, the Communist youth movement, and this got us into terrible trouble.'

'I don't understand how you coped, a cultured middle-class family living in the so-called worker's paradise.'

'Oh, you learned to develop what we called the *Deutsche Blick*, the glance over both shoulders before you spoke. When they opened the Stasi files I found out that the secret police knew more about my family than I knew myself. I read in the files, for example, that my daughter had been unfaithful to her husband.

But that is the characteristic of totalitarianism. It does not allow you to have a private life.'

'I thought you said the house was destroyed.'

'Yes, it was, and my husband wanted to rebuild it, this family house from the last century, but because we were classified as capitalists we were the very last in the queue to be given materials. As capitalists we were always the last for everything. When we went on holiday, because we were not members of a workers' trade union we always got the worst rooms.'

'You mean it wasn't illegal to have private property?'

'No, but they punished you for it. In the end we made a choice. If we surrendered both the factories – mine and Rudolf's – to the state and became state employees, as directors of the factories we would be granted building materials, and after some years of discussion that is what we decided to do. We decided to rebuild this house. And I hope you agree that we did a good job. Rudolf had to use old photographs and not everything is exact but we did our best. It took fourteen years.'

'So who owns the factory now?'

'A good question. It was still in production until the end of the Communist era, then of course absolutely no one wanted GDR-era cold cream when you could buy something from France or America. Production ceased. You know, two of the women had worked there since they were teenagers, under your grandfather. It was their whole lives, that factory, and their retirement is full of difficulties. I must say, I was very surprised to experience the indifference of the West towards us. There was a lady who worked for me who had to have her leg amputated and could not afford the medicines and when she wrote to her own relatives in Munich and Frankfurt, whom she had not seen for sixty years, it seemed they could not care less about her fate. The factory is empty now and every month my son-in-law goes and removes the graffiti. We had no crime under the Communists, or if there was, they never told you about it, everyone was kept too busy. When I went to put in my papers to the Claims Conference I knew that it was very possible that there would be other rightful heirs, the children of Lotte and Ernst, but I also knew that it was imperative to make an application before the deadline. The factory belongs to the Dorfs and their descendants. It was stolen first by the Nazis and then by the Communists. As I am not legitimate I do not expect you to honour my inheritance. I did not do this for myself, I did it for my father, who always loved me, so that something could be returned of his past in Dresden. You will, I'm sure, take advice from your lawyer. You will understand now why my granddaughter had no interest in posting the letters. She thinks the whole business is a total waste of time.'

'Frau Koeppen, I don't know what to say.'

'It is a lot to absorb.'

'Yes.'

'You should go and see the factory, you know. I will give you the address. Also, your mother's house.'

'What? You mean that's still there too?'

'Absolutely. Blasewitz was more or less unaffected by the bombing. Unfortunately I could not make an application to the Claims Conference as the house has nothing to do with me. Frau Rebick, you have been here for two hours. It has been a very wearing conversation, even though I have prepared all the details for you many times in my mind over nearly ten years. I would be grateful if you would go now. I hope the coffee was good. I apologise for having no cake. I'll give you my telephone number. Do let me know how you get on.'

'Excuse me, before I go, are you looked after well yourself?'

'Yes, yes. Once a day I have a visitor, which is quite a lot, and some days I am glad to see no one. They bring my meals for me and clean the house, and if I need to go to an appointment at the hospital they take me. The only difficulty comes if there is something wrong with the television but since my Dieter bought me the Sony the picture is excellent, very clear.'

'What do you watch?'

'Mainly shows from America. *LA Law*, I like, and *Friends*. But my favourite is *The Simpsons*. Are you also a fan?'

'I don't know, I've never seen it. I don't watch much TV.'

'My husband was the same. Before the Wende there was little to see. They called us here in Dresden inhabitants of the Valley of the Clueless, you know, because we were one of the few cities in the GDR unable to receive signals from the West due to our geographical position.'

'Do you know what happened to the cleansing cream?'

'I know what happened. It has not existed for more than fifty years, since the night of the bombing.'

'Ah, but you're wrong, it does still exist.'

She sits in wonder as I tell of the restoration to life of her father's business. 'Do you think,' she asks, 'that any of the ladies who play in *Friends* might use it? Fraülein Aniston has beautiful skin as well as shiny hair.'

'In all likelihood, I don't see why not.'

'It is curious,' she says, 'what endures and what does not. I see God's work in this.'

'I don't.'

We rise and I walk towards her to shake her hand, but bend down and kiss her, one Dorf to another. Her blue eyes are dry. A smell comes off her, of old age and urine. 'How old are you?' I ask.

'Eighty-eight. If I can live another six years I will be here for the eight-hundredth anniversary of the city of Dresden. You must come back for the celebrations. You must meet your cousins.'

Radeburgerstrasse 380.

A long, low, two-storey red-brick building, exactly as Mamma had described it. A wooden sign, which once contained the name of the enterprise, concealed by a single brush of black paint.

Row of twenty windows, three boarded up. The glass is bearded with dust and dirt. Through them, peering inside, metal vats, a rudimentary production line. A stack of empty glass jars. A broom upright in a corner. Tiles hanging from the roof. Weeds with yellow flowers growing up in front of the padlocked door. Nettles. Ants. Smells of rot. Warm damp patch on the grass. Odour of urine. Remains of a fire. Charred bones. A couple of dozen flattened cola cans tied together with wire. A child's emerald green coat eaten by moths.

Who would want this, Mamma?

'What are you thinking?' Joseph asks me.

'All this trouble, just over face cream.'

'Does it mean anything to you, looking at it?'

'I just can't believe it's still here and I can't think of what use it could be put to, it's totally undistinguished as a building . . . when do you think it might have been built?'

'I dunno, maybe 1910?'

'Yeah, probably. What's its point? It's like that thing in movies, the McGuffin. The Maltese falcon was a McGuffin, something the whole plot revolves round, but actually it's of no significance in and of itself. It's not like the buildings I'm involved in restoring, there's nothing here. What can I say other than "This was once a factory in Jewish ownership"? So what? In the end it's just a pile of bricks.'

'That's my living you're talking about.'

'Come on. You know what I mean.'

'Yeah, I know what you mean.'

'Its only significance is that, after all these years, it's still here. And that's not enough to warrant anyone's attention.'

'You're determined not to make it into a symbol, aren't you?'

'That's right.'

'So what are you going to do about it?'

'Give it to her, of course.'

'And will you have fulfilled your mother's dying wish?'

'She wanted something restored to us of Germany. Well, she got more than she bargained for. She got relatives, German relatives. Non-Jewish German relatives. How about that?'

'What do you think your cousin Peter is going to make of it?'

'And Lauren. Don't forget Lauren.'

'Your brother made a fool of himself over her for a couple of weeks.'

'So you noticed.'

'He asked me what I thought.'

'What did you tell him?'

'At first I told him she was trouble.'

'Perhaps trouble was what he was looking for?'

'He only thought he was. He's like me. He's not built for it. Anyway, he did try it on with her but she completely rebuffed him. Wasn't in any way interested. Apparently she's wild about her husband, though God knows why. She's desperate to have a baby with him and they're running around all over the place having fertility treatment.'

'I know. She told Melanie the reason they were so mad to get their share of the Dorf fortune was so they could pay the hospital bills.'

'I've never seen a guy back off so quick as when Sam heard that.'

'Just what he needs. He had a plan, you know, to run away to America.'

'We discussed that. I told him he was an idiot.'

'Why?'

'You don't walk out on a woman like Melanie.'

'What's so special about her?'

'Take it from me, she's special. These mid-life crises men and women have, you gotta resist them. You don't know what it is you're throwing away. The important thing is to figure out what is waste and what isn't.'

A dog is howling. A man walks past in leather jeans, pushing a stroller with a large-headed infant inside it. The taxi driver lights another cigarette. What is it with this place, that it won't disappear? All around it there are flats: flats flung up after the war when the urgent need was to house the thousands of homeless; flats executed in the sixties brutalist style as a statement of the supremacy of the workers with tiled murals of the rise and rise of the proletariat; flats built since the Wende in glass and brushed steel, where the new technocrats from Siemens live. Some things go on surviving long after they have served their purpose yet here we still are. And there is my aunt with all her infirmities, hunched over *The Simpsons*. What's *she* for? To show the example of rectitude, I suppose, which is a lesson we need reminding of repeatedly.

And myself. What remains? Lust. You can't kill it in me.

The phallic right, the phallic entitlement to which everything else must submit – brutal, simple, magnificent – this is what thirty years of feminism had battled to overthrow, and where had it got us, the generation that took to the streets? What did we wind up with? Empty cunts. What's the resolution? The resolution is that there is no resolution, no catharsis, no moving on, no release. Submission and acceptance, or refusal to submit and accept. Both ways are intolerable. There is no point in looking for consolation in gardening, knitting, good works, pets, travel, cookery, country walks, fishing, antique collecting, fine art, house plants. The revelation of your life is that you're going to have to live with pain that is not consolable.

Yet there is also the example of Marianne Koeppen. What a fucking awful time to be born in the twentieth century, she had the worst of everything: war, inflation, fascism, more war, firestorm, Communism in its most deadened form, liberation into an indifferent world. And somehow she remains entirely morally intact, undamaged in every respect by the contamination of multiple evils, a blaze of love still alight inside her for her dead husband. How does she do it? I need to know. I have to admit that my generation, born after the war, has had the easiest ride in the whole of history. Look at us, and all our tawdry toys. What gives us the right to think we should be immune from sorrow and loss? Now a light of affection is in *me* for that old lady, my aunt, stiff and proud in her chair, still smoking her cigarettes, sharp as a needle, her brown wig clamped on to her head. A care package of Rose Rosen's finest products will, I think, be an initial gesture of renewal and reconciliation between our families. Mamma, listen. I've done what you asked, I got the factory back for you. Are we finished, is the tragic past over and done with? Are we done with heartbreak, already? We are property owners in Germany once more; the Dorfs can hold their heads up high as they step out through the streets of Dresden, because here we are, back in the heart of Europe, where we belong – let them try to get rid of us a second time. In all directions the plains and the fields and the mountains and the cities radiate out, from the Urals to the Atlantic, and on every metre we are entitled to step. As for America? A delusion. I am not an American born or bred. I am not Augie March and hence also not at liberty, like him, to go at things freestyle. I know that what the heart craves it does not invariably get, and this is what we understand as Europeans, chiefly: that there is so much that is not possible. You can yelp *I want, I want, I want, I want, I want, I want, I want, I want,* as much as you like because however deep the want goes, there are things that will always elude you.

Enough? Peace at last?

Mamma. The last time I will say your name.

My mother is dead and in her grave, my father too. Nothing can bring them back to me. But my aunt, by some miracle, is still here and perhaps it is true that of the many different kinds of love that there are, this lesser love, that of a middle-aged woman for an old lady, is all that will be granted to me. And no, it's not enough, how could it be?, but it is still love. I have to say I find it a little humiliating, not to mention embarrassing, but what can you do? This is my fate. I'm just not lovable.

'Come on,' Joseph says. 'Let's go. You want to go have a look at your mother's house?'

'Not now. Tomorrow.'

'I'll buy you dinner.'

'Thanks.'

'You like seafood? There's a good seafood restaurant here.'

'That would be nice.'

He takes my arm and once again the heat of his blood expressed through the skin of his hand ignites my own. I break free and step into the taxi.

'You sure you're okay?' he asks me.

I take out my powder compact and draw my lips in the mirror. My mouth reappears, my big Jewish gob painted vermilion, a red pigment that contains mercuric sulphide.

'Yeah,' I say, smiling. 'Don't worry about me.'

Joseph

Erica had brought tragedy upon us by her insistence on trying to look like her own daughter. She had damaged our marriage, perhaps fatally. I was still in shock, bereft, and at times enraged. Could things be repaired? I didn't know. About the face-lift nothing could be done but she had flatly refused to gain even ten pounds. I returned to Chicago for a week and found that she had moved back into our home, was waiting expectantly for me to rejoin her. Nobody was on my side. 'If she likes what she sees in the mirror, what's it to you?' my mother said. My father told me, 'A marriage is a marriage. You know how I feel about that.' The kids thought she looked wonderful. Allison called me and said, 'Mom told me you want her to gain weight. Do you think she's some kind of odalisque in a harem? It's her body, not yours, that's rudimentary feminism, Dad. I thought you were okay with this stuff. I never had you down as a male chauvinist.' Did girls still talk this way? Apparently they do. I told her, 'I would have thought feminists of all people would understand what's going on here. It's the same as anorexia, teenagers starving themselves to look like the models they see in the magazines.' 'It's way more complex than that.' 'Well, I don't believe it.' You'd think I was Hugh Hefner the way they had me down as the oppressor of women's bodies. I didn't find any of it funny.

What was the matter with me? Why couldn't I see things the way everyone else did? Why did something that happened for a few moments in 1973 cause me to be incapable of getting over what my wife had done to herself? And every time I asked myself that, every time I looked at her, I saw the same thing: the knife executing a line along her jaw, the flap of skin raised, the blood and muscle and bone revealed beneath . . .

I couldn't bear to be in the house, hated to watch her eat – salad and diet dressing, nothing else, hated to watch her hold a tape measure round her skinny ass every day, hated feeling her stick legs in bed next to me. I tried to make love to her and totally failed. 'It's just your time of life, Joe,' she told me. 'I'll make an appointment for you at the doctor, he'll give you a prescription for Viagra.' *Fuck that.* I wanted to move back in with my parents but Michael was in my old room and had taken over the treehouse, filling it with skateboard magazines and, to my relief, copies of *Playboy* at long last, and an unbroken package of rubbers so I knew he was as normal as a sixteen-year-old could be and wondered if there was any girl he had his eye on for whom these were intended. I climbed up there one hot morning when he'd taken my mother out to the supermarket and Dad was resting and I picked up a girly magazine and opened up the centrefold. She was a blonde, a little thin for my taste and I have always preferred dark-haired women but I hadn't had sex for so long I unzipped and started to jerk off anyway. I closed my eyes and Miss August vanished, replaced by the Erica of 1973 in the youth hostel and I came very quickly. But the Erica of today, no, nothing. I was only aroused by the image of a girl who has not existed for twenty-seven years.

Me-and-Erica as-was could still drive me crazy. Me-and-Erica as-is left me as limp as a banana skin. And as empty of emotion.

I guess I'd been really lucky all these years. Many of my friends had dumped their first wives because they were no longer attracted to them; without a lissom young thing in their beds they couldn't perform. Enslaved to the wills and wants of their cocks they detonated their marriages and blew them to hell, taking everyone along with them, causing pain and hate and damage to their kids, and all because their wang told them, 'Get me something I wanna fuck.' It was embarrassing to look at them with their trophy wives, embarrassing to hear the way they deluded themselves into believing that these chicks were actually interested in them for their saggy stomachs and wrinkled buttocks. I never see any garbage collectors with young wives. Those people know they have to stick with what they've got, they have no collateral except themselves to wave around, no Porsche, no stock portfolio, and without any of those things who really wants an old man?

At fifty I had still lusted after my wife. It was unusual but I did. Now I didn't any more. So what was left? And who exactly was Erica?

At twenty-three, when I met her, she was a child of her time, of that period in the early seventies when you could feel, as we did, that the best was behind us, the whole flaming anti-war years, the civil-rights marches, that the future was someplace else, outside of the protest movement. The future, in fact, as she guessed, was private life, what people called the Me Decade when we all took up jogging and health foods and whatnot. I was as susceptible as anyone else to that retreat from politics, more

so, given my circumstances. In the middle of the mopping-up
operation at the end of the war, the part that involved months
deactivating land-mines, I found in Erica a haven, a soft breast
against which to rest my head on, in a time when I didn't want
to talk, discuss, analyse, remember. The political life that had
energised me as a student at Berkeley was what I turned my back
on now. What I wanted more than anything else in the world
was to have the things that only women can offer men, which is
everything that war is not. Life rather than death.

Back at home I looked at my wife and I tried to see her body
merely as an envelope for the woman I had known for all that
time, not just the Erica I made love to in a hostel in Tel Aviv all
those years ago, or the law student falling asleep over her text-
books and me priming the coffee percolator for her, or the young
mother with her babies in her arms, or the middle-aged woman
sitting under the tree in the yard reading her book-club assignment, but the Erica who a couple of years after we got married
had stood by my side in the cemetery, when my grandfather died,
me and my dad saying Kaddish, my cousins on my mother's side
Daniel and Ben, and their two boys, Jonathan and Richard. The
sound that disturbed us, turning, the sight of those neo-Nazi
thugs, kids in flat-tops under even flatter faces, standing a few feet
away on the green lawn screaming, 'Die, fucking Jews, die.' Me
and my cousins chasing the little freaks through the headstones
and grabbing one of them by the leg, tripping him up, delivering
what was, to my own huge surprise, an iron punch to the nuts
leaving him squealing, while Ben and I kicked him in the face
with our shiny black shoes. And walking back, seeing Erica with
her hand over her mouth, her skin white, her eyes milky. The
first time I ever thought, Joe, you gotta be really careful from now
on. That night was the first she ever turned away from me, when
my hand reached out for her breasts to cup them in my palms,
and she pretended to sleep and I lay awake and ached for her, and

knew that what I had married was a girl who knew and could name a hundred types of apple, who was, as I feebly joked, the apple of my eye, but to whom I could never fully reveal myself if she was to go on giving herself to me in the way I wanted.

So we built ourselves a marriage. We were as easy with each other as any man and woman could ever know how to be, stayed up at night talking and worrying about our kids, our finances, our health, our friends, the government. We were the Shields. I *was* a shield, come to think of it. That was my job, what I'd willingly taken on, to protect my family and my people. When we walked into a room, at a party, say, what did people see? I suppose they saw a couple who were doing okay financially, who dressed well, or at least as far as we could with our expanding waists (just when did I stop wearing a size thirty-four in pants, what was *that* memorable date?), who donated to all the right charities, who voted Democrat, obviously, who built a house that was featured in a magazine, who gave parties and liked to try new restaurants, particularly any kind of new cuisine, who drank moderately, but always had a few good bottles of wine around. Who argued and stormed out in a rage occasionally but always made it up. On the whole we were good-humoured people, both of us, and the parts of me that weren't I kept well away from her. There were certain things about me she'd never understand – nothing to do with having fought a war, but what she sensed was a lack of liberalism over certain matters. After the incident in the cemetery she gave me some pamphlets for the Anti-Defamation League she'd sent away for; she said that this was a better way of fighting prejudice, 'with the pen, not the sword'. 'Thanks,' I told her, 'I'll certainly read them.' But I threw them out.

You know what the secret is? The anti-Semites are right, we *are* powerful in the media, we *have* wormed our way into government. In fact, we have woven ourselves so inextricably into everything that matters in America, not so we can rule the world but because there's *no way* now that they can march us off to the gas chambers and get away with it. It ain't going to happen.

These are not popular views. All my friends wince when they hear them. So what?

And there are things in her that I don't get either. The long hankering for a dog. Invite another species into your home? What for? They should go out and earn their own living. But gradually she won me over because, she said, the kids would learn something, which was how to have a loving nature, how to care for someone who needs you, who can't get food without your help, who can't be healed without you take it to the vet, who can't tell you through speech what its needs are. So we got a dog and she was right. The kids each grew up a year or two when that mutt arrived in the house. I kept my distance, the smell of the stuff in cans we had to feed it turned my stomach, but I watched her in the yard playing for hours with the dog, doing stuff with sticks and whatnot, and I thought, This is all I want, I have everything, the whole world is here and I don't believe there's anything that can take this from me. I had a normal life. And when you have seen men frying in front of your eyes it was as if God had parted the clouds and bent down and kissed my head.

She was my Promised Land flowing with milk and honey.

So much for Promised Lands. The one I'd fought for hasn't turned out so well, either. They're throwing stones at us now. We're firing back with live rounds. God knows what kind of mess that's going to turn into, I don't even want to think about it, and when I turn on the TV and watch the news, I find myself looking for another channel.

In the history books, that war only lasted three weeks, but for those of us who were there, it has consumed the whole of the rest of our lives.

I couldn't believe it the first time that thought came to me, ten days ago. I was *sure* the war was finished. Done. It was behind us. Maybe because I left Israel and came back to America, I didn't have what other Israelis had – a band of brothers from the army you stayed with over decades, all of whom knew exactly what you knew. Had I remained, I know I would have gone from time to time to the grave of Saidi whom I saw with my own eyes leap into the air before he fell to earth again, the whole of the back of his head shot away. My lieutenant Yishai, I hung out with him while he was completing his master's degree in engineering, and he came to the airport to see me off when I left the country. Cesare, who ran the clothing store on Dizengoff Street until they built the new mall, him I would have known too: he'd have got me into one of those imported Italian suits that his uncle in Rome sent over far quicker than it took back in America when the realisation finally broke that in my line of work you have to keep up appearances. But I only saw them on family trips back to Israel, once every five or six years, more for the kids' sake than ours (particularly after '82 when we went into that quagmire called Lebanon), so they could hear Hebrew spoken as a living language and do the obligatory float in the Dead Sea.

We keep away from the Negev. I never take them to Eilat. I never want to see the Sinai again as long as I live. I'm not even all that happy about beach vacations.

I'll just say there was a battle. A total fucking nightmare. We had a whole army concentrated in one place on the edge of the Suez Canal, which is a violation of the most basic rule of any kind of military strategy. All the Egyptians had to do was to start lobbing artillery from the other side, which of course they did, and they were shooting at sitting ducks. Men and armour were arriving round the clock twenty-four hours a day and stopping at the Canal because they couldn't go any further and stuff was beginning to build up three or four miles back into the desert, all of us camped there with nothing to do. There was nothing going on behind us, we had secured all that already, everything that needed doing was *across* the Canal and sure enough the Egyptians opened up with an artillery barrage that went on for three days. I read subsequently that it was the most concentrated artillery fire in the history of warfare; it exceeded anything from the First World War, Verdun, any of that stuff. How can you grasp it? This was three whole long, terrible, terrifying days of around-the-clock artillery shells falling, 155 mm howitzers, a shell about the size of the chest of drawers in the room in the Albert Dock apartment, and if one of them hit a house it would knock it down completely, and this kind of stuff was falling out of the sky, twenty-four hours a day for three days, no let-up. It turned our side of the Canal into a kind of moonscape, everything was cratered like we had left earth and were wandering lost in the debris and devastation of a dry dead planet bombarded by comets and meteors. Stars and solar systems and galaxies rained down on us and the desert shrugged, shifted its shape and our dead vanished beneath its surface. We all disappeared into the sand. The only way to protect yourself was to dig a foxhole, make it as deep as you could and hunker down inside it and stay there. I was crouching in something the width and depth of a fireplace, sitting huddled up in a foetal position to keep my arms and face covered because once one of those shells lands and explodes, it turns into shards of shrapnel, which are pieces of molten hot steel flying at the speed of a travelling bullet. This was going on night and day, trucks and tanks were going up outside, like fifty-ton firecrackers bursting into one massive explosive force – dozens of Big Bangs in our desert universe.

Sleep in the foxhole. It wasn't real sleep, it was a sleep of a kind of emotional exhaustion, you fell unconscious for twenty minutes because you were so tired of the noise, the incessant whistling shriek coming overhead followed by a momentary pause of nothingness, then a really loud thud in which the ground shook, and you started playing these mental games inside your head trying to calculate where that shell fell relative to where you were. And it was going on all the time, incredible explosions, and not only that, there were also the ammunition explosions where sometimes a shell would strike an ammo or petrol dump. The pallets would be stacked up four or five high and when they were hit by shells the bullets would explode individually like someone dropped a match inside a box of firecrackers going off on the Fourth of July. The smell of cordite was in the air all the time, that substance which is the propellant they stuff in the back of the cannon, which explodes and becomes gas and forces the projectile out. The burnt smell of the cordite was everywhere mixed with the stench of singeing human flesh.

I killed a lot of people during those few days. You fired into the distance and a shadow crumpled but it didn't feel like killing. A couple of days later I shot someone at close range. That did.

We were in a village on the other side of the Canal. The houses are very typical of the region, made of mud bricks with wooden doors, one window. In Hebrew or Arabic it's the same – you call these people Falashin, really poor dirt-farmers engaged in the most meagre subsistence living. Our job was to clean out the enemy. I advanced on the first house I was responsible for clearing, the door opens and there's an Egyptian soldier standing in front of me and I could see that he was trying to figure out what I was going to do. I was advancing in firing position, I was covering myself. He had opened the door with his hand, he didn't kick it open with his foot, he came out like he was opening the door to bring in the paper. Maybe he was expecting to be shouted at in Arabic, 'Okay, Ahmed, the war is over for you, put your hands up,' maybe he really did think that he was going to be taken prisoner because he certainly wasn't prepared for any confrontation. But I was so surprised at the door opening and his coming out that I just pulled the trigger and shot him in the chest and he collapsed like a house of cards.

I don't see his face in my dreams. I can't conjure him up at all, though I can still feel the heat of the sun on my back and the smell of the palm groves and dust in my mouth and the ever-present stench of decaying flesh heavy in the air. I am not haunted by him. The only thing that matters to me morally is that I could not afford to give him the benefit of the doubt. It wasn't a chess game. I had no way of knowing whether he was somebody who had incredibly fast reflexes. For all I knew he might have been a crack shot, he could have been some Egyptian gun-slinger who was capable of assessing a situation that he had played badly and correcting it sufficiently to make it a satisfactory outcome for him. So he was dead and I was alive. I suppose somewhere in Cairo there's a faded photograph of this man. He was somebody's son and somebody's brother and probably somebody's husband. I guess I have this in common with a few people still living in Egypt, that we are all bound together in some form of intimacy, and it's curious that it is me, not his loved ones, who knows exactly how he died, who witnessed his final moments. But I can't help that. Because if I hadn't pulled the trigger first it would have been my photo on the bureau of my parents' house in Chicago and my parents saying Yiskor for me every Yom Kippur and this Cairene in his fifties who maybe once in a while turned his mind to the guy from the Zionist entity he gunned down all those years ago, because he had quicker reflexes than me. It turned out different. I'm still here, he isn't. There's nothing I can or would want to do about it, to have the positions reversed, so it was me in my grave and not him.

Erica never knew any of this. I didn't tell her. Of course she knew I'd killed, though maybe not in cold blood. Why didn't I ever sit down with her and say, 'Okay, this is how it was'?

I know, and I suppose I have always known why I never said

anything. Because she couldn't take it. She would have left me. And, what's more, I fell for her because I understood in my heart of hearts that I *couldn't* tell her about the war, however much she asked. She was the type who would crumple up. She thought she had totally left behind the Canadian farm girl but she hadn't really. I'd watch her watching the news; she'd say, 'All this killing and for what? If women ran the world there'd be no more war.' How do you talk to someone who thinks that way, who knows nothing of grudges and grievances that go back centuries, of tribal conflicts that will remain until the end of time? Why can't we all just love each other? she asked of the nightly news. I don't know, I really don't, I wish I did.

Growing up in the orchards, among the apple trees, she had never once eaten the fruit of the Tree of the Knowledge of Good and Evil. She was Eve unsullied, happy in ignorance, and I was happy for her to remain there.

When the war finished I wanted to be married. That was my goal. Get married. Stay married, just like my parents, find my Promised Land. So I married someone for whom the war would never become an issue – something that might threaten to destabilise our relationship – because you wouldn't even start to explain to someone like her what it was all about. I married Erica because I knew that I would always have to maintain my silence and so I would never risk that time in combat ruining my personal life.

And now that I was no longer attracted to her physically, what remained?

Just the silence.

The hotel was nearly finished. The delays, the sabotage, all the local problems that had been bogging down the project were resolving themselves. I stood on the street in Liverpool watching the water fill the pool that surrounds my hotel – the finishing touch which makes the statement that was always in my mind, the sense of the kind of place this is – and all the workmen were hanging around in their hard hats also watching and some of them even cheering too. The newspapermen had been allowed in and had taken photographs, and I was running around going to receptions. Alix had fixed everything for me, I totally have her to thank for all she did. Brian Humphreys, sitting in his jail cell, got a visit from his mom and as a result of that meeting he gave me his blessing. Everything changed overnight; it was like I was gliding on smooth tracks into the future.

Now I was up to my ears in all the really fun stuff: choosing door handles and mirrors, staying up till two or three in the morning looking at catalogues from my European suppliers. Soon the whole thing will be handed over to the boutique chain that commissioned me, and my baby will be born and I will pocket a satisfying cheque, pay off my loans, bank the profits and move on to the next project, wherever that's going to be. For weeks I'd been taking round tours of travel agents and looking in on meetings where the manager they had appointed a month ago was hiring the first staff, and that was something else altogether because the candidates they keep sending him really do not have the service mentality we're used to in the States but insist on calling people 'love' and behaving with a kind of warm familiarity I've never seen before in the hospitality industry. One lady who came to see him about a job in housekeeping said she was coming back to work having nursed her dying father. 'I'm sorry,' he said. 'Was it a long illness?' 'Yeah, Alzheimer's, the old Alcatraz. It's often the butt of jokes but it can have its serious side, Mr Thomson.' 'But that will be the charm of the place,' he told me, 'it's true Liverpool.' Okay. I'm not concerned with the human-resources side. People are very unlike buildings: they're clumsy, the wrong shape, they sometimes smell. I just stick to bricks and mortar and concrete and glass, which I can form according to my will.

Here in the Hotel Kempinski everything is fake and phoney, *trompe l'oeil* everywhere, which I can't stand, though absolutely luxurious and the staff, all these former Soviet-controlled robots, have half the world's supply of hair gel on their heads and they're always smiling and it seems as though they really are very happy to serve you, which I guess they would be after fifty years of totalitarian governments. Outside is even worse: on the one hand you have high German baroque, which isn't my thing at all, and on the other you have the world's worst post-war architecture – cheap, ugly, utilitarian, soulless, charmless. A travesty of what the great Modernists were interested in, hateful stuff, though at least without the bombast of those Stalinist showcase monstrosities they put up all over the place in Russia. In the centre of the public square, the Altmarkt, there's a theatre with a mosaic mural on the back and some green netting over it, so as not to offend the eyes of all the tourists, and round the GDR symbol of the hammer and the sheaves of corn a lot of men with red armbands and rifles and clenched fists do all kinds of heroic stuff with as much animation as is possible when you're made up of thousands of little bits of coloured ceramic. There's some kind of slogan running all the way through: *Life will become our programme, our path.* It was the kind of thing we spouted for five minutes back in the sixties before we realised that life was holding down a job and getting on with your wife and trying not to scream at your kids when they were annoying you. Mundane or what?

So what was I doing here?

To be honest, I think the truth is that I just wanted to see Alix Rebick. I really missed her. I liked her humour and her honesty and her caustic remarks. I still couldn't forget how she behaved that day in Ritchie Sylvester's office, and how she looked either.

I tried to imagine Erica in that room, with the lap-dancers, and I couldn't. No way. She would have totally freaked out – in fact the very thought of Erica in Liverpool was inconceivable. There was no possibility that she would be able even to navigate the idea of such a city for all the time she'd lived in Chicago. It was true that she adored Europe, but by that she meant Venice and Florence and Paris, places with no edge to them. Because that's who Erica was, all the time I knew her, a woman without edges, round, like an apple.

I didn't want to fuck Alix, not at all. I just thought it would do me good being around her, and if anyone could give me any perspective on what Erica had done she was that person, *she* was the one I could talk to about the whole mess, *she* would help me grope my way through it. When she asked me, in the lobby, what was I doing there and I replied, 'Perversity', I have really no idea what I meant. Not perversion, obviously, but rather I seemed to be saying that I was doing something I knew I shouldn't do and that baffled me because I was perfectly clear what I was after. I told her that time on the beach that I'd rather be her friend than her lover and I meant it. I thought we could become good friends: that is, when I went back to Chicago we'd keep up an e-mail exchange, I'd send her any jokes I heard, let her know about my projects, and when I was in London, as I often am, maybe we could meet up for a drink or dinner. It isn't usual for men to have this kind of relationship with a woman but that doesn't mean it can't be done. You just have to want to enough. Sam, when I told him this – I was quite open with him about it – said, 'Okay. If you think so.' So I'll take that as support.

What is it about Alix? All the time we were in that old woman's apartment I was watching her. I had a hazy kind of idea of what the old lady was saying, I understand German a little, though I can't speak it, because when I lived in that apartment in Haifa across the hall there was an Austrian lady, what they call in

Israel a Yekke, one of the immigrants from the thirties, very proper and correct, always dressed immaculately in a dress and stockings and hat despite the heat, very formal, and she and Marianne Koeppen could have been sisters, the same autocratic imperiousness, the same hopeless passion for high culture. She never spoke Hebrew if she could help it, thought it was a barbaric language, and when we had our rows about the garbage cans or our cat crapping near her door she would let out a torrent of German which, after a while, I didn't find too difficult to understand, though my own attempts to speak it back to her were barked at because of my atrocious grammar so I just gave up. But I used to listen to her talking to her brother, who had not got out when she did, early on in the thirties, had stayed behind and gone to the camps from where he found his way to Israel in 1949. And I saw him once, standing at the open door of her apartment with his hand on the jamb and his sleeve riding up his arm so you could quite clearly catch sight of the number tattooed there, watching me lugging my rifle up the stairs when I'd just got back from a month's reserve duty, my hair in a ponytail, and he turned to his sister and said, 'Look, even the children are armed now.'

So I let Frau Koeppen and Alix talk on and didn't interrupt too much, happy to get the gist of what the two of them were saying and pick up the detail later. What I was hugely impressed by was that Alix simply fell silent. There was a great stillness in her as she listened, she seemed to absorb all this information without rejecting or deflecting it. It must have been a big shock discovering who this woman was, her own aunt, and although she registered an exclamation of surprise, she was unfazed by anything she heard. These details – of the night of the fire-bombing – she took in without flinching or crying out, 'How horrible,' or asking all the usual questions people have, the brain-dead, 'How did it feel? Weren't you frightened?' Hardly anybody knows how to ask questions and really listen to the answers, *really* listen. There is a particular talent that you come across occasionally, something good journalists have (and I ran into one or two of them during the war, I mean really first-rate correspondents not the celebrity-obsessed nincompoops who pass for scribes these days), to be able to interrogate someone's experience without getting personal or emotional, without groping around to find the right language, stumbling around over words. Most normal people can't do it and I would put my own family into that category.

But Alix Rebick sat and listened. She didn't take her eyes off Marianne Koeppen; she hardly moved a muscle. I was trying to relax in the same kind of hard, upright chair as she was and my back was killing me, but she continued to sit, not shifting around; she was like a black hole absorbing information. I can't believe that nothing could have been disrupted inside her – after all, here was a whole family history having to be completely reorganised, your own past shifting like tectonic plates inside your head – but she just sat there and took it. She retained detail, I noticed, because when we talked about the meeting afterwards she recollected it in very precise ways. She also told me something about her grandfather, Frau Koeppen's father, and it seemed that far from being the loving pre-war papa of sacred memory, he had been in his old age a bitter, broken man and the whole family had been infected in a way by its dissolution as a result of the escape from Germany.

Now we sat in this restaurant, she was eating lobster Thermidor. The pink flesh was raised to her lips. A ceiling spotlight right above her head cast shadows on her face that didn't flatter her and I wished we could switch places because I knew she wouldn't want to be seen this way. A long shadow like a dark veil against her skin hung on her neck with diamonds sparkling through it and drew my eyes down to her dress, which was red, and her breasts rose inside the dress as she spoke.

She was saying, 'I wish I could decide whether or not there is such a thing as evil.'

I replied, 'Why? Do you think about it a lot?'

And she said, 'Yes, from time to time.'

What came to mind was a little incident in the street in Liverpool when she dropped me off after our tennis game and a woman had come up to us and asked if we would sign a petition so that those two ten-year-old boys who murdered the little kid a few years back would not be released from jail. 'Because,' as the woman had said, 'they're evil through and through.'

But Alix had shook her head and stood her ground and refused to accept the clipboard and the pen that were offered to her, which caused an altercation there on the street with other people putting in their two-cents' worth and sounding off at her for defending murderers. It had impressed me enormously, the way she stood her ground like that, and was perhaps part of that quick urge I'd had on the beach to kiss her.

'You didn't think those kids that murdered the little boy in Liverpool were evil.'

'No, I don't think *they* are evil. The matter that engages is me is whether the actions, what actually happened to the child they killed, were evil. The question is whether evil can be independent of intent.'

Which sent a shock right through me.

'What do you mean?'

'Oh, just that evil begets evil, it becomes separate from its original source.'

'Like?'

'A child who is abused who grows up to be an abuser. A people who have been the victims of genocide, who in fighting for their survival are so conditioned and traumatised by the apparently irreparable damage done to them that they are no longer able to distinguish between self-defence and aggressive indifference to the fate of others. The fuck-you mentality that's prevalent today among so many Jews, the adoration of the Jewish tough guy, whether it's Dutch Schultz or Ariel Sharon, a disease from which I'm not myself immune, of course.'

And, boy, did she go red when she said that.

I watched her eat dessert.

She said, 'And now I am replete. My greed is sated.' I wondered if she ate as a substitute for sex. Women do, apparently, according to the kind of people who appear on *Oprah* (for whom Erica had a sneaking admiration because of her struggle with her weight, and always hoped that living in Chicago she'd run into her one day to which I replied, 'Yeah, might get run over by her limo driver, that's as close as you're likely to get').

I picked up the check after we'd finished our coffee, saying, 'It's my pleasure', and we walked through the quiet streets, across the cobblestones that caused her to hobble in her high-heeled red shoes.

'I got upgraded to a suite,' I told her.

'Me too.'

'What's yours like?'

'Pretty luxurious. Two bathrooms, a little sitting-room area with a CD player.'

'Mine's the same, maybe they're all like that.'

'Could be.'

'Wanna have a nightcap and listen to some music? They got Bach in my room, the Contrapuntals.'

She looked at me sharply. What could be going through her mind other than there would be a repetition of that ignominious scene on the beach? I thought she was going to refuse but instead she didn't say anything. We got to the lobby and she walked straight to the elevators. I stood next to her as she punched the button for her floor and I leaned across and punched the button for mine. 'I'm not going to kiss you this time.'

'A threat or a promise?' she replied, shrugging.

'Ah, come on. Just a drink. Or we could order up coffee or anything else you want.'

'Okay.'

We walked along the hallways. There were ashtrays filled with sand and some poor former-Soviet robot had to come along every five minutes and redraw on the surface the logo of the hotel.

She slid into the room behind me, sat down on a sofa and pointed at the mini bar. 'Do they have any good vodka in there? I haven't looked in mine.'

'I'll check it out. There's some Russian stuff, that okay?'

'Thanks, with tonic.'

'So here we are.'

'Yeah.'

'Getting to know each other.'

'That's right.'

The light was much kinder here, like the candles on the table when I first came to dinner at her brother's place and I'd had that sudden revelation of us all when we were younger, unlined, innocent of tragedy. She crossed her legs and looked at me, and I felt like Ritchie Sylvester must have done when she fixed her eye on him.

'So can I ask you something?'

'Go ahead.'

'I gather from what you've said you were in the Israeli army and you fought in a war, which must have been '73.'

'That's correct.'

'So tell me, what was the worst thing that happened to you?'

It had come. At last.

Odd, that in nearly thirty years this was the one question nobody had ever posed. Maybe they felt it was too blunt a demand, that no one with any degree of sensitivity would probe so openly. Maybe they simply didn't want to hear whatever it was

I had to say. Hardly anyone of my generation has known combat, no one I was with in college or high school who got their draft papers went, everyone found a way out of it one way or the other. Either we opposed the war on principle, as in my case, or we thought too highly of ourselves to want to parade around in a government-issued suit being told what to do by some southern redneck sergeant. We had plans for our lives that didn't include surrendering our will to the politicians. It was just me who, instead of going to cold Canada or cold Sweden, thought that there was an easier way out, to tail it to the country I'd visited as a kid with my parents where the sky was blue and there were palm trees and you got a little frisson just thinking how Jews can go anywhere now, we can get any job we want, we're not scared of anybody. Of course, in my innocence, I didn't see the war coming. It caught me totally by surprise. I'd done my three years, I thought that was it.

So here she is asking me this question and I'm looking at her wondering what to say. I could have avoided it. There were plenty of half-assed answers I could have given her about ammo explosions, rocket attacks, tanks on fire, but because she didn't speak, didn't rush to fill the silence, I opened my mouth and inside I was trembling, my guts were shaking with fear. Of what? Not judgement, or even disgust, but that she wouldn't understand what I was talking about.

'I can never decide,' I said, 'if this is nothing or something. In nearly thirty years I haven't been able to make my mind up, but I know it was the worst thing for me. I shot someone in close combat and I'm not bearing any guilt for that. I lived through a terrible artillery bombardment down by the Suez Canal and I was pretty frightened but it doesn't give me nightmares. There was just this . . . Do you know what C rations are?'

'Combat rations.'

'Yes. You got a cardboard box and when you opened it usually what you found inside was a can of hummus, a can of okra in tomato sauce, a sachet of strawberry powder, which you poured into your canteen and shook up to make a drink, a package of dried biscuits, a pack of gum, a chocolate bar, a tin of chocolate spread, packages of coffee and a main meal, which on Friday was always a large tin with a boiled chicken inside in aspic, tinned corn, a tin of fruit like pears or peaches or apples, and as you would expect these things became currency. The Ashkenazis would trade four tins of hummus for the one tin of the chicken that the Sephardim wouldn't in a million years think of opening. And the tinned fruit was a particular prize because that was really the only edible thing in there. Tinned fruit became the currency with which you bought your way out of guard duty. If you found yourself pulling the three to five a.m. stint a couple of tins of apples would usually be enough to get somebody to swap with you.'

'Are you trying to tell me that the worst thing that happened to you in the Yom Kippur war was the meals? How Jewish is that?'

'No, no, no.' She'd made me laugh. Out of all the horror there is always laughter. You have to keep on remembering God's eleventh commandment: Thou shalt laugh. Especially at thyself. 'We were on the Egyptian side of the Suez Canal. Just hanging around, waiting for orders. We'd finished eating lunch, which this time was a couple of sardines on a dry biscuit, a chunk of halva and coffee brewed in a can that a few minutes before had held preserved grapefruit slices. The lieutenant reminds us to bury our garbage and a guy called Saidi, this very tough Tunisian, says he'll get up and dig a hole so he grabs a shovel and starts laying into the sand. As he starts to excavate the hole we all stand round lobbing our garbage into it like we're playing some kind of horizontal basketball, the kind of thing you do in offices, throwing balled-up pieces of paper into the waste-basket, and this makes Saidi really pissed off because as fast as he can dig, the hole is filling up again with sardine cans and candy wrappers. And then suddenly he stops digging altogether and he's just standing there but that doesn't stop us, we're acting like kids, scooping up more and more garbage, the Dixie cups from our coffee, the biscuits no one wants, all this detritus is being used so that a bunch of fairly frightened soldiers in the middle of a pretty nasty war can let off a bit of steam and our lieutenant joins in, we're all at it, and Saidi is still standing there doing nothing.

'Finally someone walks over, and underneath the pile of garbage something is visible. We bend down and start to pull away the sardine cans, out of the hole, and emerging from this refuse tip is the rotting corpse of an Egyptian soldier. We clear away the crap from his face. We dig some more. I find a pair of pants riddled with small-calibre fire, stained with faded claret blotches, and a parched brown leather wallet containing two carefully folded letters, which I open up and show to Saidi, who looks at them and reads the Arabic and says they're from the guy's father. But now everyone is digging and everyone is making his own discovery. A pair of canvas desert boots with cardboard soles. A shaving kit with a couple of razor blades, still sharp, wrapped in greaseproof paper. A shirt. A notebook. A kit-bag. A mess kit with bits of food baked to the knife and spoon. Every time someone found something, he held it up, wordlessly, for everyone else to see. We were silent in our industry. The lieutenant stood and watched this bizarre mime being acted out by his men. I guess there was nothing in Officers' School to prepare him for this.

'We cleared out the garbage, re-dug the hole, reburied the Egyptian and put a handkerchief over his face. A couple of days later, returning back to the Sinai, we passed the spot again. His grave had been washed open by the surging waters of the Canal, and he lay there, the handkerchief gone. He was only one of, I think, a dozen rotting corpses I saw on both sides of the Canal: men fighting and dying in anonymity and worthlessness and you can say to me, what did you do? You did nothing. But we did do something. We turned a man into a garbage dump. All of us did. And I still see his face, the decaying eyes and lips, the bones of his skull pushing through the rotten flesh of his cheeks. I look at people's faces sometimes and that's what I see and I suppose that it was because of this that I decided to study architecture, because all I wanted to do was work with materials that are non-corruptible.'

'So you want to know whether I think that was evil?'

'I suppose.'

'You'd value my opinion?'

'Yes.'

'Then absolutely it was an evil act, as evil as anything the Nazis did when they referred to us Jews as *stücke*, pieces. The question is whether you yourself actively and knowingly participated in this evil and, of course, the answer is no. Once you realised you were throwing garbage on to a corpse you stopped, where others might have continued.'

'I'm off the hook?'

'Also no. Because in my view the act remains evil in and of itself. Take those kids, ten-year-old boys, were they evil? No, how could they be? They had no fully-developed understanding of the moral consequences of their actions, there was no active choice between right and wrong, no pleasure in defying the ethical order of the world. They hadn't taken sides, they weren't in league with the devil . . .'

'The devil?'

'A metaphor. Yet what they *did* to the child, what happened to him, that was evil and as a result they were contaminated by the horror of his death. It's the same with you. You were touched by evil. I'm not surprised, by the way, that you consider this the worst thing to have happened to you in the war.'

'You understand?'

She looked at me and her voice softened. 'My father always told me that we have only one goal here on earth, only one way to fulfil our destiny, which is to be human. Not gods but human. Each act makes us more or less so. Our aim isn't to get into heaven as angels but to be fully human here on earth. My father struggled with this problem more than most. When they made abortion legal he was one of the few doctors in Catholic Liverpool who would sign the consent form and it grew to be a great burden to him because he signed so many forms, far more than anyone else. But he looked at the women and particularly the teenage girls who came to him, and he saw *them* as the embryos with the potential for life, not the fertilised egg growing inside them. He knew that something barely begun could be damaged beyond capacity for any further growth. My father was in other ways, I have only recently found out, a far from perfect man. My parents' marriage wasn't what I thought it was. I've had to deal with many difficult things lately, things it's not for me to tell you. But I know that for all our flaws, and we are all deeply flawed people, every one, what redeems us is one thing only, the knowledge of good and evil, the revelation that expelled us from paradise. If I say to you, you've done nothing wrong, you live in innocence and ignorance and both of those are bliss. But it *is* wrong. You turned a man into a thing and you remain a man yourself by understanding that you have done wrong, even if you didn't will it.'

'So what do I do?'

'If I were a rabbi, I'd say you go to *shul* on the Day of Atonement and recite whatever it is you recite. But as I'm not a rabbi, and I'm not religious, I can only say, it's something you live with. What have other people told you?'

'I never told other people.'

'You never told your parents, your wife?'

'No.'

'So why are you telling me?'

'I don't know.'

'Come on, that's not good enough.'

'Okay, then. Because I thought maybe you could handle it. That you wouldn't be shocked and horrified and wouldn't see me in some other light, as a trained killer, like the Vietnam vets.'

'Oh, really, what nonsense.'

'You'd be surprised.'

'You remained silent about this, all these years?'

'Yes.'

'What did you tell your family about the war?'

'Nothing.'

'Didn't they ask?'

'Yes. But I resisted.'

She considered this for a moment. 'You know the Hebrew poet Haim Bialik?'

'Of course.'

'He had something pertinent to say about this in reference to another atrocity, the Kishniev massacre in 1903, which brought us running out of Eastern Europe, the beginning of the exodus to America: "*And who else is like God on earth and can bear this in silence?*"'

She'd got me there.

'You know what?' she said. 'I think you need to be brought to justice.'

'Justice?'

'Yes. A trial is needed. I will try you. So, Mr Defendant-at-the-bar, I've heard the evidence, that is *your* testimony. The prosecution doesn't have the time here tonight to subpoena witnesses but I think I've got enough to go on. I've carefully considered my verdict and I pronounce you guilty as charged but I'm prepared to take into account mitigating circumstances, also previous good character, and I'm going to be merciful. I sentence you to life.'

'Thank you.'

'You're welcome.'

'Is that it?'

'Yes. Justice has been done and has been *seen* to be done, at least by me. You can tell anyone you like, I'm not imposing any reporting restrictions.'

I went to the bar and poured us both another drink. We sat there for a while, each of us with our own thoughts, I don't know what hers were. I knew it was time now to move on, I should start to talk about Erica and the face-lift, about how when she told me what she had done I was suffused with horror, thinking of her skin lifted to reveal beneath it what I'd seen in the desert. That the face of the dead Egyptian was imprinted now on *her* face, that I couldn't look at her. That everything had become a bad movie, the kind my doltish son would watch where people morph into monsters in front of your eyes. But as I thought of this I began to berate myself. What was this nonsense? I simply didn't like the way my wife looked any more. The sexual impulse towards that scrawny, bony rag of a woman was totally extinguished. Alix was right about the incident in the Sinai; it was just going to be something I'd have to continue to live with but it had nothing at all to do with the sudden collapse of my marriage. I thought about the house in Chicago, the kids, my parents, the whole edifice of what I'd built since I came back to America like it was one of my own projects, and it seemed to me to be riddled with faults, as my buildings were not, and this didn't matter, but what mattered was that it was no longer rooted in the solid foundations of the erotic desire I had felt for Erica these past twenty-seven years. Which left things where? I didn't know. Who was I in love with? Or maybe the question was what? There was that Bob Dylan line about giving shelter from the storm. All I'd ever wanted was that, I'd have married anyone who offered it. It just happened to be her, the girl from the apple orchards in Canada, who willingly did what I desired, remade herself for me, abandoned her past for me. How could I not still love her?

The truth was, I didn't. I just didn't. The harvest was over, the leaves had fallen and the branches were bare. The outline of their shape stood out against the sky.

'Are you okay?'

I looked up at her.

'What?'

She was still sipping her drink, and once again I didn't know what to make of her, how calm she was when confronted with horror. She absorbed it, it didn't bother her at all. Her arm was resting on the back of the chair, her forearm was strong but a fold of flesh fell from it. The skin had a sheen. It was toothsome. I wanted to bite it. I had a need to sink my mouth on to her flesh and suck it. For a second she looked . . . yes, it *was* there, she was voluptuous. Everything Erica had destroyed was still present in Alix, bruised, knocked out of shape, but fleshiness she certainly possessed. The breasts really were magnificent and she flaunted them, the skin was freckled but the pigmentation was gold under the light. I couldn't take my eyes off her. What did I feel? It wasn't anything complicated, just sexual desire.

'What?' she said again.

'I don't know.'

'What don't you know?'

My fingers reached out, touched her face, and she flinched.

'Oh, for God's sake, not that again.' She turned her head away from me.

My fingers reaching out to her breasts.

'What are you doing?' she cried, recoiling from me.

'Don't do that. Come here. Please.'

'Don't humiliate me.'

'I wouldn't do that for the world. Not in a million years. I want to make love to you.'

Her face altered beyond recognition. Hot lights came on in her eyes.

'Why are you saying this? What do you mean?'

'What do I mean? I want to fuck you.'

'You said you didn't.'

'Well, now I do.'

'Why?'

'What does it matter?'

My hand was right inside her dress. A muscle moved in her cheek.

'Of course it matters.'

'I want to fuck you because I want to fuck you. That's the only why that's important. Because you look amazing and are amazing and I want you.'

'Are you hard?' She reached across and felt my cock. 'Yes. It seems you are.'

Reaching behind her, I unzipped her dress and unhooked her bra. Her breasts fell away and my head was full of some kind of erotic musk her skin gave off. I took her nipple in my mouth. She was unzipping my pants and I felt her warm hand clasp my cock. My mouth moved to the other breast and licked and bit the nipple. Her finger ran along the dark vein and down to my balls.

'Suck me,' I said.

Her head bent and she took my Jewish cock in her Jewish mouth and it silenced her. Her tongue executed spiralling circles. I looked down and the great head of auburn hair was engulfing me. My hand was inside her panties, on her cunt. My finger pushed inside her and she withdrew her mouth from me and shuddered.

'Fuck me,' she said. 'Now.'

I pushed her back on the couch and pulled her panties off. I didn't look at them, they dropped to the floor. Underneath me, she unbuttoned my shirt and licked my chest.

A hot flush was all across her skin. The lipstick she wore was gone and her eyes were smeared. I pushed myself into her and she let out a scream.

'Am I hurting you? I don't want to hurt you.'

'No, no.'

Harshness was in her throat, she was holding on to my arms, I saw she was going to come very quickly and this excited me. There is a taste in women's mouths that changes when they are about to come and it was here on her lips and on her tongue. She was all around me, I had got myself deep inside her. This extraordinary woman was taking her pleasure and the sight of her aroused me like there was no tomorrow and I came too.

When I opened my eyes again, her fingers were loose on my hands. She lay there, passionate and radiant and serene in my arms, smiling.

And looking at her I thought for a moment of the words of Rabbi Hillel in *The Ethics of the Fathers*. 'If I am not for me, then who will be? If I am only for me, then what am I?' That hoary old rabbinical formulation struck me now as posing a new set of questions. And I asked myself, If not her then who? And if not her, then why not her?

This train of thought was interrupted by her sudden laughter.

'What are you laughing at?' I asked, my hand touching her mouth.

'I remembered a good joke,' she said. Listening to her begin to recount it, I thought, Why not her?

Just try and stop me!

Acknowledgements

Above all else, I would like to express my deepest appreciation to my dear friend Judah Passow for our discussion of military matters, his account of the Yom Kippur War and for always aiming his photographer's lens in the best possible light. My warm thanks also to Michael and Hillary Swerdlow, for their abundantly generous hospitality at their Albert Dock flat during my stays in Liverpool and for their insights into the current state of the city. Kath Viner and Bill Mann forced me to look again at what I thought I had forgotten. Bill Maynard, at Urban Splash, filled me in on the background to the city's urban regeneration, and Robert Broudie detailed the ballistics case in which Sam Rebick made his legal reputation. Thanks also to Dick Mosse who explained German restitution law and to Esther Freud for the introduction to him.

My very warm appreciation goes also to Frau Armgard Ehlech, who, like Marianne Koeppen, survived with great dignity some of the worst abuses to befall twentieth-century Dresdeners, and who shared with me her memories of both the Allied bombing raid firestorm and life in the city during the post-war period. My thanks, too, to James Marsh who acted as my interpreter during my meeting with her.

Books and articles I have consulted include Morris Beckman's *The 43 Group*; Tony Kushner's 'Anti-Semitism and austerity: the August 1947 riots in Britain' in *Racial Violence in the Nineteenth and Twentieth Centuries* edited by Panikos Panayi; Peter Aughton's *Liverpool: A People's History*; Quintin Hughes' *Liverpool: City of Architecture*; and Alexander McKee's *The Devil's Tinderbox: Dresden 1945*. Details of Brownlow Hill in the twenties come from a short typewritten manuscript by Jack Levy, dated July 23, 1990, which I found amongst my mother's papers after her death.

My agent Derek Johns, as always, has been a calm and intelligent influence and Natasha Walter has been the most supportive friend and reader I could wish for. Appreciation, too, to Annabel Arden for the modelling assignment. Finally, Lennie Goodings at Little, Brown has been the most formidable editor I have ever encountered. Her determination to wring from me the best possible book, her dedicated work when others (myself included) would have collapsed exhausted long ago, was breathtaking and chastening. I would like to thank wholeheartedly her and the other staff at Little, Brown who have worked so hard to bring this book to fruition.